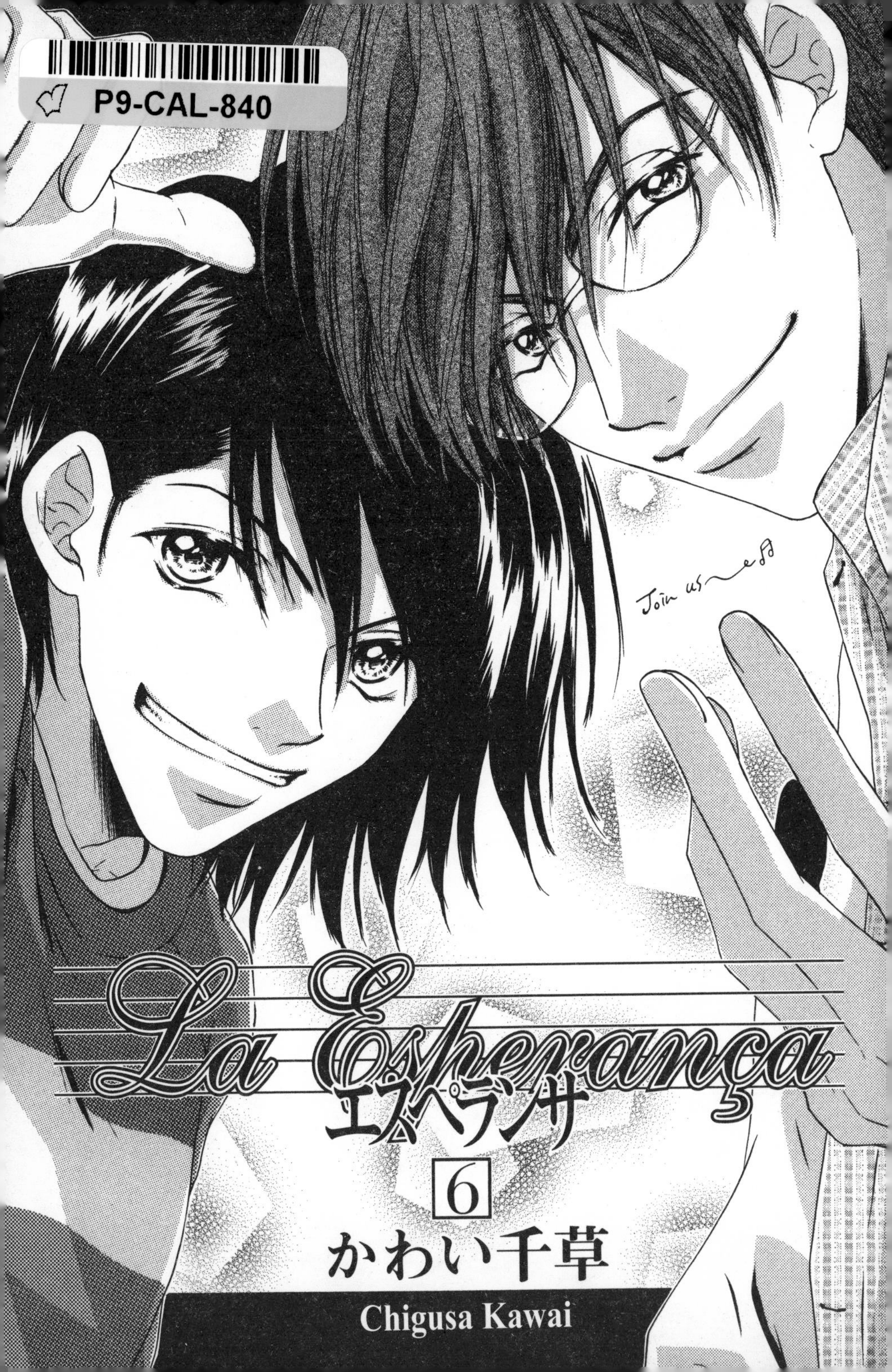
Join us~
La Esperança
エスペランサ
6
かわい千草
Chigusa Kawai

La Esperança

6

ROSARIO
3

Promenade
188

Translation	Sachiko Sato
Lettering	Replibooks
Graphic Design	Fred Lui
Editing	Stephanie Donnelly
Editor in Chief	Fred Lui
Publisher	Hikaru Sasahara

English Edition Published by
DIGITAL MANGA PUBLISHING
A division of DIGITAL MANGA, Inc.
1487 W 178th Street, Suite 300
Gardena, CA 90248

www.dmpbooks.com

First Edition: February 2007
ISBN-10: 1-56970-848-7
ISBN-13: 978-1-56970-848-4

1 3 5 7 9 10 8 6 4 2

Printed in China

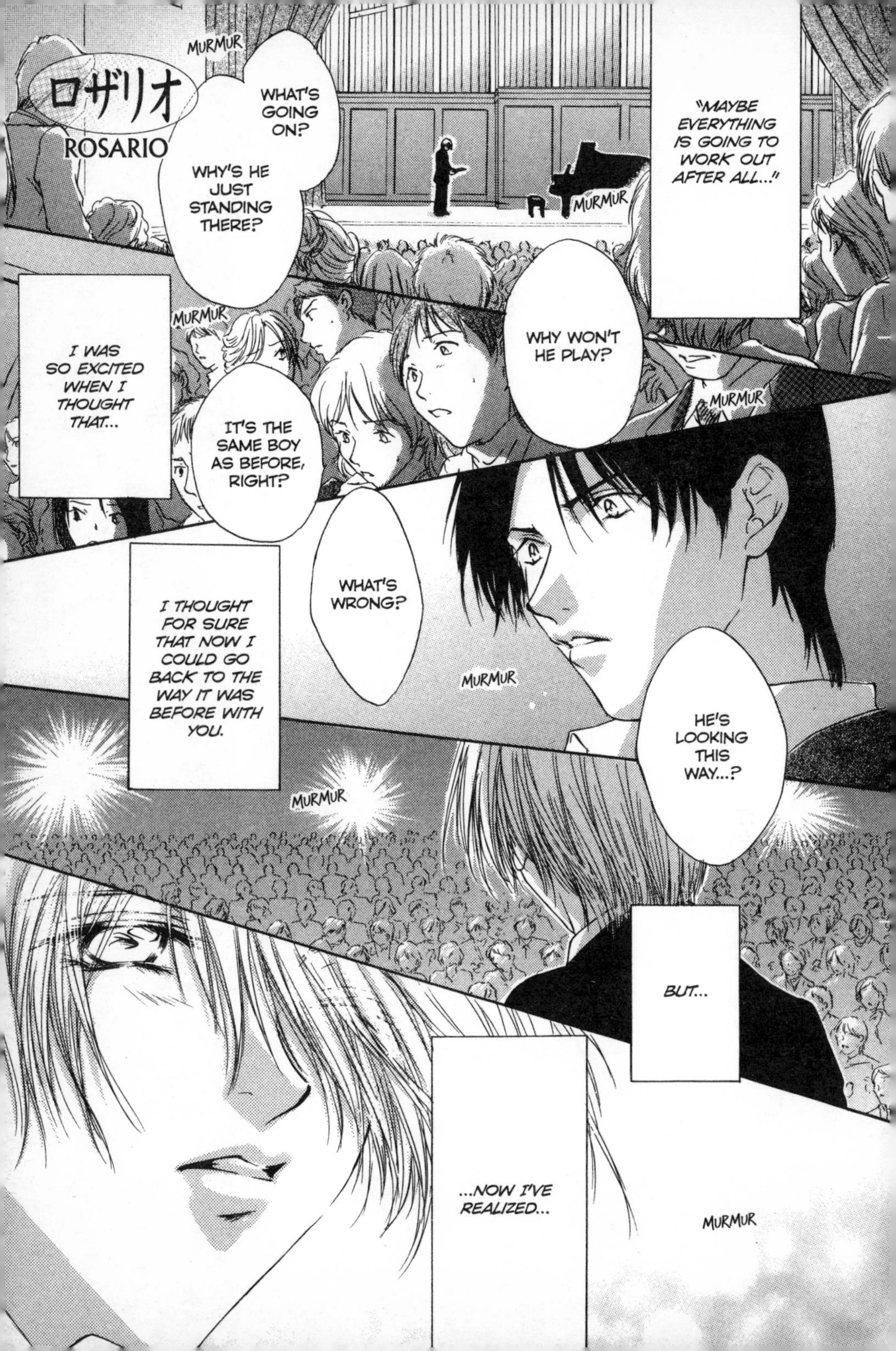
ロザリオ
ROSARIO
"MAYBE EVERYTHING IS GOING TO WORK OUT AFTER ALL..."
MURMUR
MURMUR
WHAT'S GOING ON?
WHY'S HE JUST STANDING THERE?
MURMUR
WHY WON'T HE PLAY?
IT'S THE SAME BOY AS BEFORE, RIGHT?
MURMUR
I WAS SO EXCITED WHEN I THOUGHT THAT...
MURMUR
WHAT'S WRONG?
I THOUGHT FOR SURE THAT NOW I COULD GO BACK TO THE WAY IT WAS BEFORE WITH YOU.
HE'S LOOKING THIS WAY...?
MURMUR
BUT...
MURMUR
...NOW I'VE REALIZED...

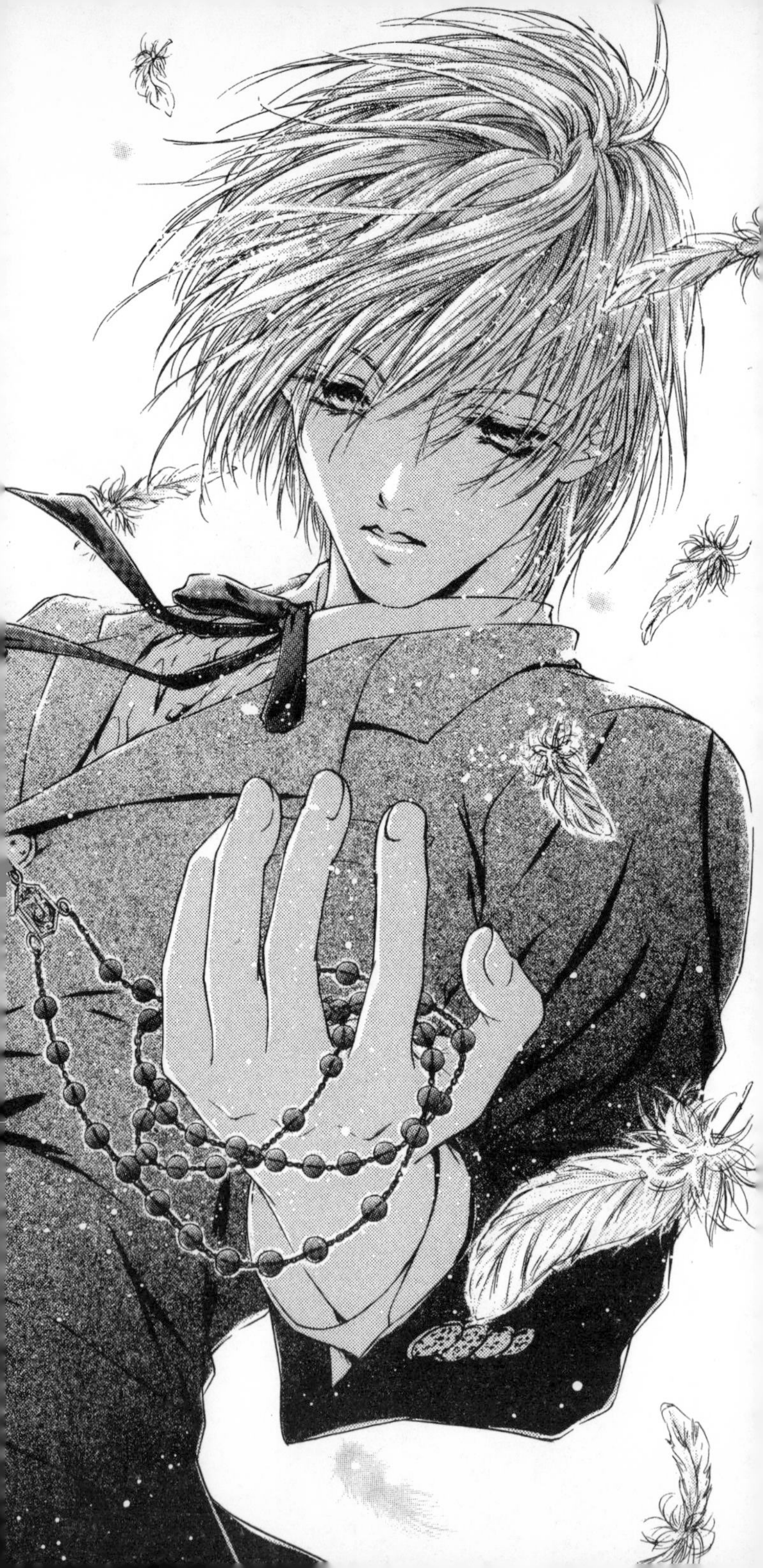

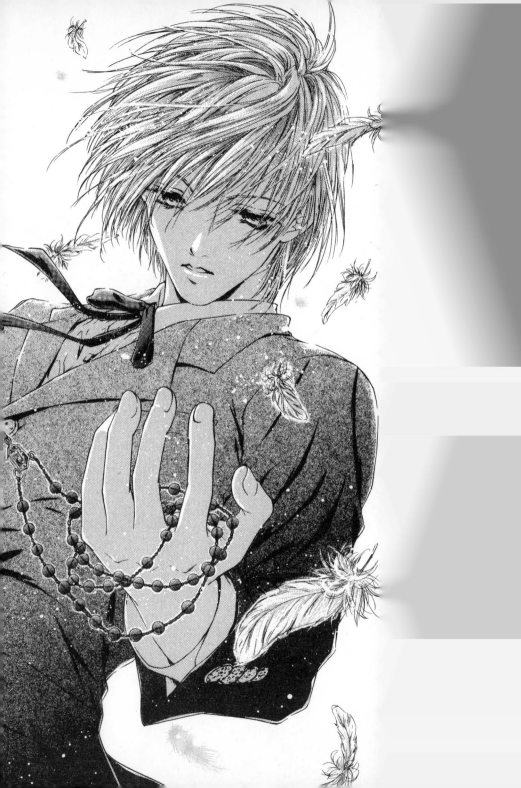

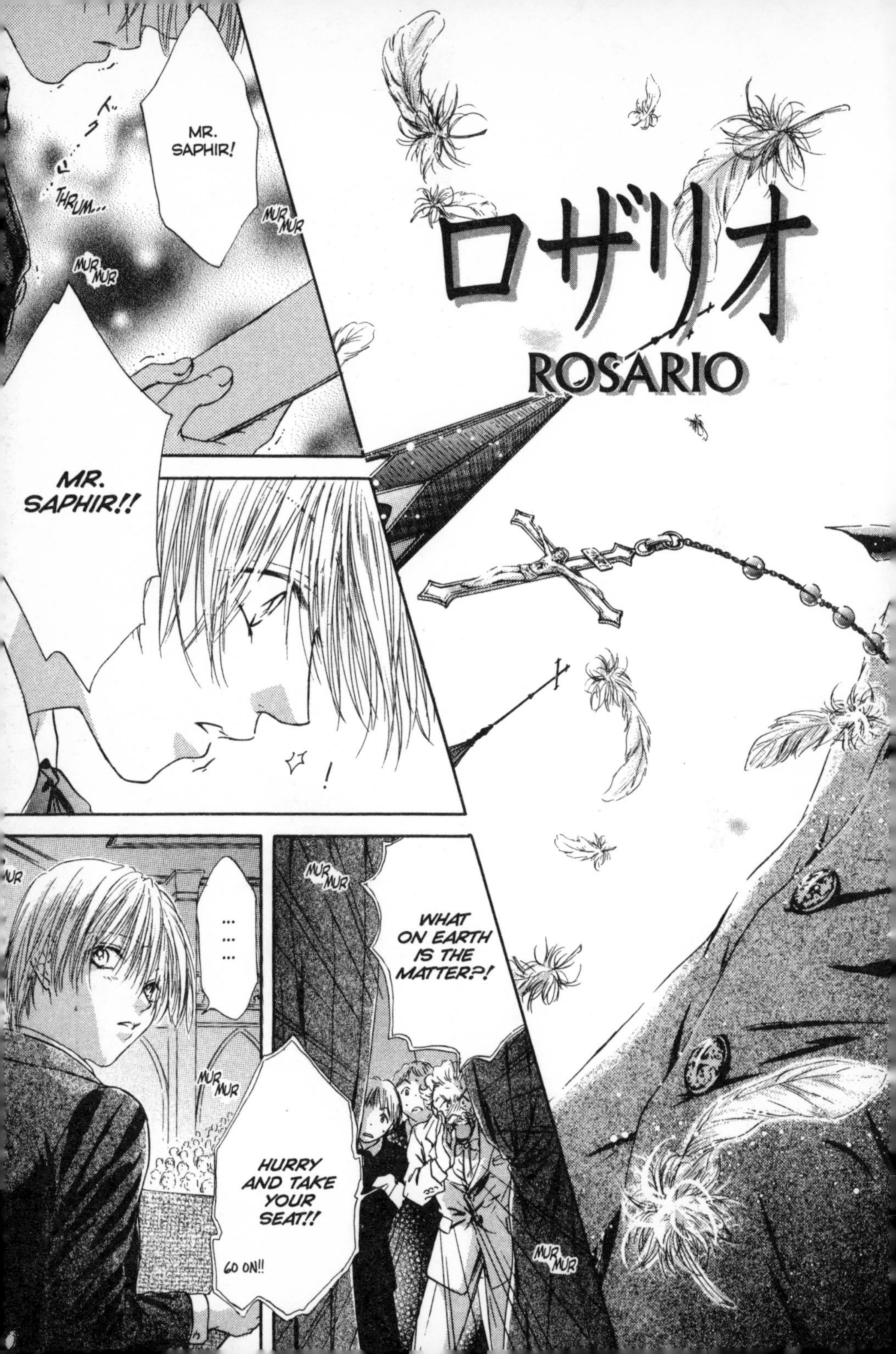
ロザリオ
ROSARIO
MUR MUR
MR. SAPHIR!
THRUM...
MUR MUR
MUR MUR
MR. SAPHIR!!
MUR MUR
WHAT ON EARTH IS THE MATTER?!
HURRY AND TAKE YOUR SEAT!!
GO ON!!
...
...
...
MUR MUR
MUR

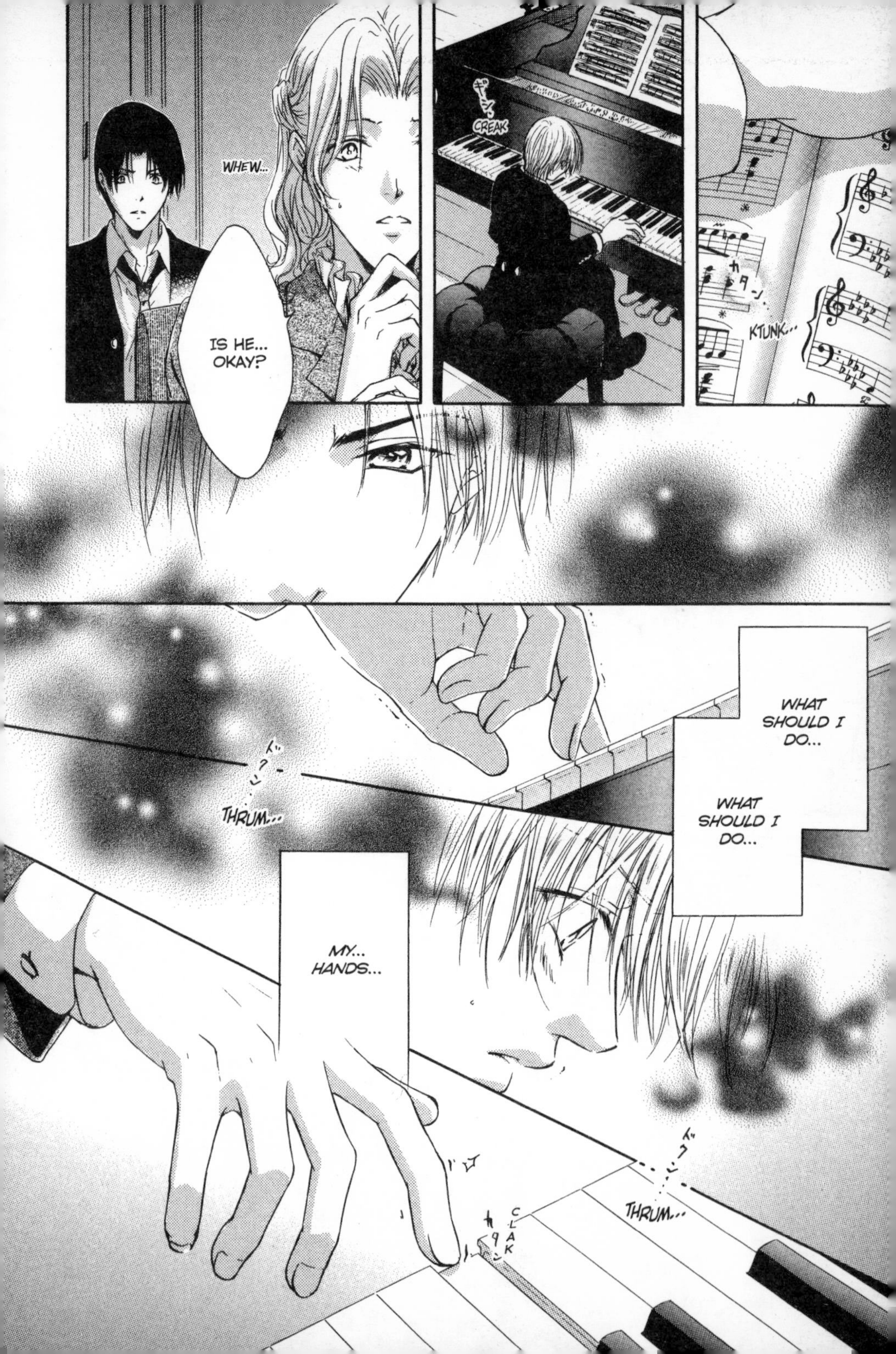
KTUNK...
CREAK
WHEW...
IS HE... OKAY?
WHAT SHOULD I DO...
WHAT SHOULD I DO...
THRUM...
MY... HANDS...
THRUM...
CLAK

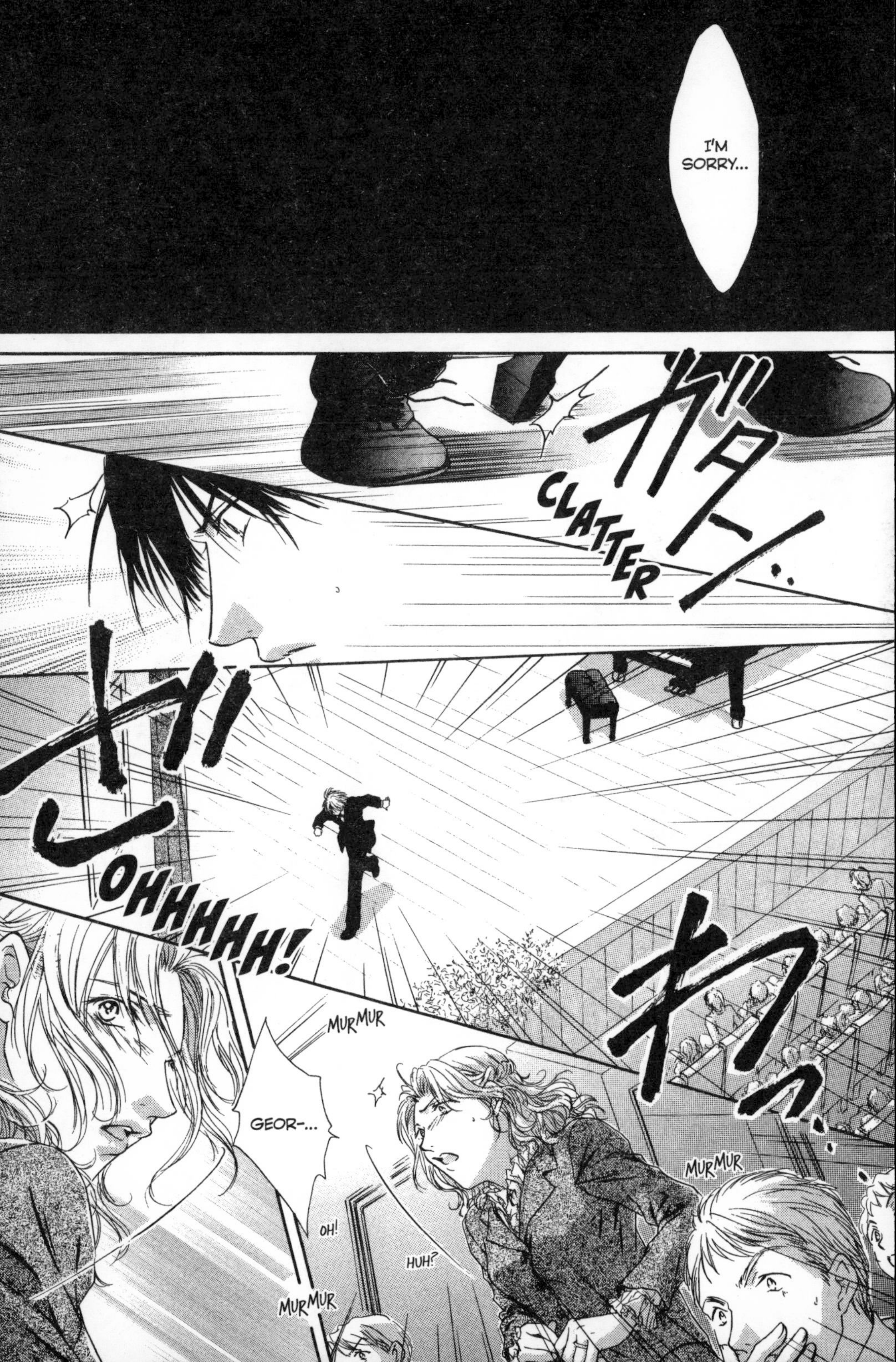
I'M SORRY...
CLATTER
OHHHHHH!
MURMUR
MURMUR
GEOR-...
OH!
HUH?
MURMUR

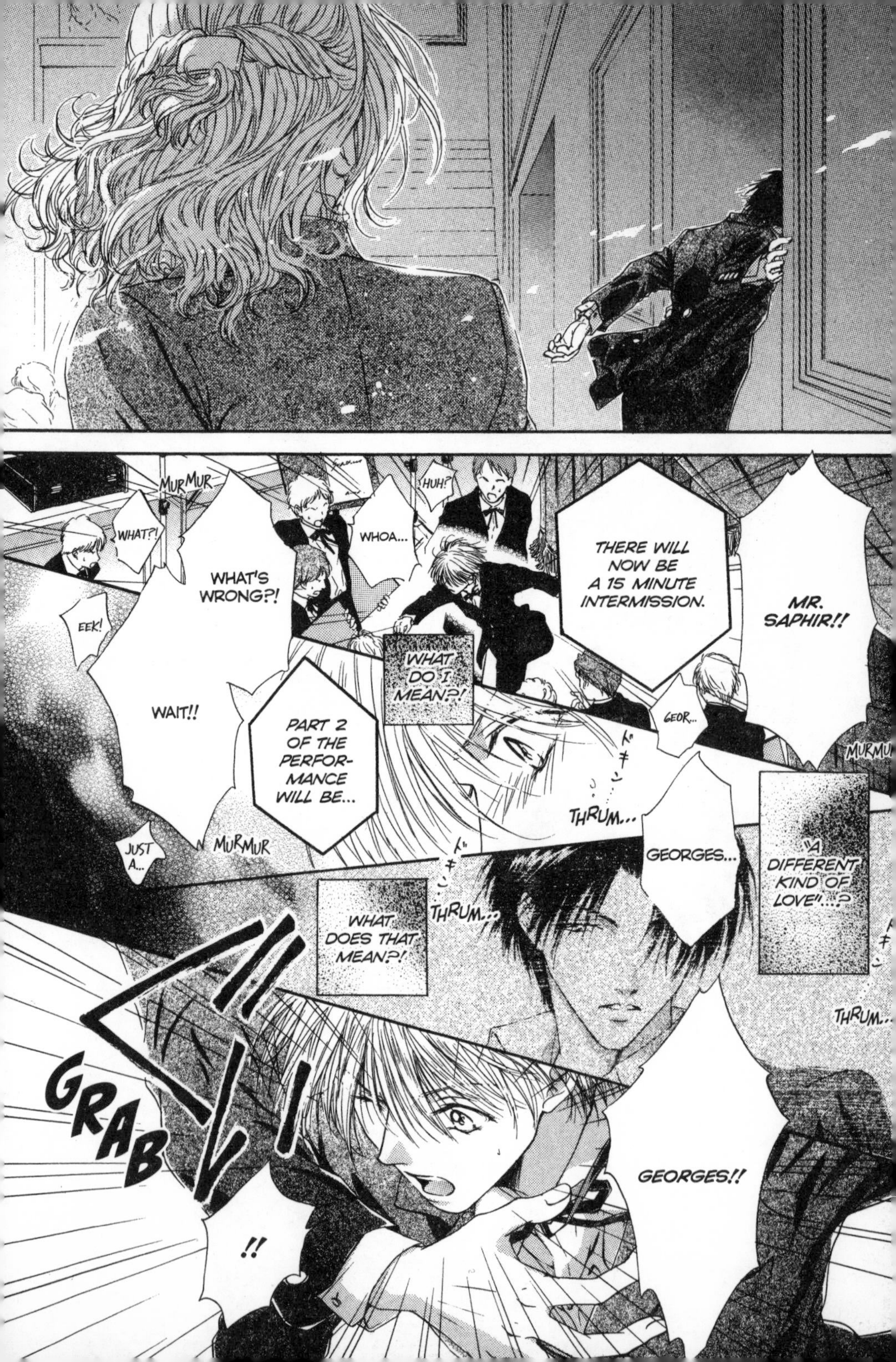
MR. SAPHIR!!
THERE WILL NOW BE A 15 MINUTE INTERMISSION.
HUH?
WHOA...
MURMUR
WHAT?!
WHAT'S WRONG?!
EEK!
MURMU
GEOR...
WHAT DO I MEAN?!
PART 2 OF THE PERFORMANCE WILL BE...
WAIT!!
THRUM...
MURMUR
JUST A...
"A DIFFERENT KIND OF LOVE"...?
GEORGES...
THRUM...
THRUM...
WHAT DOES THAT MEAN?!
GEORGES!!
GRAB
!!

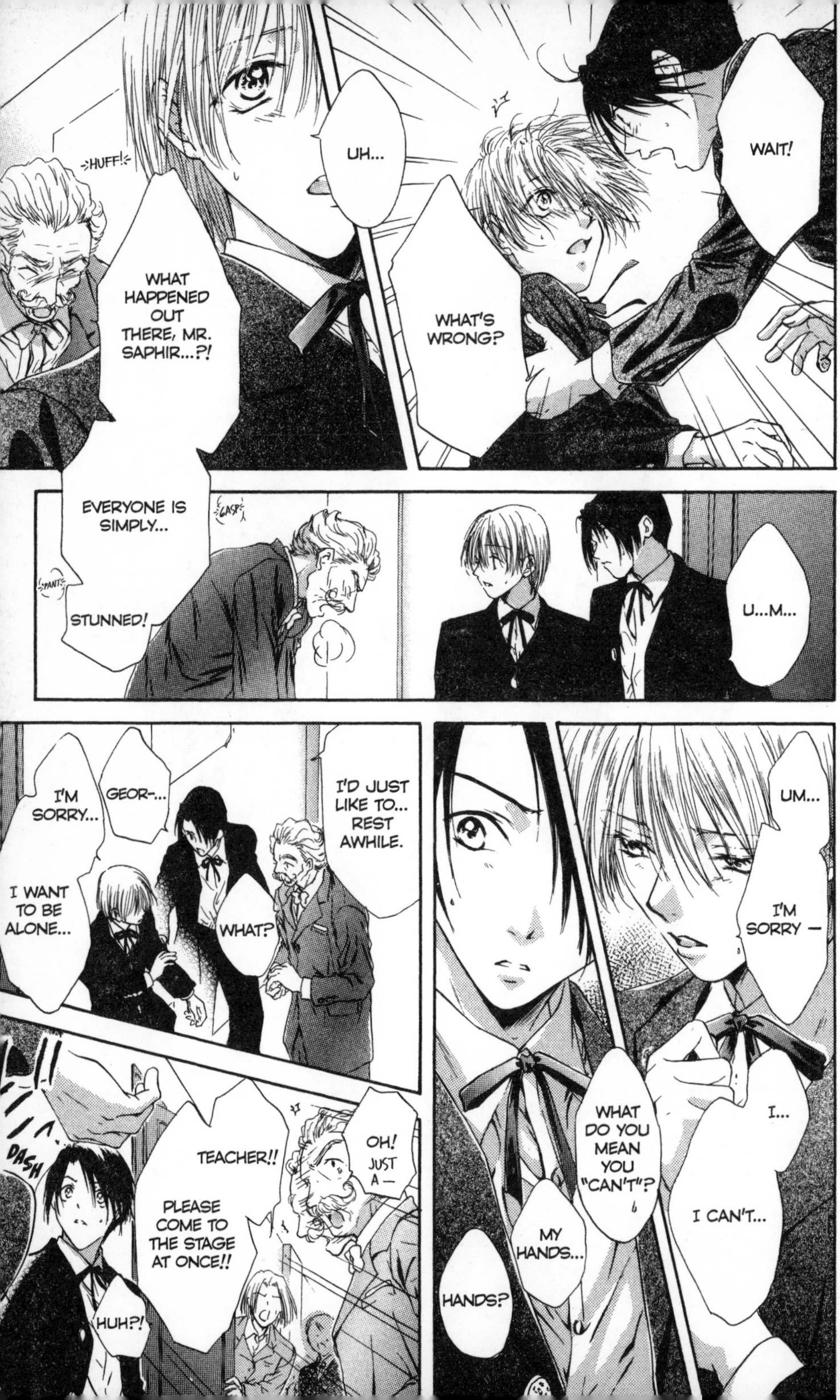
WAIT!
WHAT'S WRONG?
UH...
-HUFF!-
WHAT HAPPENED OUT THERE, MR. SAPHIR...?!
U...M...
GASP
EVERYONE IS SIMPLY...
PANT
STUNNED!
UM...
I'M SORRY —
I...
I CAN'T...
WHAT DO YOU MEAN YOU "CAN'T"?
MY HANDS...
HANDS?
I'D JUST LIKE TO... REST AWHILE.
GEOR-...
I'M SORRY...
I WANT TO BE ALONE...
WHAT?
OH! JUST A —
TEACHER!!
PLEASE COME TO THE STAGE AT ONCE!!
DASH
HUH?!

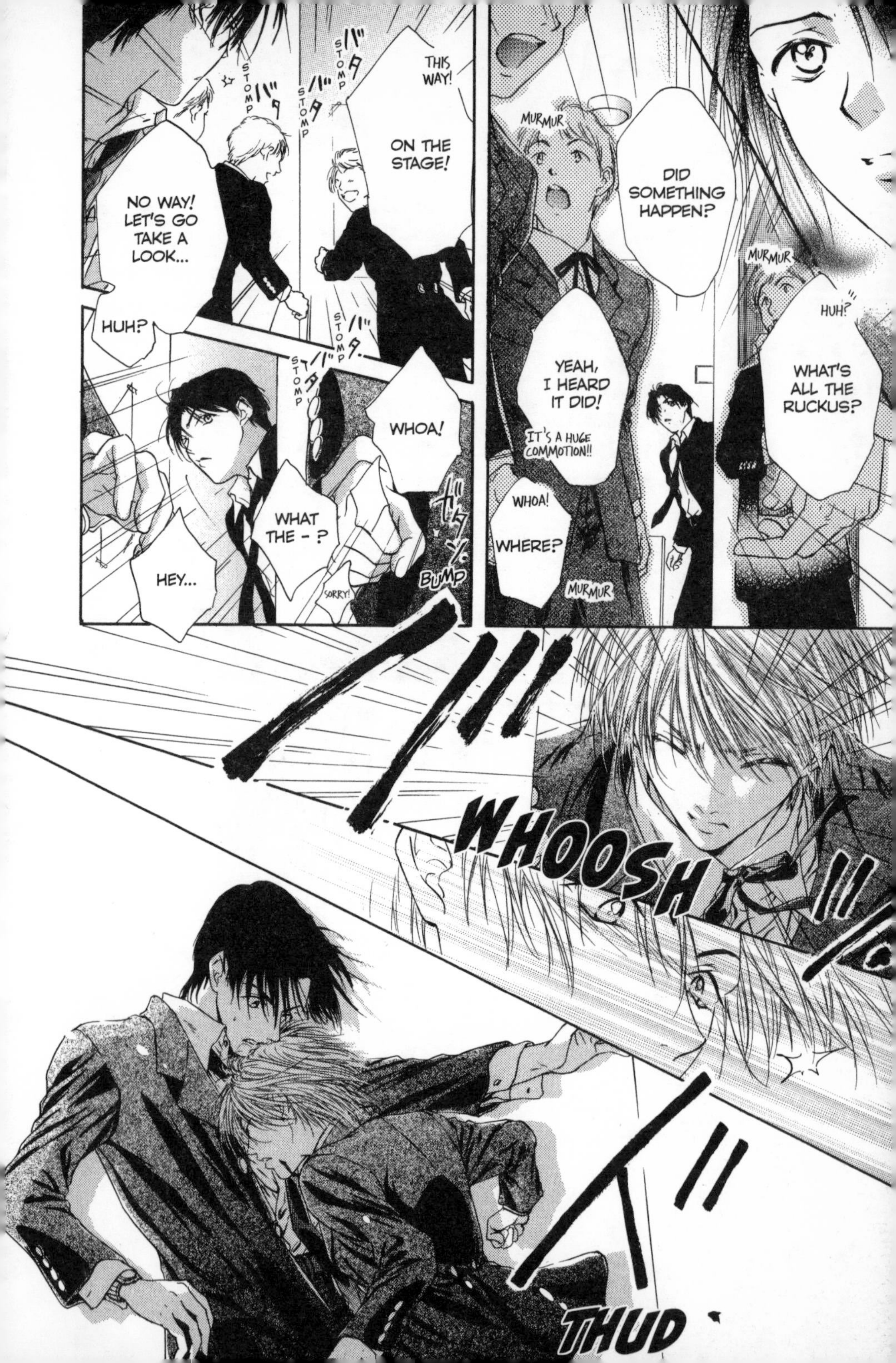
MURMUR
DID SOMETHING HAPPEN?
MURMUR
HUH?
WHAT'S ALL THE RUCKUS?
YEAH, I HEARD IT DID!
IT'S A HUGE COMMOTION!!
WHOA!
WHERE?
MURMUR
THIS WAY!
ON THE STAGE!
STOMP
STOMP
STOMP
NO WAY! LET'S GO TAKE A LOOK...
HUH?
STOMP
STOMP
WHOA!
WHAT THE - ?
HEY...
SORRY!
BUMP
WHOOSH
THUD

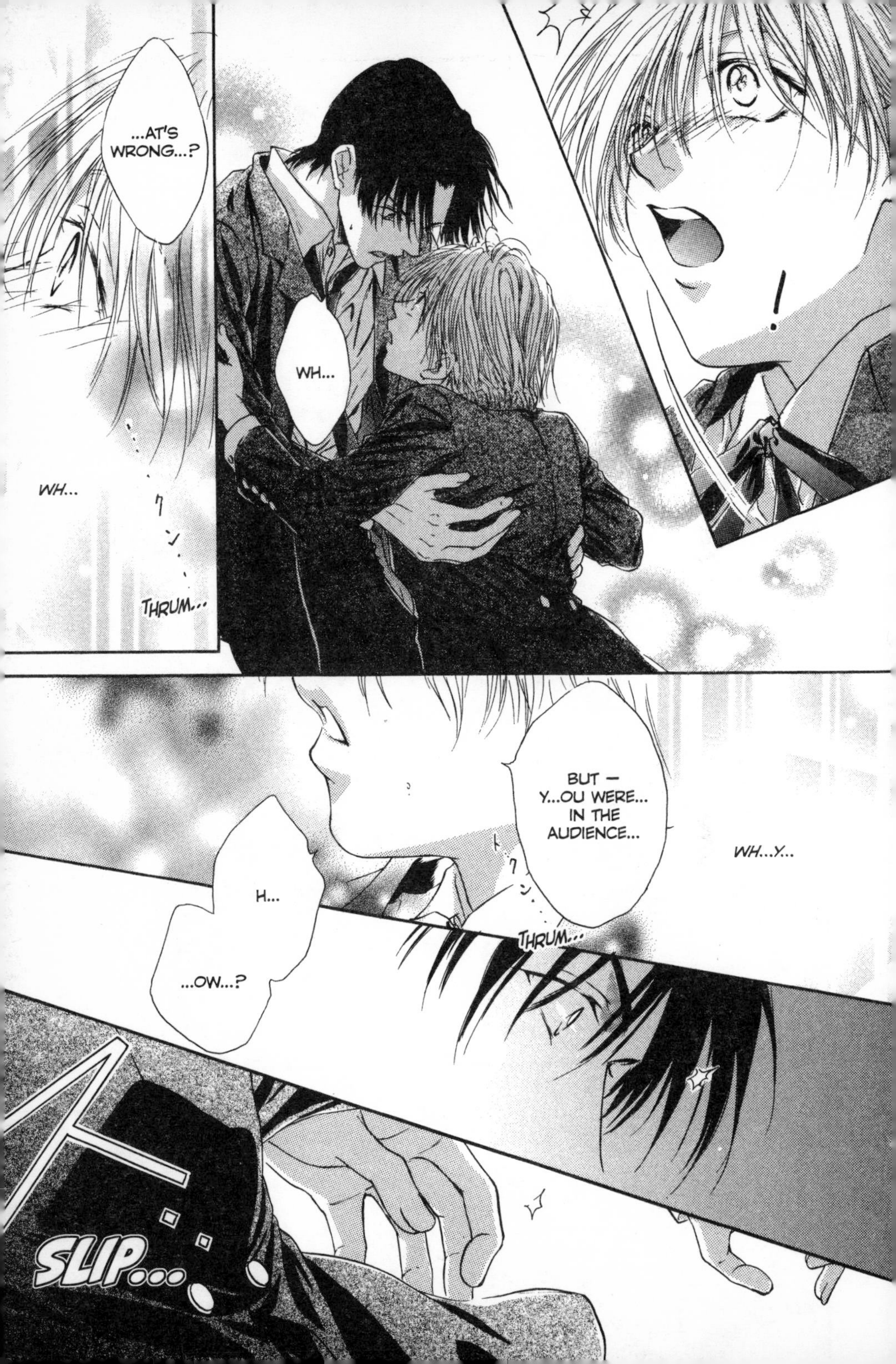
WH...
...AT'S WRONG...?
WH...
THRUM...
WH...Y...
BUT — Y...OU WERE... IN THE AUDIENCE...
THRUM...
H...
...OW...?
SLIP...

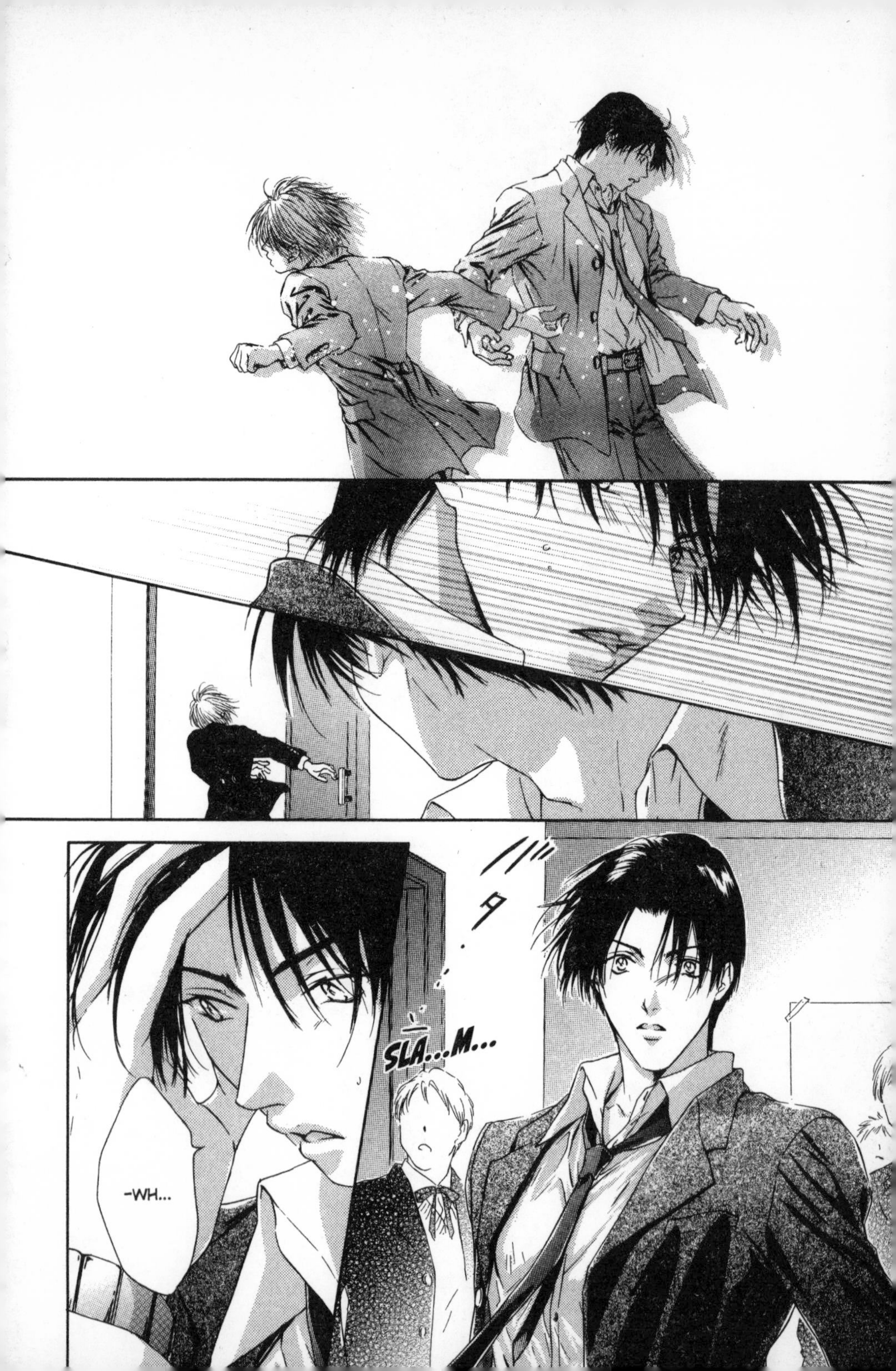

SLA...M...
-WH...

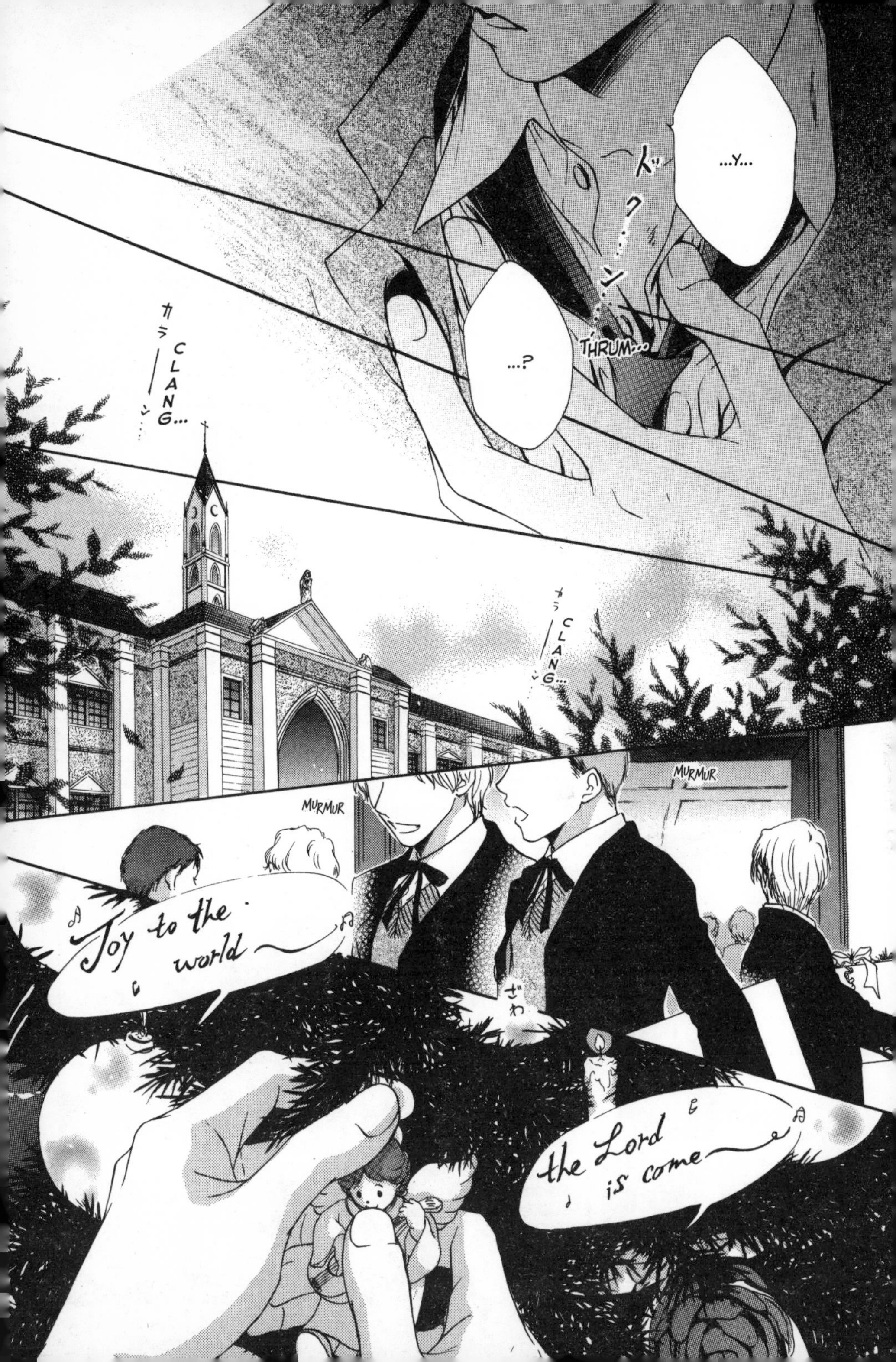
...Y...
ドクン……
THRUM...
...?
カラン…
CLANG...
カラン…
CLANG...
MURMUR
MURMUR
ざわ
Joy to the world
the Lord is come

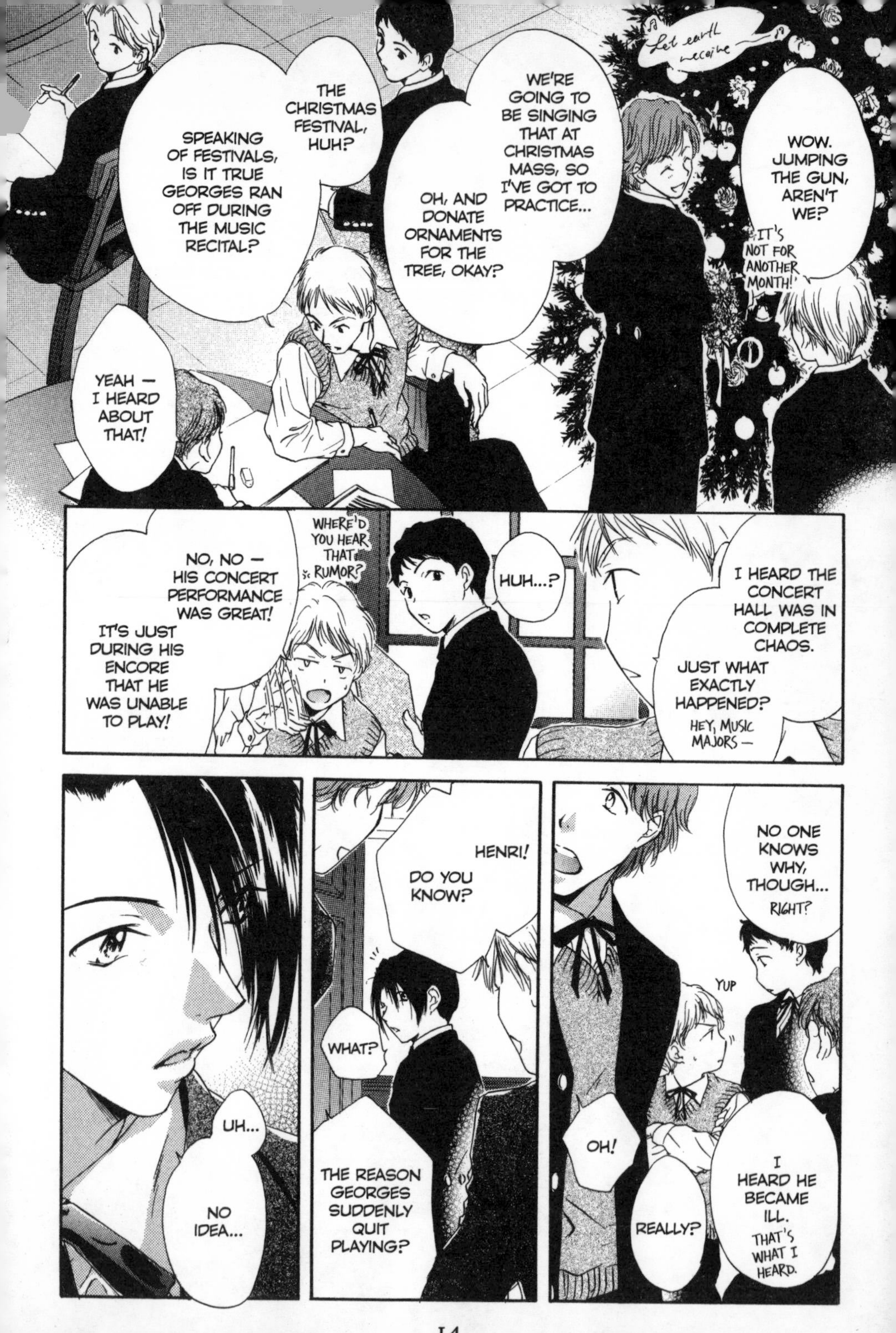

Let earth receive —
WOW. JUMPING THE GUN, AREN'T WE?
IT'S NOT FOR ANOTHER MONTH!
WE'RE GOING TO BE SINGING THAT AT CHRISTMAS MASS, SO I'VE GOT TO PRACTICE...
OH, AND DONATE ORNAMENTS FOR THE TREE, OKAY?
THE CHRISTMAS FESTIVAL, HUH?
SPEAKING OF FESTIVALS, IS IT TRUE GEORGES RAN OFF DURING THE MUSIC RECITAL?
YEAH — I HEARD ABOUT THAT!
I HEARD THE CONCERT HALL WAS IN COMPLETE CHAOS.
JUST WHAT EXACTLY HAPPENED?
HEY, MUSIC MAJORS —
HUH...?
WHERE'D YOU HEAR THAT RUMOR?
NO, NO — HIS CONCERT PERFORMANCE WAS GREAT!
IT'S JUST DURING HIS ENCORE THAT HE WAS UNABLE TO PLAY!
NO ONE KNOWS WHY, THOUGH...
RIGHT?
YUP
I HEARD HE BECAME ILL.
THAT'S WHAT I HEARD.
OH!
REALLY?
HENRI!
DO YOU KNOW?
WHAT?
THE REASON GEORGES SUDDENLY QUIT PLAYING?
UH...
NO IDEA...

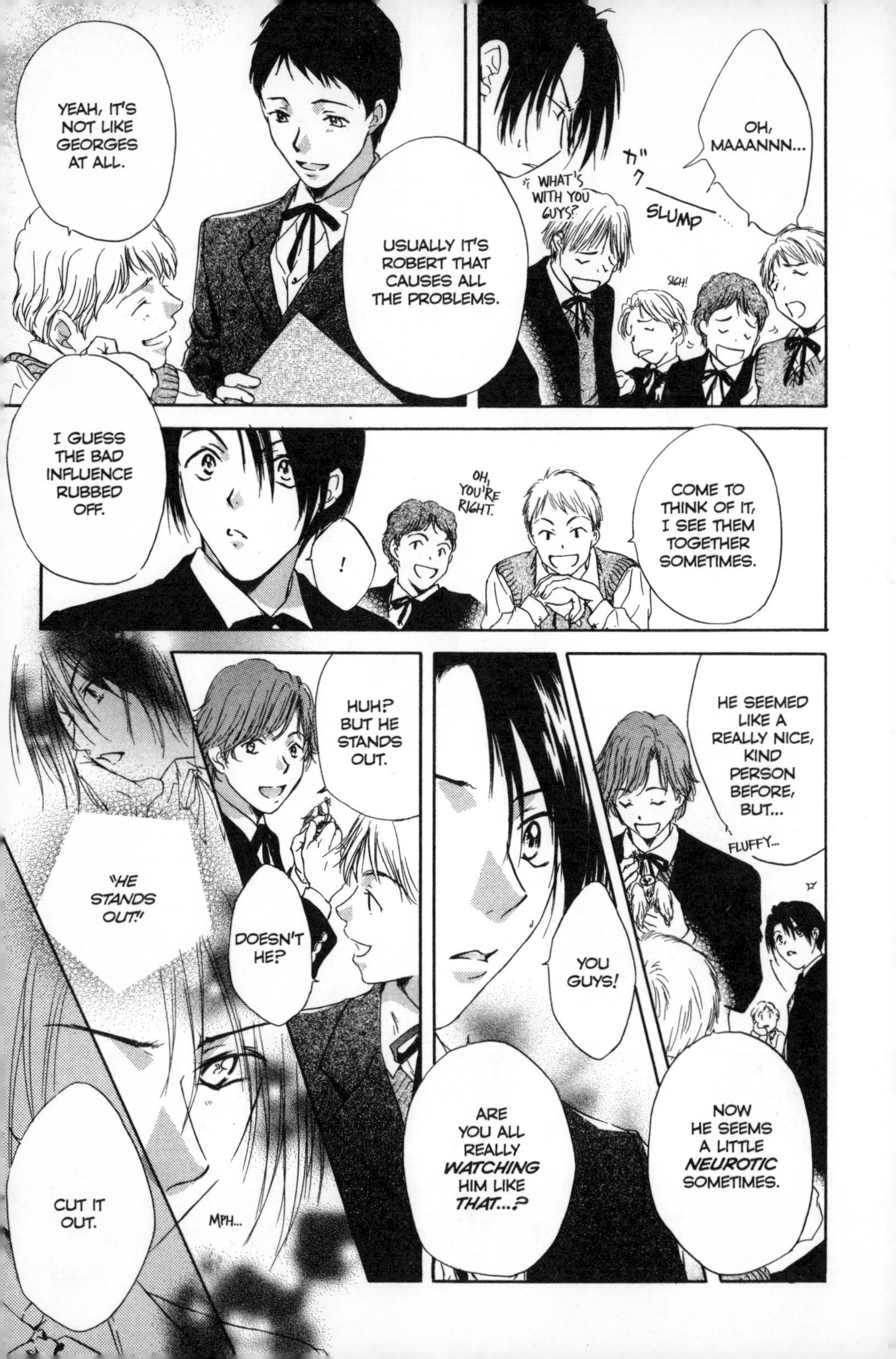
OH, MAAANNN...
ガク
SLUMP
WHAT'S WITH YOU GUYS?
SIGH!
YEAH, IT'S NOT LIKE GEORGES AT ALL.
USUALLY IT'S ROBERT THAT CAUSES ALL THE PROBLEMS.
COME TO THINK OF IT, I SEE THEM TOGETHER SOMETIMES.
OH, YOU'RE RIGHT.
!
I GUESS THE BAD INFLUENCE RUBBED OFF.
HE SEEMED LIKE A REALLY NICE, KIND PERSON BEFORE, BUT...
FLUFFY...
NOW HE SEEMS A LITTLE NEUROTIC SOMETIMES.
YOU GUYS!
ARE YOU ALL REALLY WATCHING HIM LIKE THAT...?
HUH? BUT HE STANDS OUT.
DOESN'T HE?
"HE STANDS OUT!"
MPH...
CUT IT OUT.

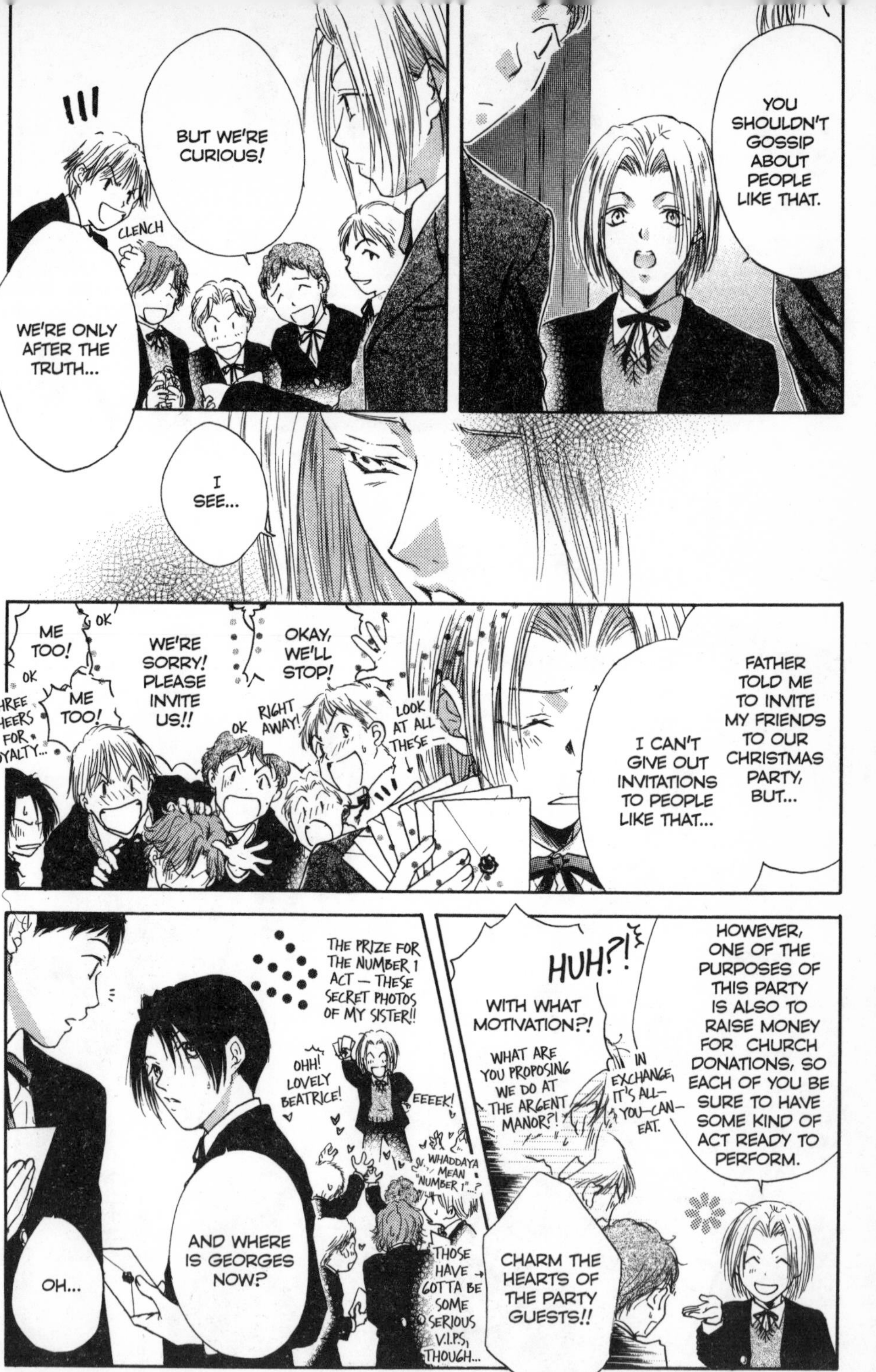
YOU SHOULDN'T GOSSIP ABOUT PEOPLE LIKE THAT.
!!!
BUT WE'RE CURIOUS!
CLENCH
WE'RE ONLY AFTER THE TRUTH...
I SEE...
FATHER TOLD ME TO INVITE MY FRIENDS TO OUR CHRISTMAS PARTY, BUT...
I CAN'T GIVE OUT INVITATIONS TO PEOPLE LIKE THAT...
LOOK AT ALL THESE—
OKAY, WE'LL STOP!
RIGHT AWAY!
OK
WE'RE SORRY! PLEASE INVITE US!!
OK
ME TOO!
OK
ME TOO!
THREE CHEERS FOR ROYALTY...
HOWEVER, ONE OF THE PURPOSES OF THIS PARTY IS ALSO TO RAISE MONEY FOR CHURCH DONATIONS, SO EACH OF YOU BE SURE TO HAVE SOME KIND OF ACT READY TO PERFORM.
HUH?!
IN EXCHANGE, IT'S ALL-YOU-CAN-EAT.
WITH WHAT MOTIVATION?!
WHAT ARE YOU PROPOSING WE DO AT THE ARGENT MANOR?!
CHARM THE HEARTS OF THE PARTY GUESTS!!
THE PRIZE FOR THE NUMBER 1 ACT — THESE SECRET PHOTOS OF MY SISTER!!
OHH! LOVELY BEATRICE!
EEEEK!
WHADDAYA MEAN "NUMBER 1"...?
THOSE HAVE GOTTA BE SOME SERIOUS V.I.P.S, THOUGH...
AND WHERE IS GEORGES NOW?
OH...

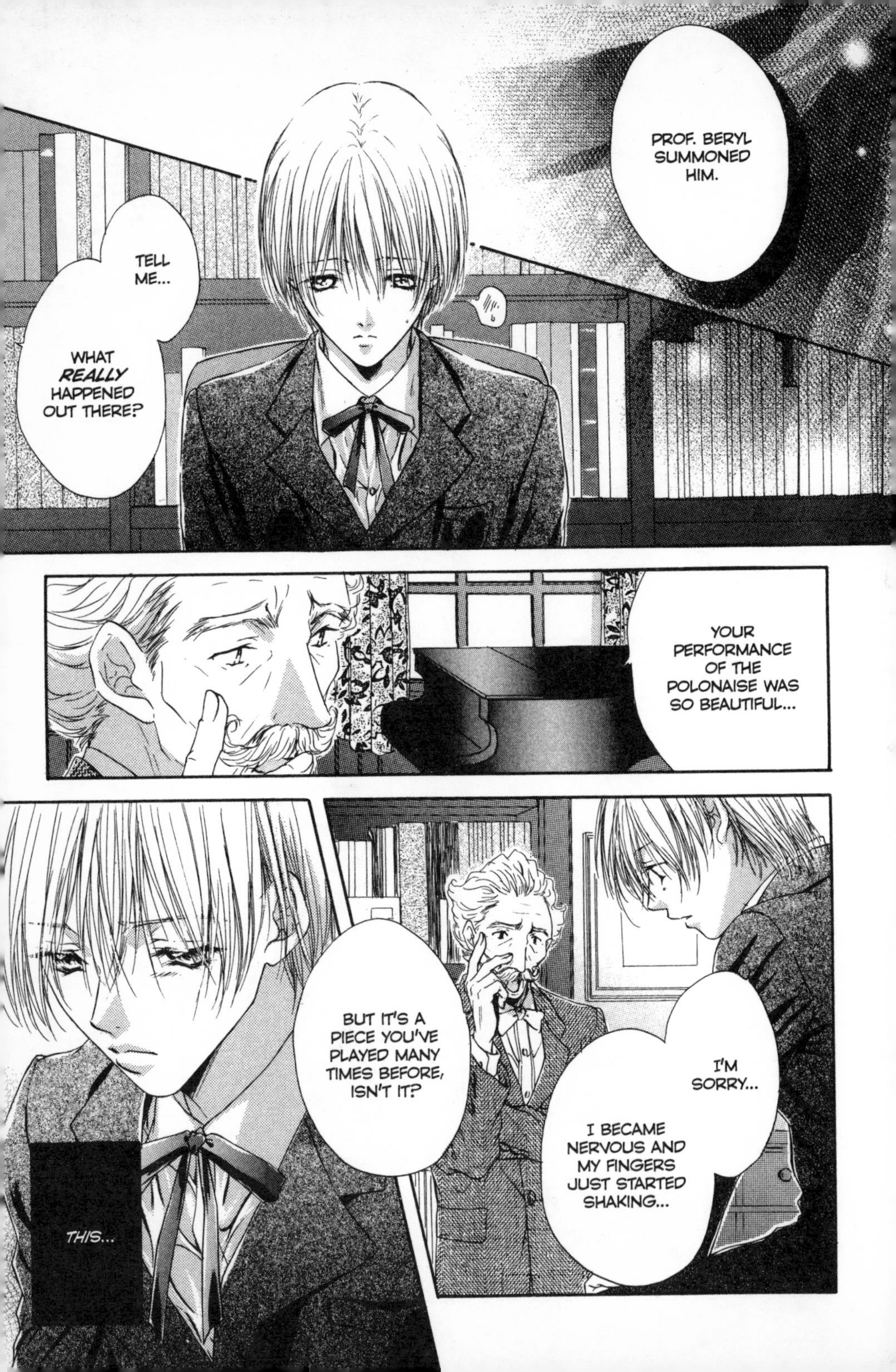
PROF. BERYL SUMMONED HIM.
TELL ME...
WHAT *REALLY* HAPPENED OUT THERE?
YOUR PERFORMANCE OF THE POLONAISE WAS SO BEAUTIFUL...
BUT IT'S A PIECE YOU'VE PLAYED MANY TIMES BEFORE, ISN'T IT?
I'M SORRY...
I BECAME NERVOUS AND MY FINGERS JUST STARTED SHAKING...
THIS...

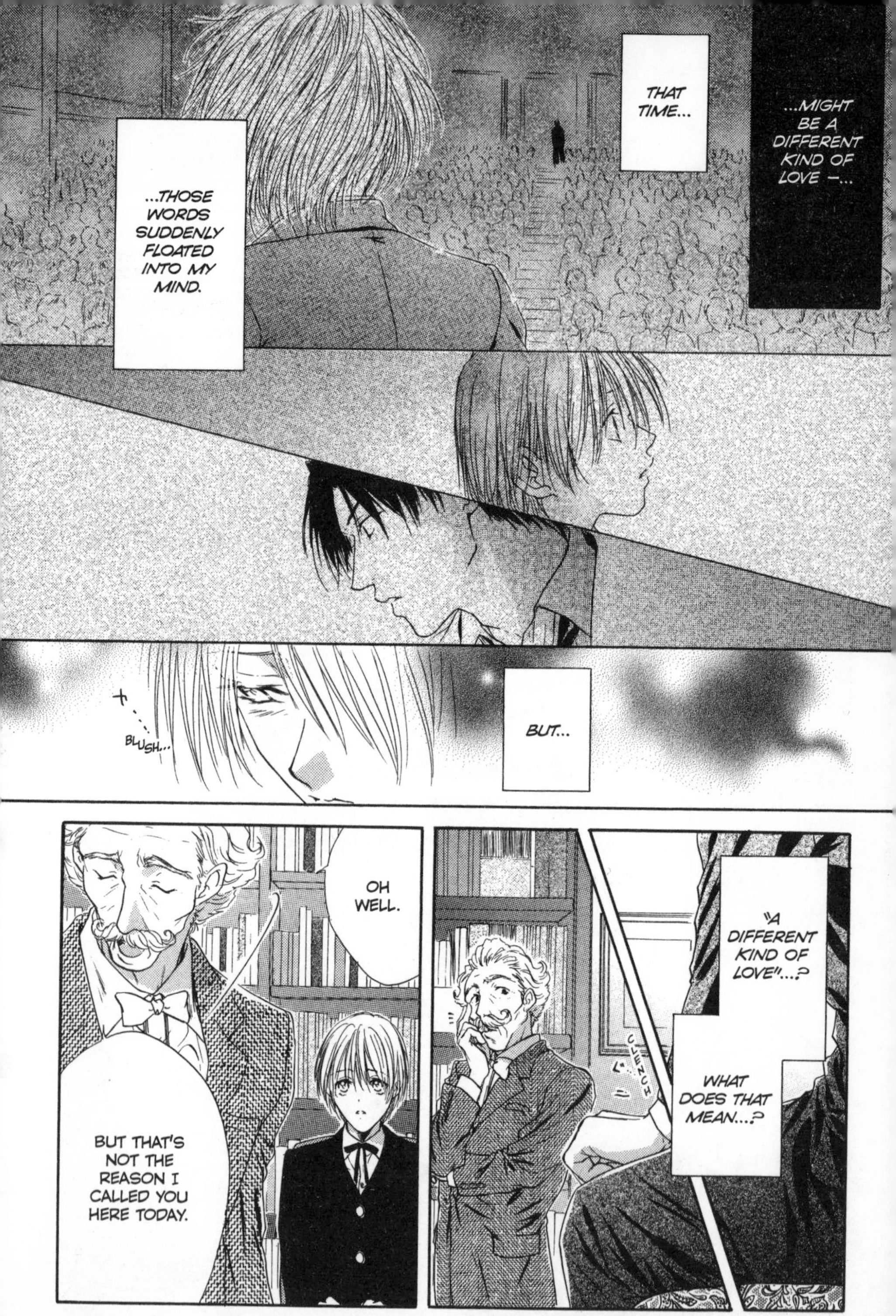
...MIGHT BE A DIFFERENT KIND OF LOVE —...
THAT TIME...
...THOSE WORDS SUDDENLY FLOATED INTO MY MIND.
BUT...
BLUSH...
"A DIFFERENT KIND OF LOVE"...?
WHAT DOES THAT MEAN...?
CLENCH
OH WELL.
BUT THAT'S NOT THE REASON I CALLED YOU HERE TODAY.

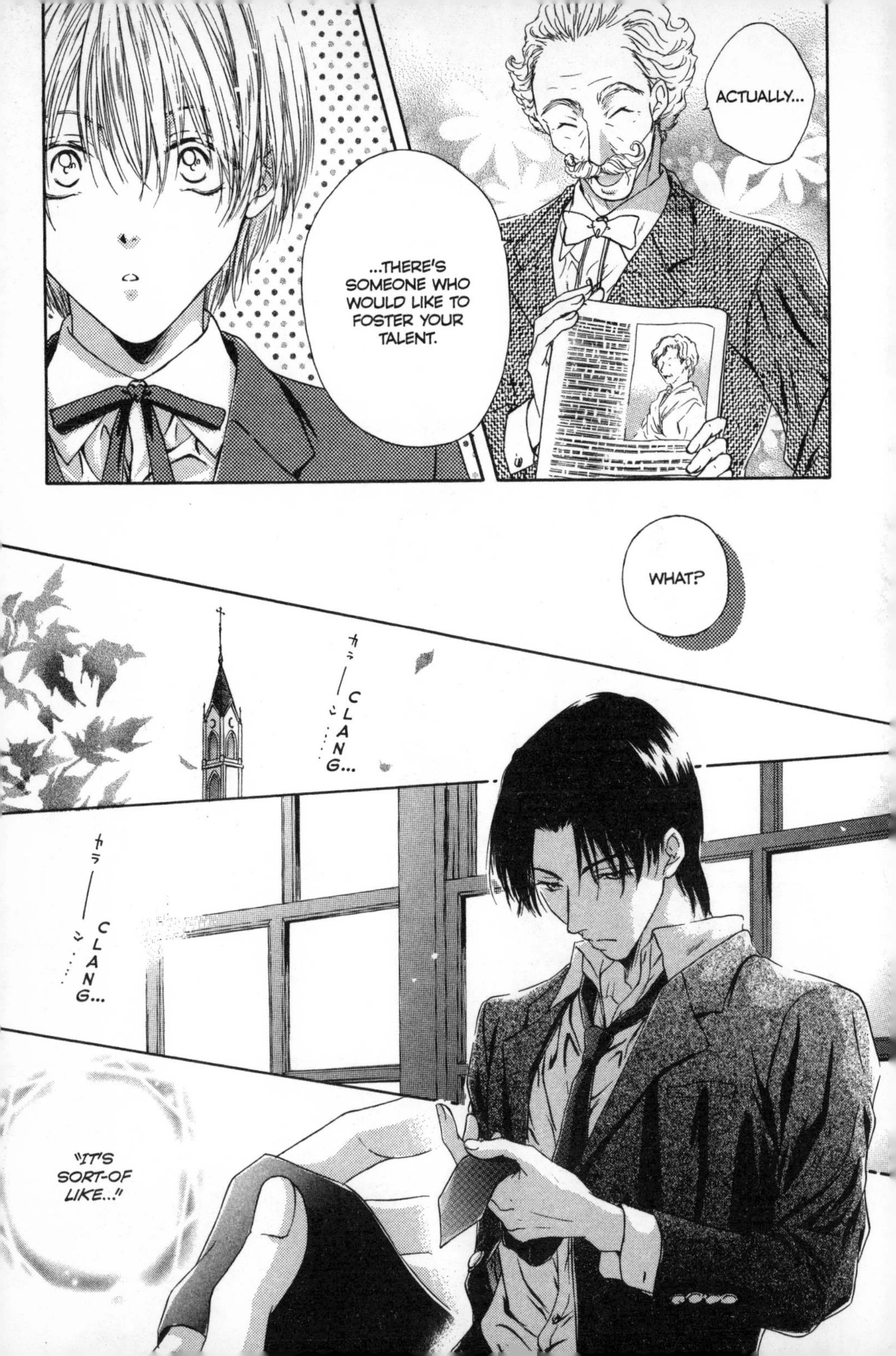
ACTUALLY...
...THERE'S SOMEONE WHO WOULD LIKE TO FOSTER YOUR TALENT.
WHAT?
CLANG...
CLANG...
"IT'S SORT-OF LIKE...!"

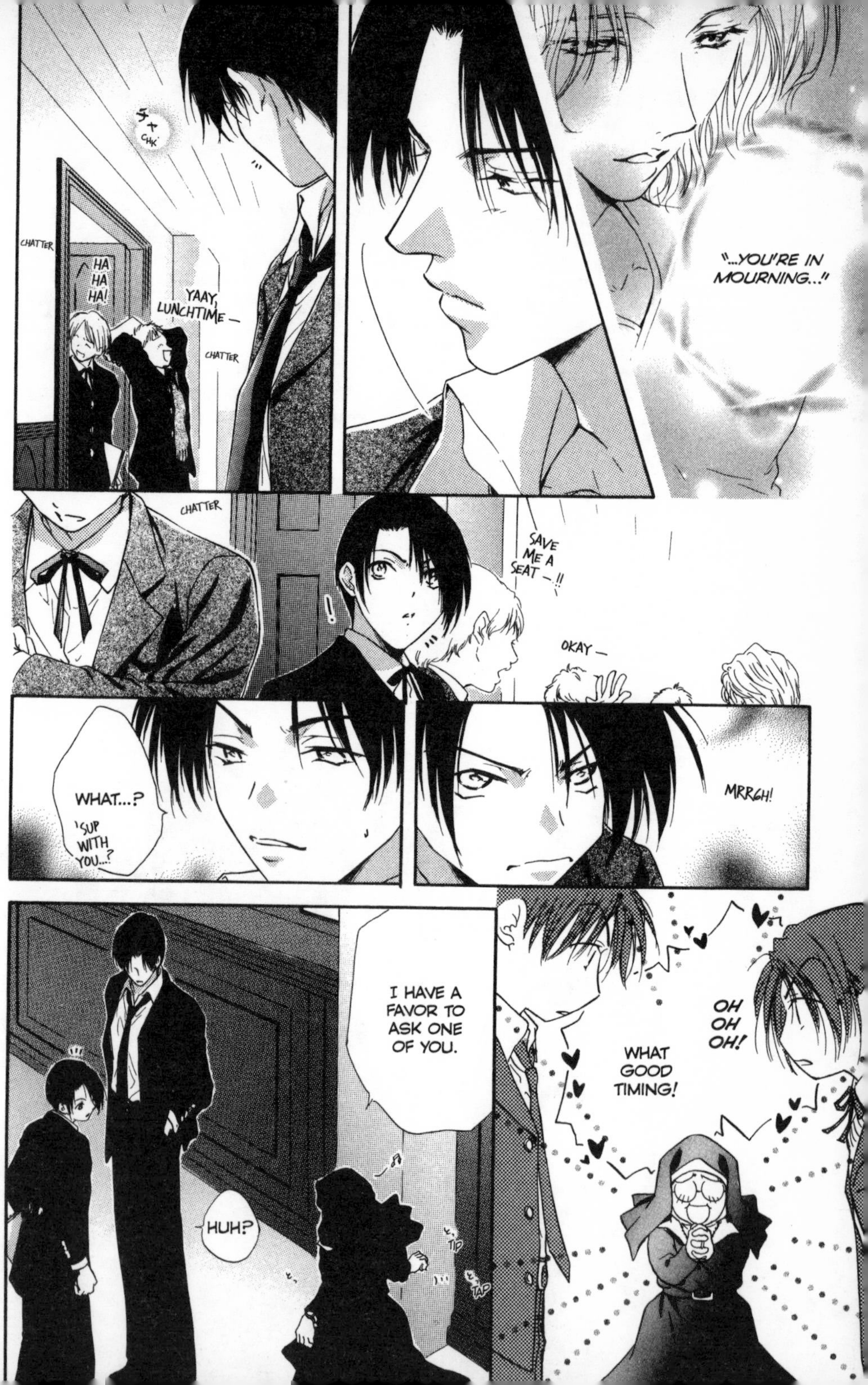
"...YOU'RE IN MOURNING...!"
チャ
CHK
YAAY, LUNCHTIME —
HA HA HA!
CHATTER
CHATTER
SAVE ME A SEAT —!!
OKAY —
!
CHATTER
MRRGH!
WHAT...?
'SUP WITH YOU...?
OH OH OH!
WHAT GOOD TIMING!
I HAVE A FAVOR TO ASK ONE OF YOU.
TIP
TAP
HUH?

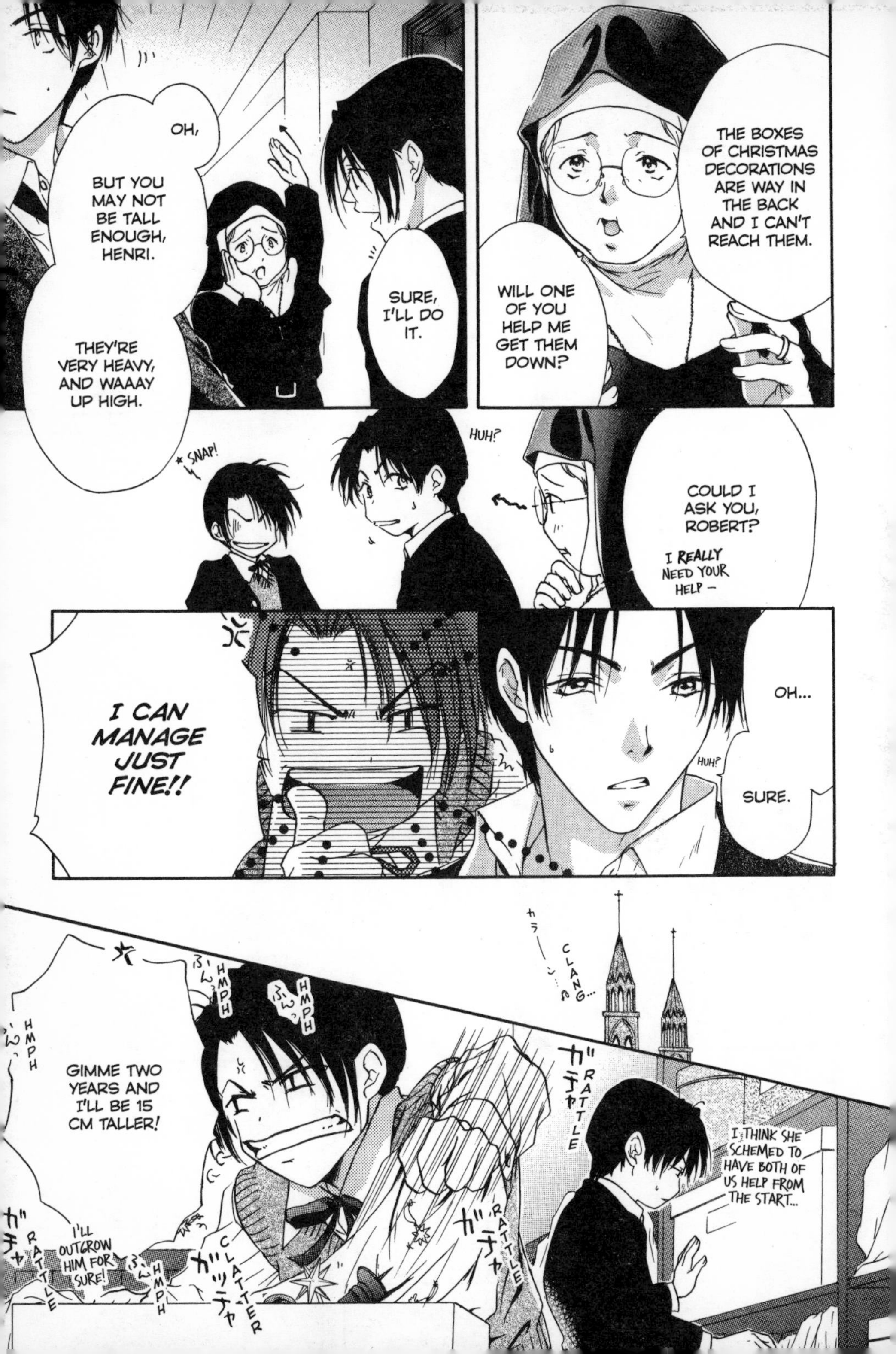
THE BOXES OF CHRISTMAS DECORATIONS ARE WAY IN THE BACK AND I CAN'T REACH THEM.
WILL ONE OF YOU HELP ME GET THEM DOWN?
SURE, I'LL DO IT.
OH,
BUT YOU MAY NOT BE TALL ENOUGH, HENRI.
THEY'RE VERY HEAVY, AND WAAAY UP HIGH.
COULD I ASK YOU, ROBERT?
I REALLY NEED YOUR HELP —
HUH?
SNAP!
OH...
HUH?
SURE.
I CAN MANAGE JUST FINE!!
CLANG...
I THINK SHE SCHEMED TO HAVE BOTH OF US HELP FROM THE START...
RATTLE
HMPH
HMPH
GIMME TWO YEARS AND I'LL BE 15 CM TALLER!
HMPH
RATTLE
CLATTER
HMPH
I'LL OUTGROW HIM FOR SURE!
RATTLE

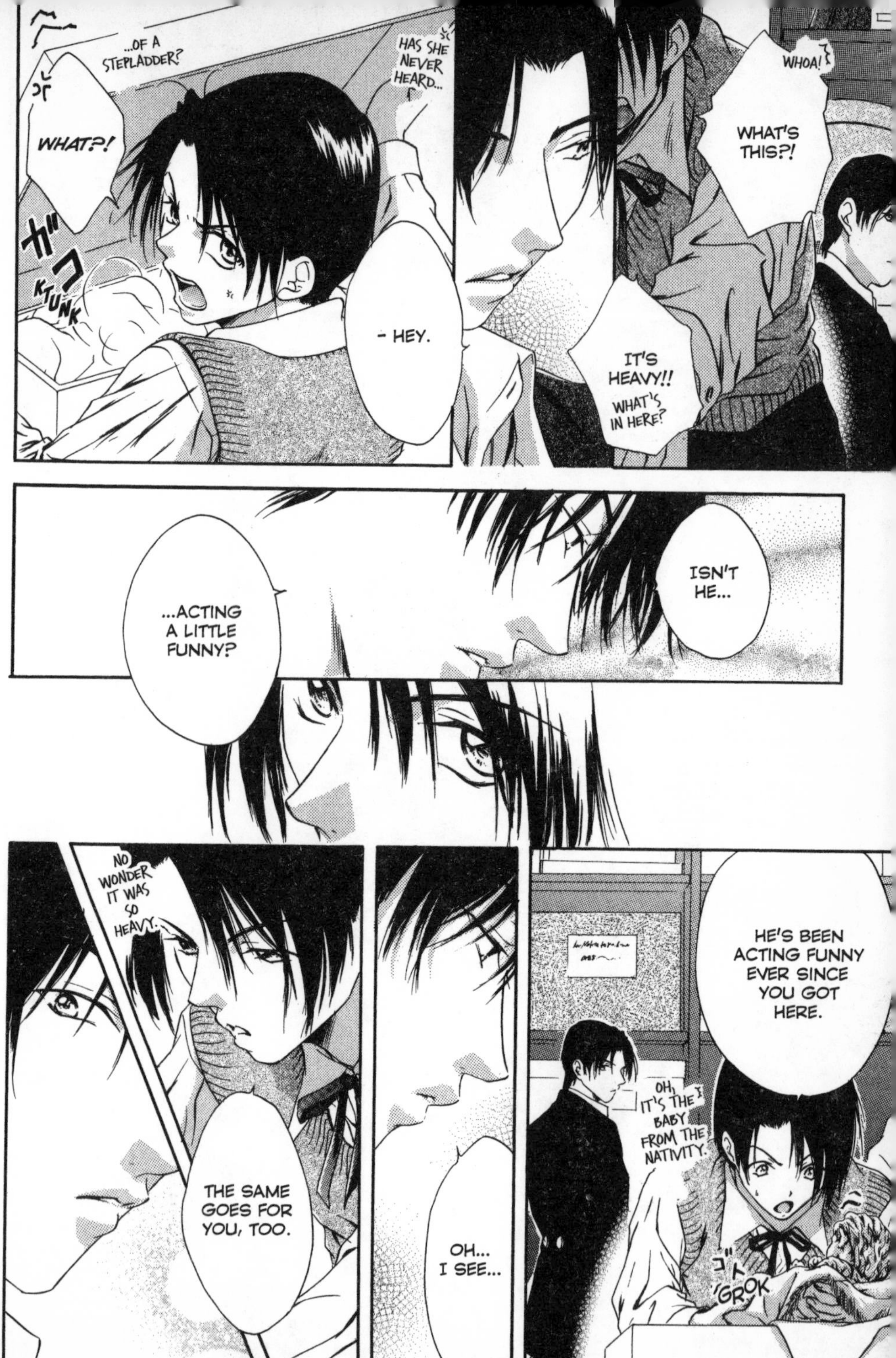
WHOA!
WHAT'S THIS?!
IT'S HEAVY!! WHAT'S IN HERE?
- HEY.
HAS SHE NEVER HEARD...
...OF A STEPLADDER?
WHAT?!
KTUNK
ISN'T HE...
...ACTING A LITTLE FUNNY?
HE'S BEEN ACTING FUNNY EVER SINCE YOU GOT HERE.
OH, IT'S THE BABY FROM THE NATIVITY.
GROK
OH... I SEE...
NO WONDER IT WAS SO HEAVY.
THE SAME GOES FOR YOU, TOO.

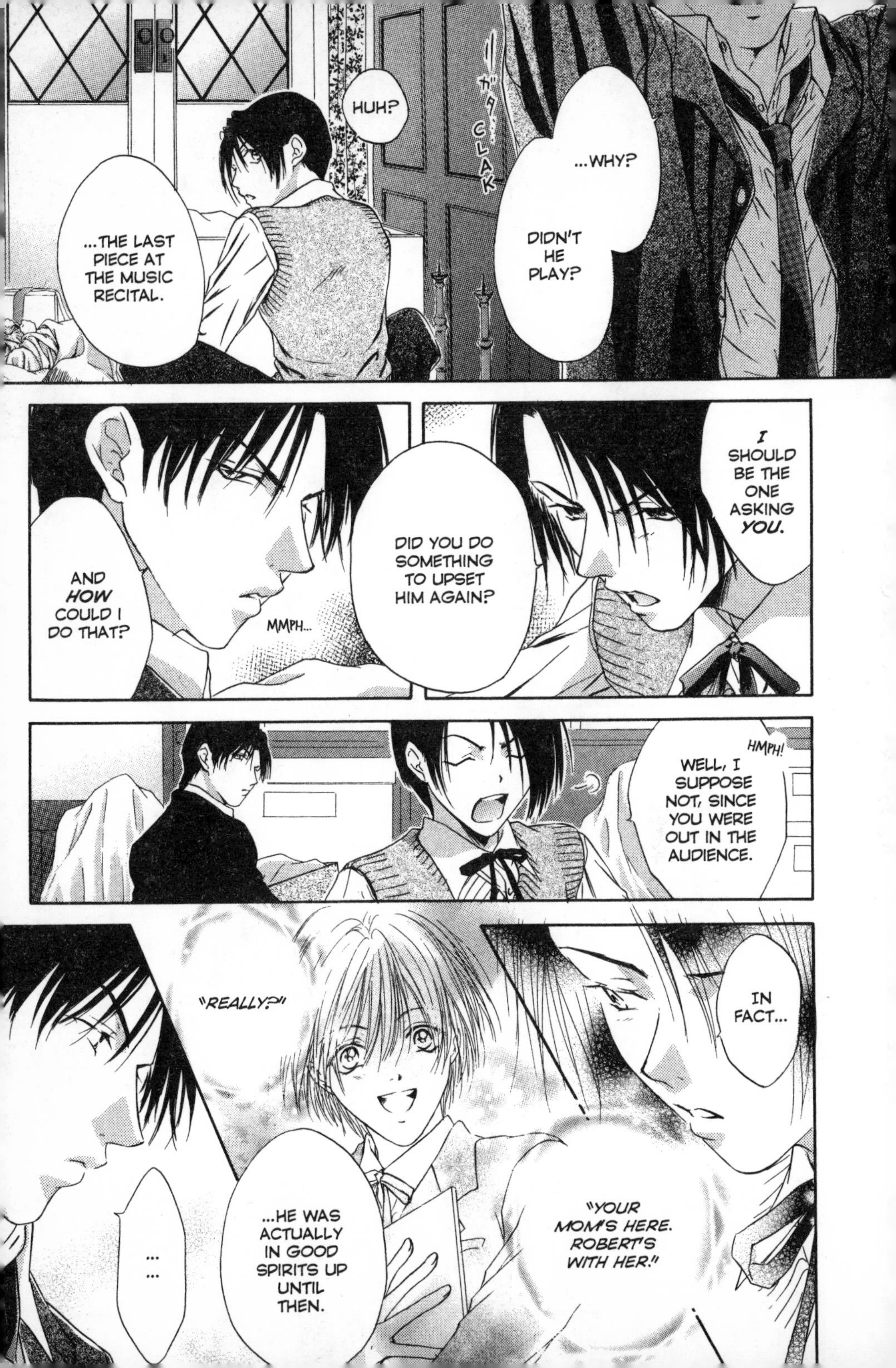
...WHY?
DIDN'T HE PLAY?
CLAK
HUH?
...THE LAST PIECE AT THE MUSIC RECITAL.
I SHOULD BE THE ONE ASKING *YOU*.
DID YOU DO SOMETHING TO UPSET HIM AGAIN?
MMPH...
AND *HOW* COULD I DO THAT?
HMPH!
WELL, I SUPPOSE NOT, SINCE YOU WERE OUT IN THE AUDIENCE.
IN FACT...
"YOUR MOM'S HERE. ROBERT'S WITH HER."
"REALLY?"
...HE WAS ACTUALLY IN GOOD SPIRITS UP UNTIL THEN.
... ...

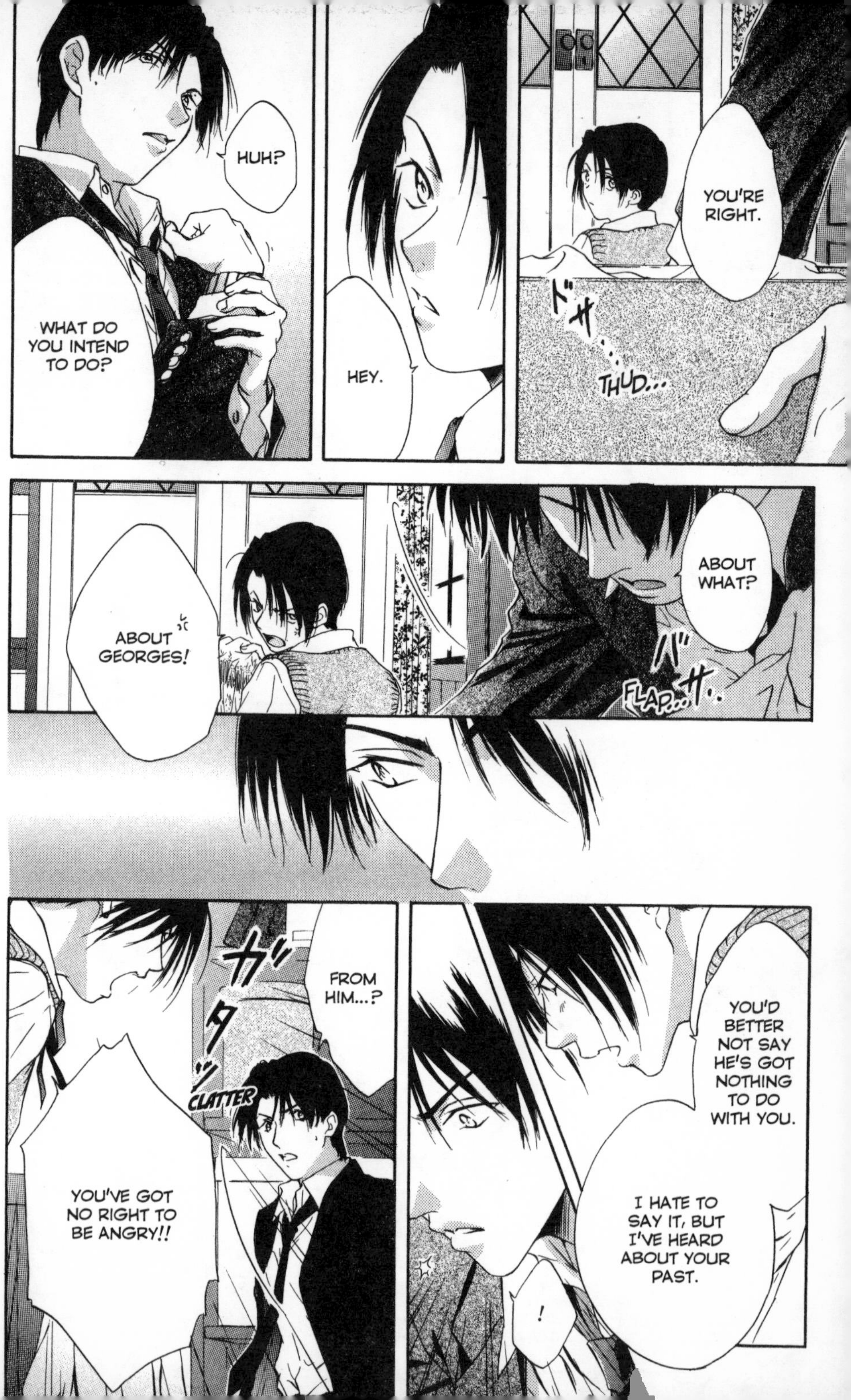
YOU'RE RIGHT.
ドサ...
THUD...
HEY.
HUH?
WHAT DO YOU INTEND TO DO?
ABOUT WHAT?
バサ..
FLAP...
ABOUT GEORGES!
YOU'D BETTER NOT SAY HE'S GOT NOTHING TO DO WITH YOU.
I HATE TO SAY IT, BUT I'VE HEARD ABOUT YOUR PAST.
!
FROM HIM...?
ガタッ
CLATTER
YOU'VE GOT NO RIGHT TO BE ANGRY!!

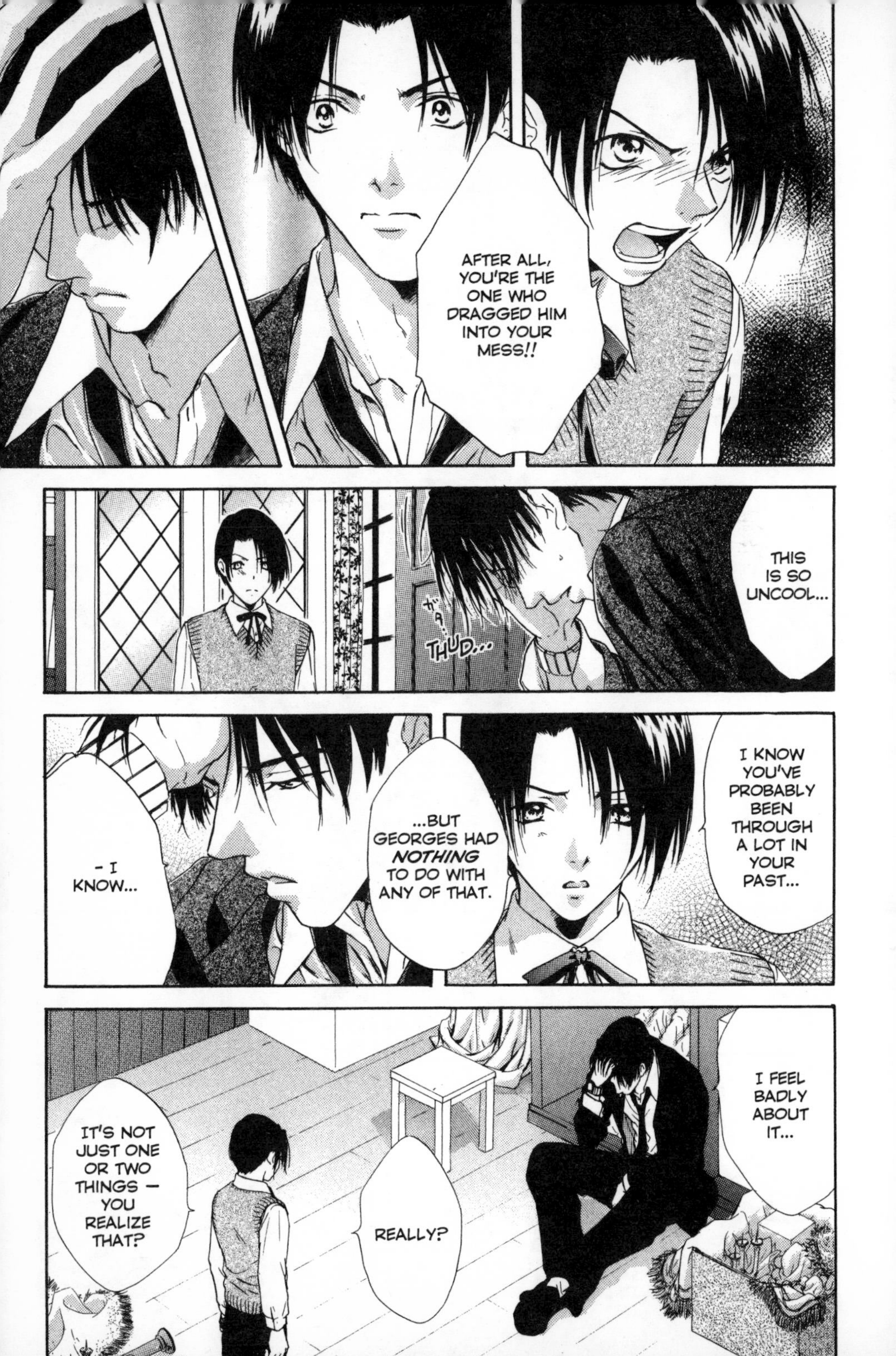
AFTER ALL, YOU'RE THE ONE WHO DRAGGED HIM INTO YOUR MESS!!
THIS IS SO UNCOOL...
THUD...
I KNOW YOU'VE PROBABLY BEEN THROUGH A LOT IN YOUR PAST...
...BUT GEORGES HAD *NOTHING* TO DO WITH ANY OF THAT.
- I KNOW...
I FEEL BADLY ABOUT IT...
REALLY?
IT'S NOT JUST ONE OR TWO THINGS – YOU REALIZE THAT?

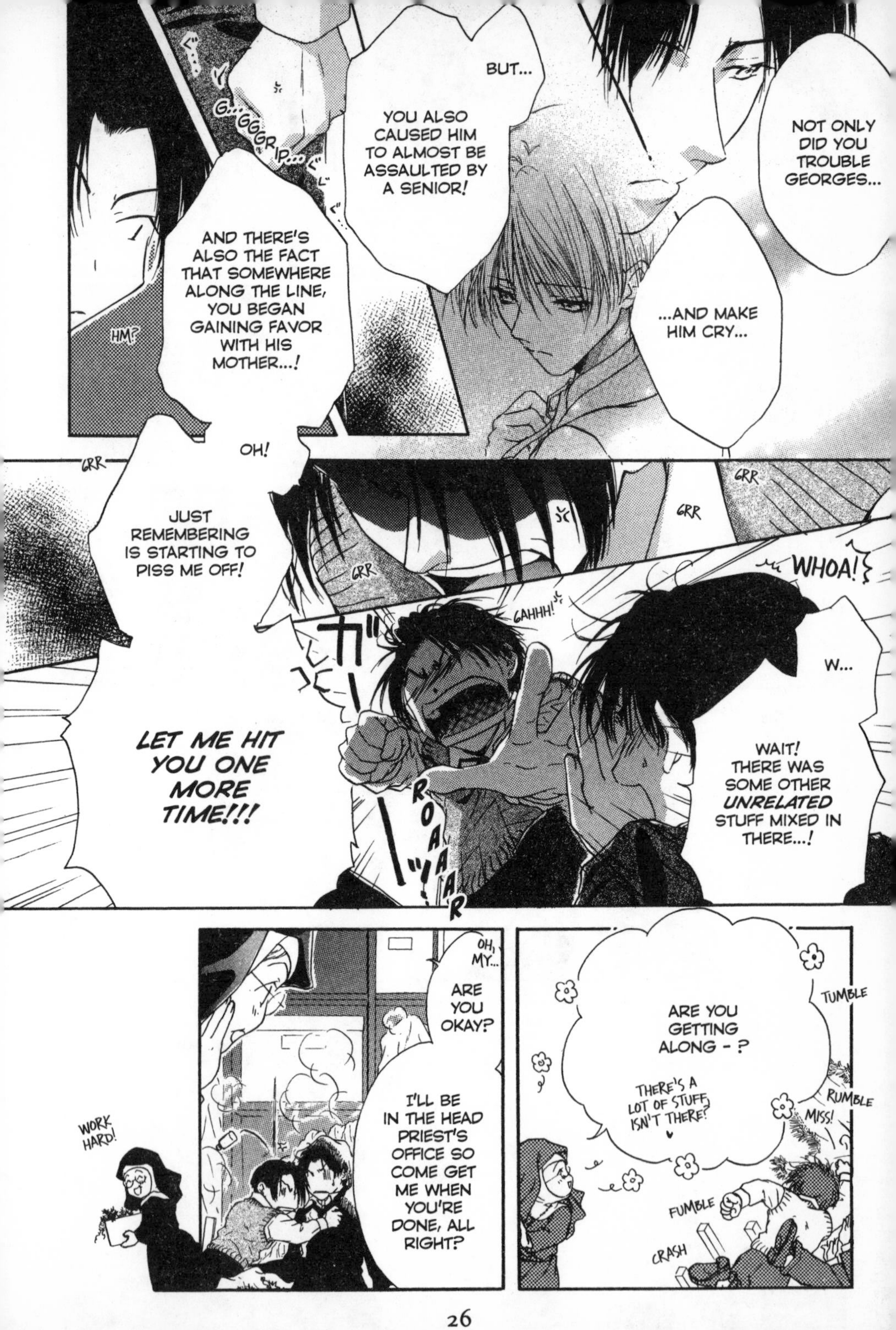
NOT ONLY DID YOU TROUBLE GEORGES...
...AND MAKE HIM CRY...
BUT...
YOU ALSO CAUSED HIM TO ALMOST BE ASSAULTED BY A SENIOR!
G...GGGRIP...
AND THERE'S ALSO THE FACT THAT SOMEWHERE ALONG THE LINE, YOU BEGAN GAINING FAVOR WITH HIS MOTHER...!
HM?
GRR
GRR
OH!
JUST REMEMBERING IS STARTING TO PISS ME OFF!
GRR
GRR
WHOA!
W...
WAIT! THERE WAS SOME OTHER *UNRELATED* STUFF MIXED IN THERE...!
GAHHH!
ROAAAAR
LET ME HIT YOU ONE MORE TIME!!!
ARE YOU GETTING ALONG -?
TUMBLE
RUMBLE
MISS!
THERE'S A LOT OF STUFF, ISN'T THERE?
FUMBLE
CRASH
OH, MY...
ARE YOU OKAY?
I'LL BE IN THE HEAD PRIEST'S OFFICE SO COME GET ME WHEN YOU'RE DONE, ALL RIGHT?
WORK HARD!

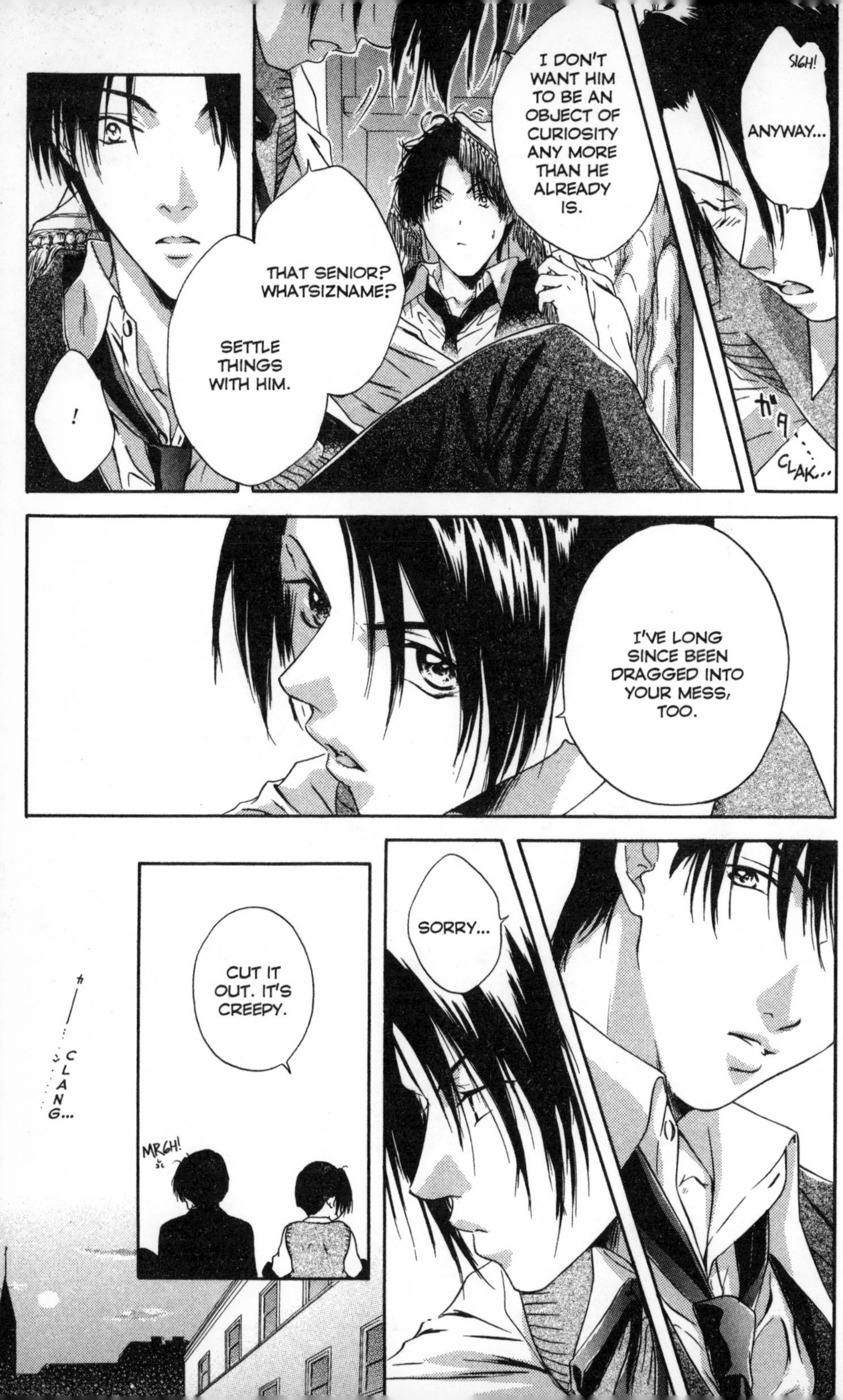
SIGH!
ANYWAY...
ガタ
CLAK...
I DON'T WANT HIM TO BE AN OBJECT OF CURIOSITY ANY MORE THAN HE ALREADY IS.
THAT SENIOR? WHATSIZNAME?
SETTLE THINGS WITH HIM.
!
I'VE LONG SINCE BEEN DRAGGED INTO YOUR MESS, TOO.
SORRY...
CUT IT OUT. IT'S CREEPY.
MRGH!
CLANG...

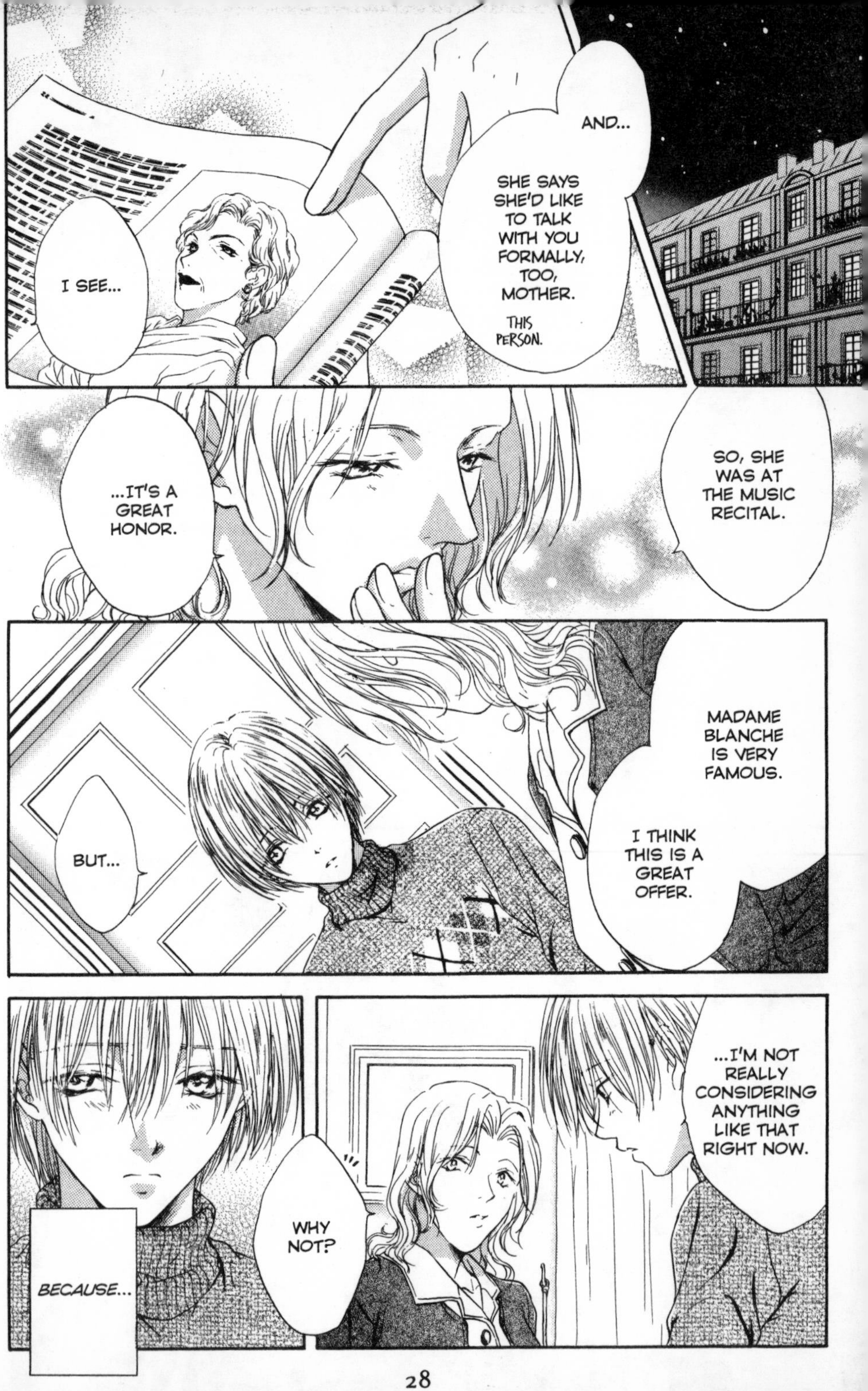
AND...
SHE SAYS SHE'D LIKE TO TALK WITH YOU FORMALLY, TOO, MOTHER.
THIS PERSON.
I SEE...
SO, SHE WAS AT THE MUSIC RECITAL.
...IT'S A GREAT HONOR.
MADAME BLANCHE IS VERY FAMOUS.
I THINK THIS IS A GREAT OFFER.
BUT...
...I'M NOT REALLY CONSIDERING ANYTHING LIKE THAT RIGHT NOW.
WHY NOT?
BECAUSE...

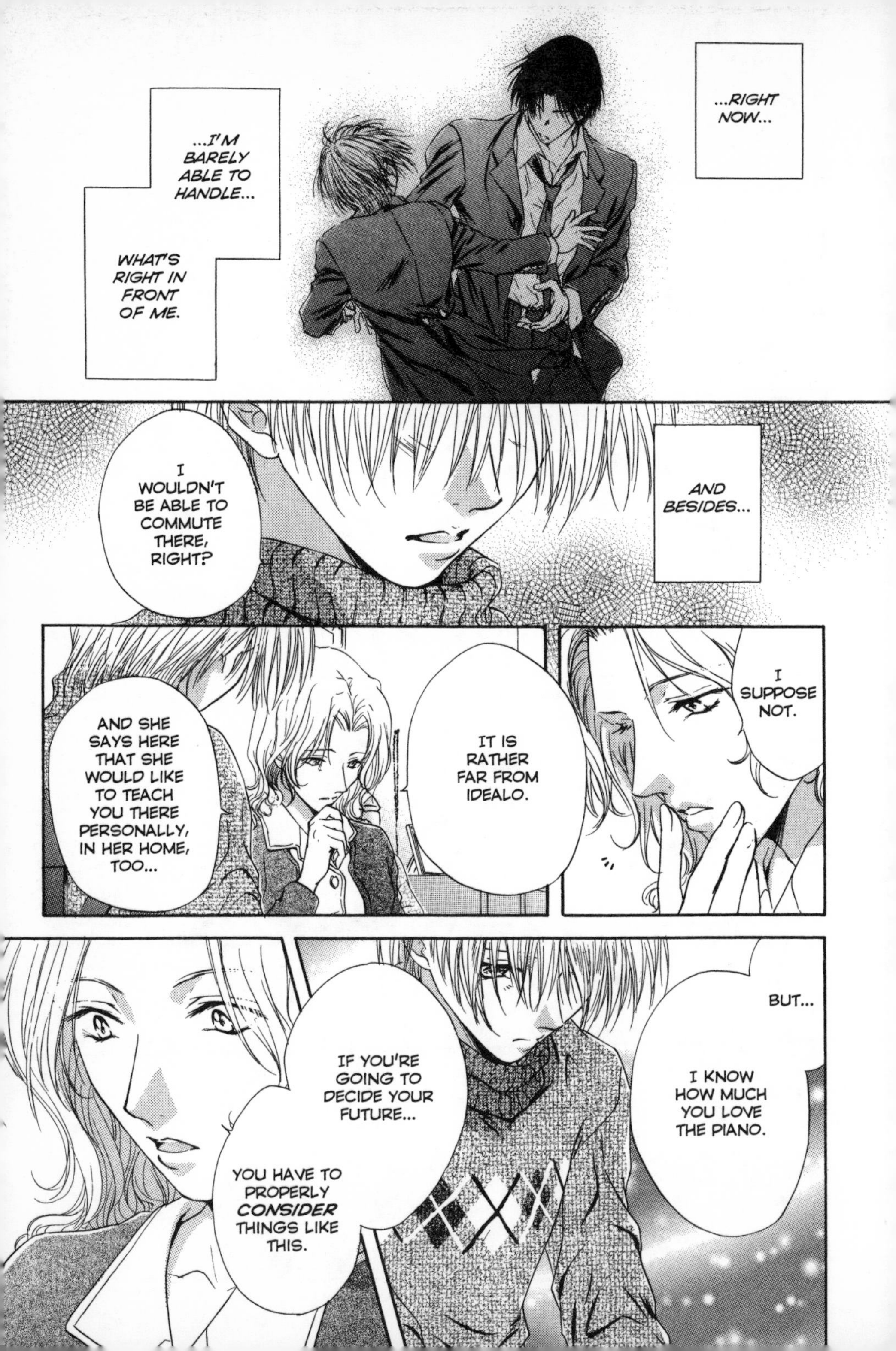
...RIGHT NOW...
...I'M BARELY ABLE TO HANDLE...
WHAT'S RIGHT IN FRONT OF ME.
AND BESIDES...
I WOULDN'T BE ABLE TO COMMUTE THERE, RIGHT?
I SUPPOSE NOT.
IT IS RATHER FAR FROM IDEALO.
AND SHE SAYS HERE THAT SHE WOULD LIKE TO TEACH YOU THERE PERSONALLY, IN HER HOME, TOO...
BUT...
I KNOW HOW MUCH YOU LOVE THE PIANO.
IF YOU'RE GOING TO DECIDE YOUR FUTURE...
YOU HAVE TO PROPERLY **CONSIDER** THINGS LIKE THIS.

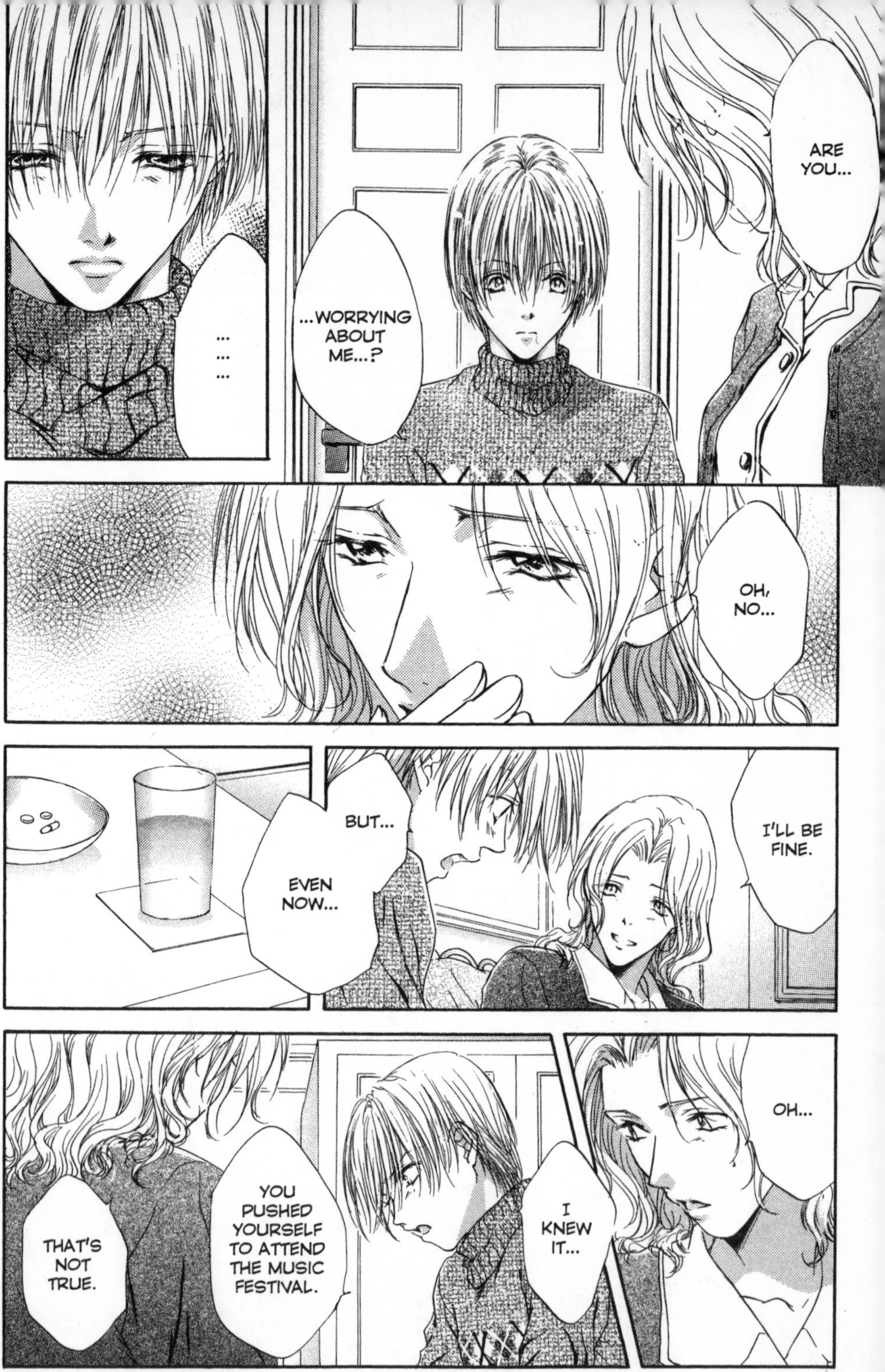
ARE YOU...
...WORRYING ABOUT ME...?
... ...
OH, NO...
I'LL BE FINE.
BUT...
EVEN NOW...
OH...
I KNEW IT...
YOU PUSHED YOURSELF TO ATTEND THE MUSIC FESTIVAL.
THAT'S NOT TRUE.

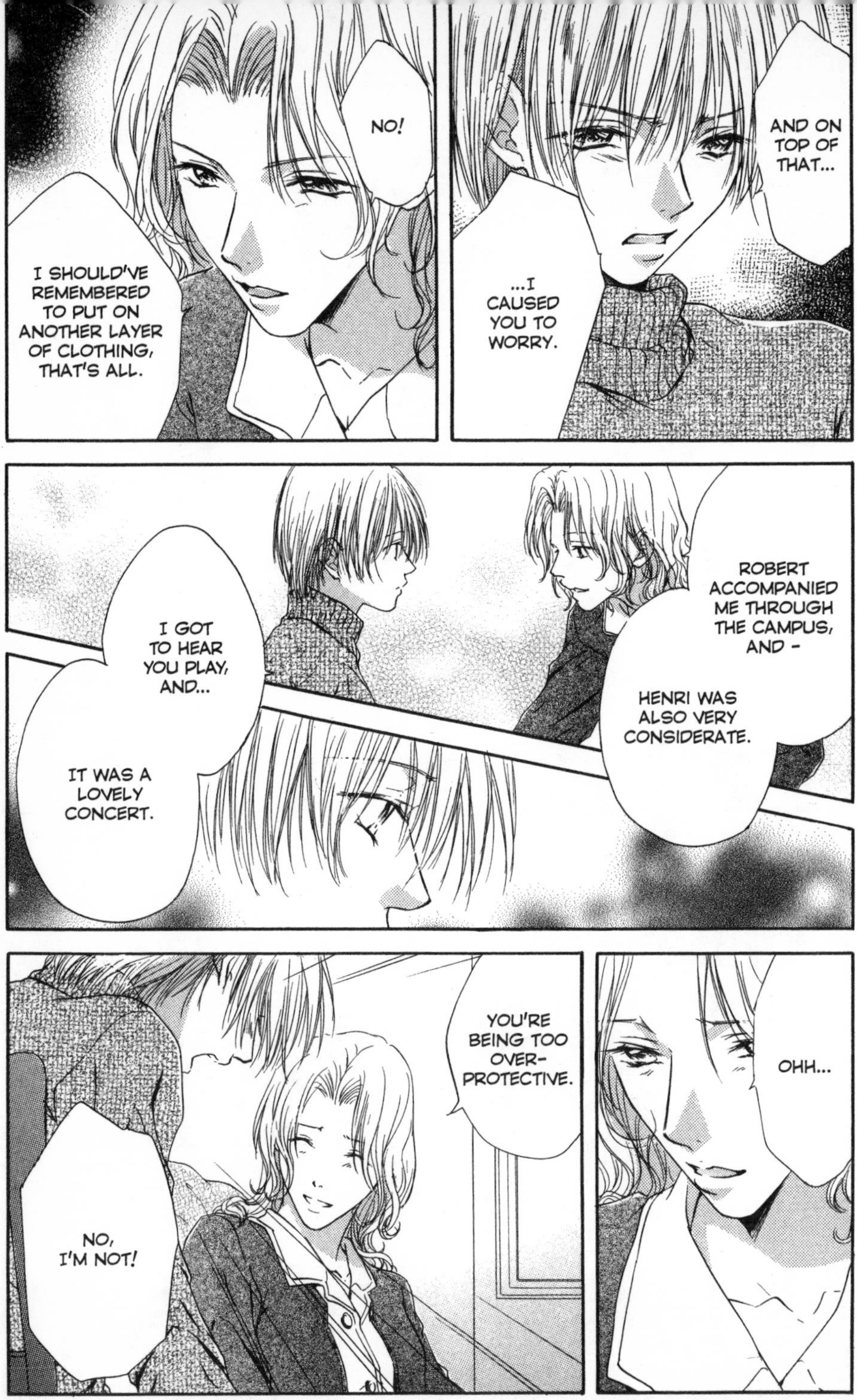
AND ON TOP OF THAT...
...I CAUSED YOU TO WORRY.
NO!
I SHOULD'VE REMEMBERED TO PUT ON ANOTHER LAYER OF CLOTHING, THAT'S ALL.
ROBERT ACCOMPANIED ME THROUGH THE CAMPUS, AND -
HENRI WAS ALSO VERY CONSIDERATE.
I GOT TO HEAR YOU PLAY, AND...
IT WAS A LOVELY CONCERT.
OHH...
YOU'RE BEING TOO OVER-PROTECTIVE.
NO, I'M NOT!

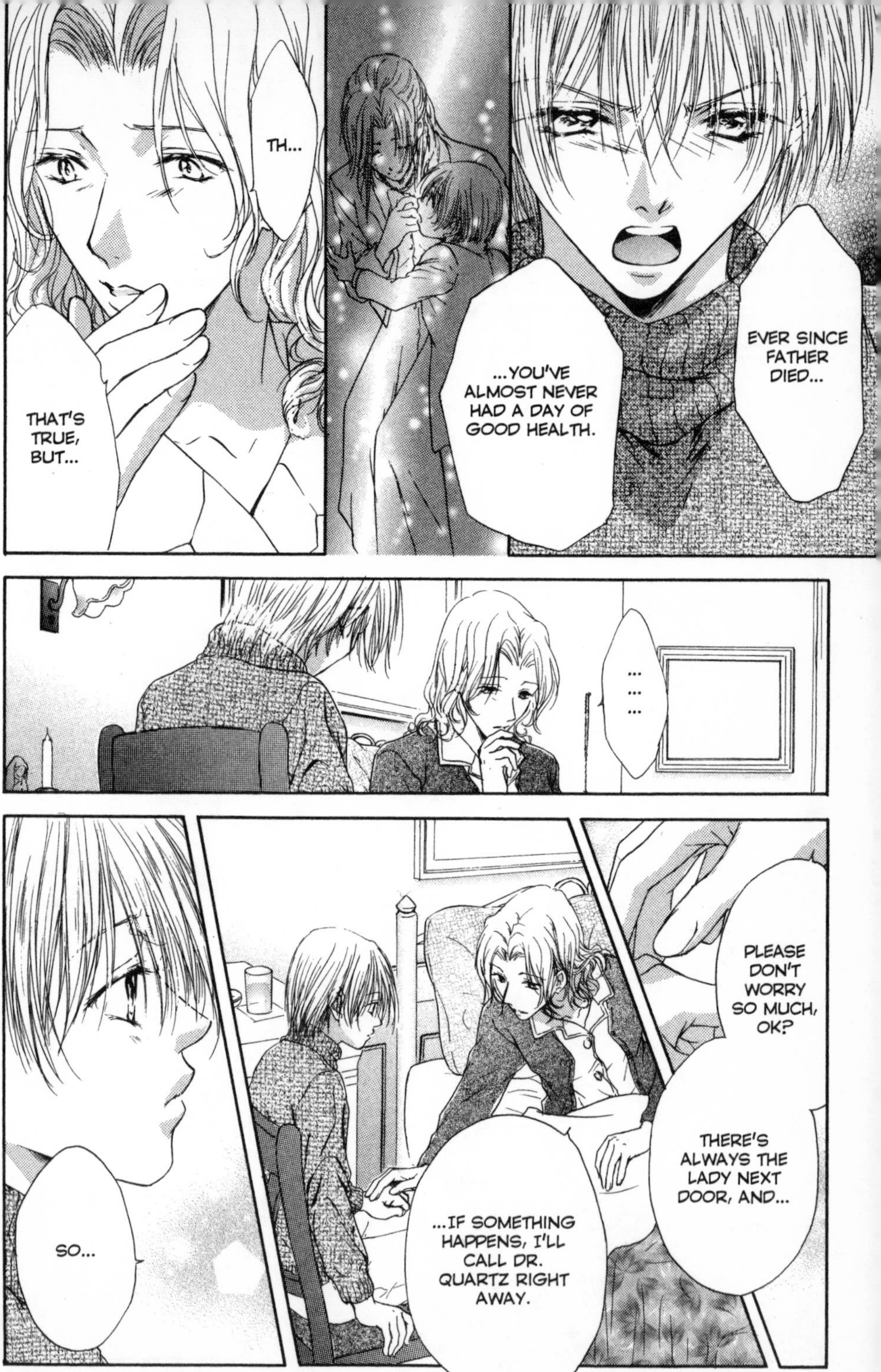
EVER SINCE FATHER DIED...
...YOU'VE ALMOST NEVER HAD A DAY OF GOOD HEALTH.
TH...
THAT'S TRUE, BUT...
... ...
PLEASE DON'T WORRY SO MUCH, OK?
THERE'S ALWAYS THE LADY NEXT DOOR, AND...
...IF SOMETHING HAPPENS, I'LL CALL DR. QUARTZ RIGHT AWAY.
SO...

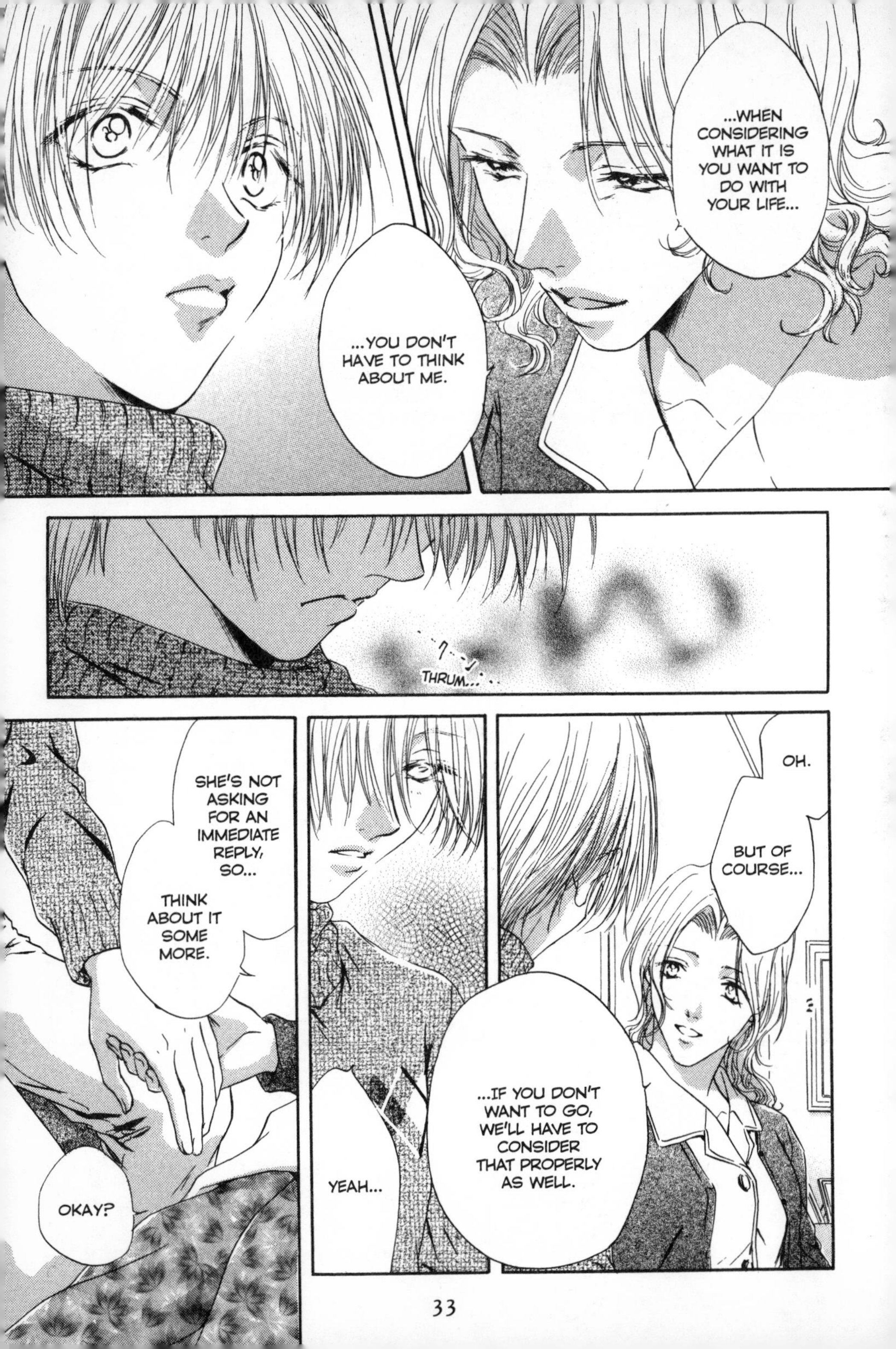
...WHEN CONSIDERING WHAT IT IS YOU WANT TO DO WITH YOUR LIFE...
...YOU DON'T HAVE TO THINK ABOUT ME.
THRUM...
OH.
BUT OF COURSE...
...IF YOU DON'T WANT TO GO, WE'LL HAVE TO CONSIDER THAT PROPERLY AS WELL.
YEAH...
SHE'S NOT ASKING FOR AN IMMEDIATE REPLY, SO...
THINK ABOUT IT SOME MORE.
OKAY?

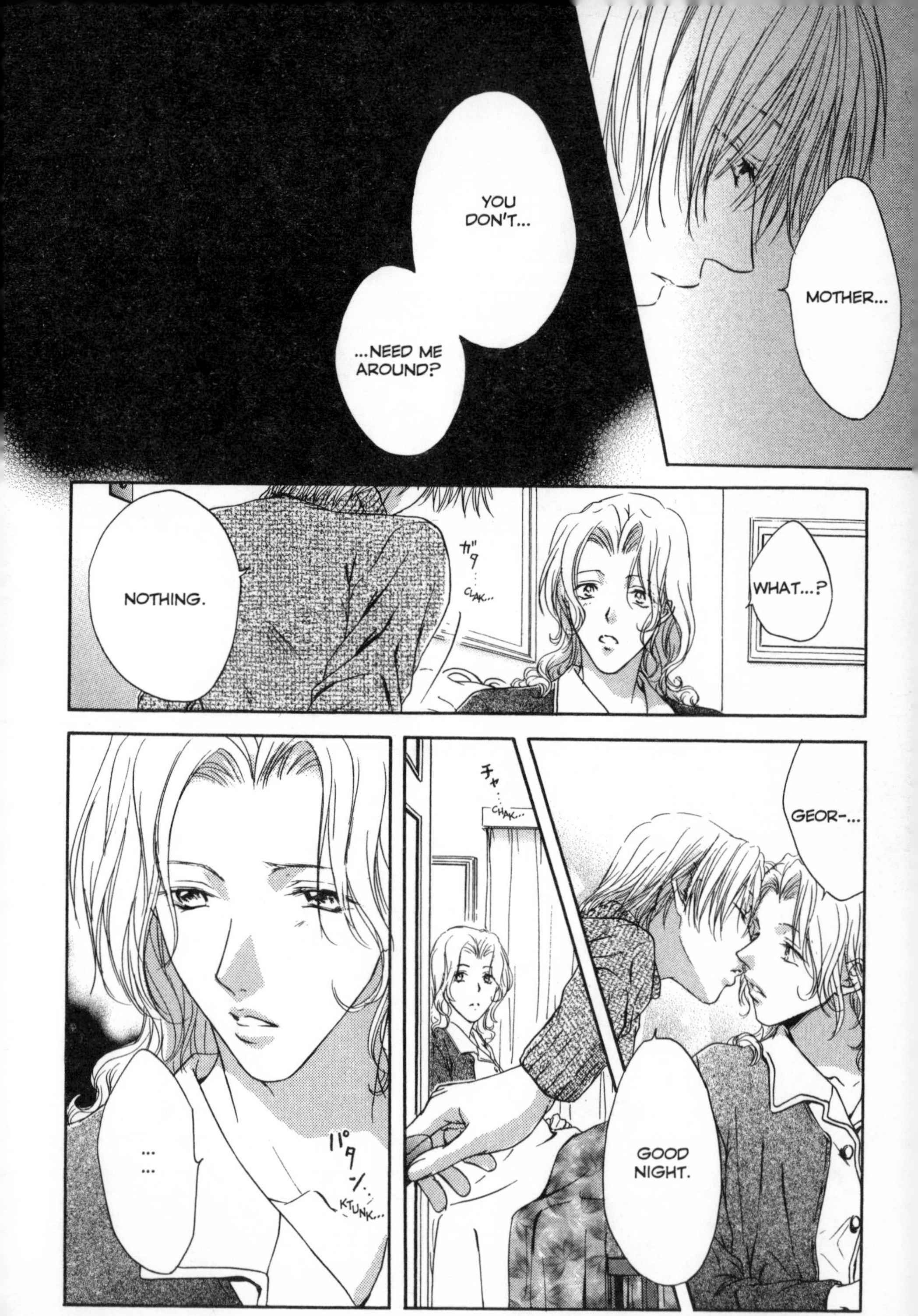
MOTHER...
YOU DON'T...
...NEED ME AROUND?
WHAT...?
CLAK...
NOTHING.
GEOR-...
CHAK...
GOOD NIGHT.
...
...
KTUNK...

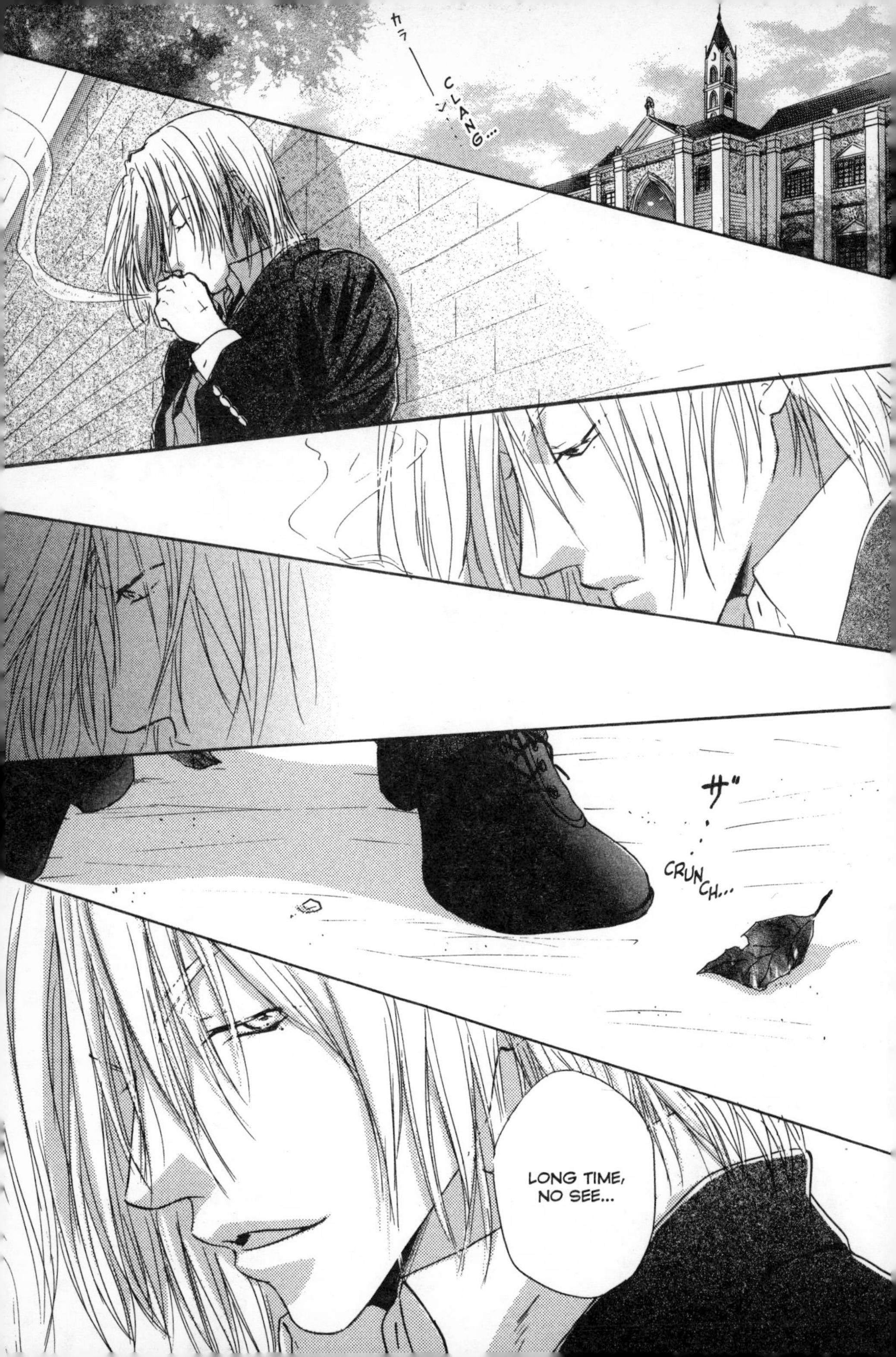
カラ——ン
CLANG...
ザ"
CRUNCH...
LONG TIME, NO SEE...

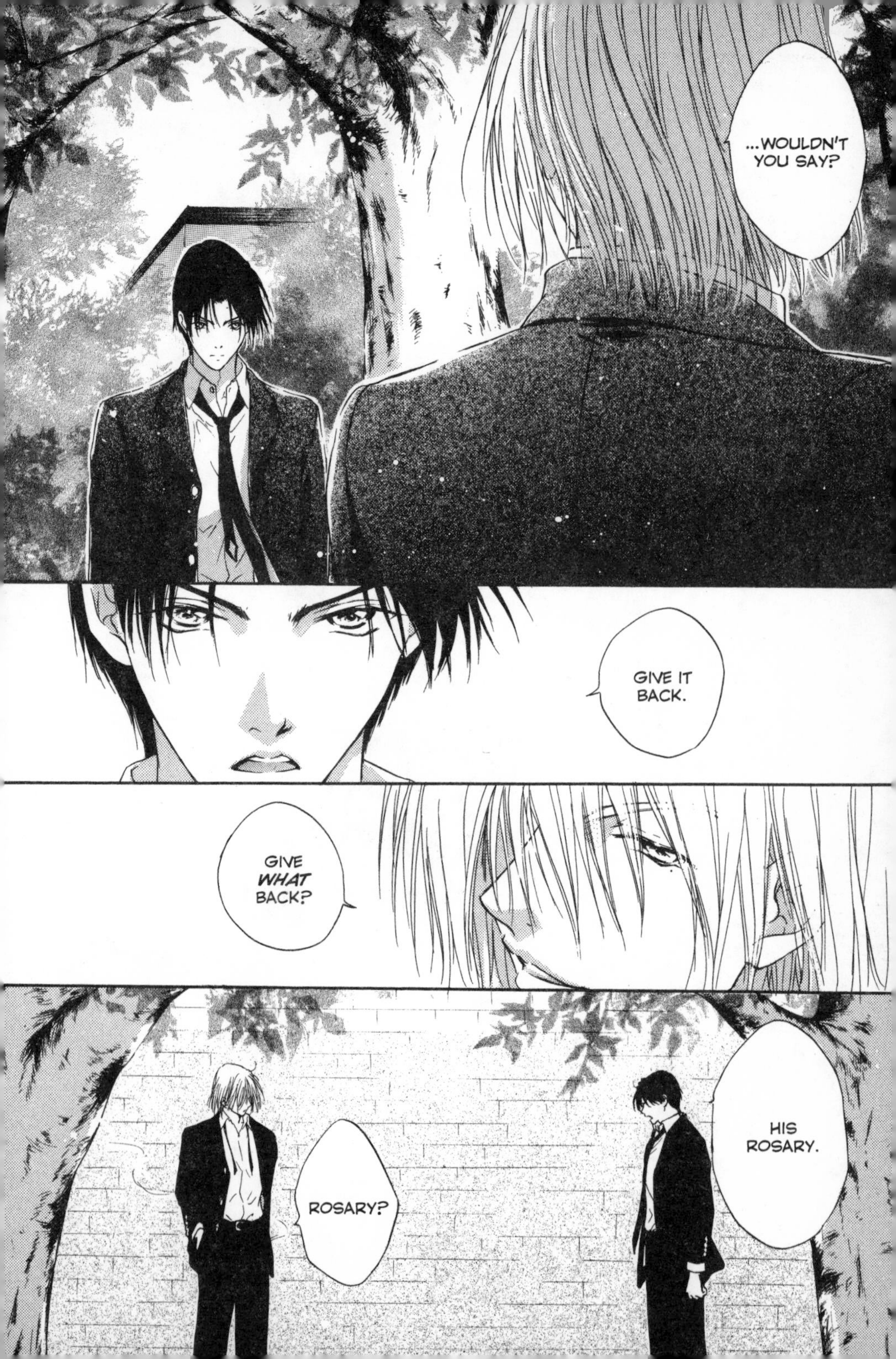
...WOULDN'T YOU SAY?
GIVE IT BACK.
GIVE *WHAT* BACK?
HIS ROSARY.
ROSARY?

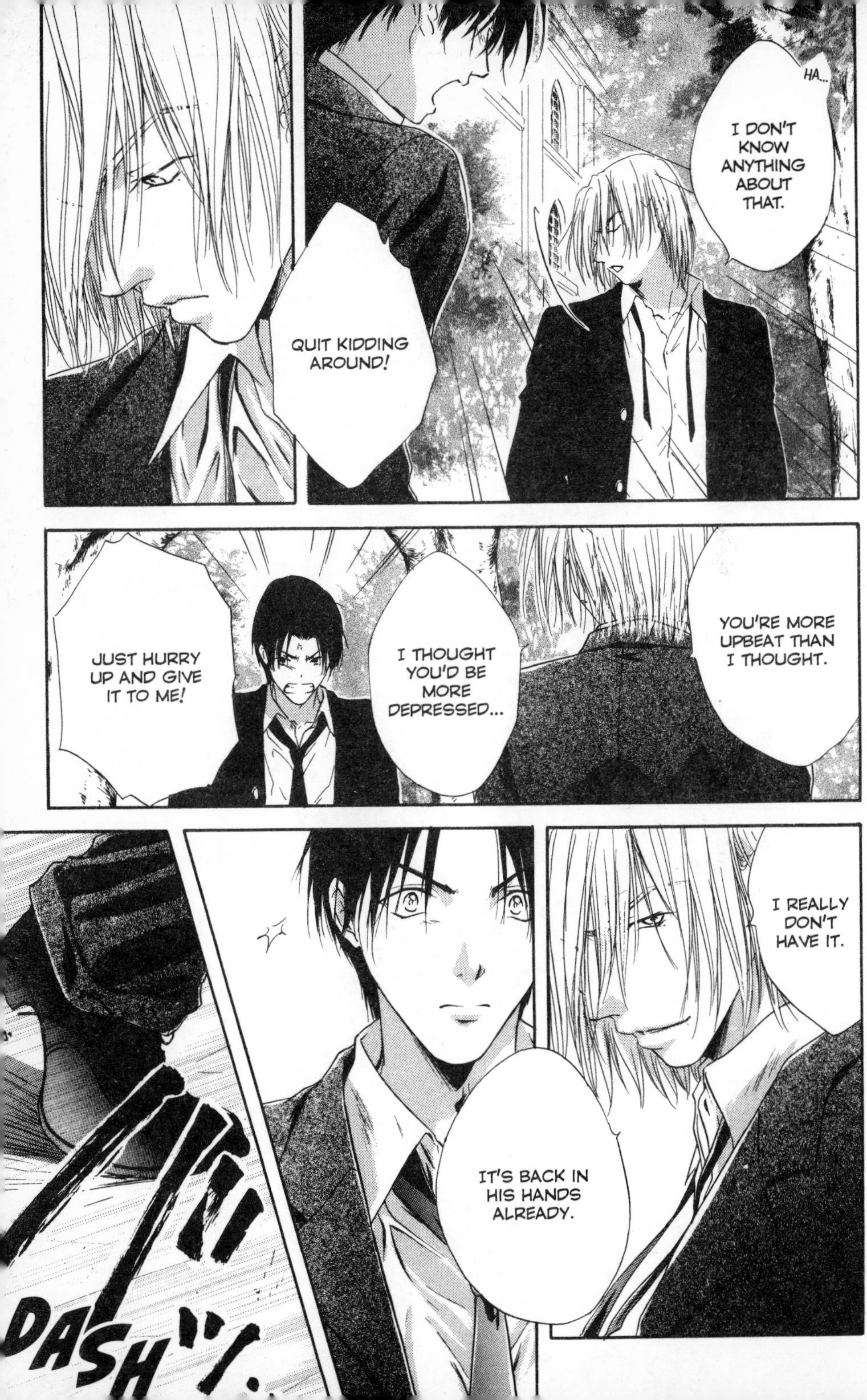
HA...
I DON'T KNOW ANYTHING ABOUT THAT.
QUIT KIDDING AROUND!
YOU'RE MORE UPBEAT THAN I THOUGHT.
I THOUGHT YOU'D BE MORE DEPRESSED...
JUST HURRY UP AND GIVE IT TO ME!
I REALLY DON'T HAVE IT.
IT'S BACK IN HIS HANDS ALREADY.
DASH!

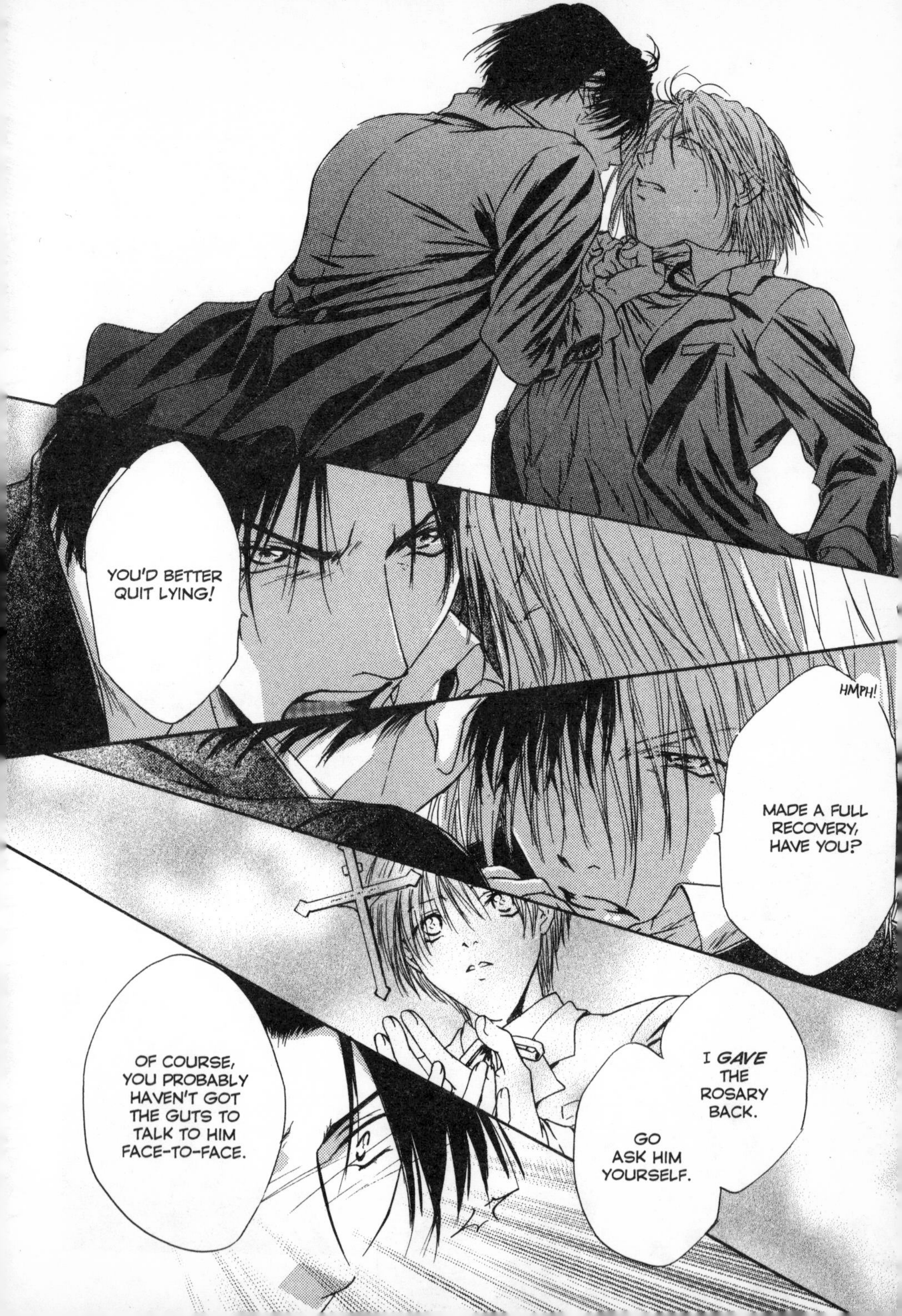
YOU'D BETTER QUIT LYING!
HMPH!
MADE A FULL RECOVERY, HAVE YOU?
I *GAVE* THE ROSARY BACK.
GO ASK HIM YOURSELF.
OF COURSE, YOU PROBABLY HAVEN'T GOT THE GUTS TO TALK TO HIM FACE-TO-FACE.

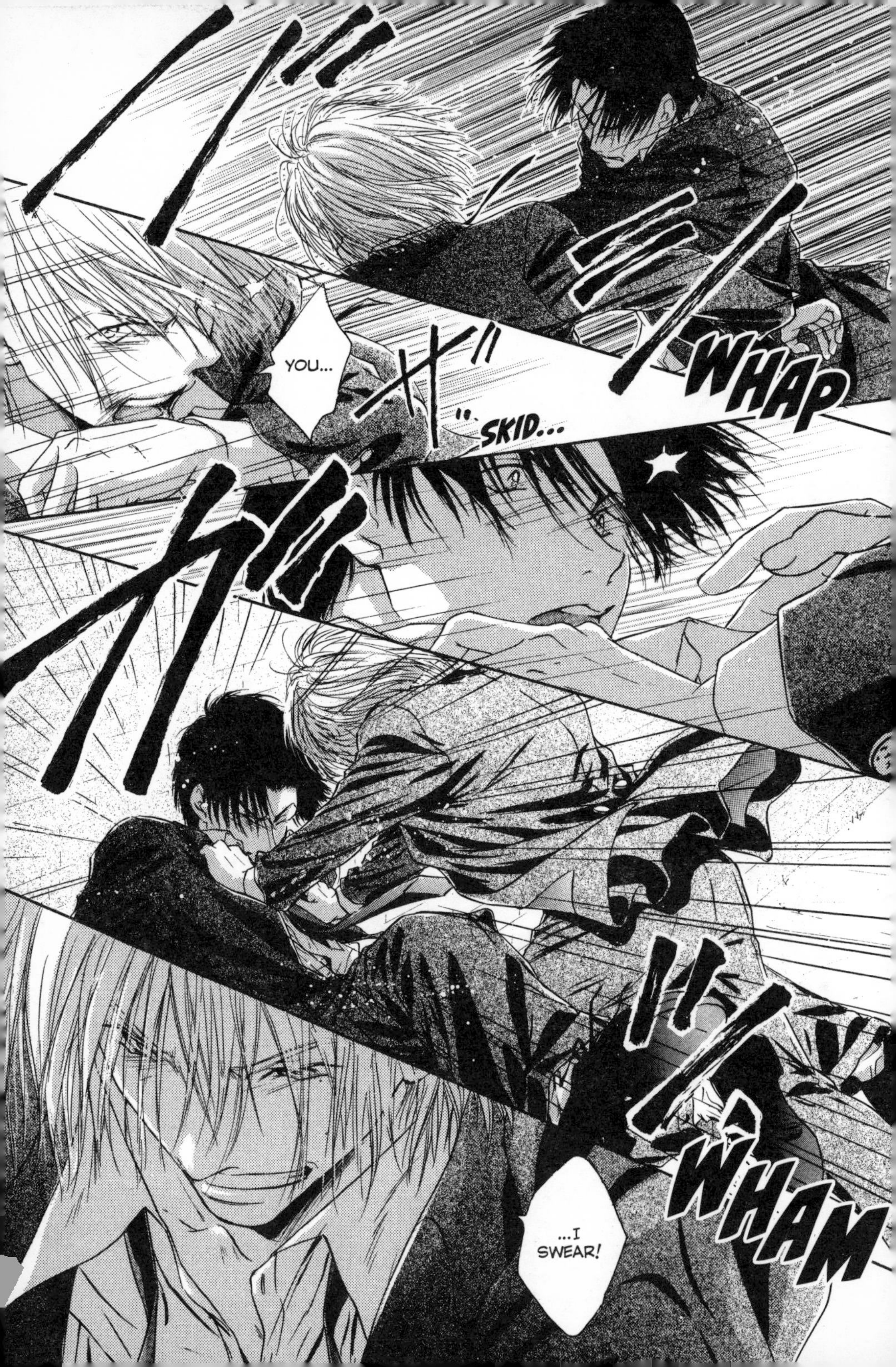
WHAP
YOU...
SKID...
WHAM
...I SWEAR!

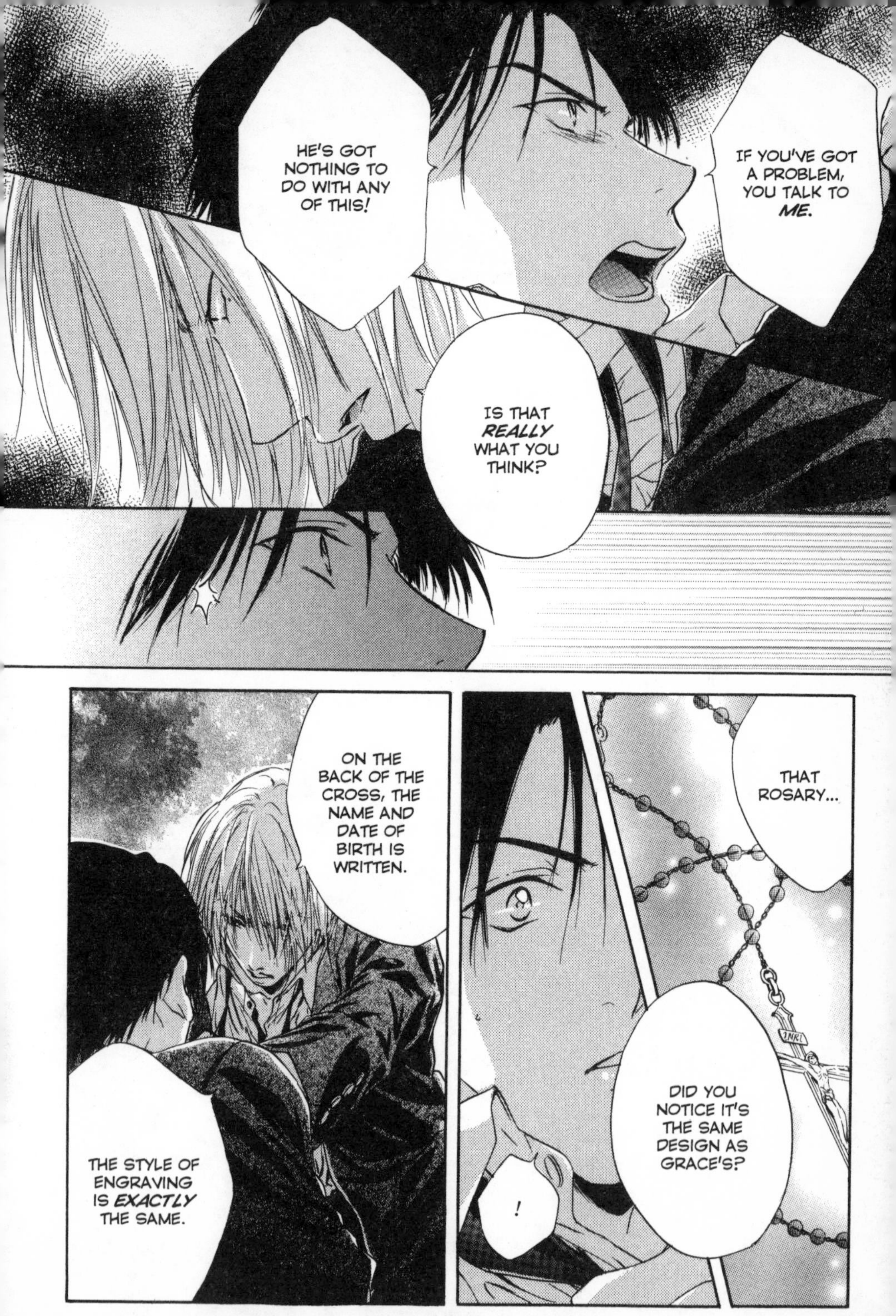
IF YOU'VE GOT A PROBLEM, YOU TALK TO *ME*.
HE'S GOT NOTHING TO DO WITH ANY OF THIS!
IS THAT *REALLY* WHAT YOU THINK?
THAT ROSARY...
DID YOU NOTICE IT'S THE SAME DESIGN AS GRACE'S?
!
ON THE BACK OF THE CROSS, THE NAME AND DATE OF BIRTH IS WRITTEN.
THE STYLE OF ENGRAVING IS *EXACTLY* THE SAME.

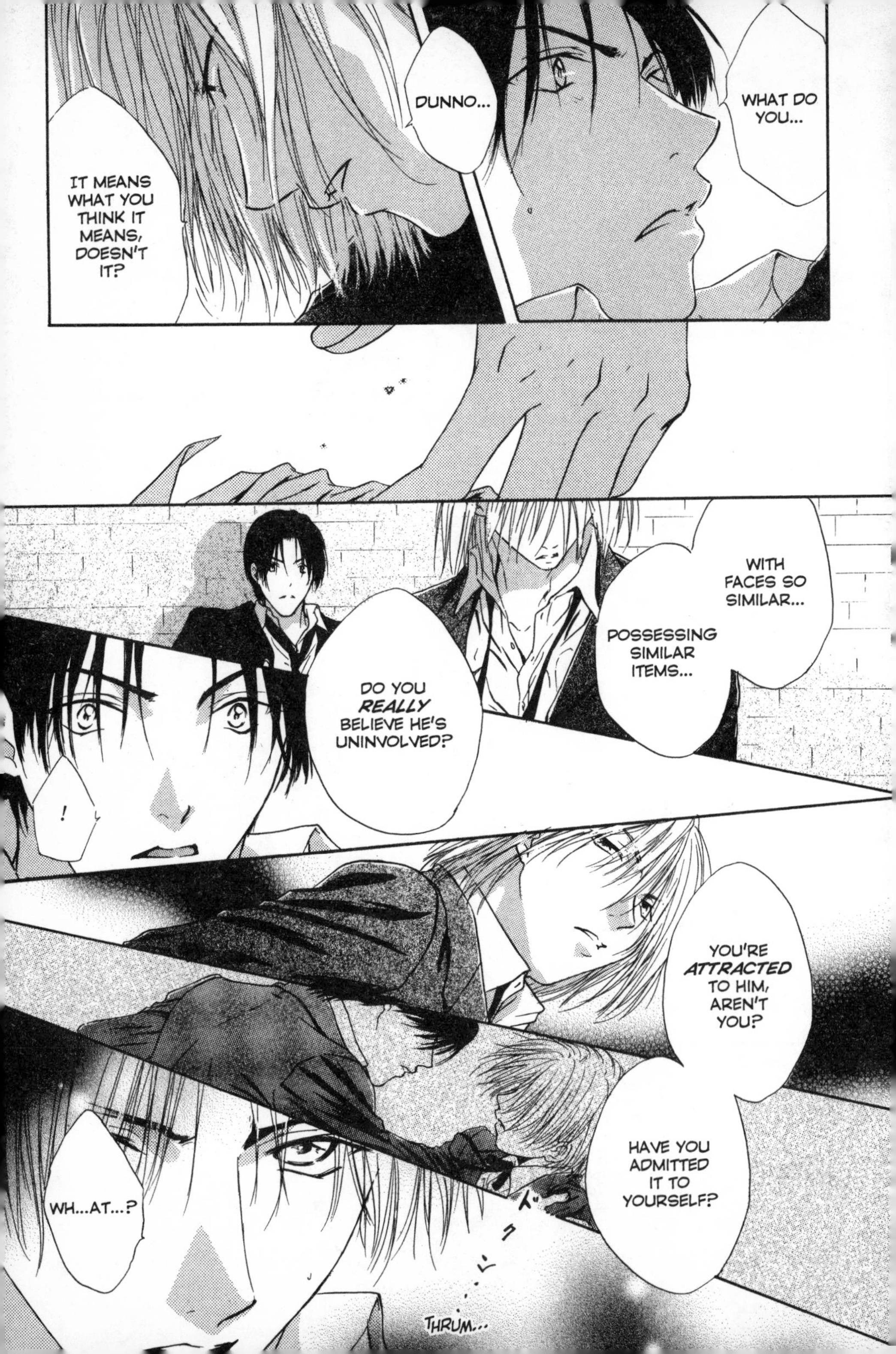
WHAT DO YOU...
DUNNO...
IT MEANS WHAT YOU THINK IT MEANS, DOESN'T IT?
WITH FACES SO SIMILAR...
POSSESSING SIMILAR ITEMS...
DO YOU *REALLY* BELIEVE HE'S UNINVOLVED?
!
YOU'RE *ATTRACTED* TO HIM, AREN'T YOU?
HAVE YOU ADMITTED IT TO YOURSELF?
WH...AT...?
THRUM...

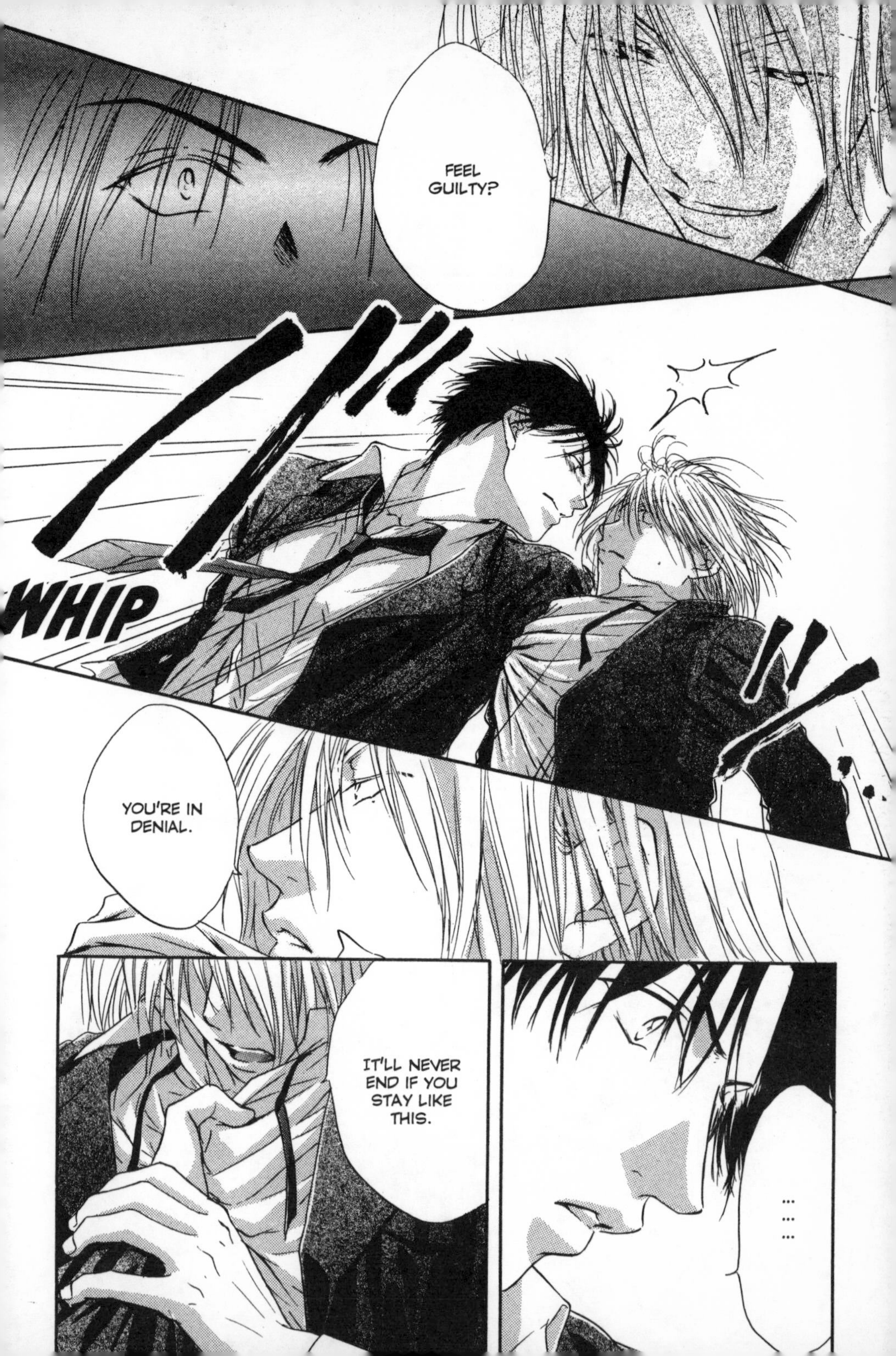
FEEL GUILTY?
WHIP
YOU'RE IN DENIAL.
...
...
...
IT'LL NEVER END IF YOU STAY LIKE THIS.

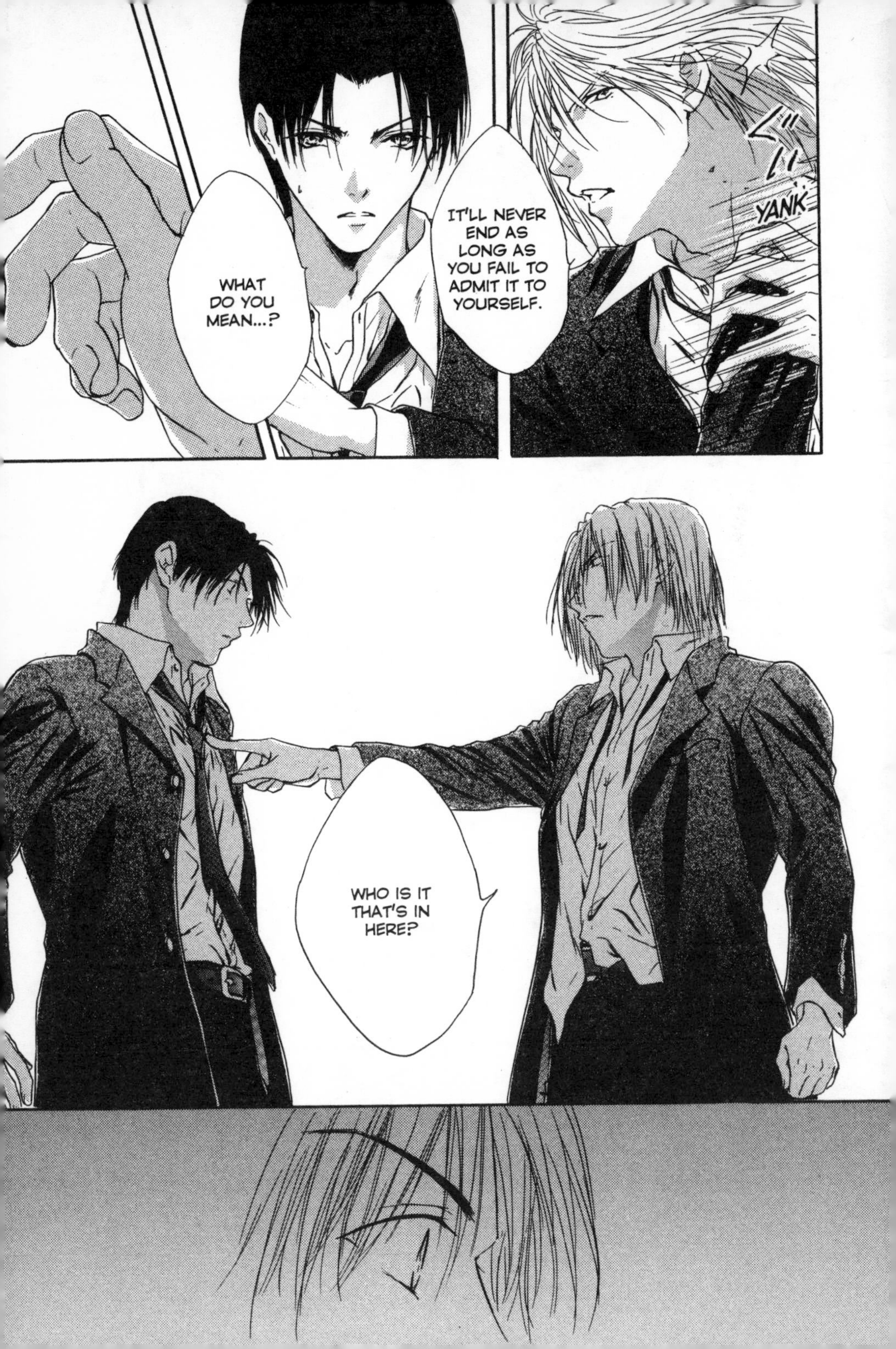
IT'LL NEVER END AS LONG AS YOU FAIL TO ADMIT IT TO YOURSELF.
YANK
WHAT DO YOU MEAN...?
WHO IS IT THAT'S IN HERE?

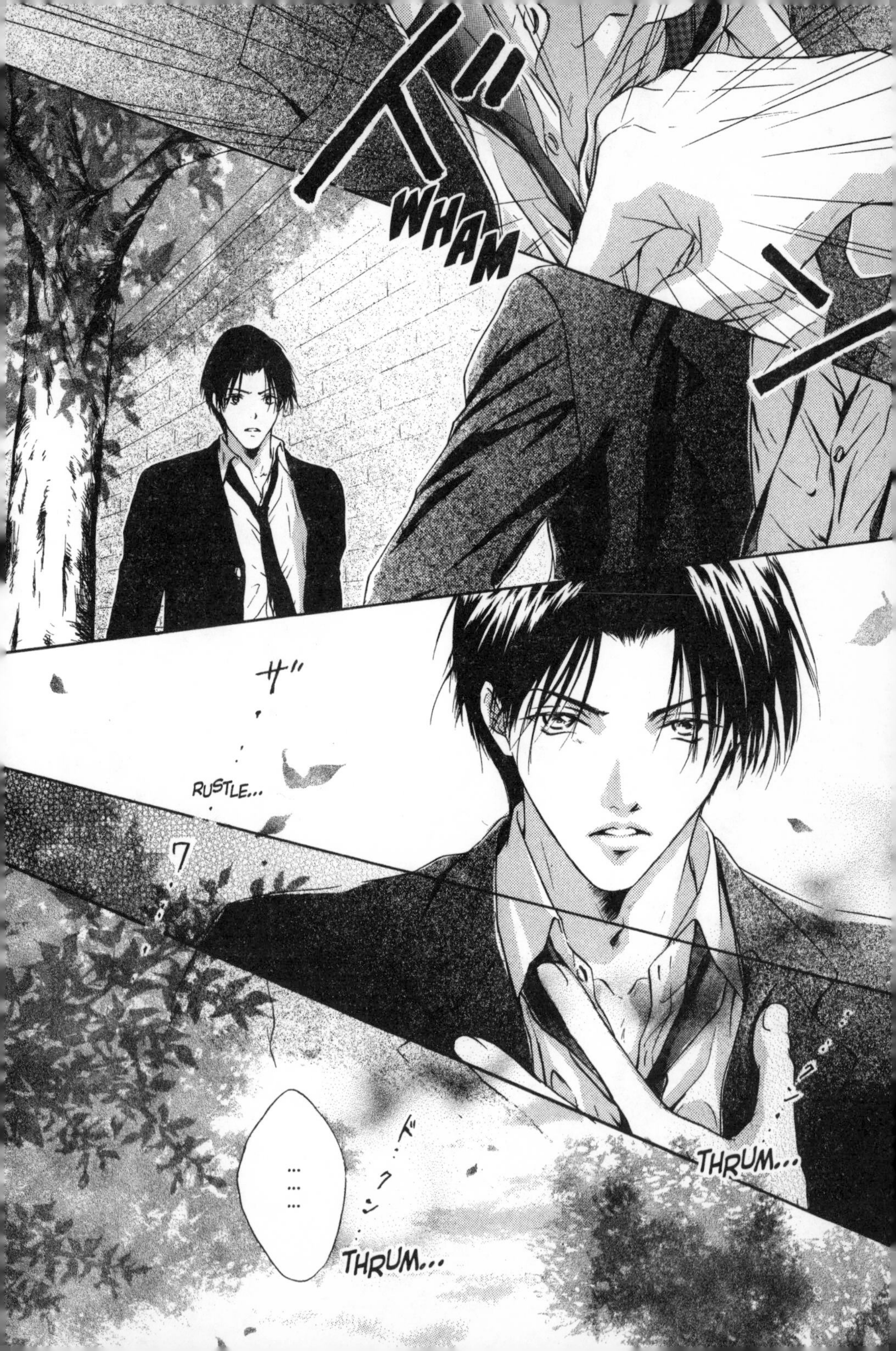

WHAM
RUSTLE...
THRUM...
......
THRUM...

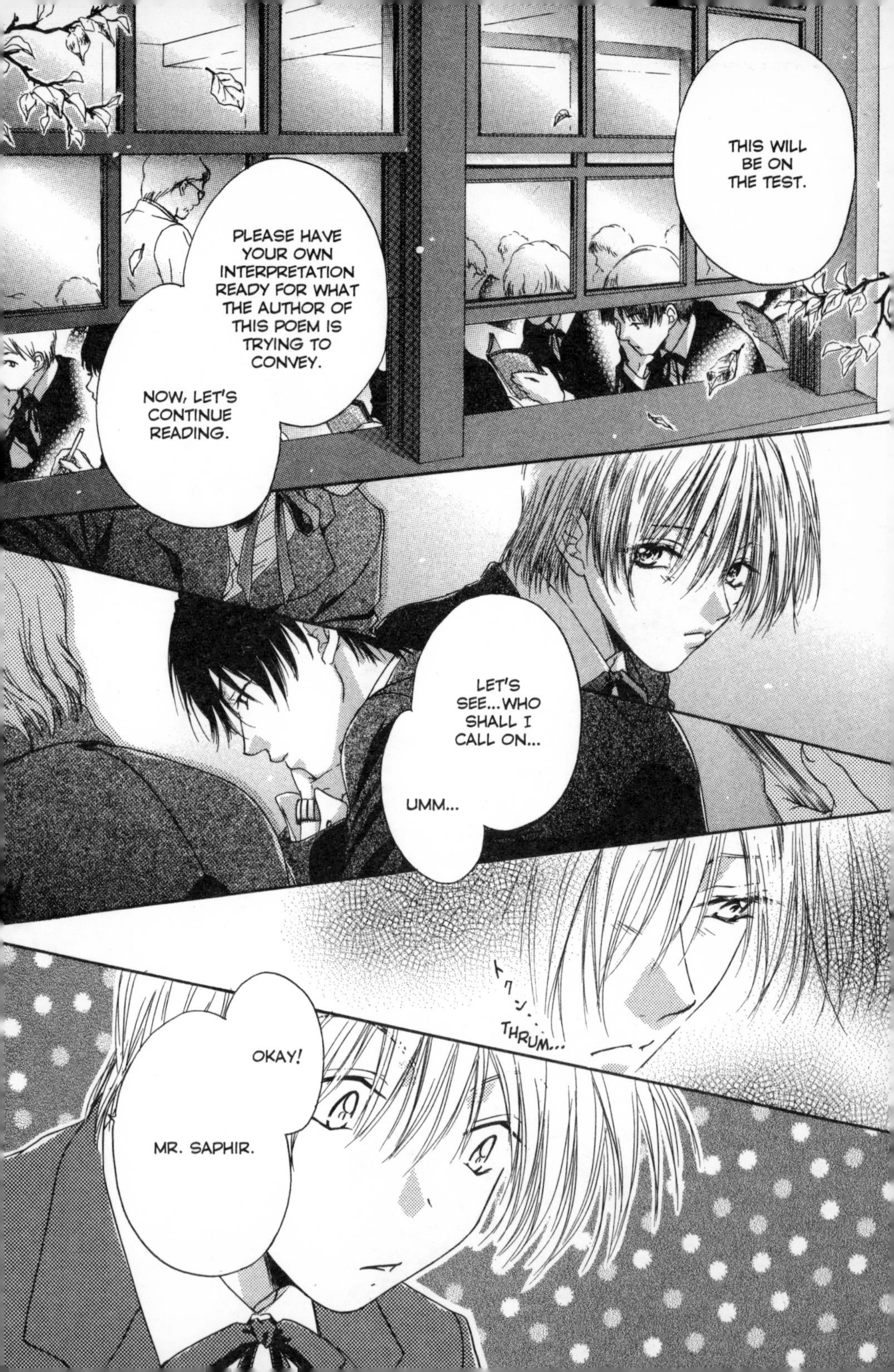
THIS WILL BE ON THE TEST.
PLEASE HAVE YOUR OWN INTERPRETATION READY FOR WHAT THE AUTHOR OF THIS POEM IS TRYING TO CONVEY.
NOW, LET'S CONTINUE READING.
LET'S SEE...WHO SHALL I CALL ON...
UMM...
THRUM...
OKAY!
MR. SAPHIR.

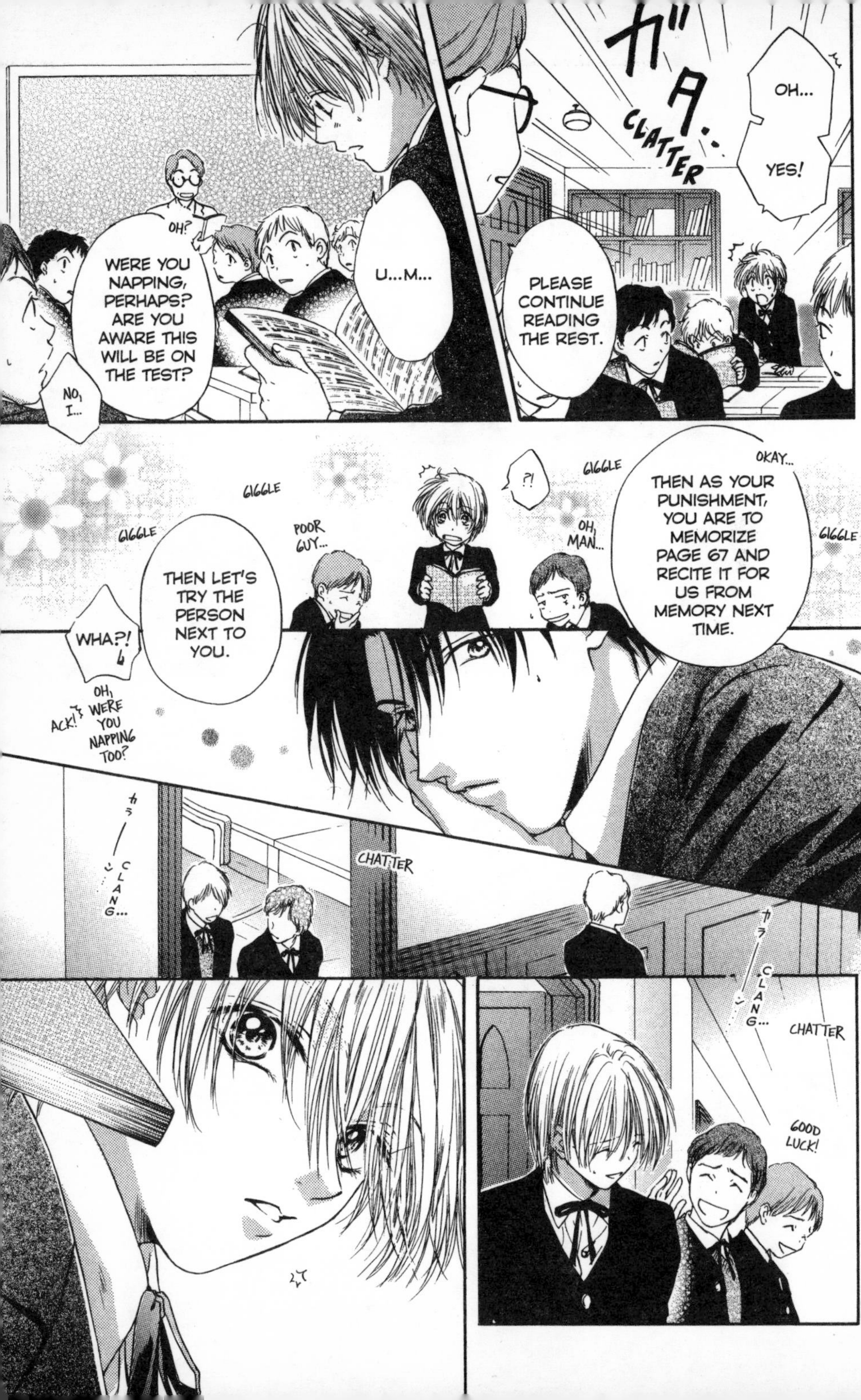
OH...
YES!
ガタ...
CLATTER
PLEASE CONTINUE READING THE REST.
U...M...
OH?
WERE YOU NAPPING, PERHAPS? ARE YOU AWARE THIS WILL BE ON THE TEST?
NO, I...
OKAY...
THEN AS YOUR PUNISHMENT, YOU ARE TO MEMORIZE PAGE 67 AND RECITE IT FOR US FROM MEMORY NEXT TIME.
GIGGLE
OH, MAN...
?!
POOR GUY...
GIGGLE
GIGGLE
GIGGLE
THEN LET'S TRY THE PERSON NEXT TO YOU.
WHA?!
OH, WERE YOU NAPPING TOO?
ACK!
CLANG...
CHATTER
CLANG...
CHATTER
GOOD LUCK!

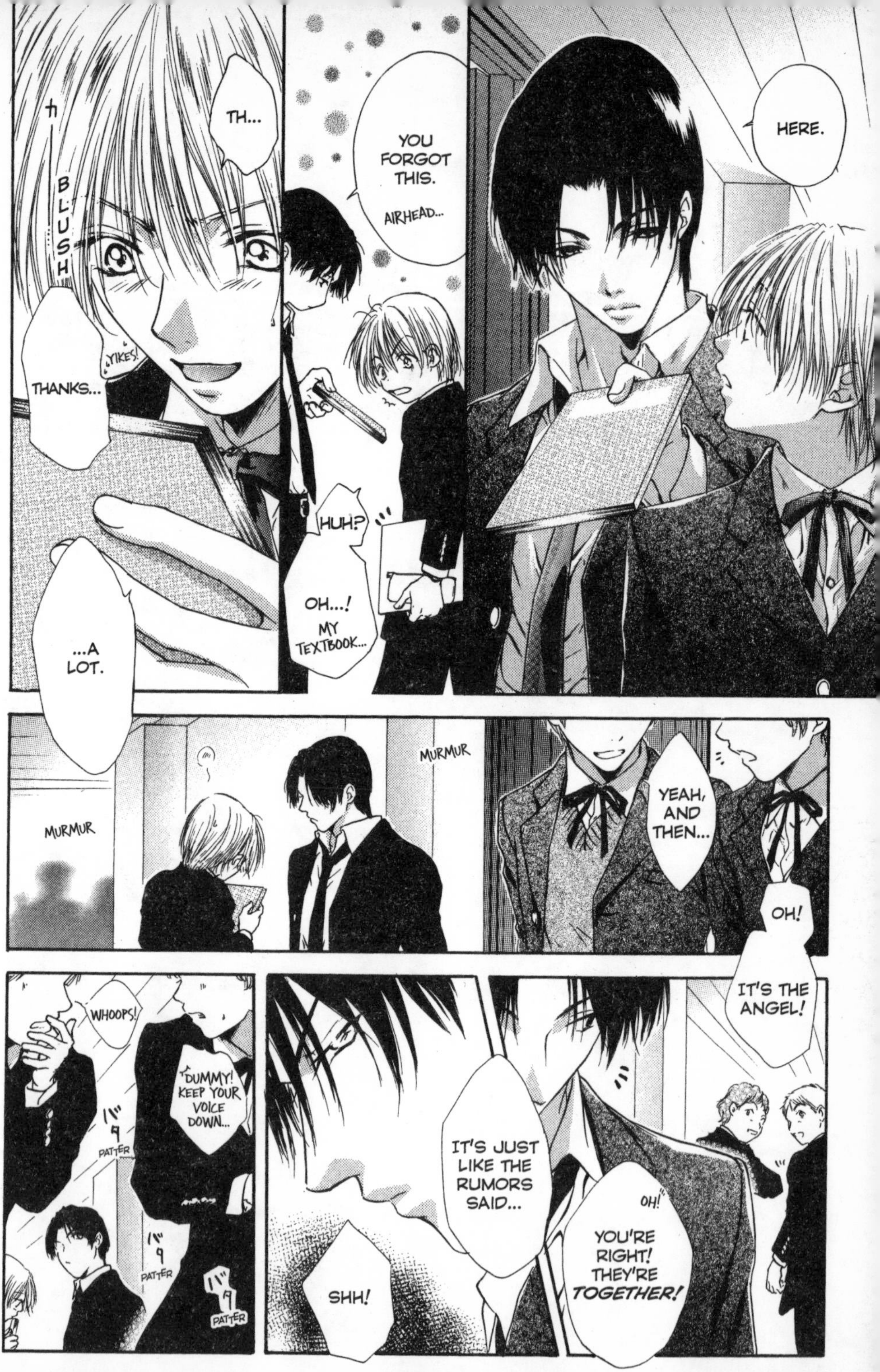
HERE.
YOU FORGOT THIS.
AIRHEAD...
HUH?
OH...! MY TEXTBOOK...
TH...
BLUSH
YIKES!
THANKS...
...A LOT.
YEAH, AND THEN...
MURMUR
MURMUR
OH!
IT'S THE ANGEL!
OH!
YOU'RE RIGHT! THEY'RE *TOGETHER!*
IT'S JUST LIKE THE RUMORS SAID...
SHH!
WHOOPS!
DUMMY! KEEP YOUR VOICE DOWN...
PATTER
PATTER
PATTER

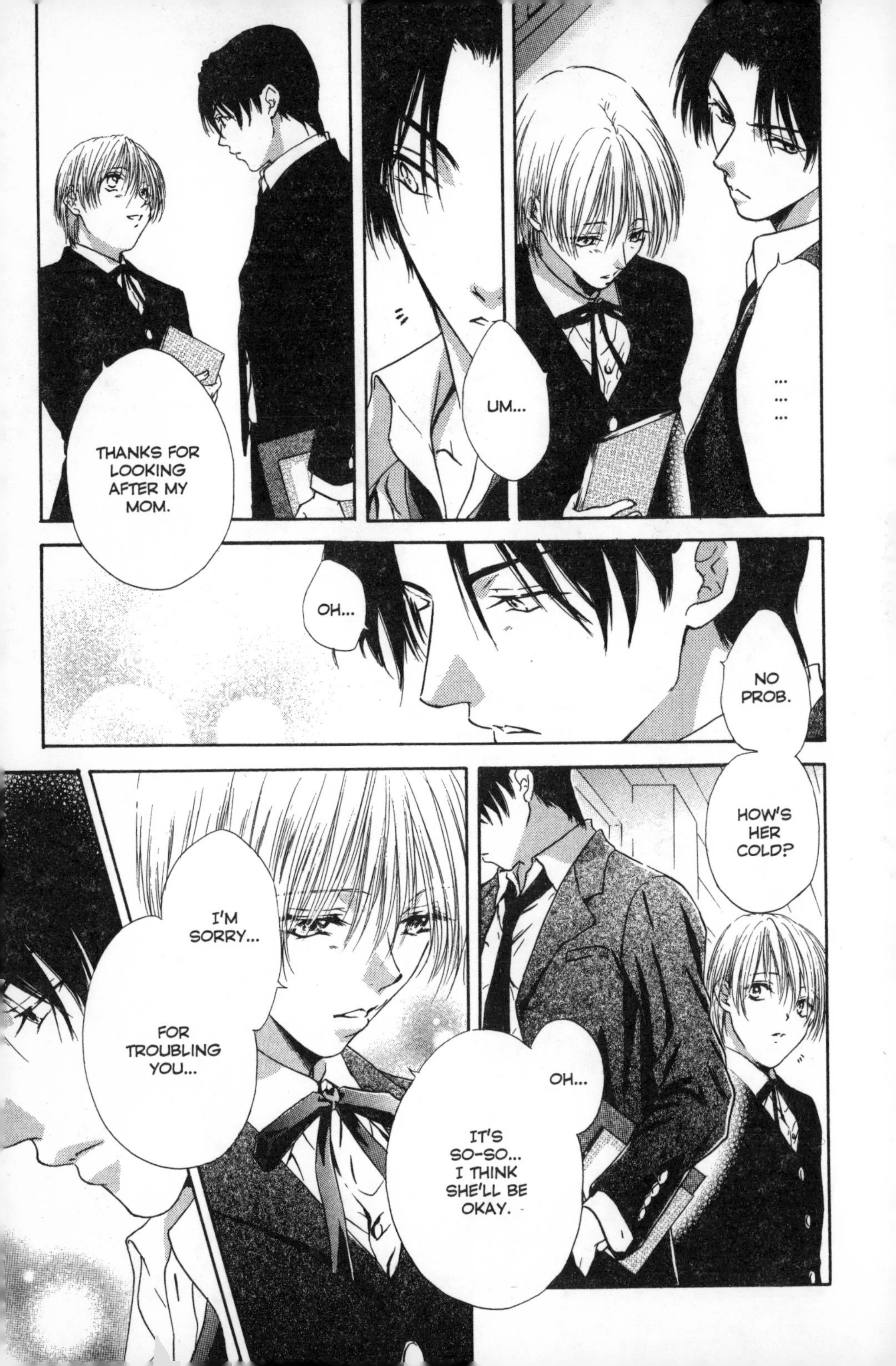
...
...
...
UM...
THANKS FOR LOOKING AFTER MY MOM.
OH...
NO PROB.
HOW'S HER COLD?
OH...
IT'S SO-SO... I THINK SHE'LL BE OKAY.
I'M SORRY...
FOR TROUBLING YOU...

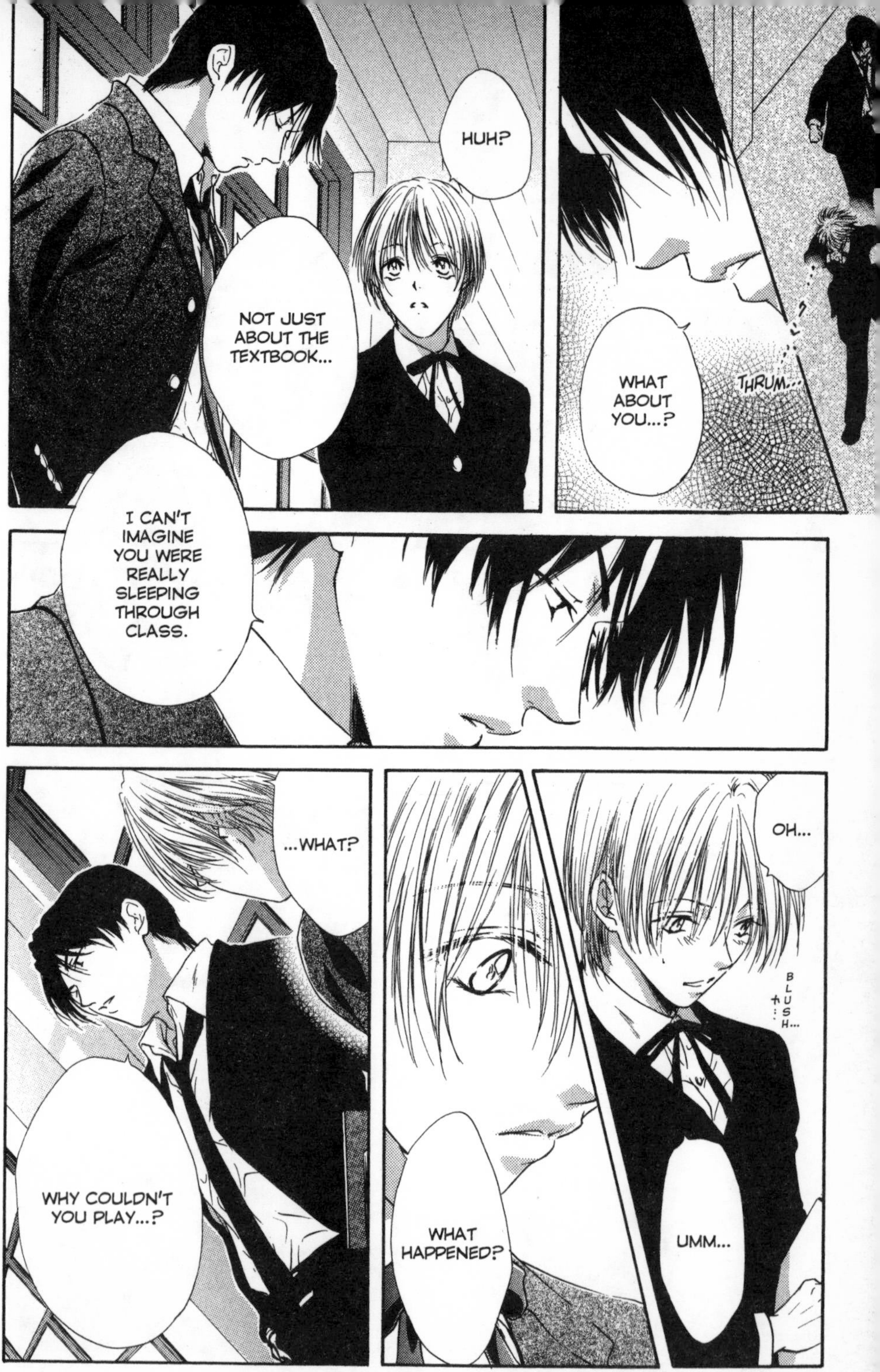
WHAT ABOUT YOU...?
THRUM...
HUH?
NOT JUST ABOUT THE TEXTBOOK...
I CAN'T IMAGINE YOU WERE REALLY SLEEPING THROUGH CLASS.
OH...
BLUSH...
UMM...
WHAT HAPPENED?
...WHAT?
WHY COULDN'T YOU PLAY...?

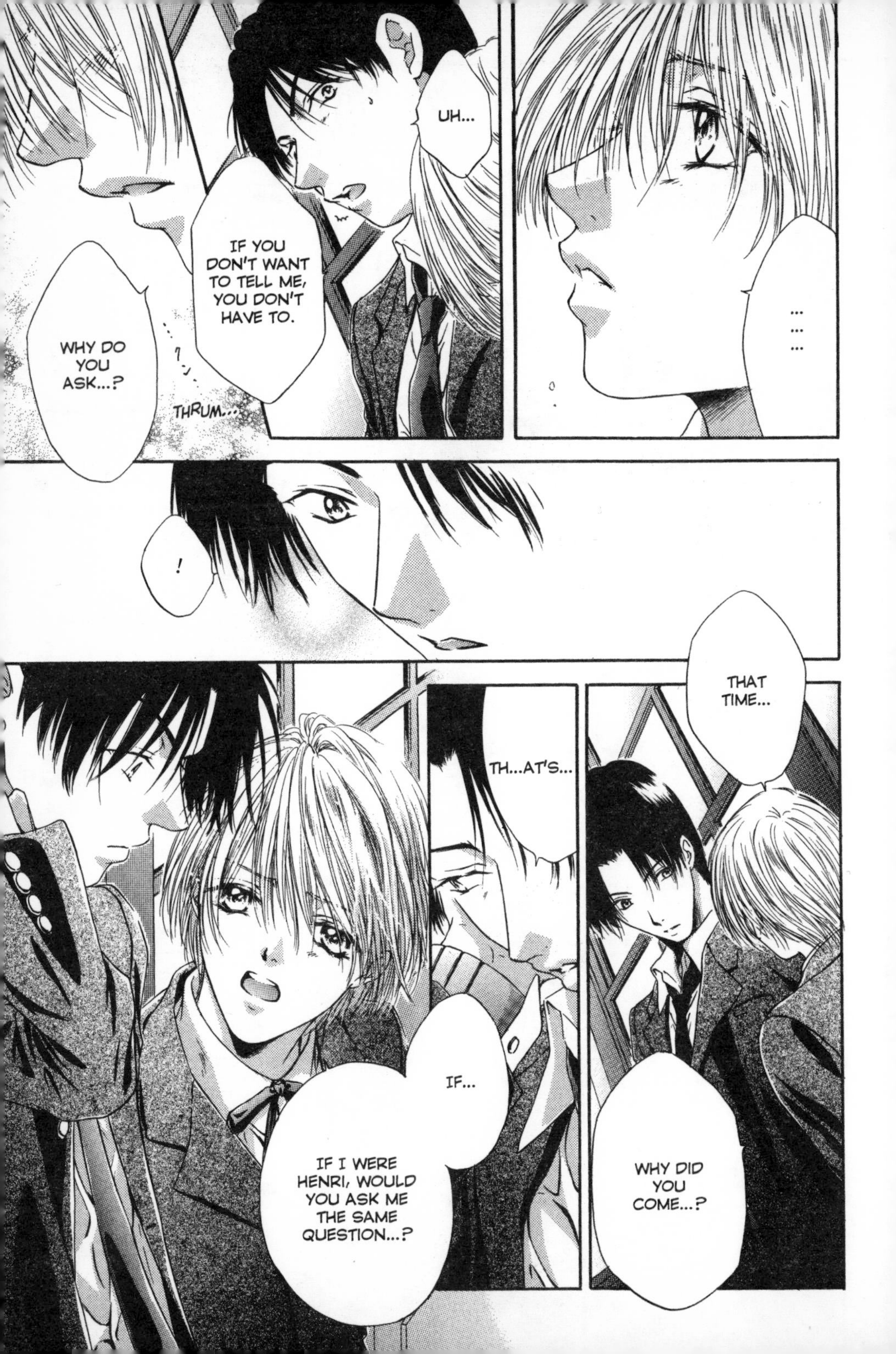
...
...
...
UH...
IF YOU DON'T WANT TO TELL ME, YOU DON'T HAVE TO.
WHY DO YOU ASK...?
THRUM...
!
THAT TIME...
WHY DID YOU COME...?
TH...AT'S...
IF...
IF I WERE HENRI, WOULD YOU ASK ME THE SAME QUESTION...?

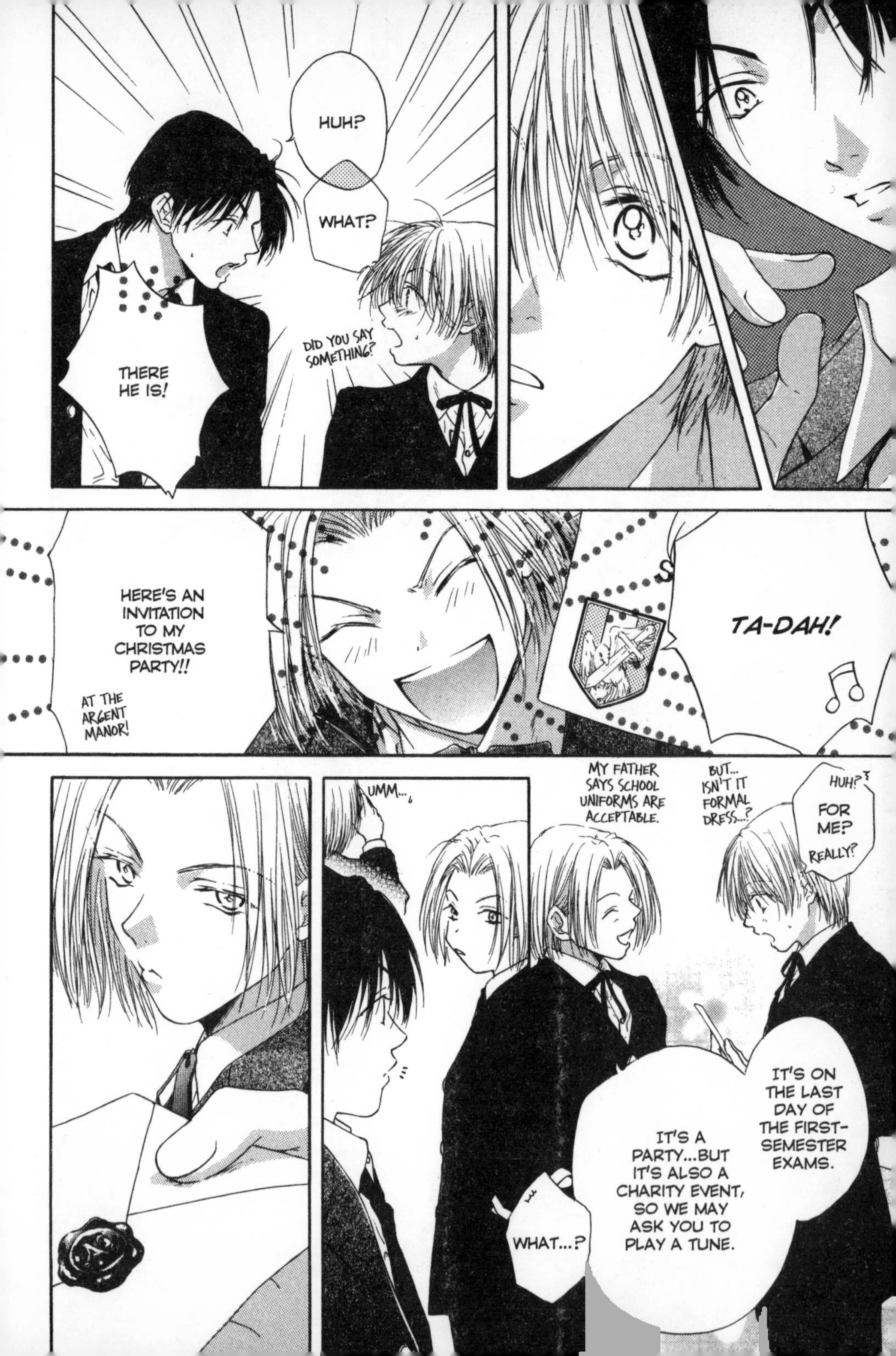
HUH?
WHAT?
DID YOU SAY SOMETHING?
THERE HE IS!
TA-DAH!
HERE'S AN INVITATION TO MY CHRISTMAS PARTY!!
AT THE ARGENT MANOR!
HUH? FOR ME? REALLY?
BUT... ISN'T IT FORMAL DRESS...?
MY FATHER SAYS SCHOOL UNIFORMS ARE ACCEPTABLE.
UMM...
IT'S ON THE LAST DAY OF THE FIRST-SEMESTER EXAMS.
IT'S A PARTY...BUT IT'S ALSO A CHARITY EVENT, SO WE MAY ASK YOU TO PLAY A TUNE.
WHAT...?

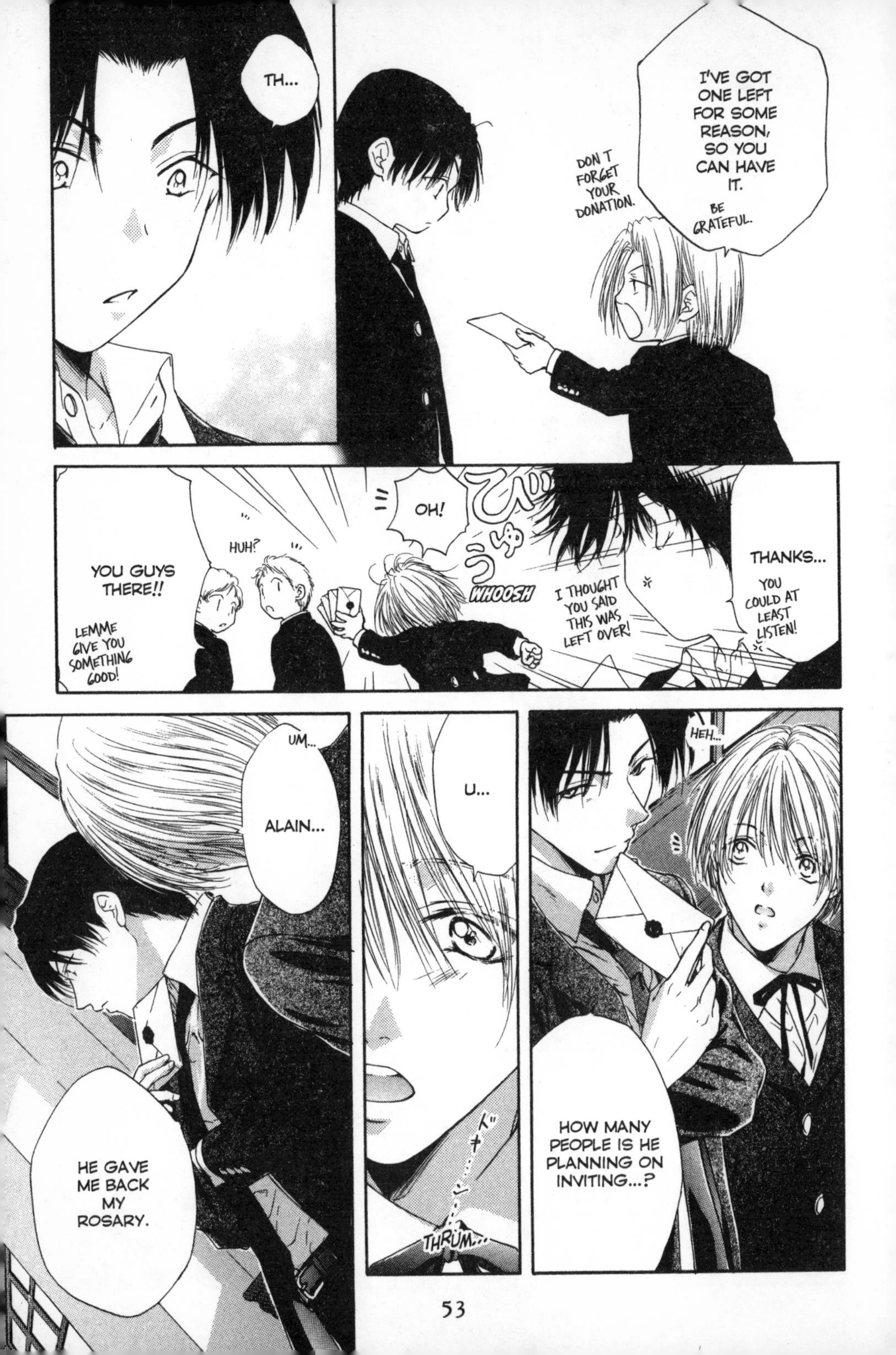
I'VE GOT ONE LEFT FOR SOME REASON, SO YOU CAN HAVE IT.
BE GRATEFUL.
DON T FORGET YOUR DONATION.
TH...
THANKS...
YOU COULD AT LEAST LISTEN!
I THOUGHT YOU SAID THIS WAS LEFT OVER!
WHOOSH
OH!
HUH?
YOU GUYS THERE!!
LEMME GIVE YOU SOMETHING GOOD!
HEH...
HOW MANY PEOPLE IS HE PLANNING ON INVITING...?
U...
THRUM...
UM...
ALAIN...
HE GAVE ME BACK MY ROSARY.

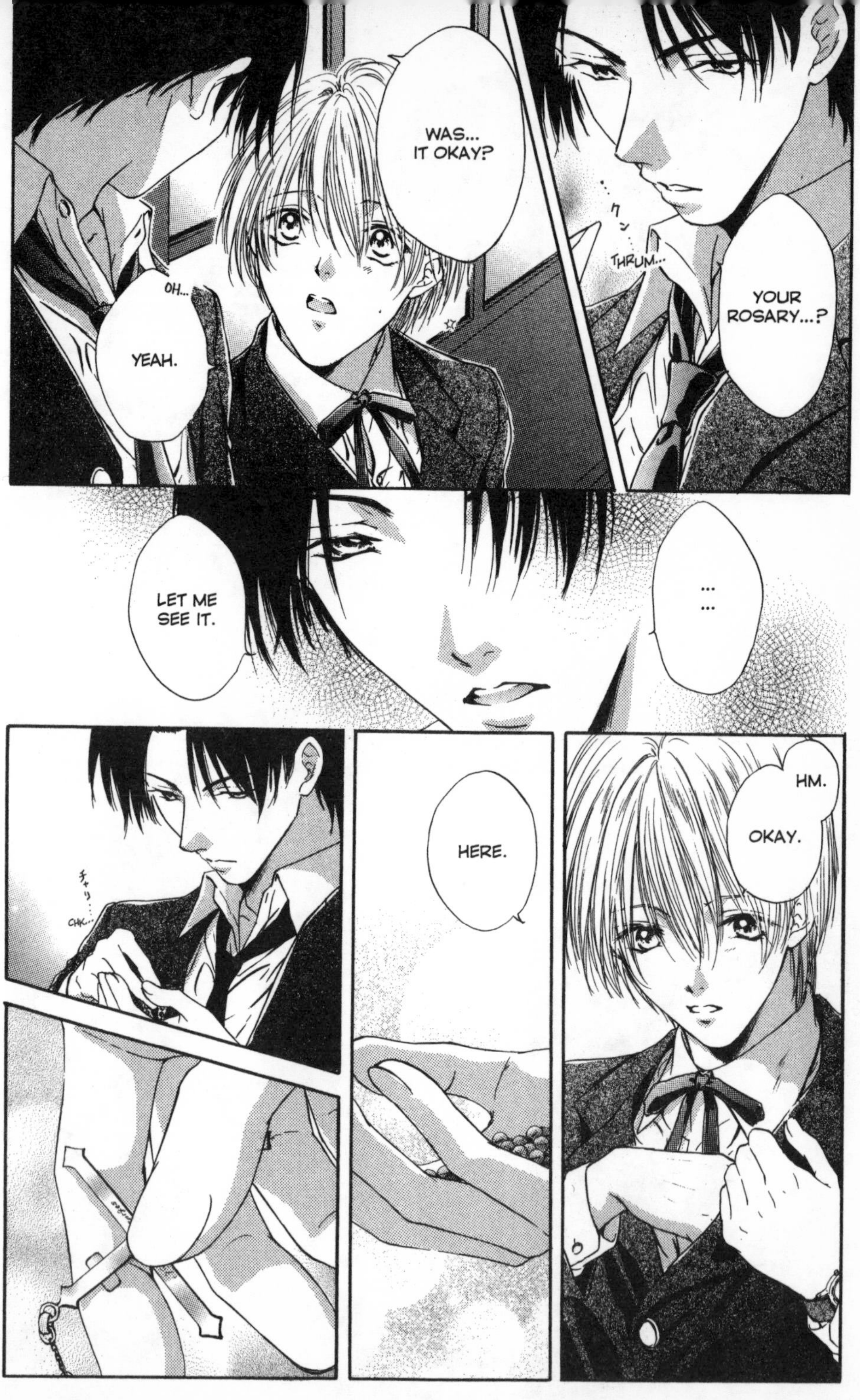
クン
THRUM...
YOUR ROSARY...?
WAS... IT OKAY?
OH...
YEAH.
...
...
LET ME SEE IT.
HM.
OKAY.
HERE.
チャリ
CHK...

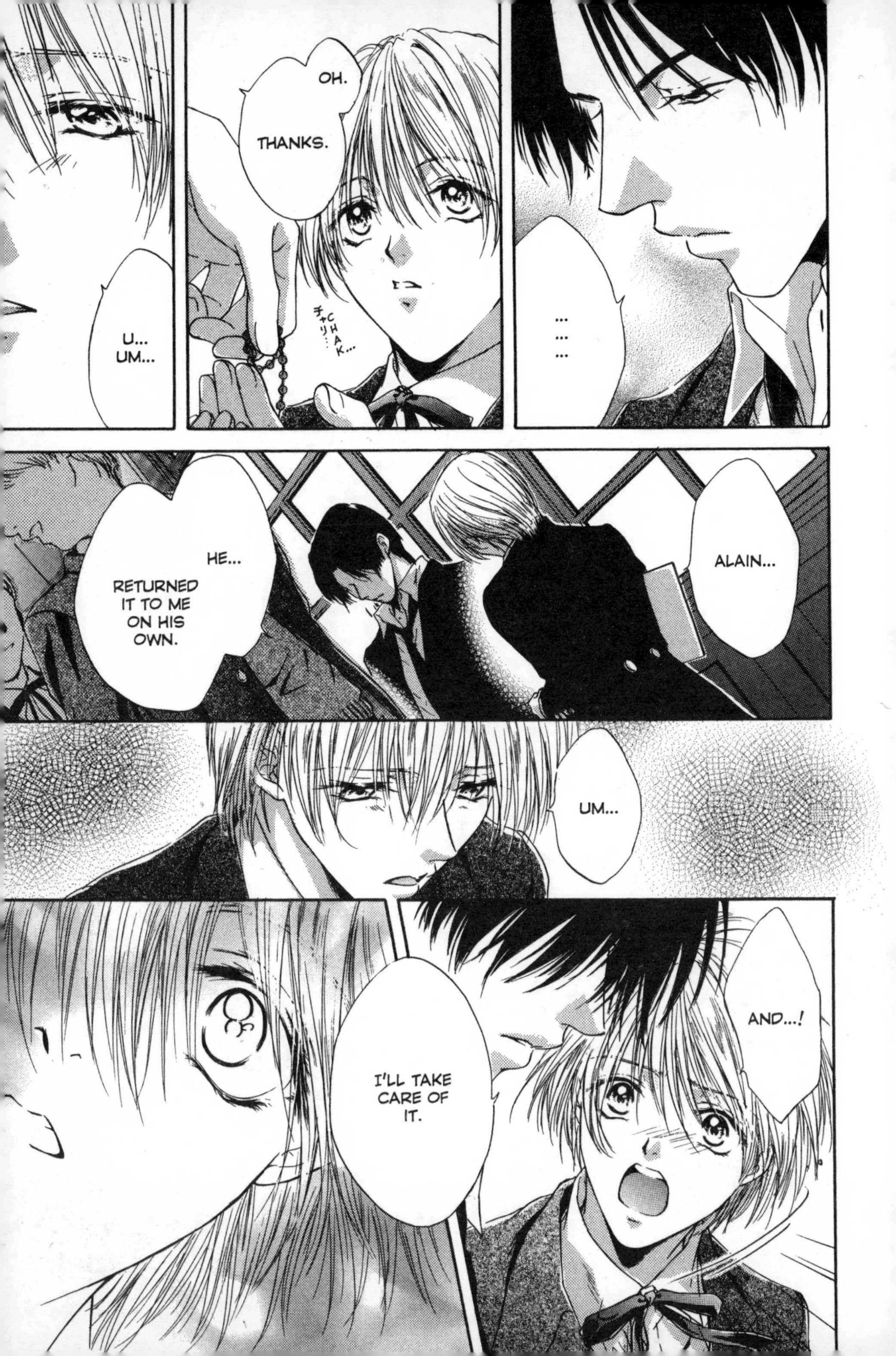

...
...
...
OH.
THANKS.
チャリ… CHAK...
U... UM...
ALAIN...
HE... RETURNED IT TO ME ON HIS OWN.
UM...
AND...!
I'LL TAKE CARE OF IT.

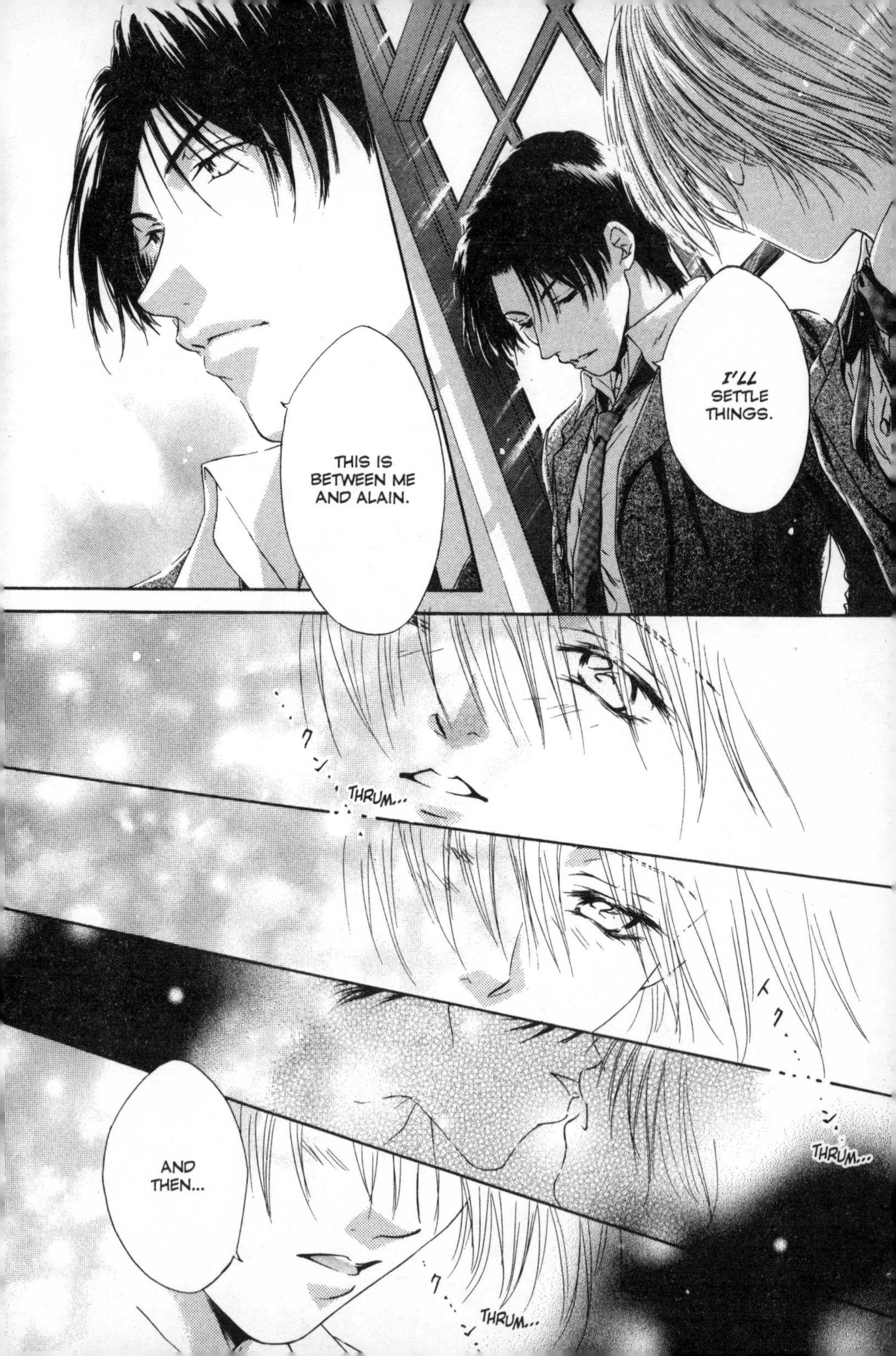
I'LL SETTLE THINGS.
THIS IS BETWEEN ME AND ALAIN.
THRUM...
THRUM...
AND THEN...
THRUM...

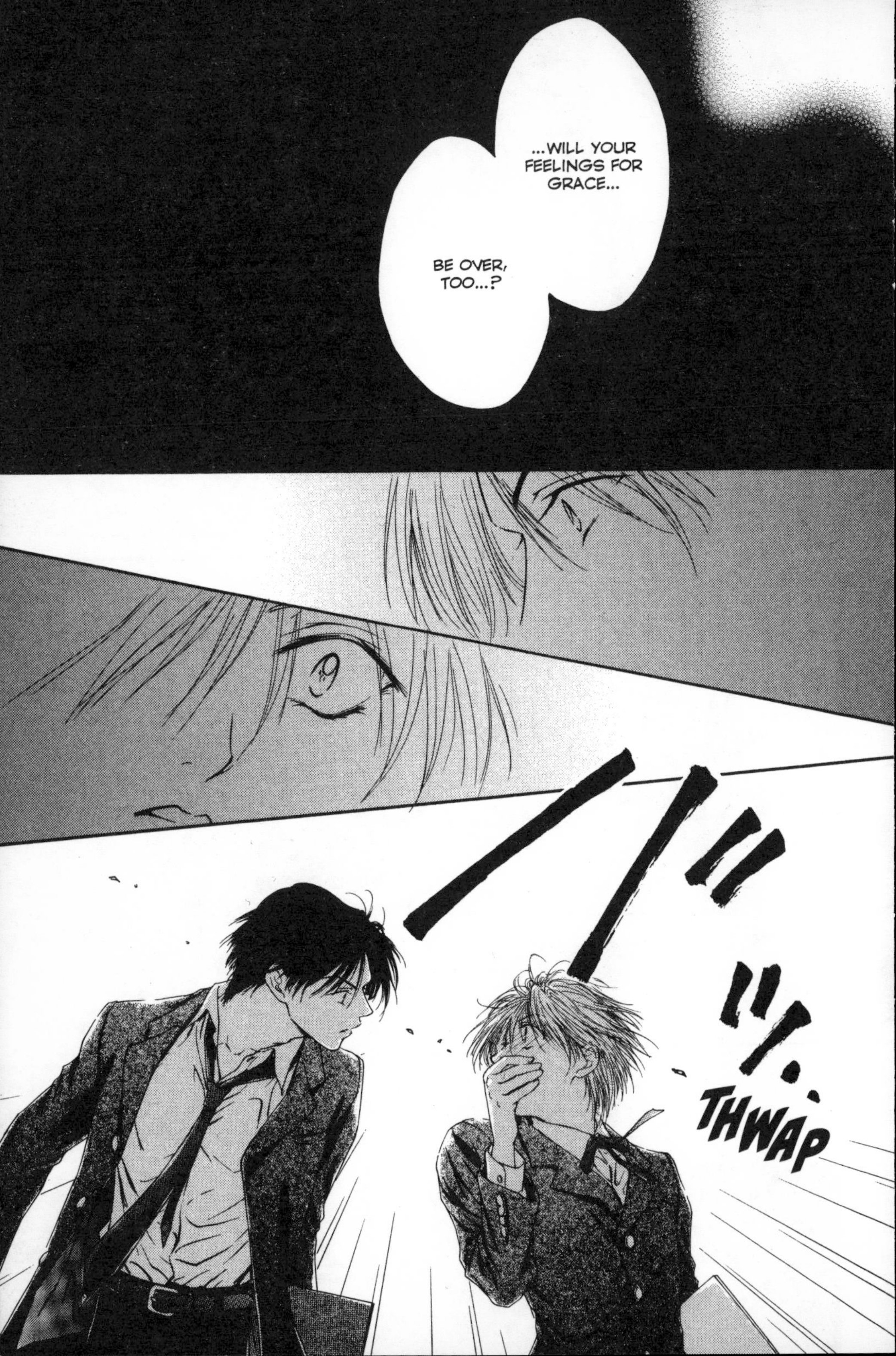
...WILL YOUR FEELINGS FOR GRACE...
BE OVER, TOO...?
THWAP

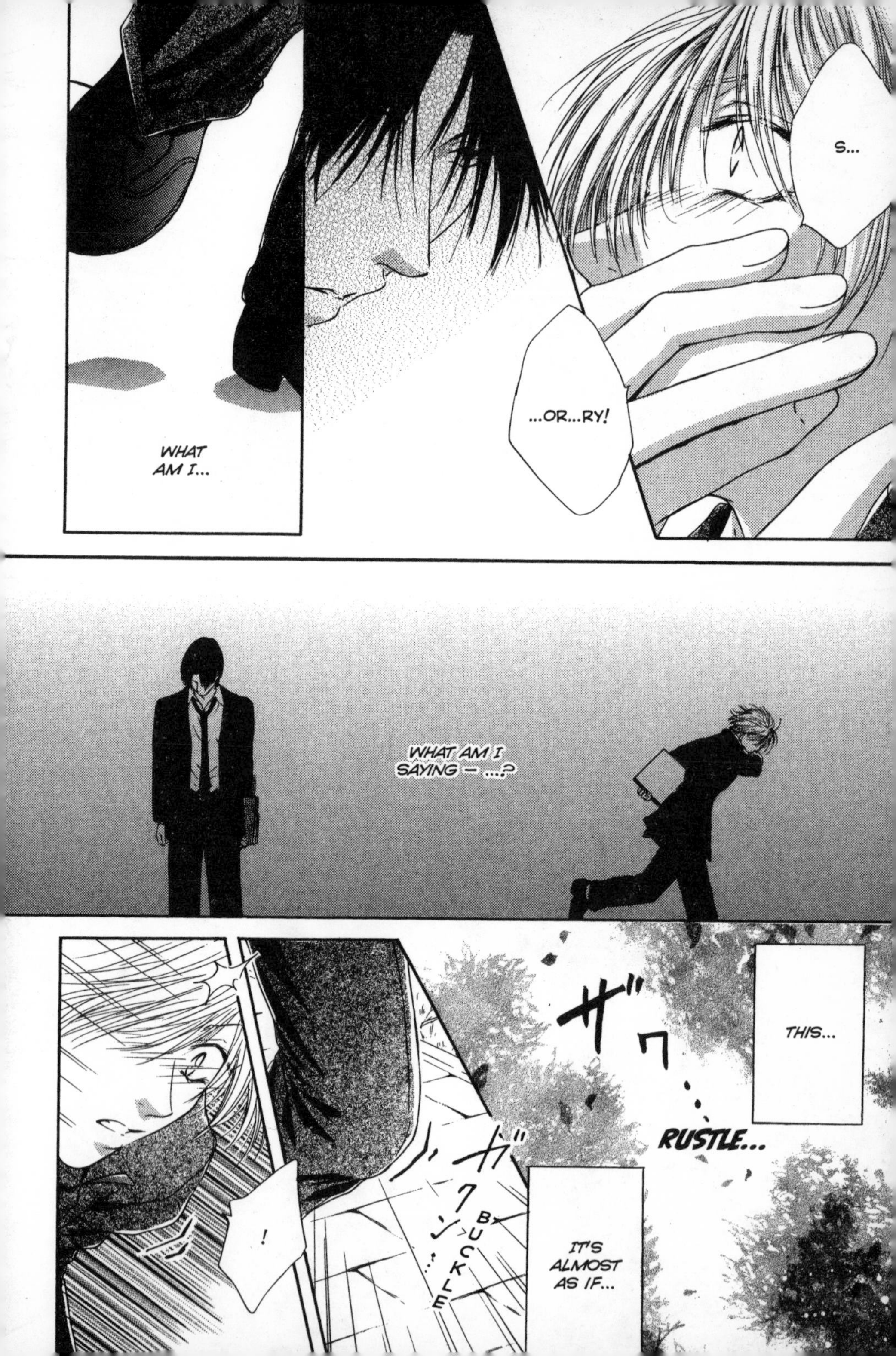
S...
...OR...RY!
WHAT AM I...
WHAT AM I SAYING — ...?
THIS...
ザワ...
RUSTLE...
IT'S ALMOST AS IF...
ガクン...
BUCKLE
!

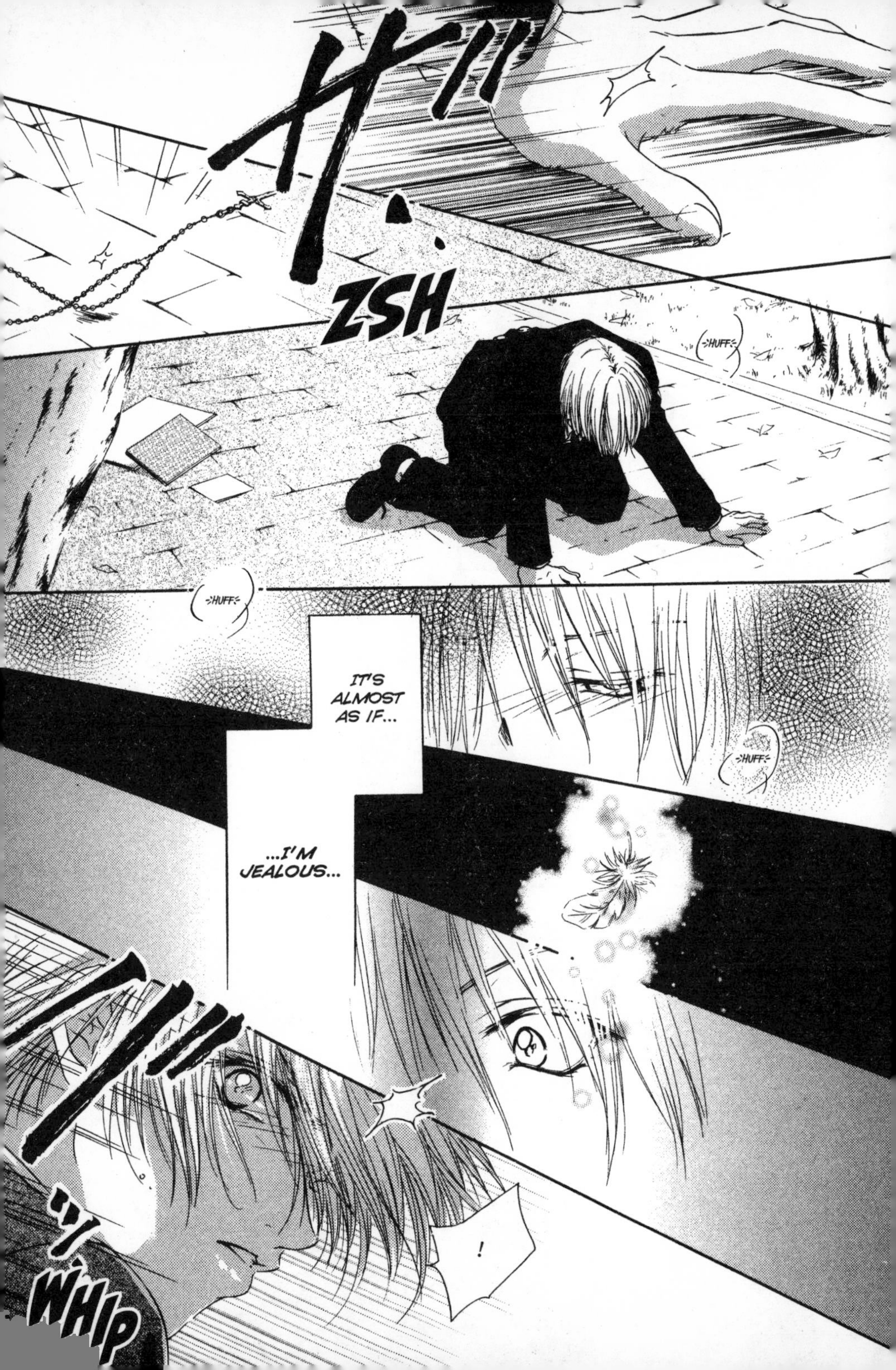
ZSH
HUFF
HUFF
IT'S ALMOST AS IF...
HUFF
...I'M JEALOUS...
!
WHIP

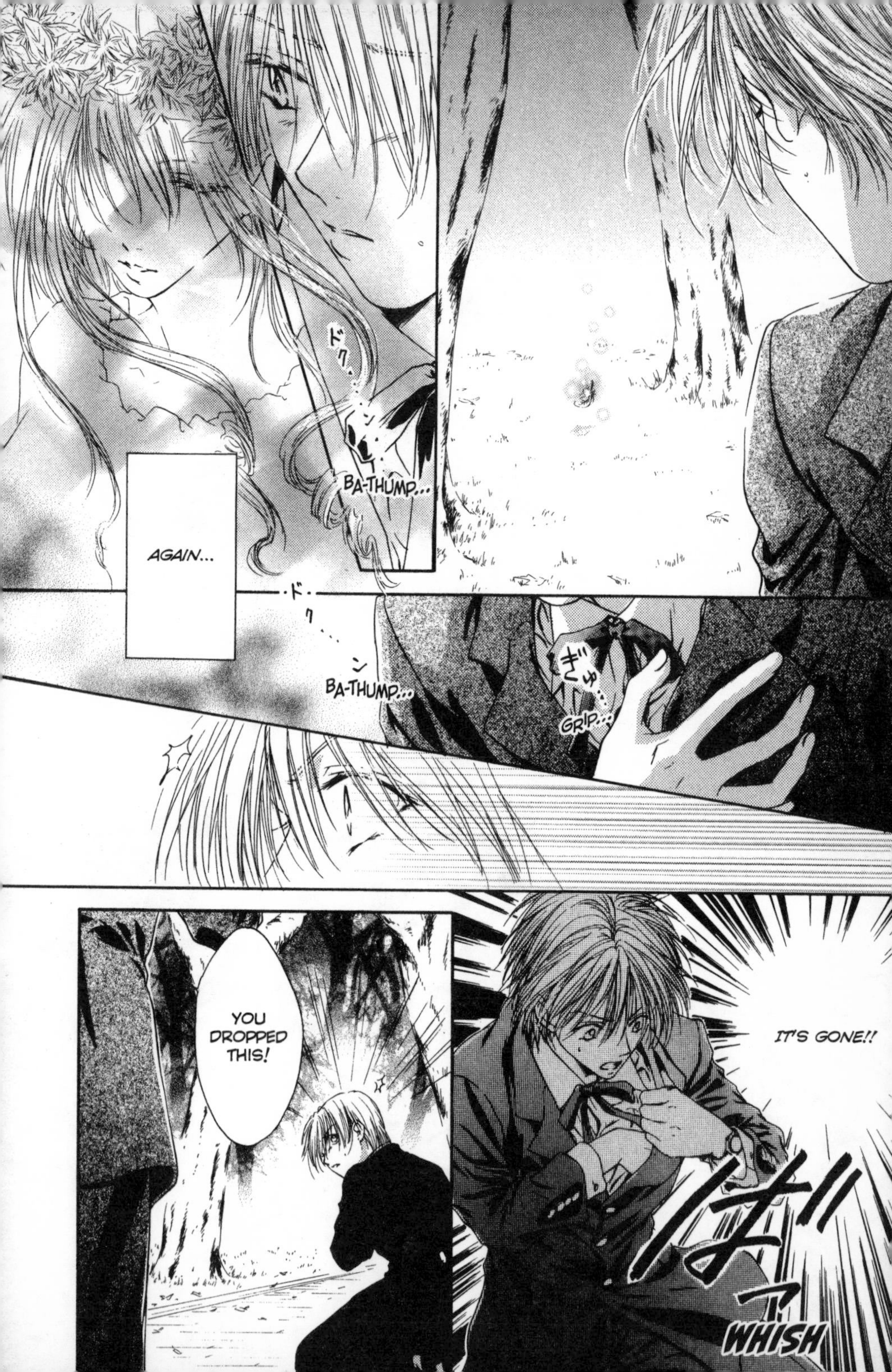
ドク…ン
BA-THUMP...
AGAIN...
ドク…ン
BA-THUMP...
ぎゅ…
GRIP...
IT'S GONE!!
はっ
WHISH
YOU DROPPED THIS!

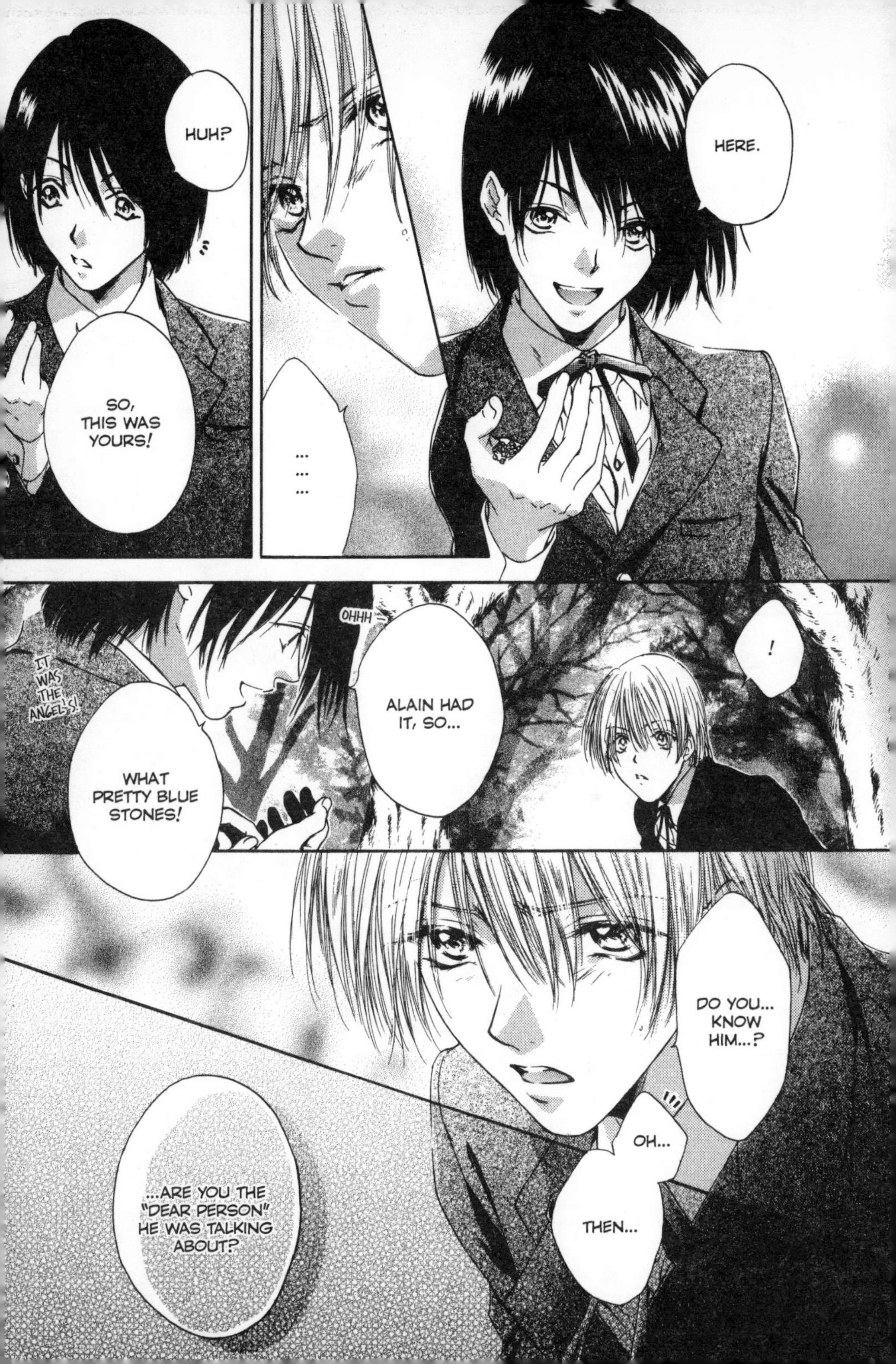
HERE.
...
...
...
HUH?
SO, THIS WAS YOURS!
!
ALAIN HAD IT, SO...
OHHH
IT WAS THE ANGEL'S!
WHAT PRETTY BLUE STONES!
DO YOU... KNOW HIM...?
OH...
THEN...
...ARE YOU THE "DEAR PERSON" HE WAS TALKING ABOUT?

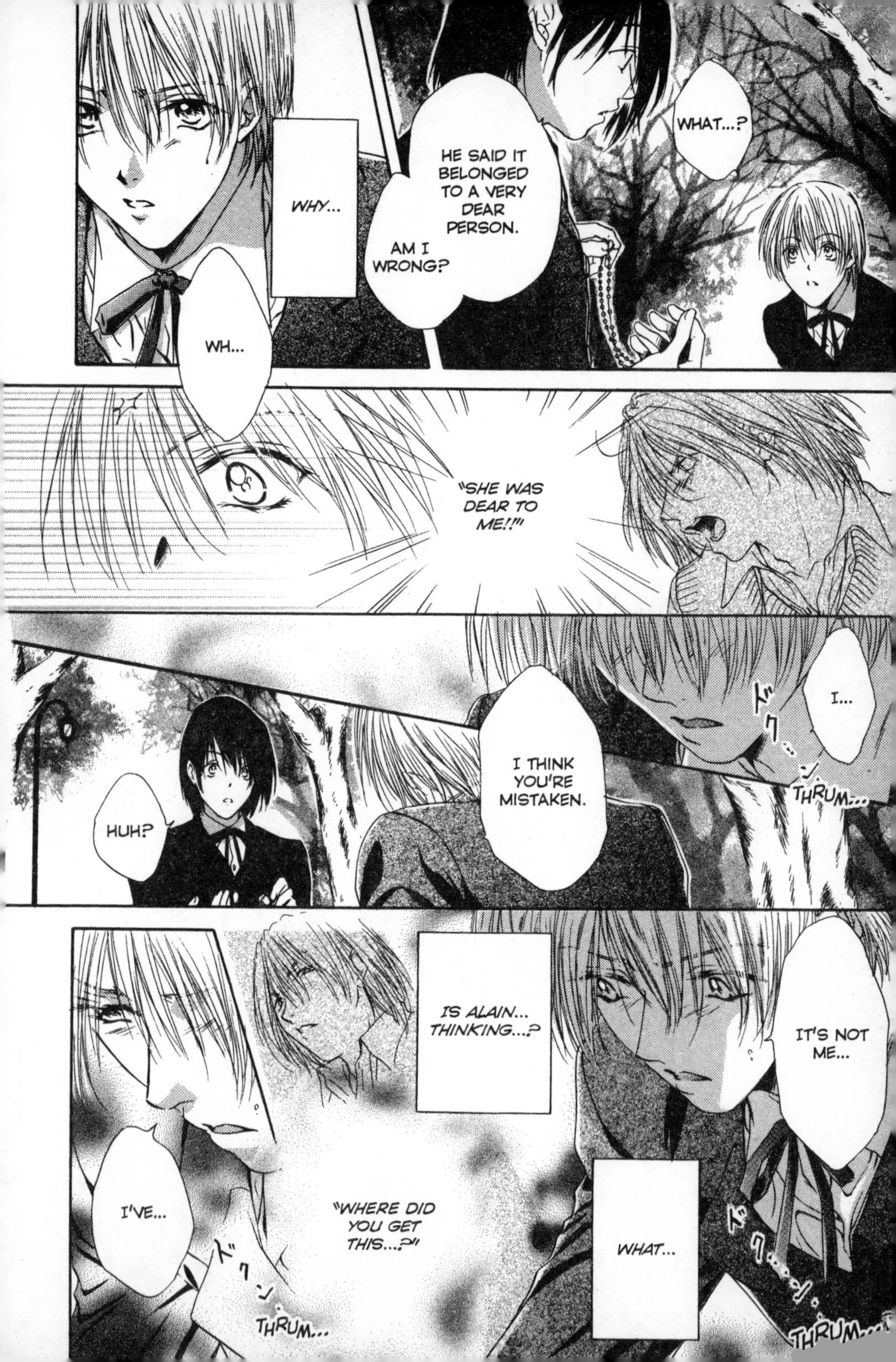

WHAT...?
HE SAID IT BELONGED TO A VERY DEAR PERSON.
AM I WRONG?
WHY...
WH...
"SHE WAS DEAR TO ME!!"
I...
THRUM...
I THINK YOU'RE MISTAKEN.
HUH?
IT'S NOT ME...
WHAT...
THRUM...
IS ALAIN... THINKING...?
I'VE...
"WHERE DID YOU GET THIS...?"
THRUM...

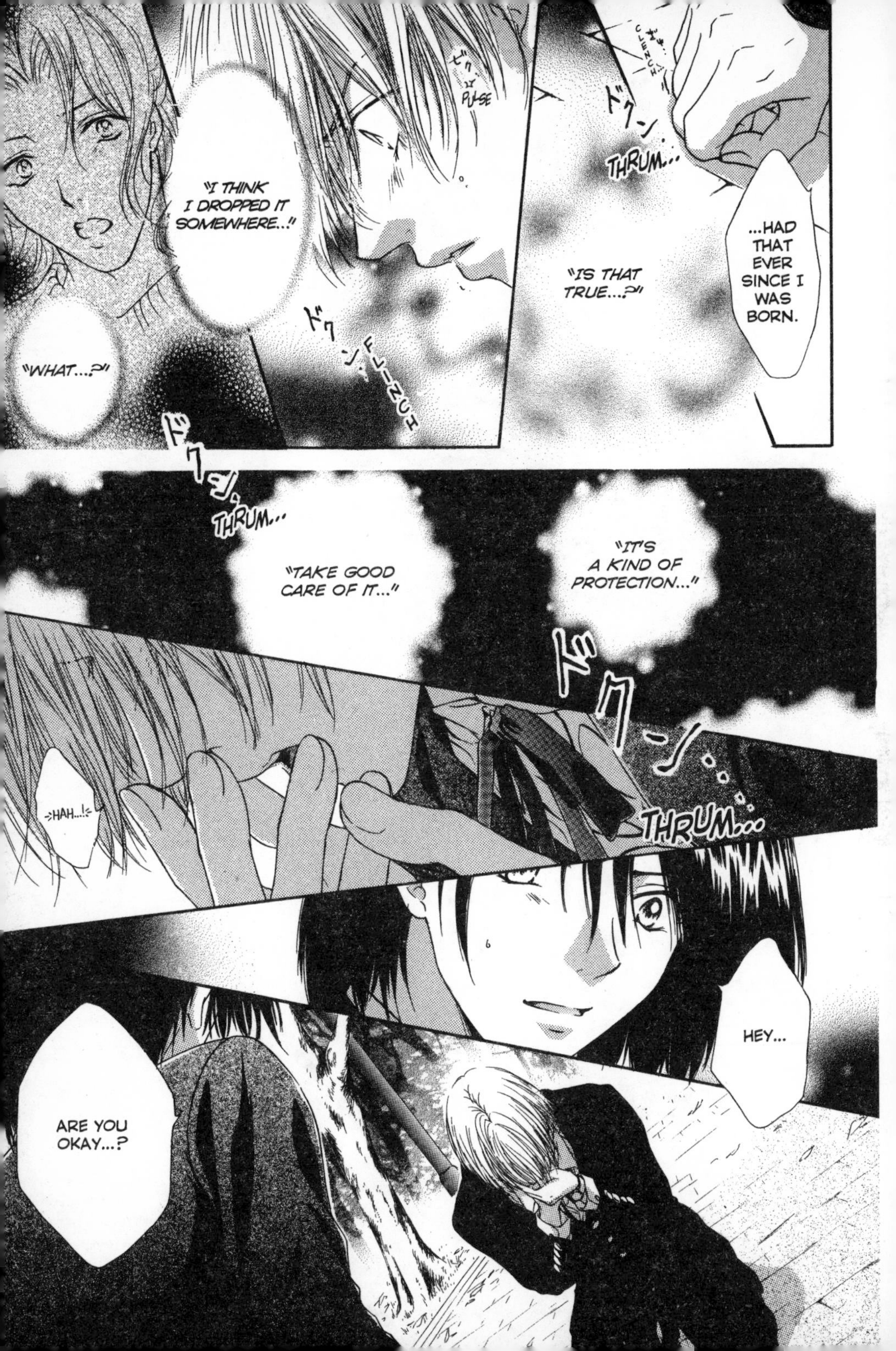
CLENCH...
THRUM...
...HAD THAT EVER SINCE I WAS BORN.
"IS THAT TRUE...?"
PULSE
"I THINK I DROPPED IT SOMEWHERE..."
FLINCH
"WHAT...?"
THRUM...
"IT'S A KIND OF PROTECTION..."
"TAKE GOOD CARE OF IT..."
THRUM...
HAH...!
HEY...
ARE YOU OKAY...?

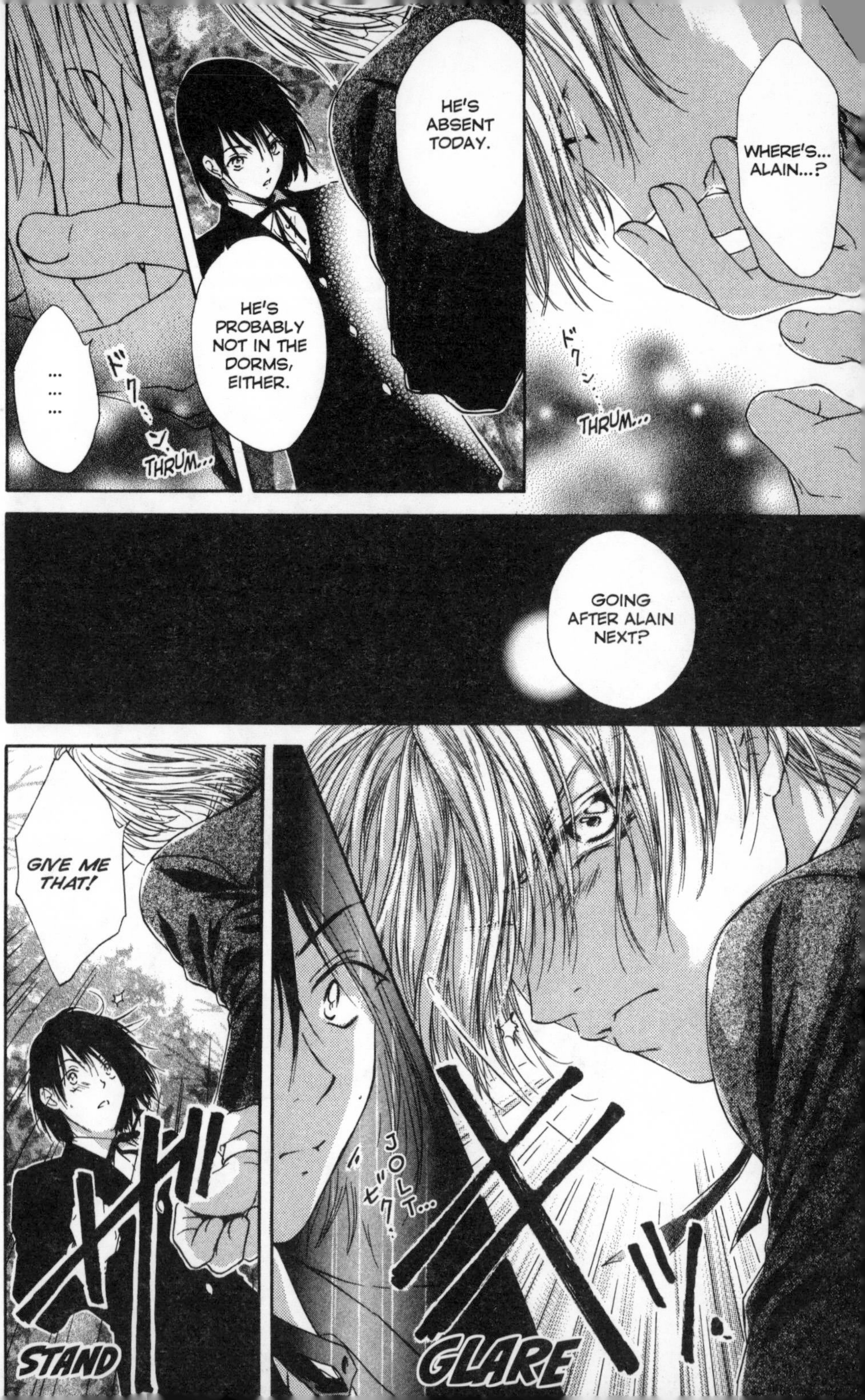
WHERE'S... ALAIN...?
THRUM...
HE'S ABSENT TODAY.
HE'S PROBABLY NOT IN THE DORMS, EITHER.
... ...
THRUM...
GOING AFTER ALAIN NEXT?
JOLT...
GLARE
GIVE ME THAT!
STAND

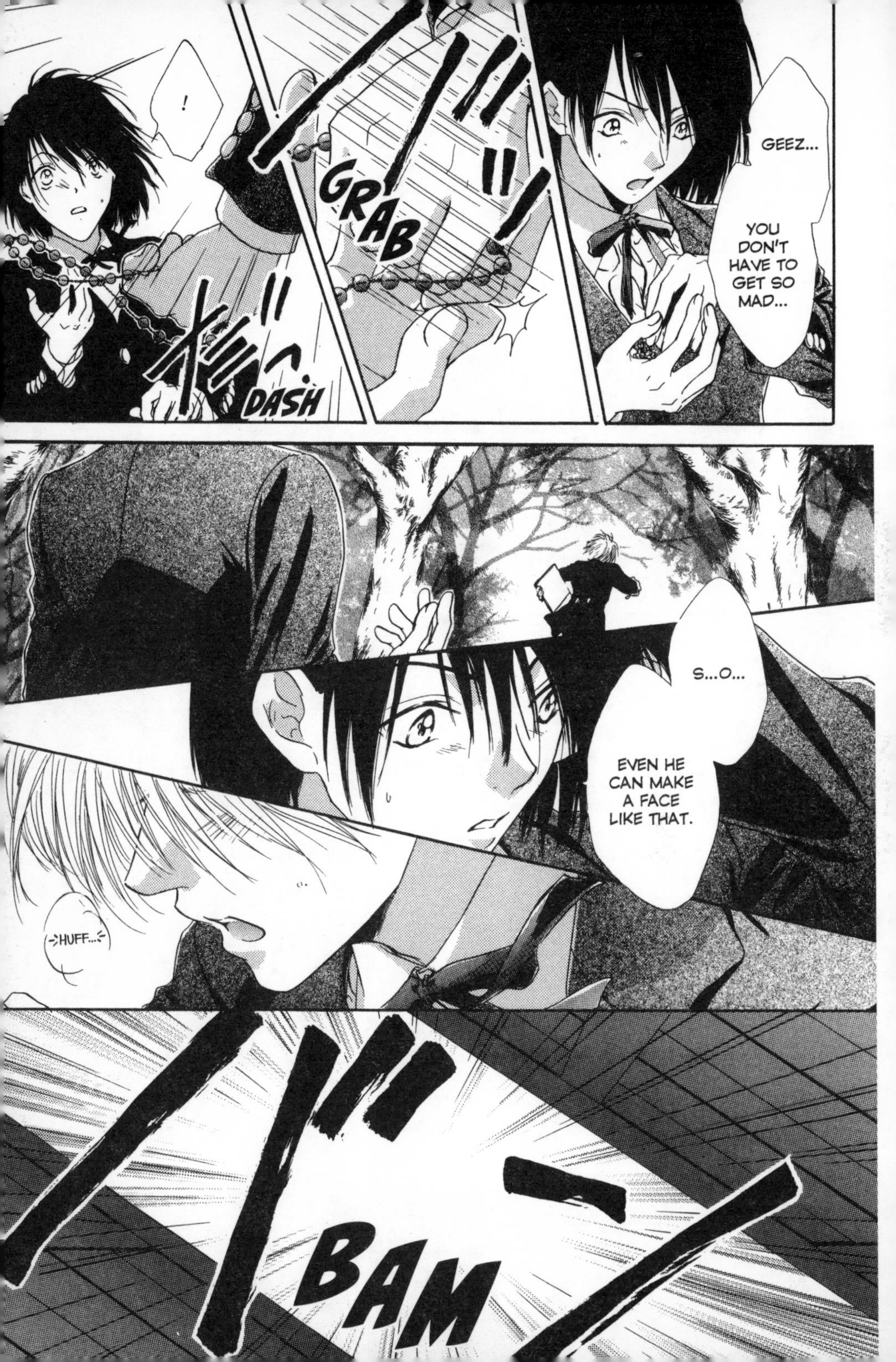
GEEZ...
YOU DON'T HAVE TO GET SO MAD...
GRAB
!
DASH
S...O...
EVEN HE CAN MAKE A FACE LIKE THAT.
HUFF...
BAM

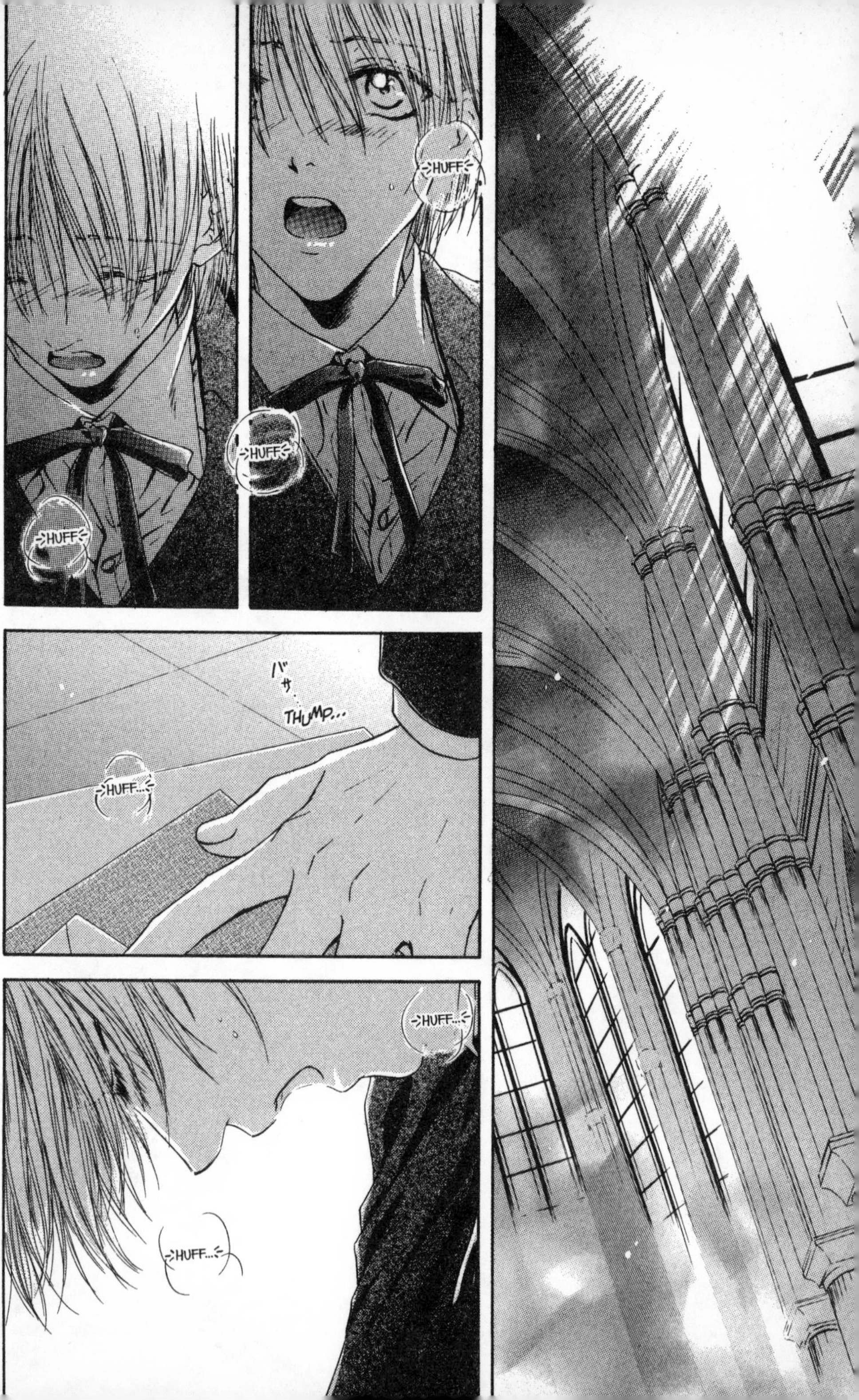
HUFF
HUFF
HUFF
バサ…
THUMP...
HUFF...
HUFF...
HUFF...

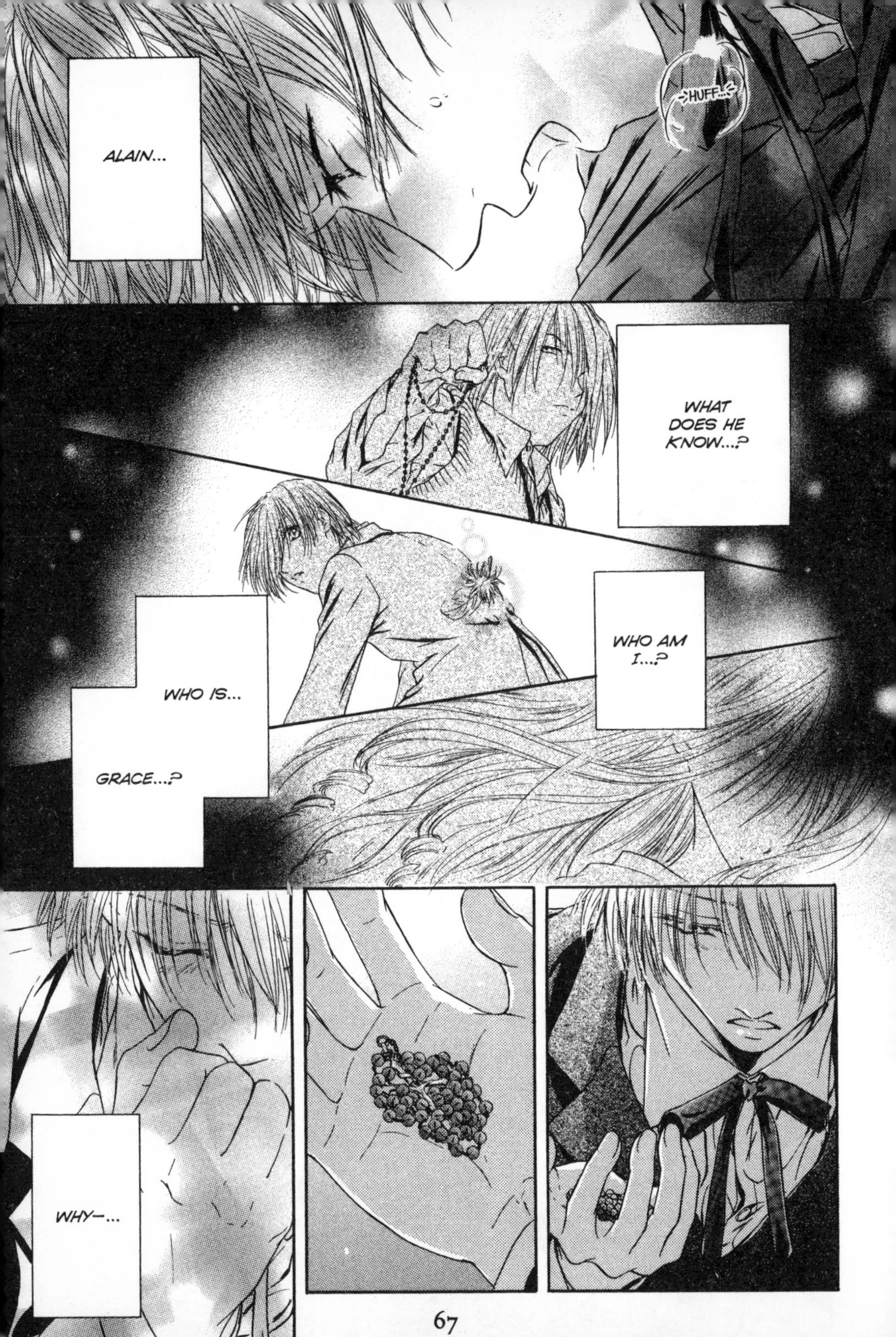
HUFF...
ALAIN...
WHAT DOES HE KNOW...?
WHO AM I...?
WHO IS...
GRACE...?
WHY-...

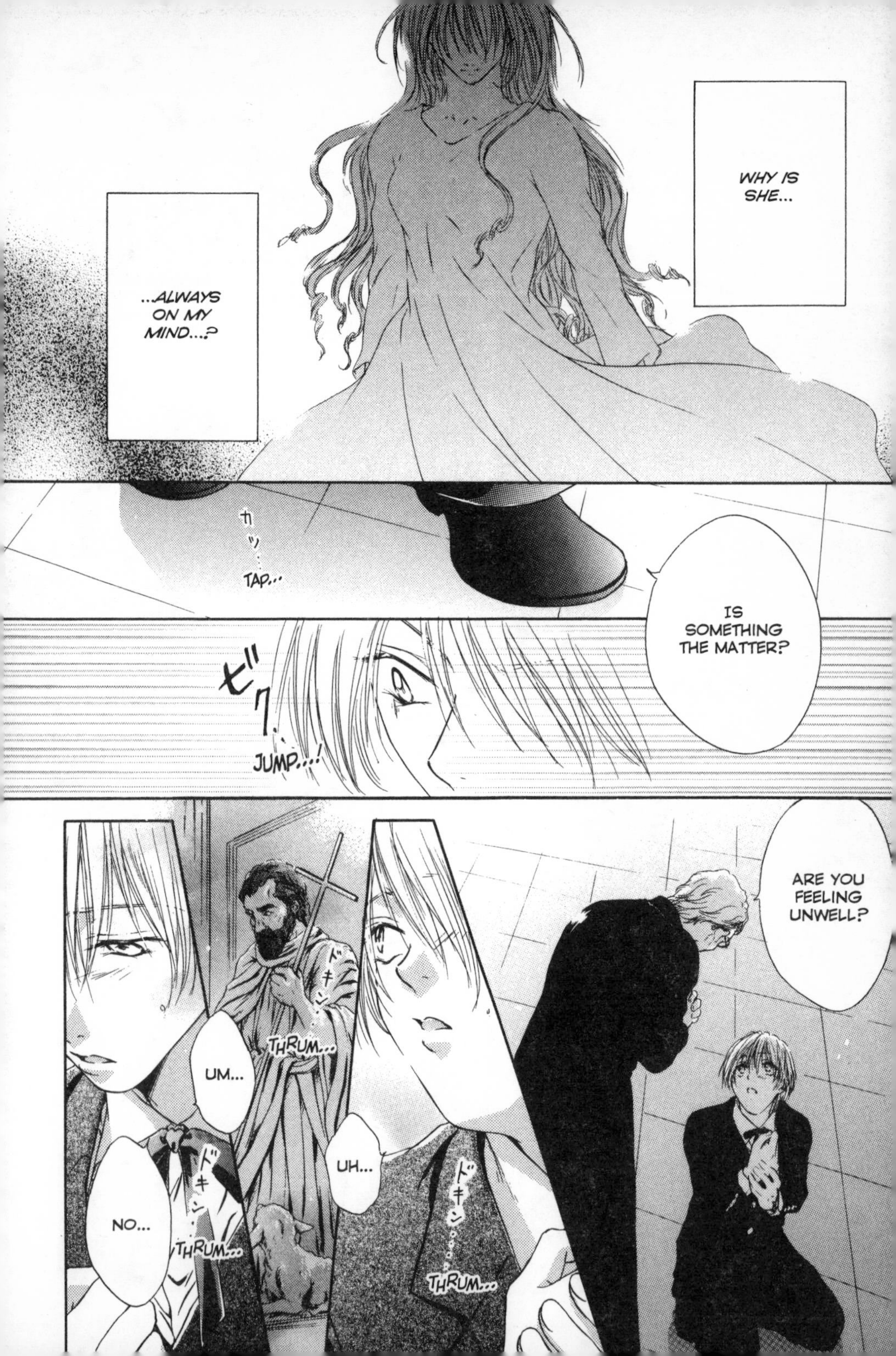
WHY IS SHE...
...ALWAYS ON MY MIND...?
カッ...
TAP...
IS SOMETHING THE MATTER?
ビクッ
JUMP...!
ARE YOU FEELING UNWELL?
ドキン...
THRUM...
UH...
ドキン...
THRUM...
UM...
NO...
ドキン...
THRUM...

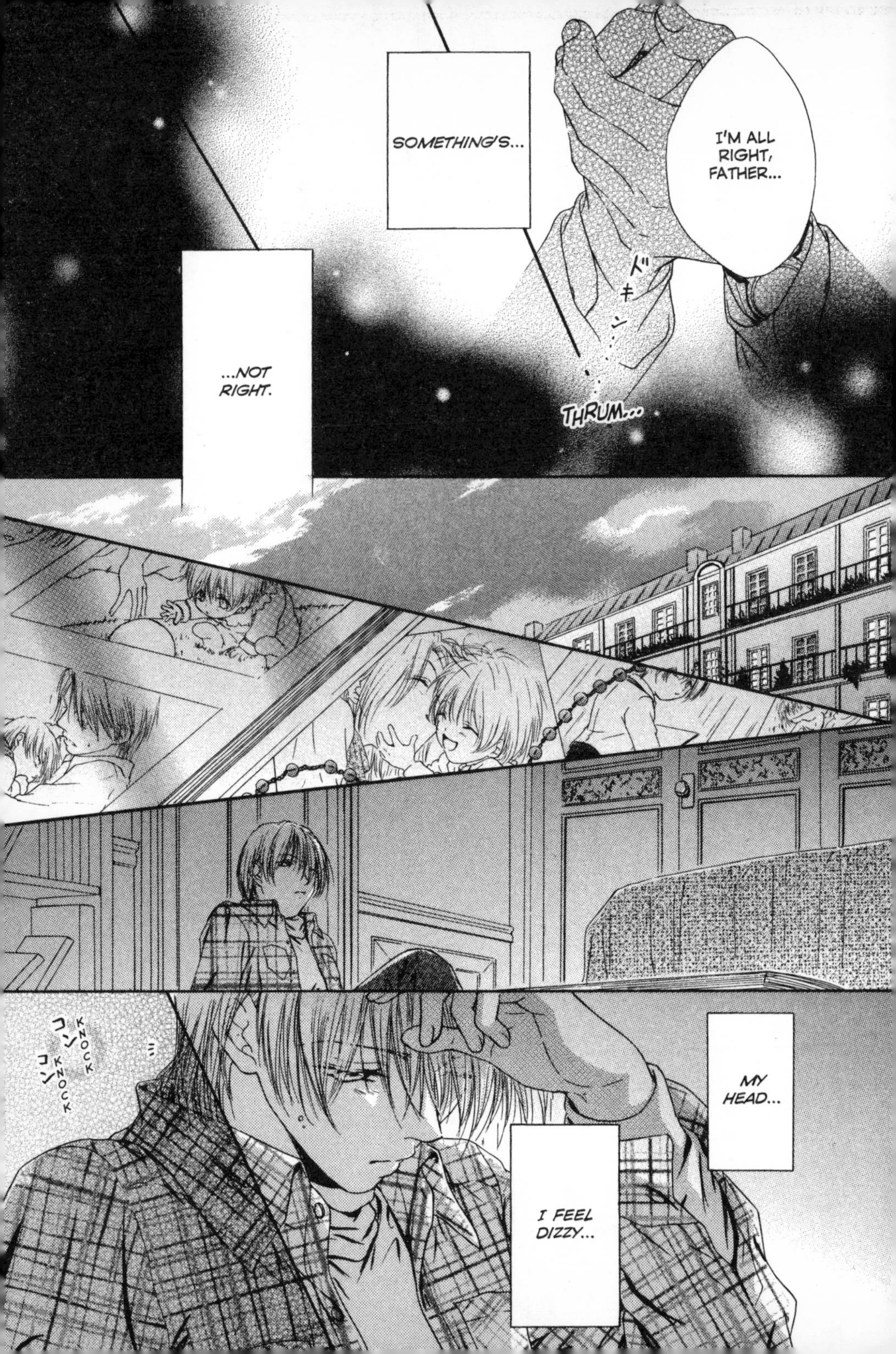
I'M ALL RIGHT, FATHER...
SOMETHING'S...
ドキン…
THRUM...
...NOT RIGHT.
MY HEAD...
I FEEL DIZZY...
コン KNOCK
コン KNOCK

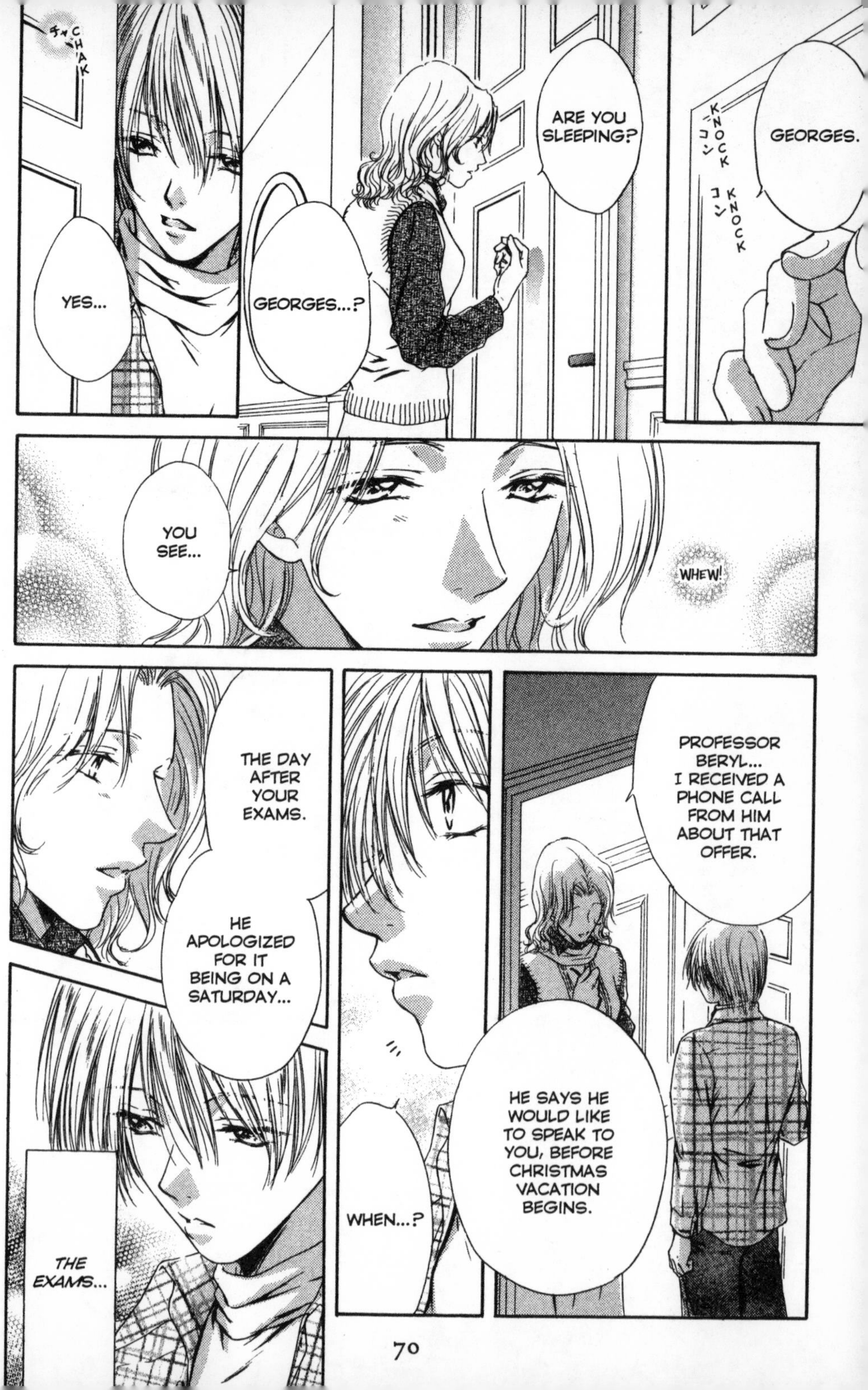
GEORGES.
KNOCK
KNOCK
ARE YOU SLEEPING?
GEORGES...?
CHAK
YES...
WHEW!
YOU SEE...
PROFESSOR BERYL... I RECEIVED A PHONE CALL FROM HIM ABOUT THAT OFFER.
HE SAYS HE WOULD LIKE TO SPEAK TO YOU, BEFORE CHRISTMAS VACATION BEGINS.
WHEN...?
THE DAY AFTER YOUR EXAMS.
HE APOLOGIZED FOR IT BEING ON A SATURDAY...
THE EXAMS...

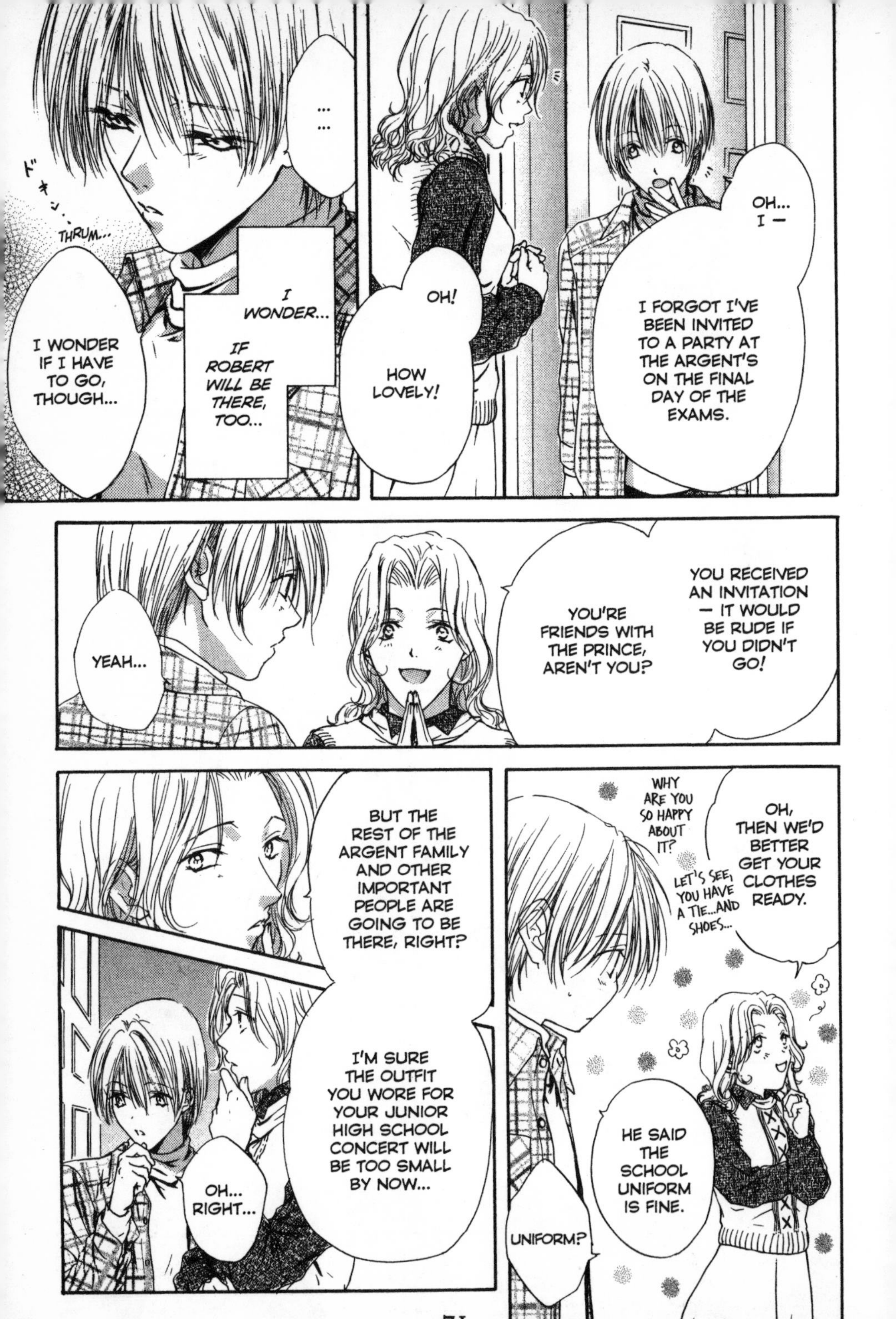
OH... I —
I FORGOT I'VE BEEN INVITED TO A PARTY AT THE ARGENT'S ON THE FINAL DAY OF THE EXAMS.
OH!
HOW LOVELY!
...
...
ドキン・・
THRUM...
I WONDER...
IF ROBERT WILL BE THERE, TOO...
I WONDER IF I HAVE TO GO, THOUGH...
YOU RECEIVED AN INVITATION — IT WOULD BE RUDE IF YOU DIDN'T GO!
YOU'RE FRIENDS WITH THE PRINCE, AREN'T YOU?
YEAH...
OH, THEN WE'D BETTER GET YOUR CLOTHES READY.
WHY ARE YOU SO HAPPY ABOUT IT?
LET'S SEE, YOU HAVE A TIE...AND SHOES...
HE SAID THE SCHOOL UNIFORM IS FINE.
UNIFORM?
BUT THE REST OF THE ARGENT FAMILY AND OTHER IMPORTANT PEOPLE ARE GOING TO BE THERE, RIGHT?
I'M SURE THE OUTFIT YOU WORE FOR YOUR JUNIOR HIGH SCHOOL CONCERT WILL BE TOO SMALL BY NOW...
OH... RIGHT...

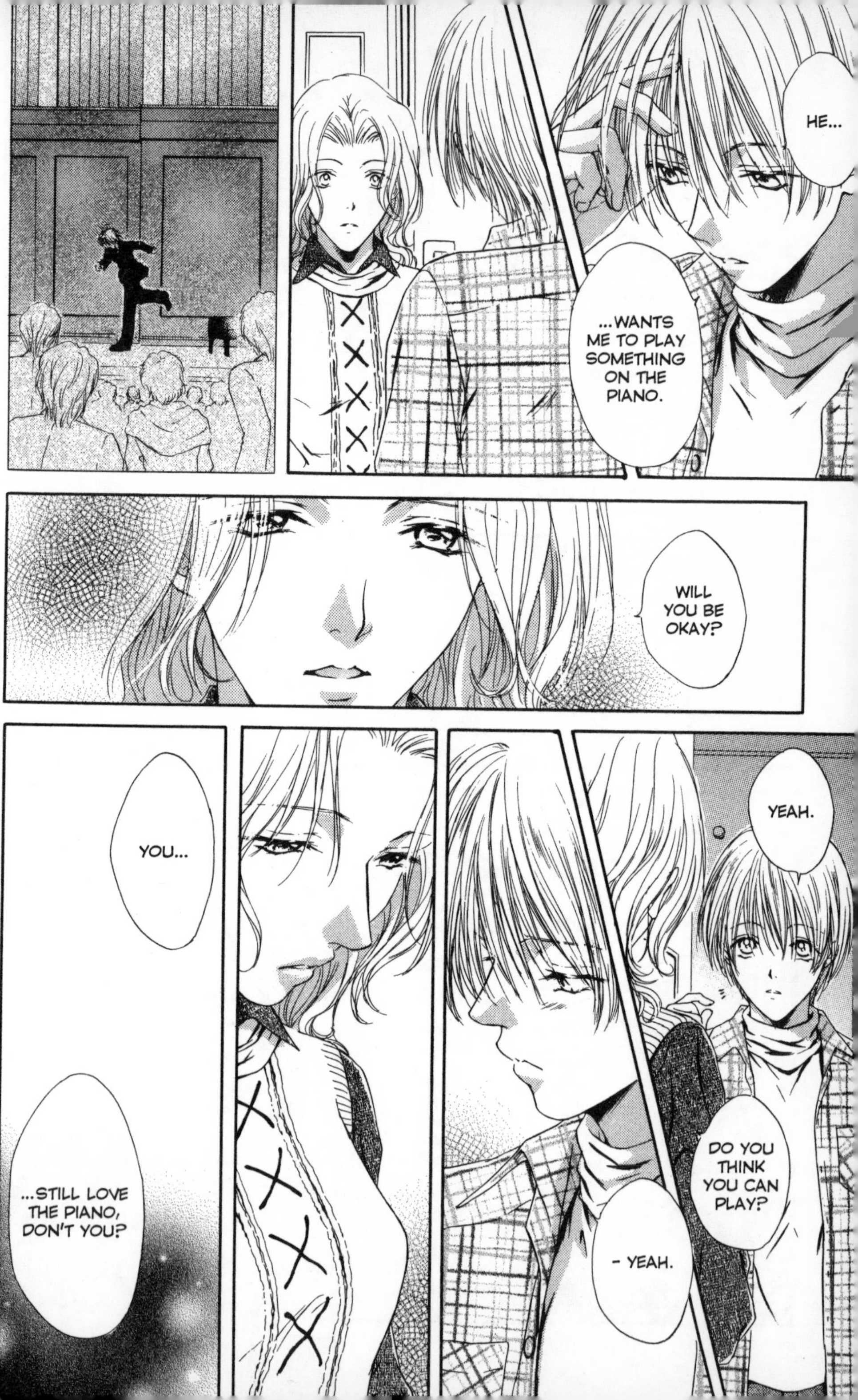

HE...
...WANTS ME TO PLAY SOMETHING ON THE PIANO.
WILL YOU BE OKAY?
YEAH.
DO YOU THINK YOU CAN PLAY?
- YEAH.
YOU...
...STILL LOVE THE PIANO, DON'T YOU?

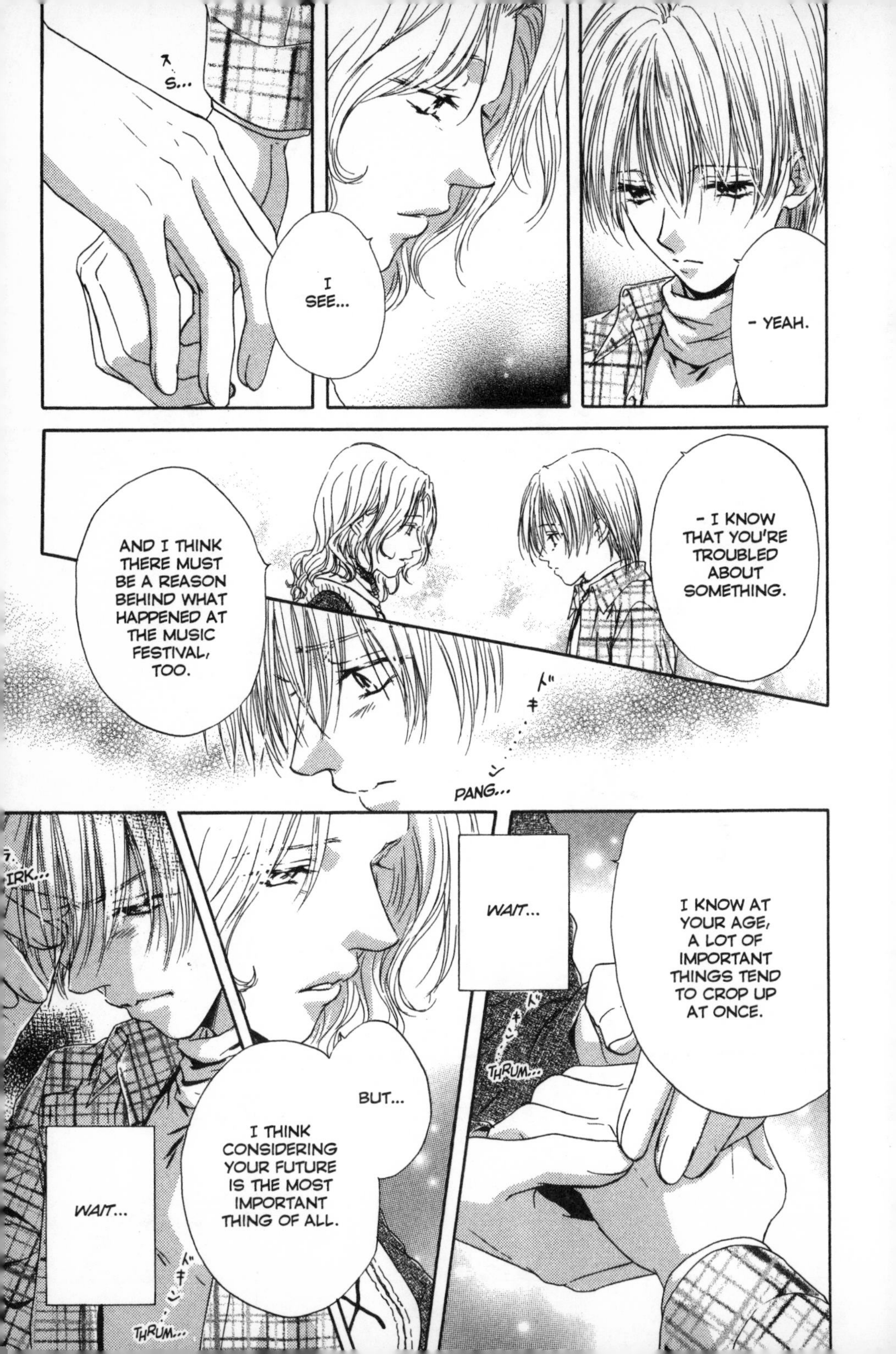
- YEAH.
I SEE...
S...
- I KNOW THAT YOU'RE TROUBLED ABOUT SOMETHING.
AND I THINK THERE MUST BE A REASON BEHIND WHAT HAPPENED AT THE MUSIC FESTIVAL, TOO.
PANG...
I KNOW AT YOUR AGE, A LOT OF IMPORTANT THINGS TEND TO CROP UP AT ONCE.
WAIT...
THRUM...
BUT...
I THINK CONSIDERING YOUR FUTURE IS THE MOST IMPORTANT THING OF ALL.
WAIT...
THRUM...
IRK...

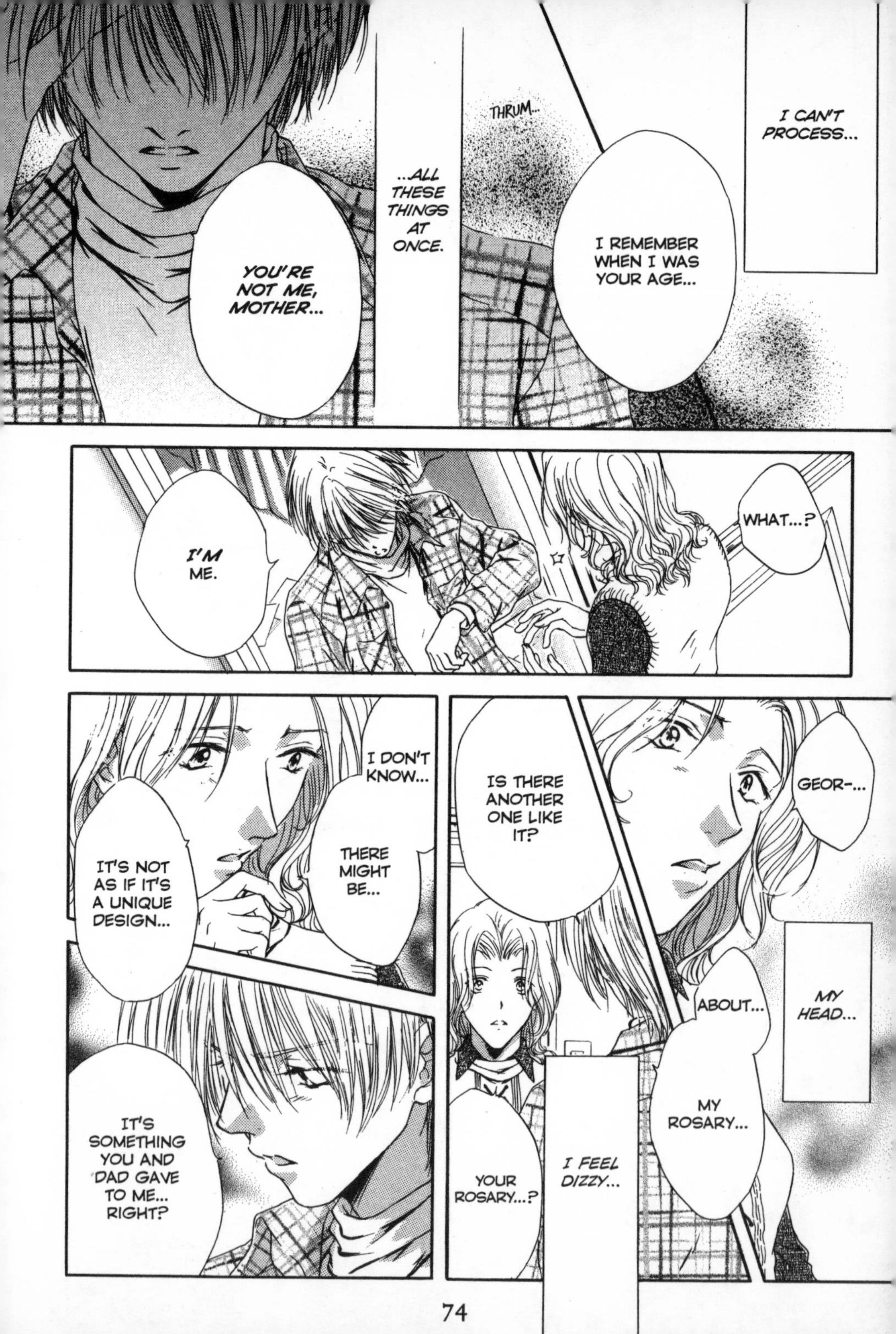
I CAN'T PROCESS...
THRUM...
I REMEMBER WHEN I WAS YOUR AGE...
...ALL THESE THINGS AT ONCE.
YOU'RE NOT ME, MOTHER...
WHAT...?
I'M ME.
GEOR-...
MY HEAD...
ABOUT...
MY ROSARY...
I FEEL DIZZY...
YOUR ROSARY...?
IS THERE ANOTHER ONE LIKE IT?
I DON'T KNOW...
THERE MIGHT BE...
IT'S NOT AS IF IT'S A UNIQUE DESIGN...
IT'S SOMETHING YOU AND DAD GAVE TO ME... RIGHT?

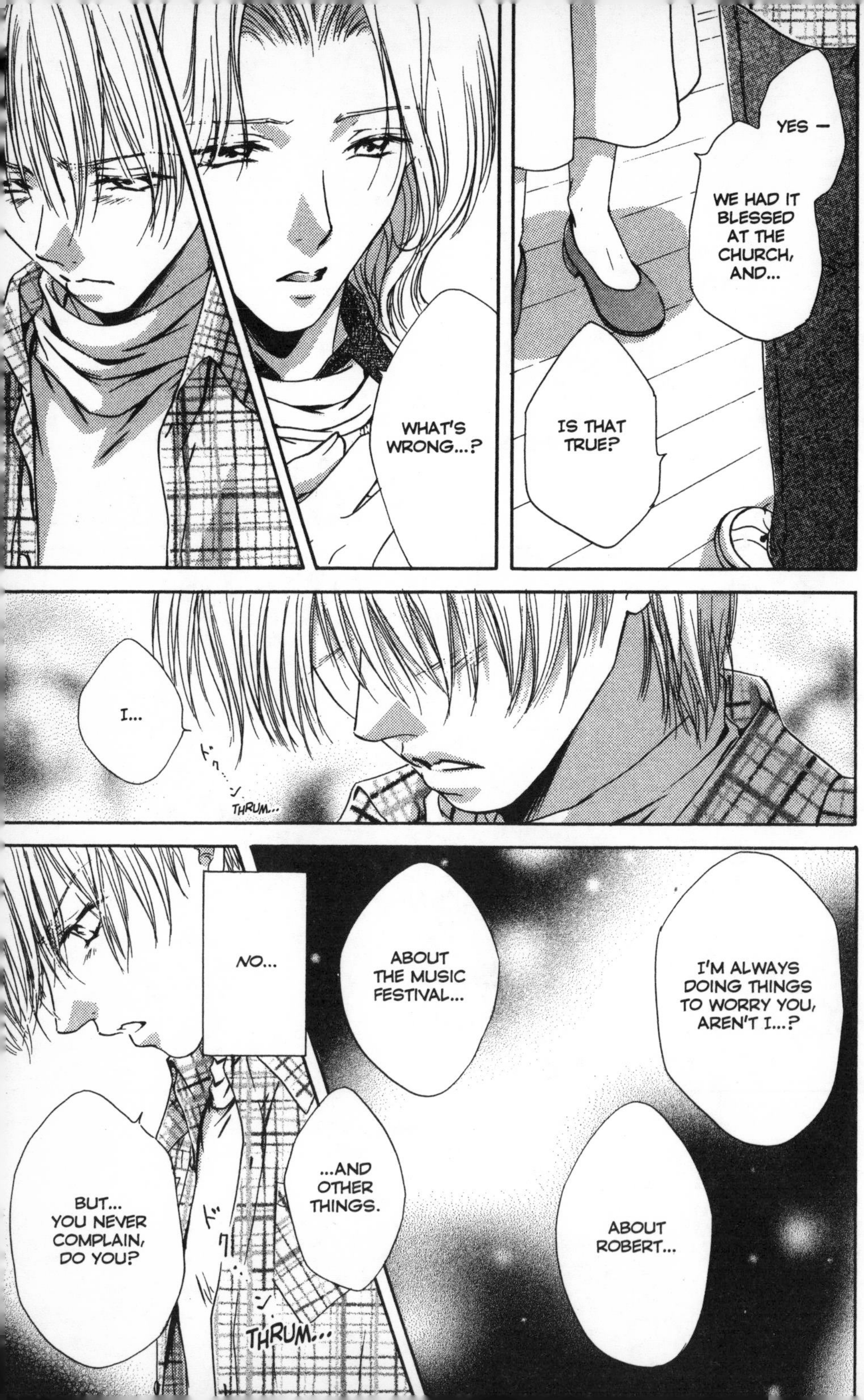
YES —
WE HAD IT BLESSED AT THE CHURCH, AND...
IS THAT TRUE?
WHAT'S WRONG...?
I...
THRUM...
I'M ALWAYS DOING THINGS TO WORRY YOU, AREN'T I...?
ABOUT THE MUSIC FESTIVAL...
ABOUT ROBERT...
...AND OTHER THINGS.
NO...
BUT... YOU NEVER COMPLAIN, DO YOU?
THRUM...

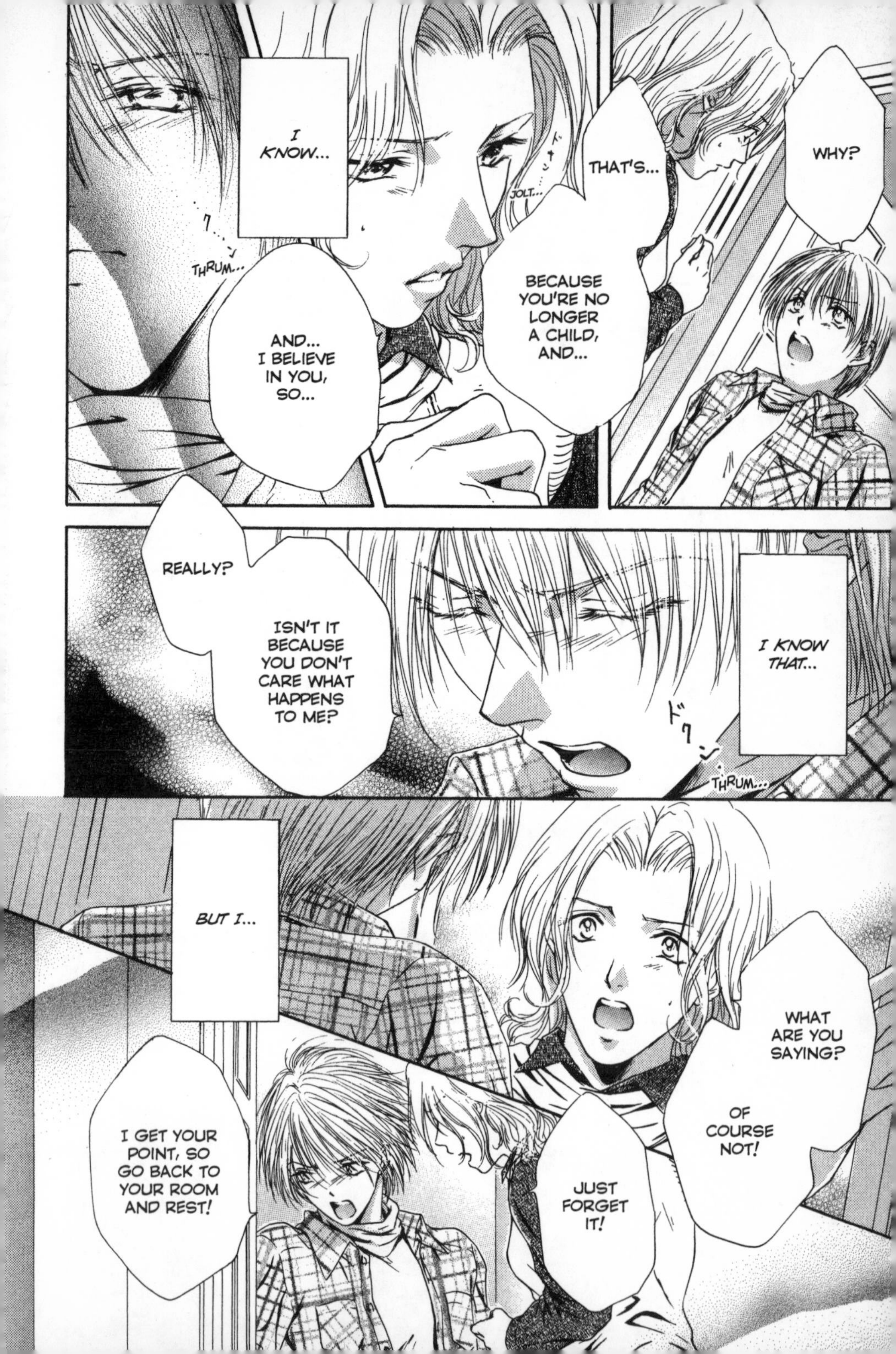
WHY?
THAT'S...
BECAUSE YOU'RE NO LONGER A CHILD, AND...
JOLT...
I KNOW...
THRUM...
AND... I BELIEVE IN YOU, SO...
I KNOW THAT...
THRUM...
REALLY?
ISN'T IT BECAUSE YOU DON'T CARE WHAT HAPPENS TO ME?
WHAT ARE YOU SAYING?
OF COURSE NOT!
JUST FORGET IT!
BUT I...
I GET YOUR POINT, SO GO BACK TO YOUR ROOM AND REST!

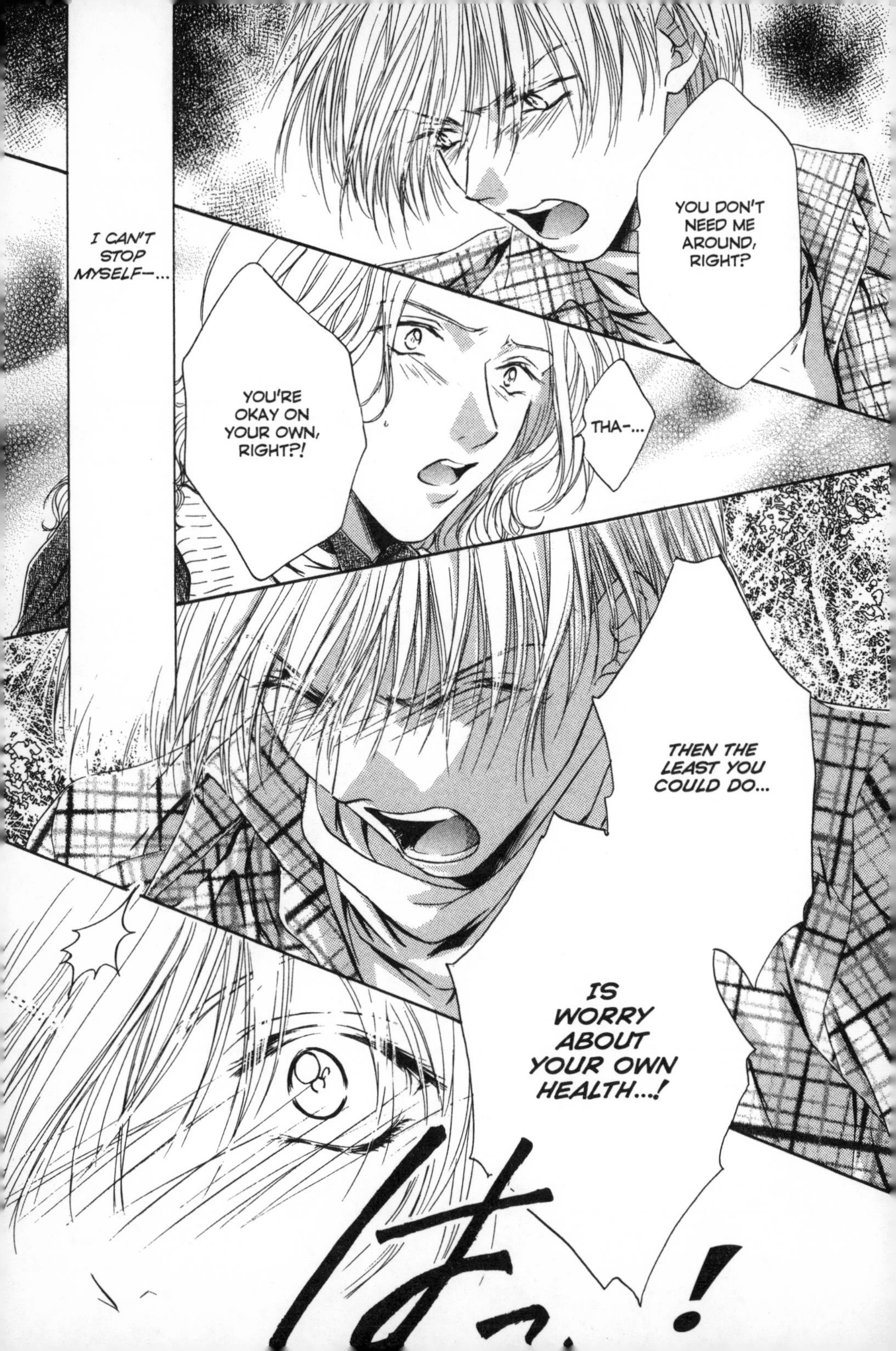
YOU DON'T NEED ME AROUND, RIGHT?
THA-...
YOU'RE OKAY ON YOUR OWN, RIGHT?!
I CAN'T STOP MYSELF—...
THEN THE LEAST YOU COULD DO...
IS WORRY ABOUT YOUR OWN HEALTH...!
はっ!

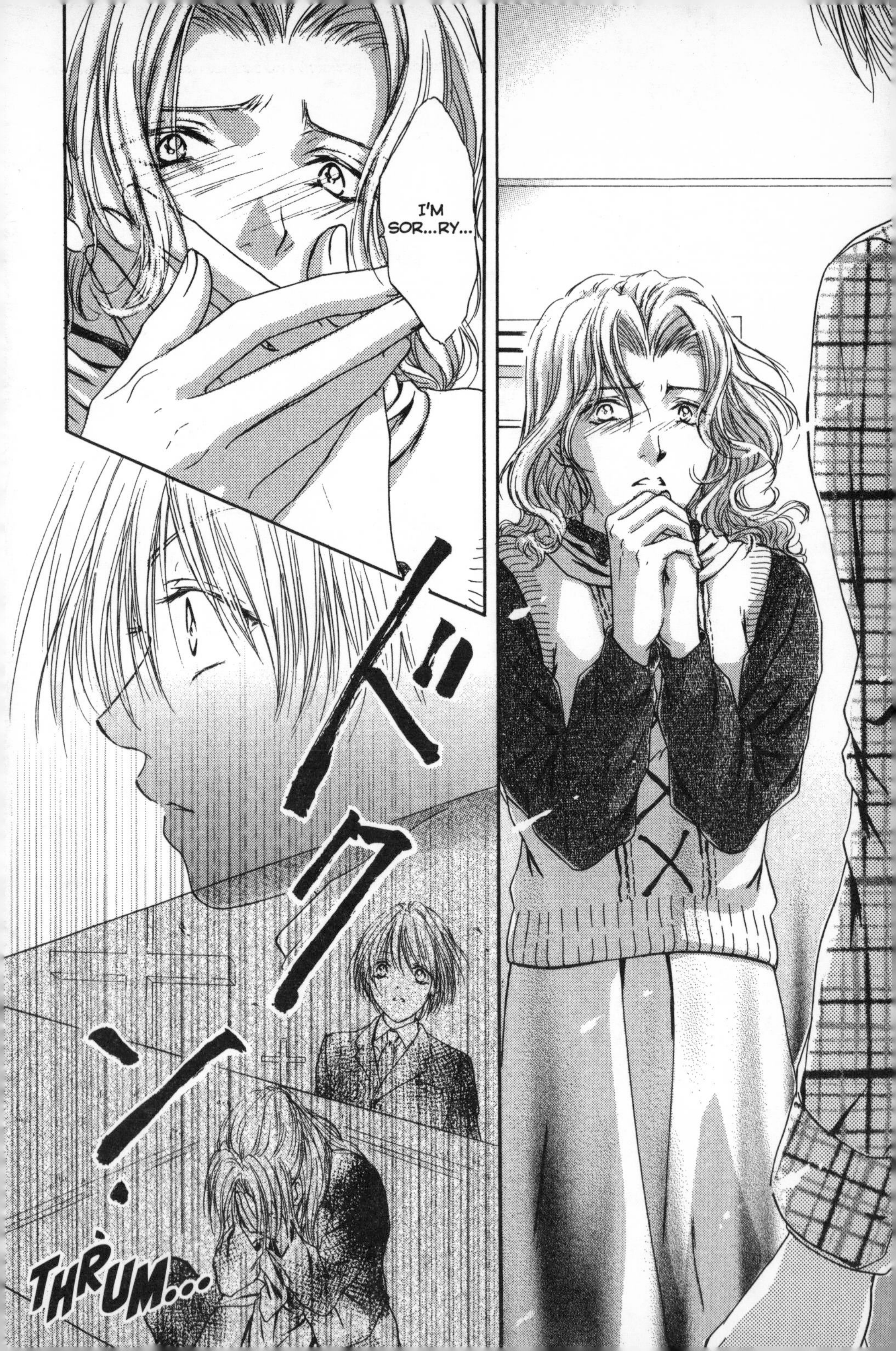

I'M SOR...RY...
ドクン…
THRUM...

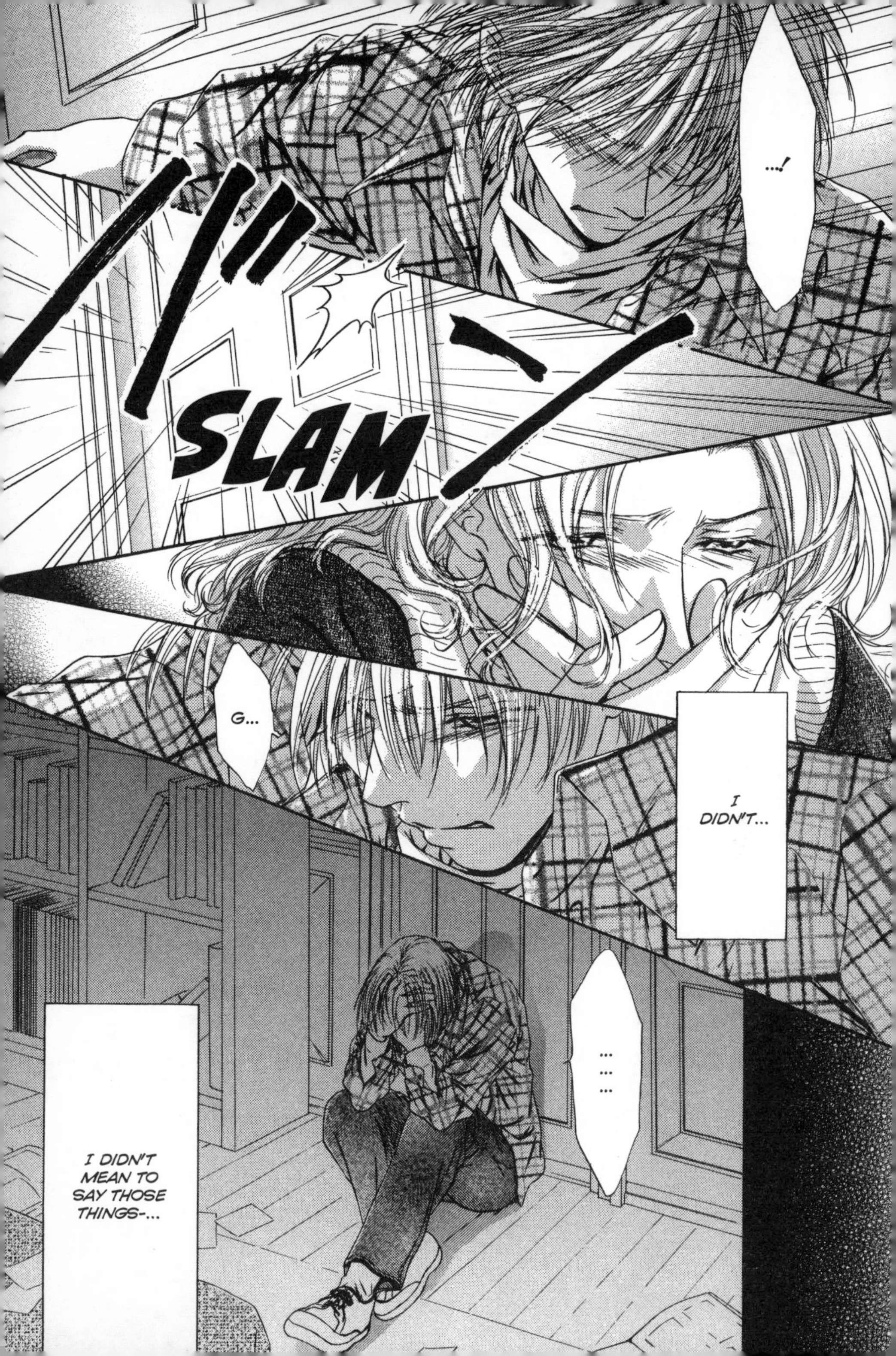
...!
SLAM
G...
I DIDN'T...
...
...
...
I DIDN'T MEAN TO SAY THOSE THINGS-...

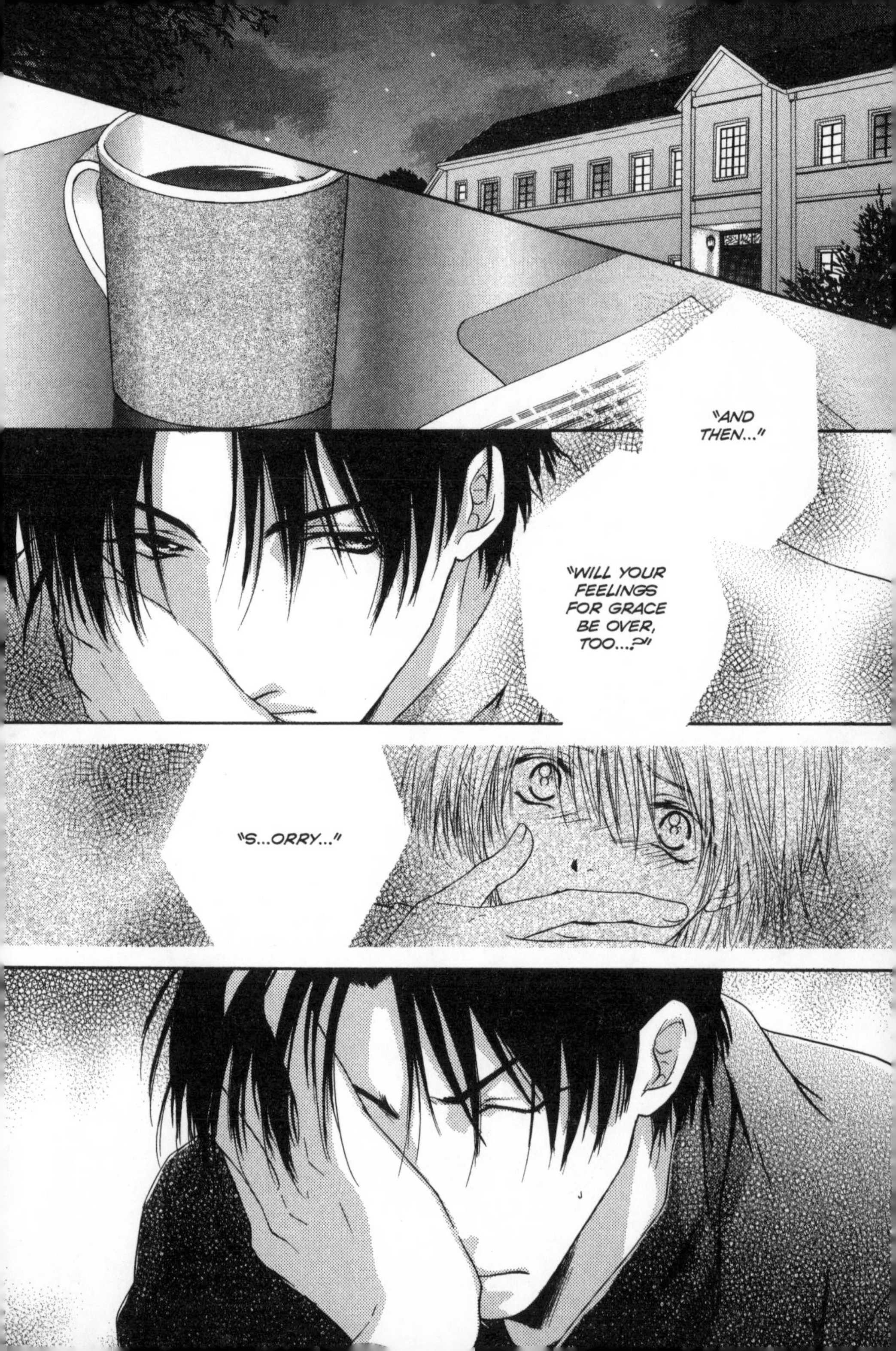
"AND THEN..."
"WILL YOUR FEELINGS FOR GRACE BE OVER, TOO...?"
"S...ORRY..."

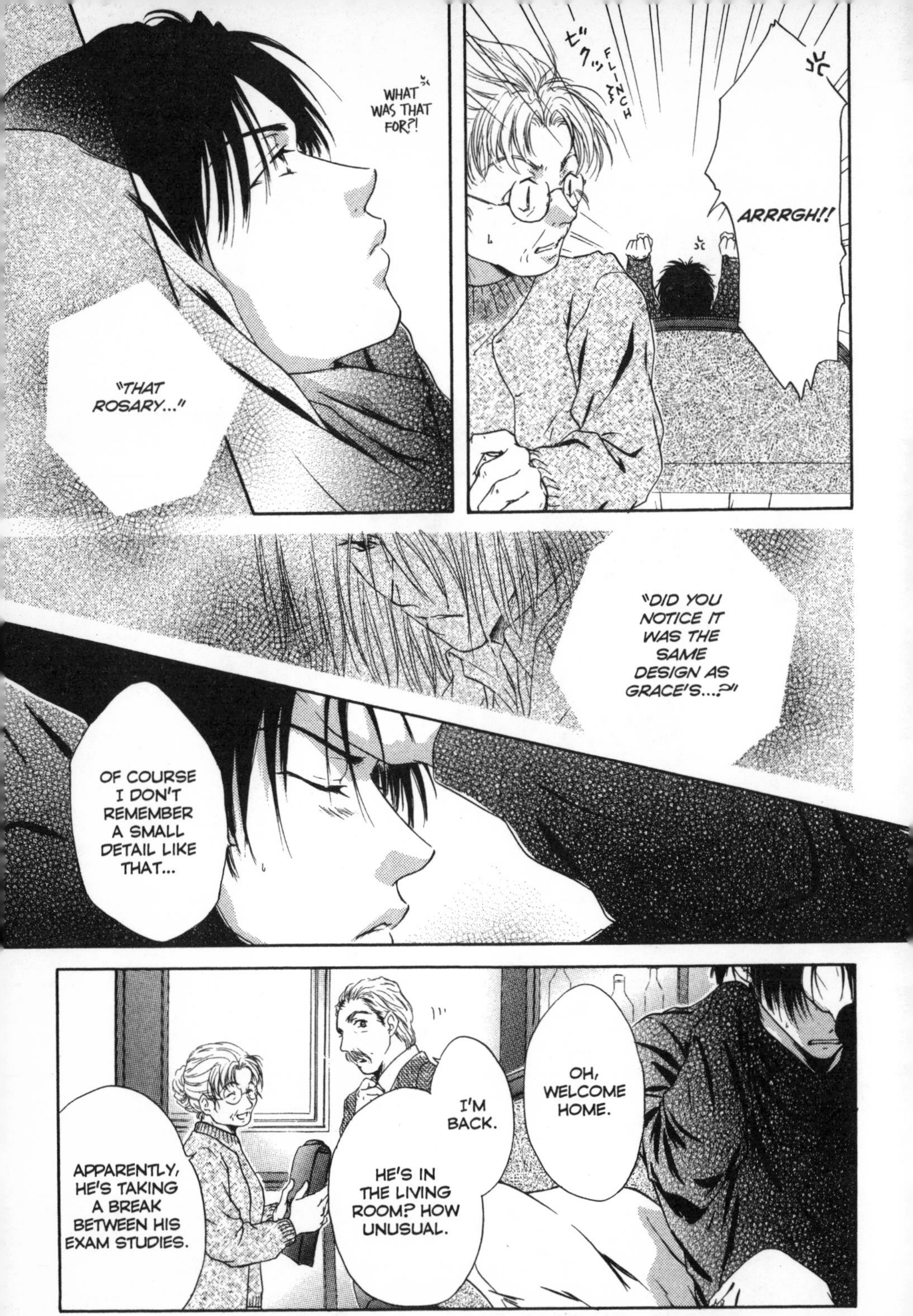
ビクッ
FLINCH
ARRRGH!!
WHAT WAS THAT FOR?!
"THAT ROSARY..."
"DID YOU NOTICE IT WAS THE SAME DESIGN AS GRACE'S...?"
OF COURSE I DON'T REMEMBER A SMALL DETAIL LIKE THAT...
OH, WELCOME HOME.
I'M BACK.
HE'S IN THE LIVING ROOM? HOW UNUSUAL.
APPARENTLY, HE'S TAKING A BREAK BETWEEN HIS EXAM STUDIES.

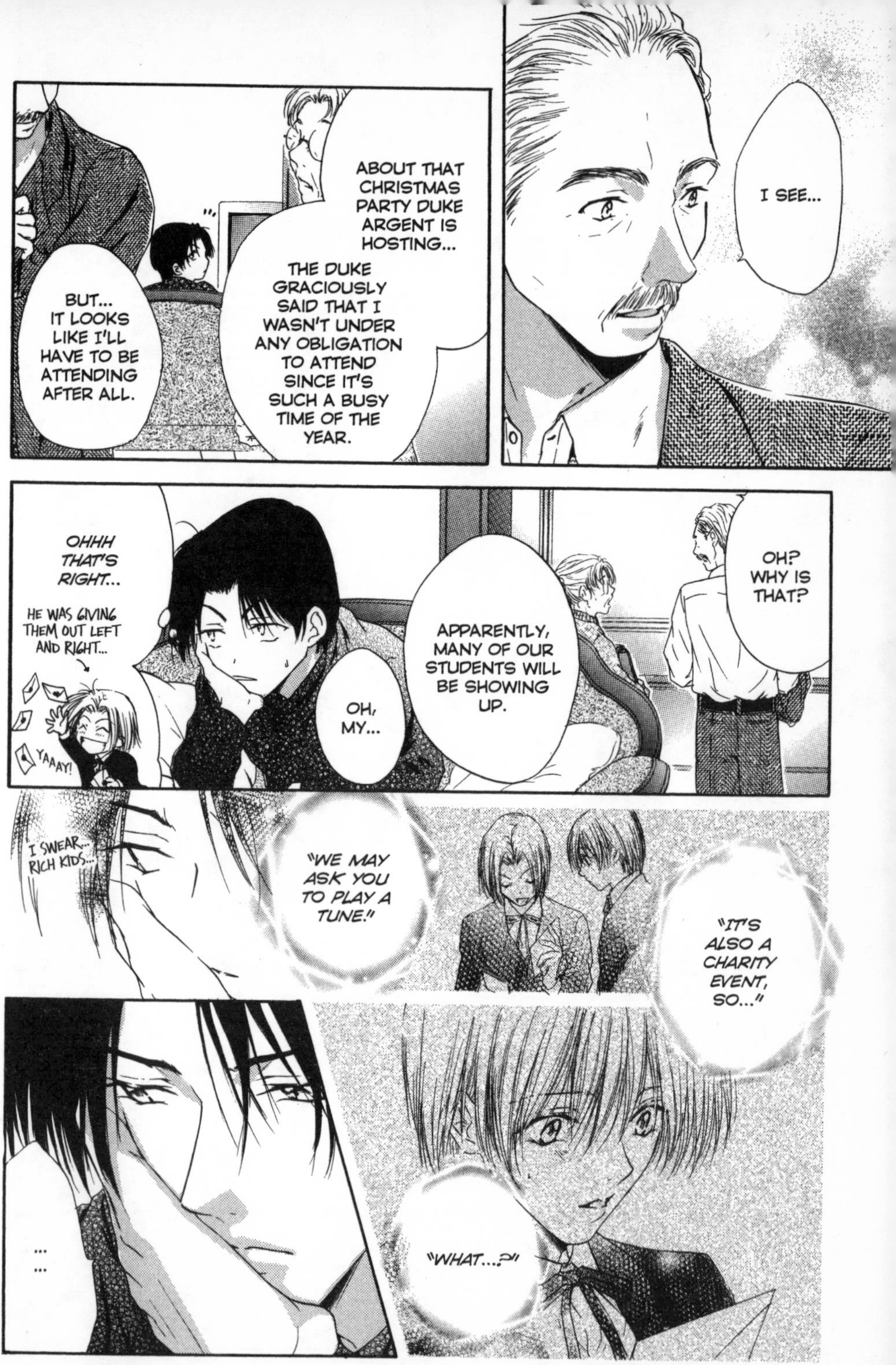
I SEE...
ABOUT THAT CHRISTMAS PARTY DUKE ARGENT IS HOSTING...
THE DUKE GRACIOUSLY SAID THAT I WASN'T UNDER ANY OBLIGATION TO ATTEND SINCE IT'S SUCH A BUSY TIME OF THE YEAR.
BUT... IT LOOKS LIKE I'LL HAVE TO BE ATTENDING AFTER ALL.
OH? WHY IS THAT?
APPARENTLY, MANY OF OUR STUDENTS WILL BE SHOWING UP.
OH, MY...
OHHH THAT'S RIGHT...
HE WAS GIVING THEM OUT LEFT AND RIGHT...
YAAAY!
"IT'S ALSO A CHARITY EVENT, SO..."
"WE MAY ASK YOU TO PLAY A TUNE."
I SWEAR... RICH KIDS...
"WHAT...?"
...
...

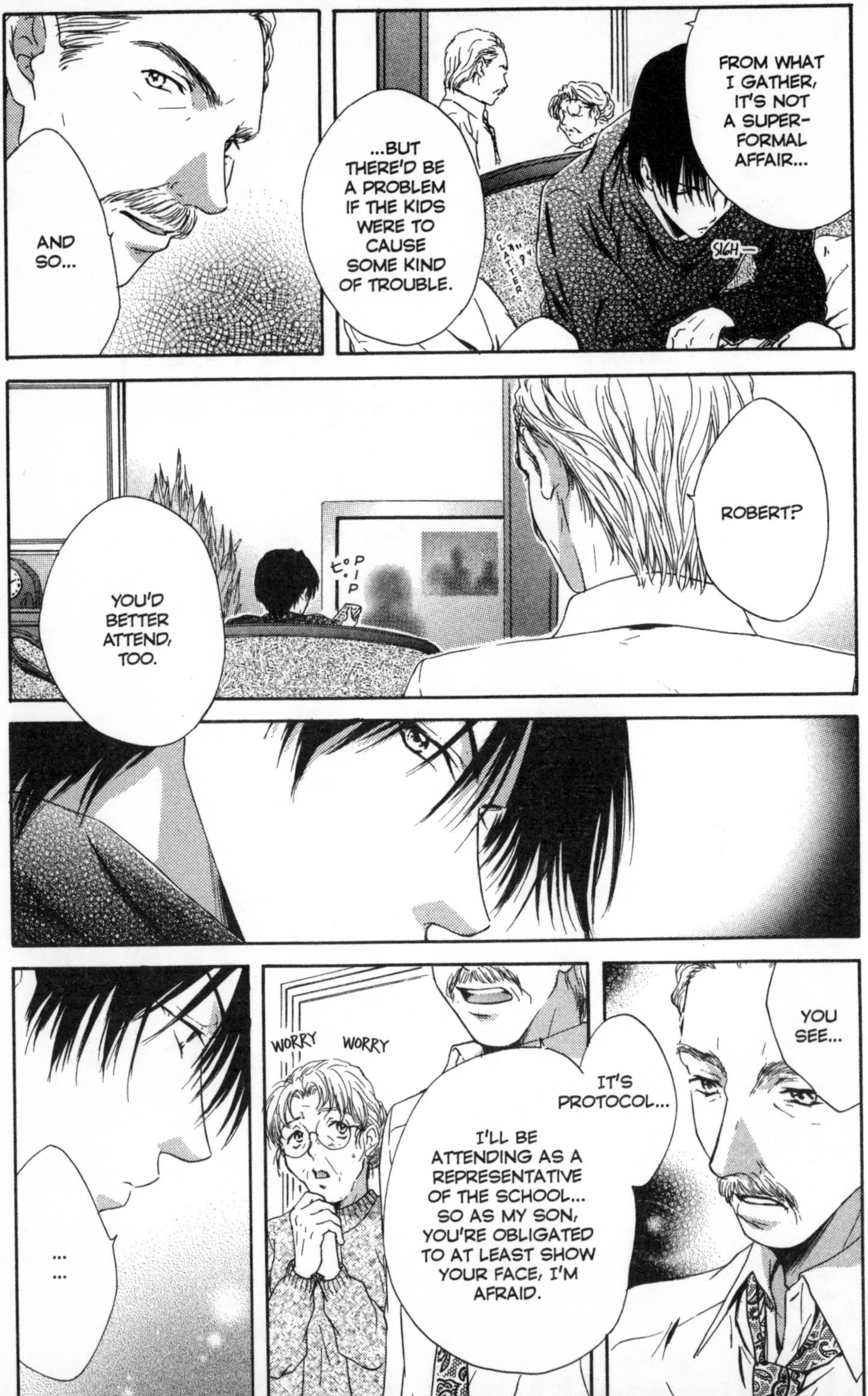
FROM WHAT I GATHER, IT'S NOT A SUPER-FORMAL AFFAIR...
...BUT THERE'D BE A PROBLEM IF THE KIDS WERE TO CAUSE SOME KIND OF TROUBLE.
SIGH—
CLATTER
AND SO...
ROBERT?
PIP
PIP
YOU'D BETTER ATTEND, TOO.
YOU SEE...
IT'S PROTOCOL...
I'LL BE ATTENDING AS A REPRESENTATIVE OF THE SCHOOL... SO AS MY SON, YOU'RE OBLIGATED TO AT LEAST SHOW YOUR FACE, I'M AFRAID.
WORRY
WORRY
...
...

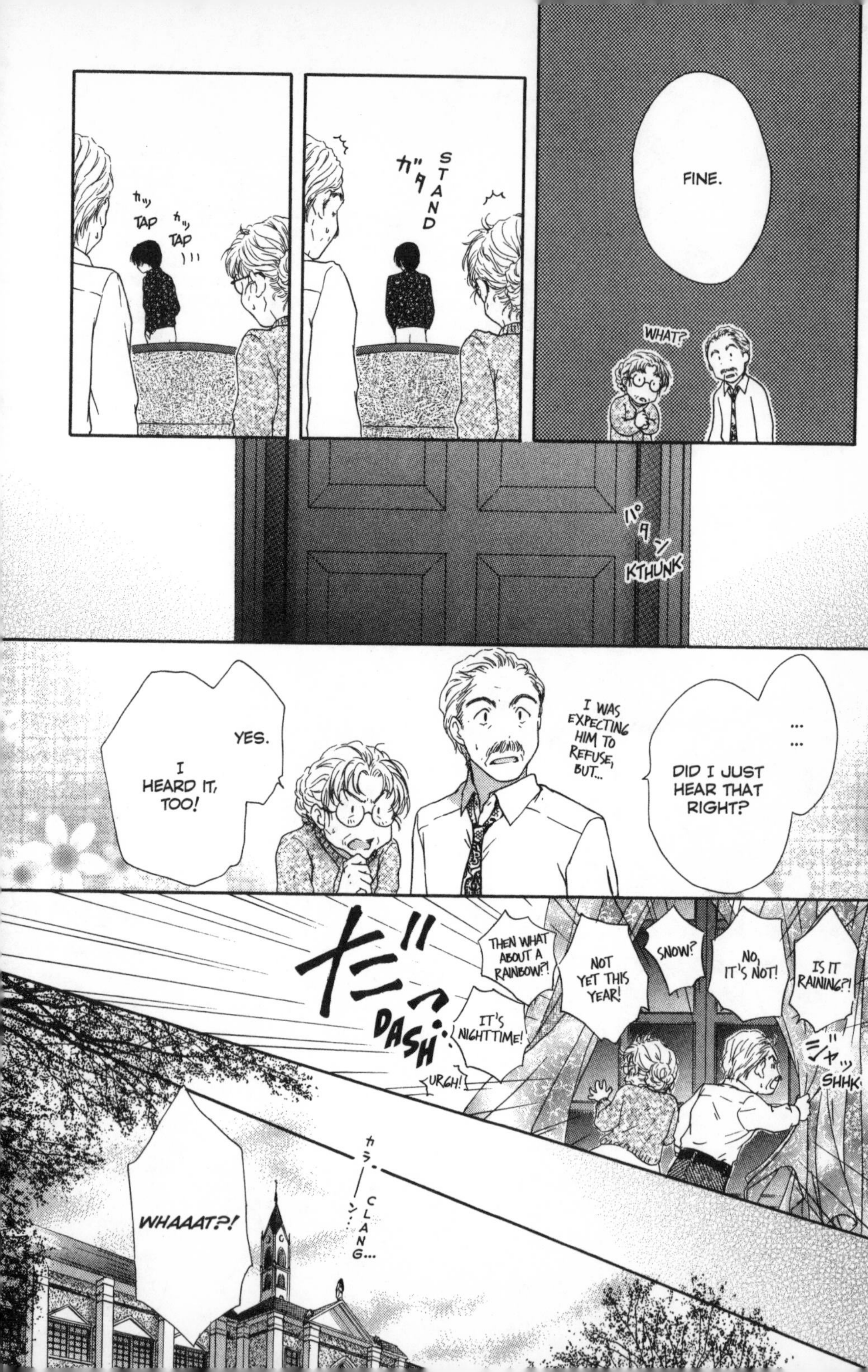
FINE.
WHAT?
ガタ
STAND
カッ
TAP
カッ
TAP
パタン
KTHUNK
……
DID I JUST HEAR THAT RIGHT?
I WAS EXPECTING HIM TO REFUSE, BUT...
YES.
I HEARD IT, TOO!
IS IT RAINING?!
シャッ
SHHK
NO, IT'S NOT!
SNOW?
NOT YET THIS YEAR!
THEN WHAT ABOUT A RAINBOW?!
IT'S NIGHTTIME!
だっ
DASH
URGH!
カラーン…
CLANG...
WHAAAT?!

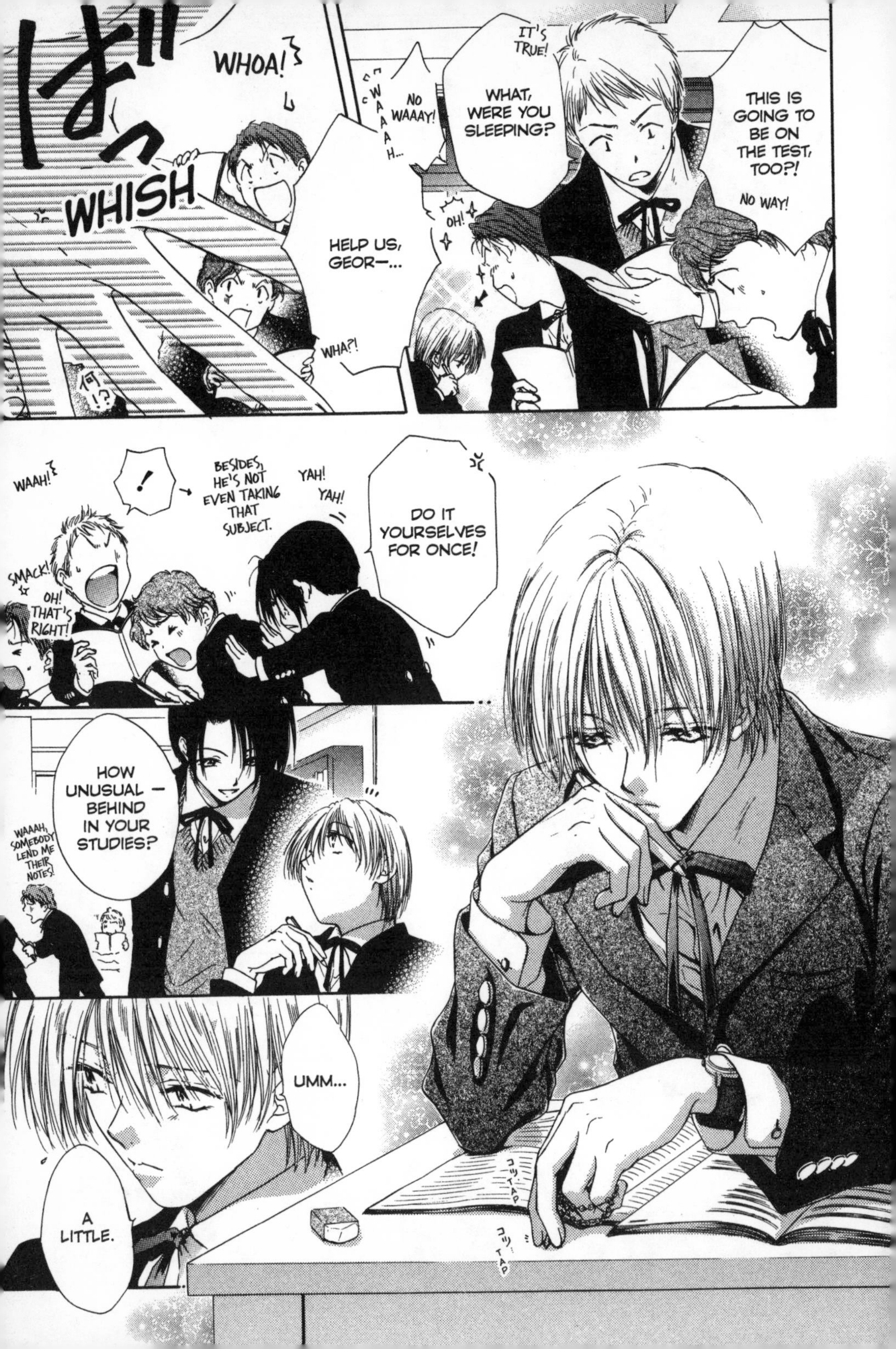
THIS IS GOING TO BE ON THE TEST, TOO?!
NO WAY!
IT'S TRUE!
WHAT, WERE YOU SLEEPING?
NO WAAAY!
WAAAH...
OH!
HELP US, GEOR—...
WHA?!
WHOA!
ばっ
WHISH
何!?
コッ TAP
コッ TAP
DO IT YOURSELVES FOR ONCE!
YAH! YAH!
BESIDES, HE'S NOT EVEN TAKING THAT SUBJECT.
!
WAAH!
SMACK!
OH! THAT'S RIGHT!
HOW UNUSUAL — BEHIND IN YOUR STUDIES?
WAAAH, SOMEBODY LEND ME THEIR NOTES!
UMM...
A LITTLE.

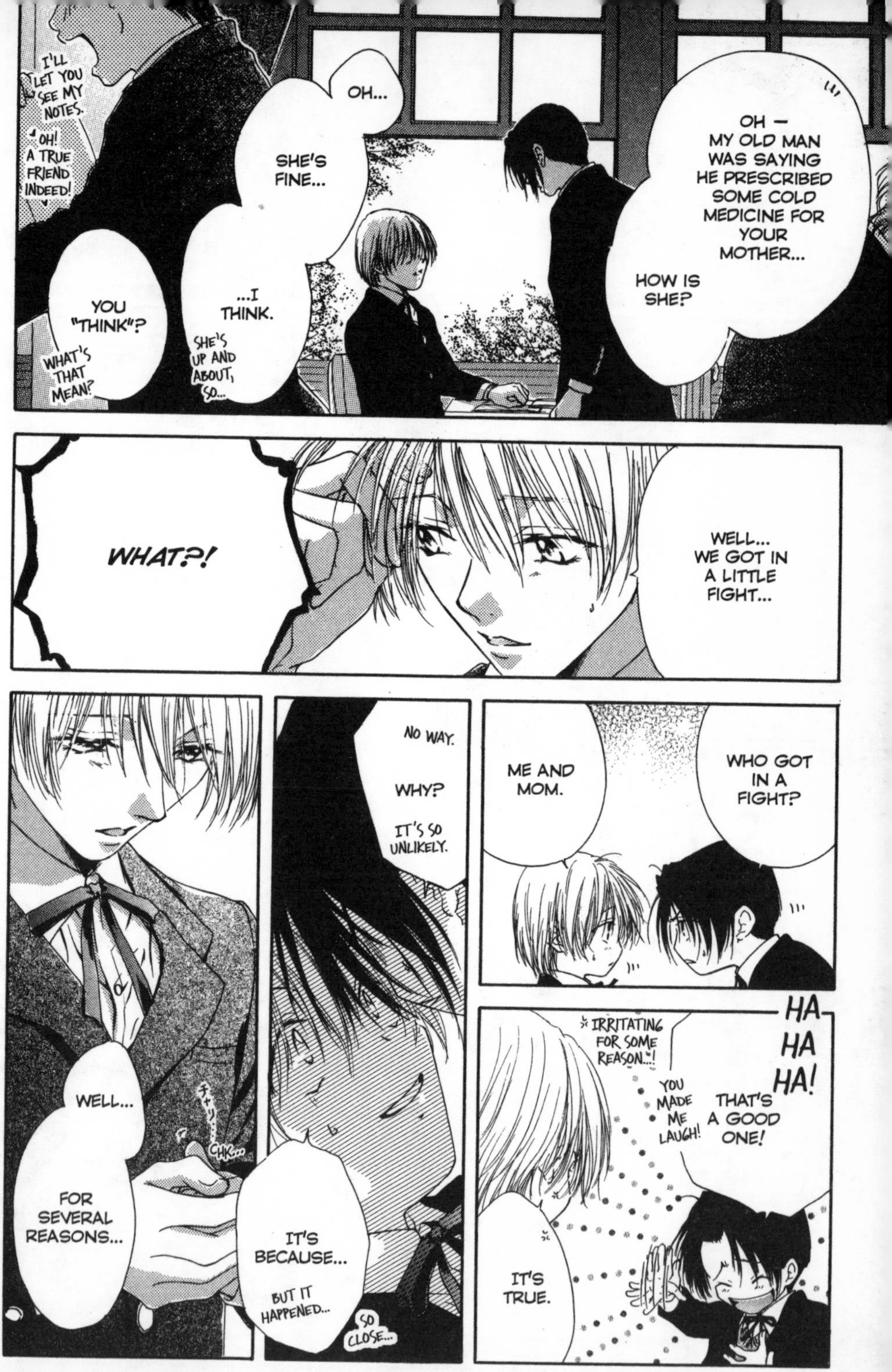
OH — MY OLD MAN WAS SAYING HE PRESCRIBED SOME COLD MEDICINE FOR YOUR MOTHER...
HOW IS SHE?
OH...
SHE'S FINE...
...I THINK.
SHE'S UP AND ABOUT, SO...
YOU "THINK"?
WHAT'S THAT MEAN?
I'LL LET YOU SEE MY NOTES.
OH! A TRUE FRIEND INDEED!
WELL... WE GOT IN A LITTLE FIGHT...
WHAT?!
WHO GOT IN A FIGHT?
ME AND MOM.
HA-HA HA HA!
THAT'S A GOOD ONE!
YOU MADE ME LAUGH!
IRRITATING FOR SOME REASON...!
IT'S TRUE.
NO WAY.
WHY?
IT'S SO UNLIKELY.
IT'S BECAUSE...
BUT IT HAPPENED...
SO CLOSE...
WELL...
チャリ...
CHK...
FOR SEVERAL REASONS...

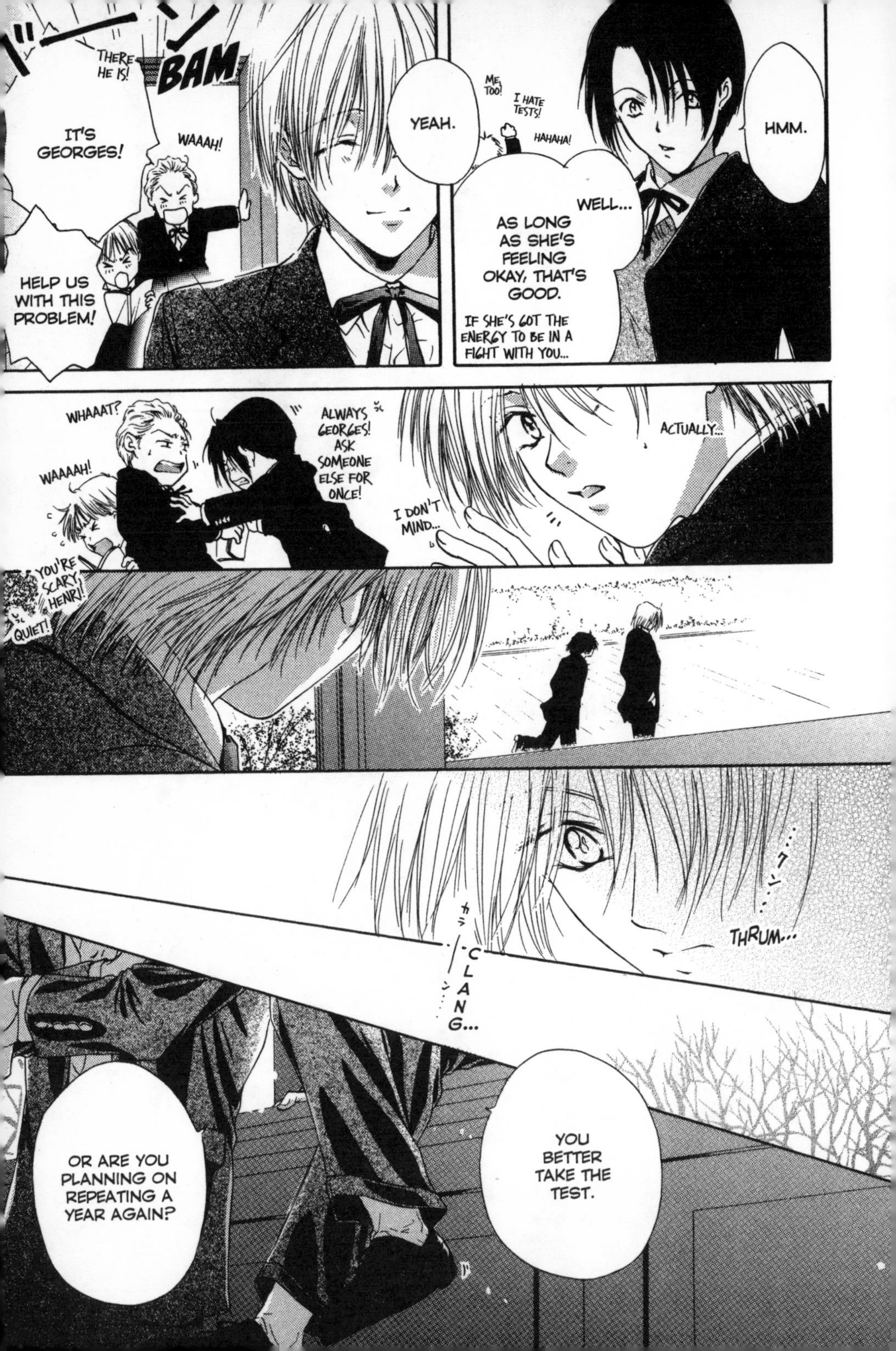
HMM.
ME, TOO!
I HATE TESTS!
HAHAHA!
WELL...
AS LONG AS SHE'S FEELING OKAY, THAT'S GOOD.
IF SHE'S GOT THE ENERGY TO BE IN A FIGHT WITH YOU...
YEAH.
THERE HE IS!
BAM
IT'S GEORGES!
WAAAH!
HELP US WITH THIS PROBLEM!
ACTUALLY...
I DON'T MIND...
ALWAYS GEORGES! ASK SOMEONE ELSE FOR ONCE!
WHAAAT?
WAAAAH!
YOU'RE SCARY, HENRI!
QUIET!
THRUM...
CLANG...
YOU BETTER TAKE THE TEST.
OR ARE YOU PLANNING ON REPEATING A YEAR AGAIN?

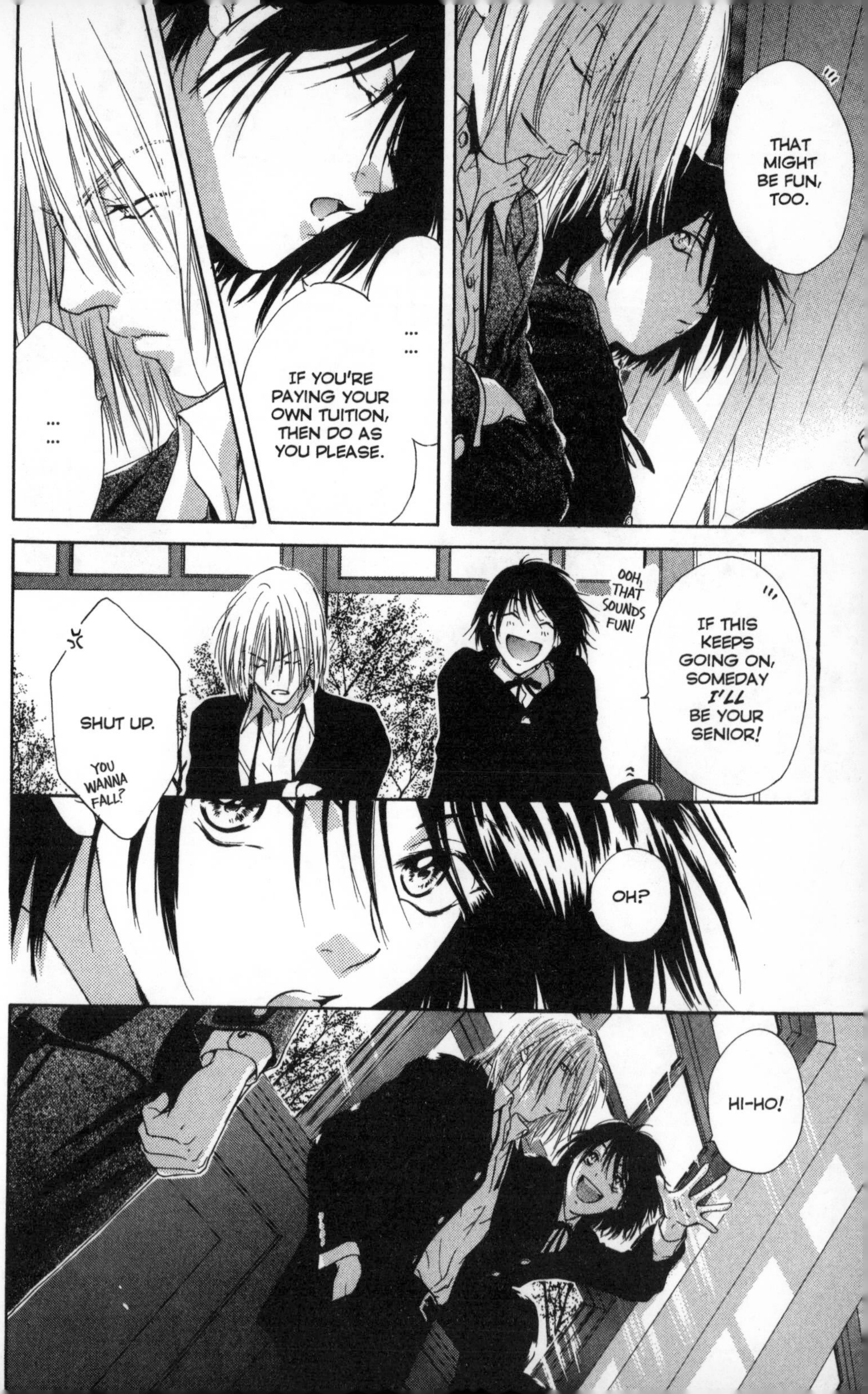
THAT MIGHT BE FUN, TOO.
...
...
IF YOU'RE PAYING YOUR OWN TUITION, THEN DO AS YOU PLEASE.
...
...
IF THIS KEEPS GOING ON, SOMEDAY I'LL BE YOUR SENIOR!
OOH, THAT SOUNDS FUN!
SHUT UP.
YOU WANNA FALL?
OH?
HI-HO!

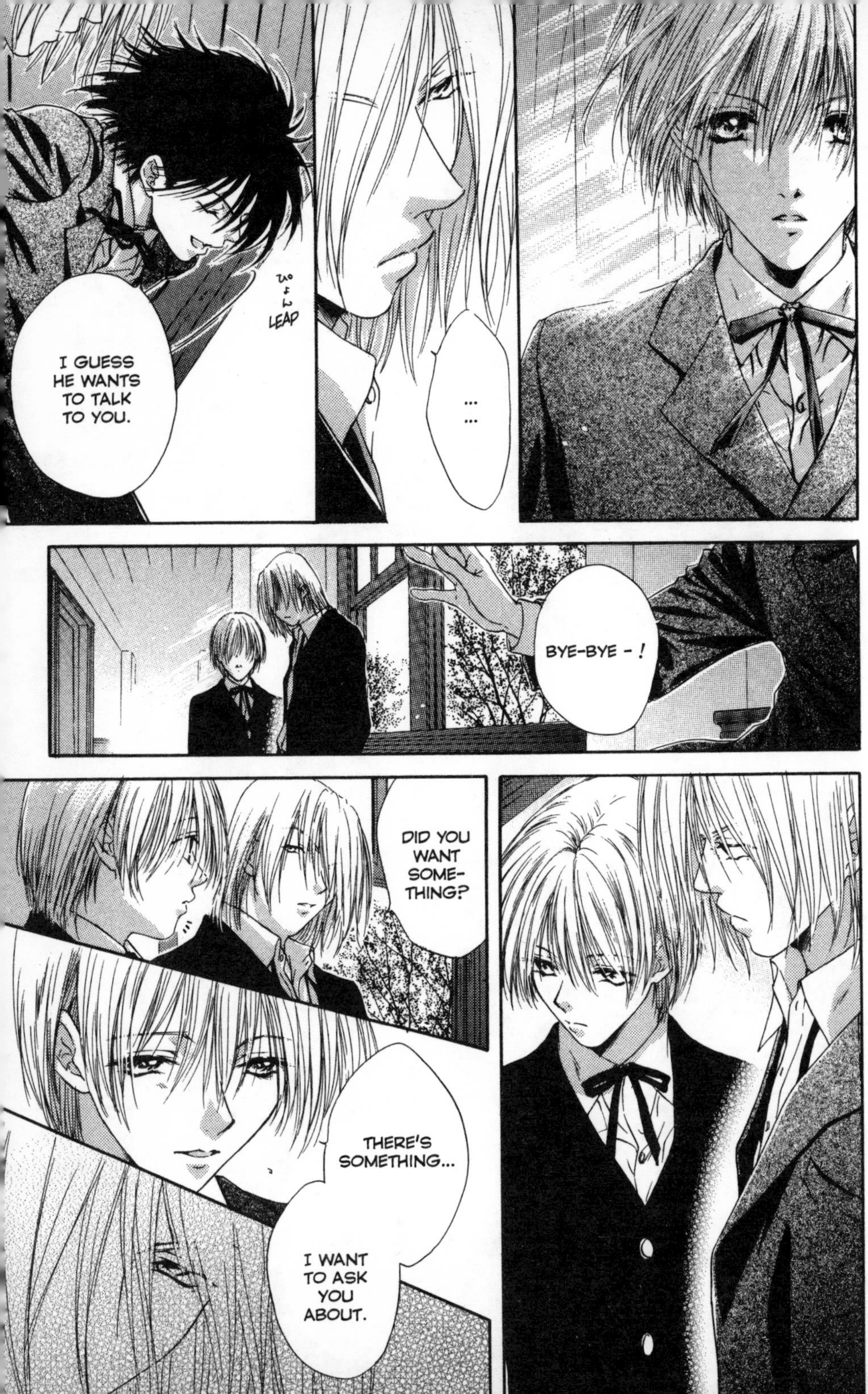

...
...
ぴょん
LEAP
I GUESS HE WANTS TO TALK TO YOU.
BYE-BYE -!
DID YOU WANT SOMETHING?
THERE'S SOMETHING...
I WANT TO ASK YOU ABOUT.

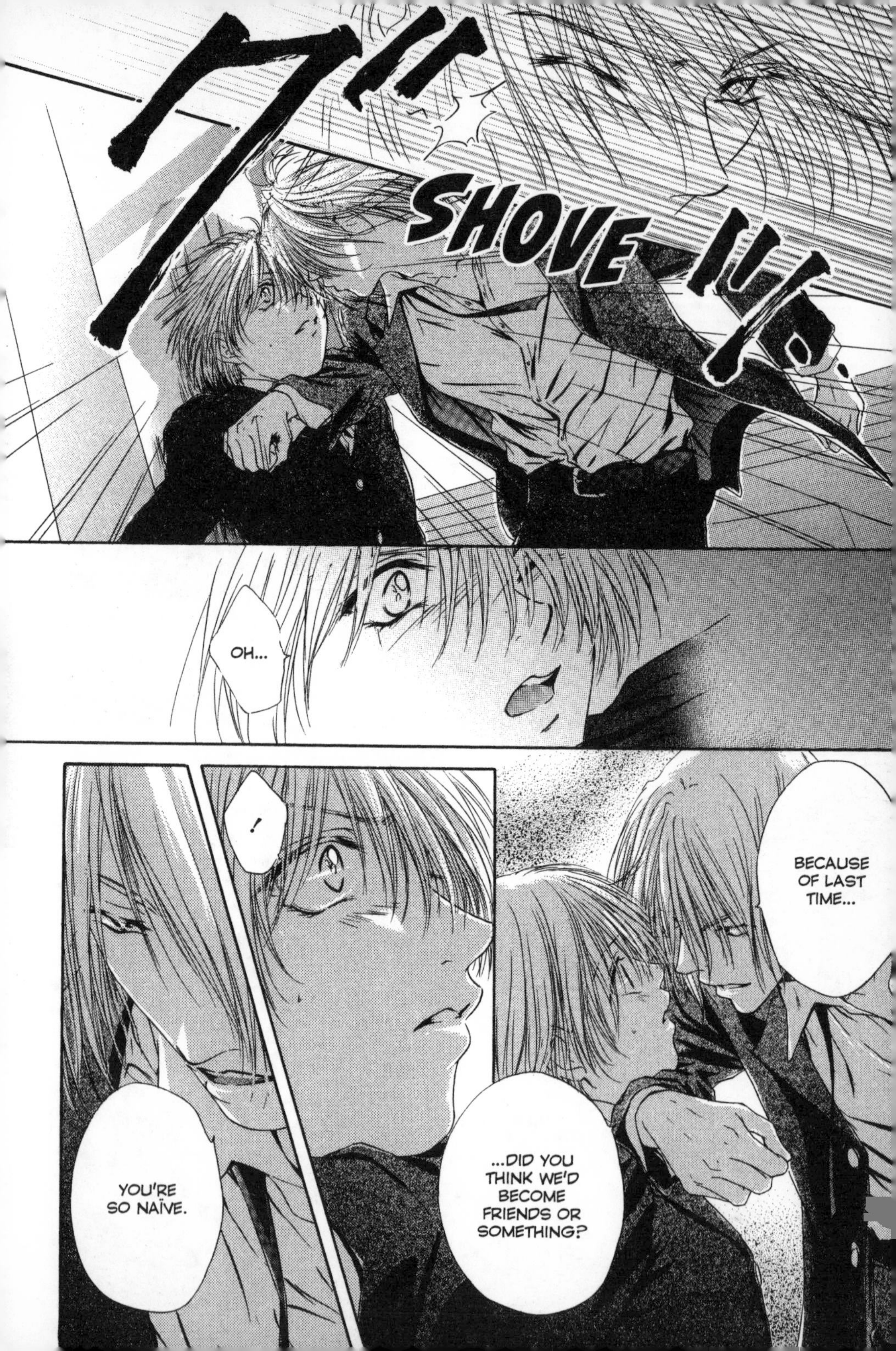
SHOVE UP.
OH...
BECAUSE OF LAST TIME...
...DID YOU THINK WE'D BECOME FRIENDS OR SOMETHING?
!
YOU'RE SO NAÏVE.

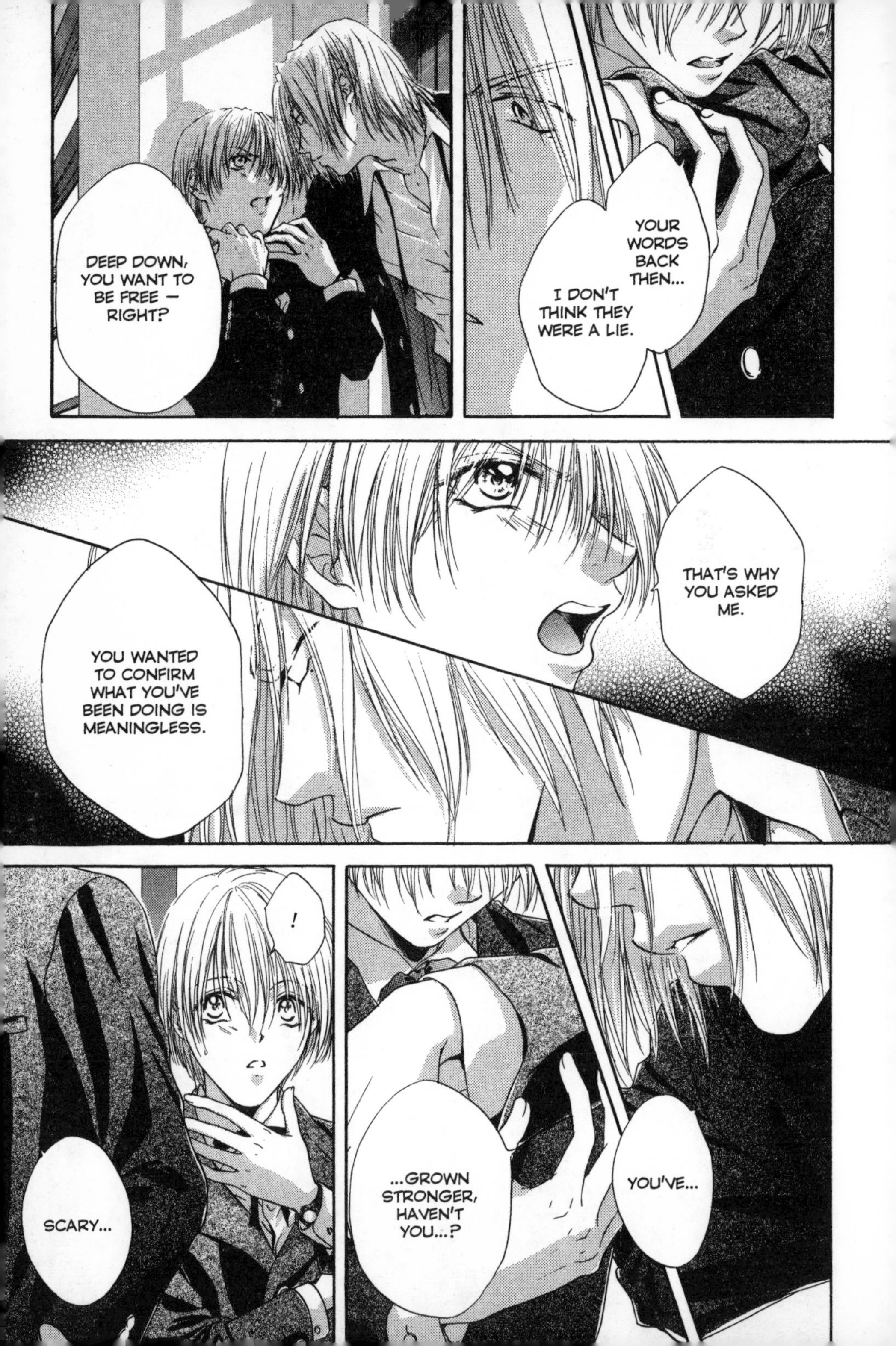
YOUR WORDS BACK THEN...
I DON'T THINK THEY WERE A LIE.
DEEP DOWN, YOU WANT TO BE FREE — RIGHT?
THAT'S WHY YOU ASKED ME.
YOU WANTED TO CONFIRM WHAT YOU'VE BEEN DOING IS MEANINGLESS.
YOU'VE...
...GROWN STRONGER, HAVEN'T YOU...?
!
SCARY...

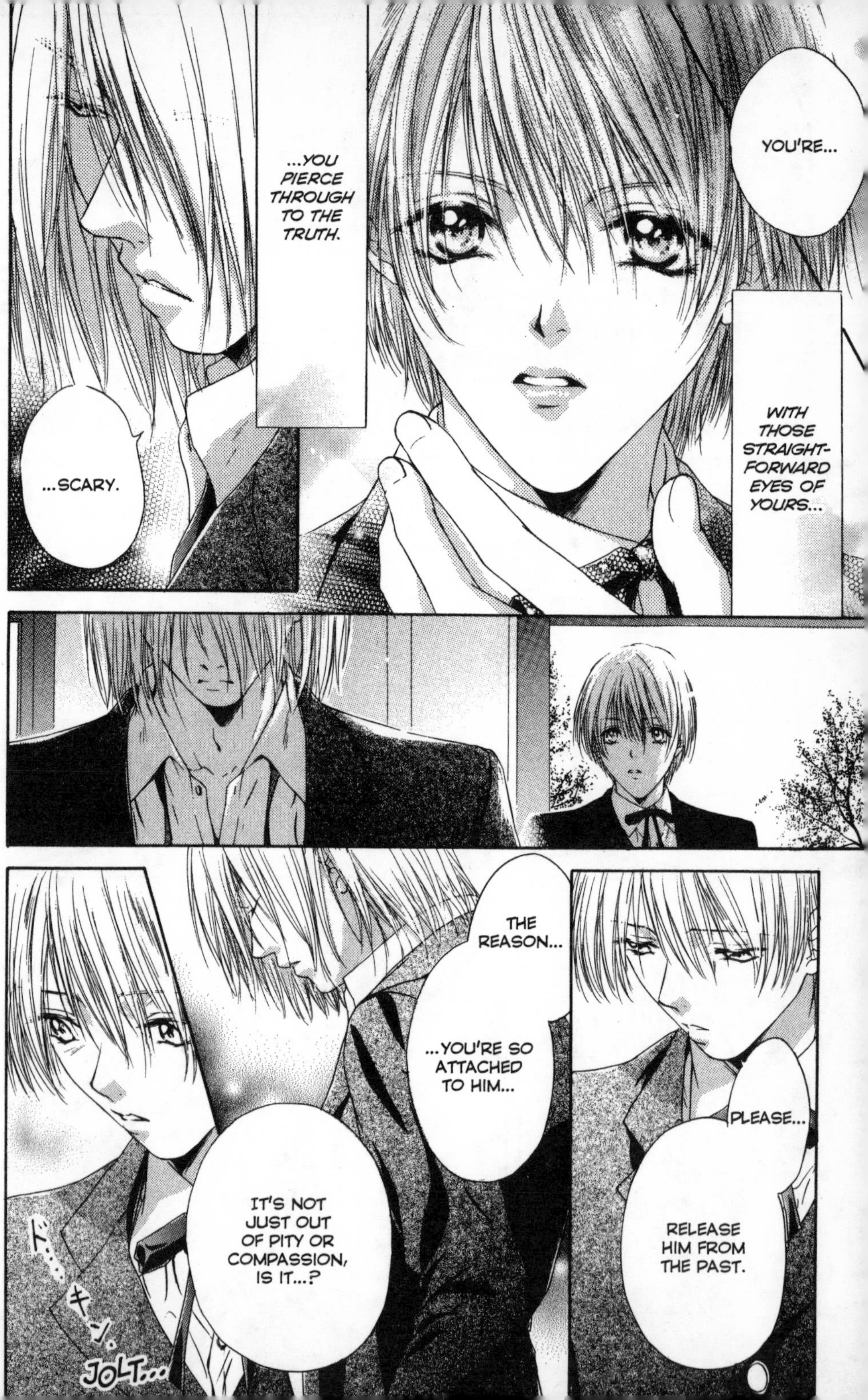
YOU'RE...
WITH THOSE STRAIGHT-FORWARD EYES OF YOURS...
...YOU PIERCE THROUGH TO THE TRUTH.
...SCARY.
PLEASE...
RELEASE HIM FROM THE PAST.
THE REASON...
...YOU'RE SO ATTACHED TO HIM...
IT'S NOT JUST OUT OF PITY OR COMPASSION, IS IT...?
ド…キン
JOLT...

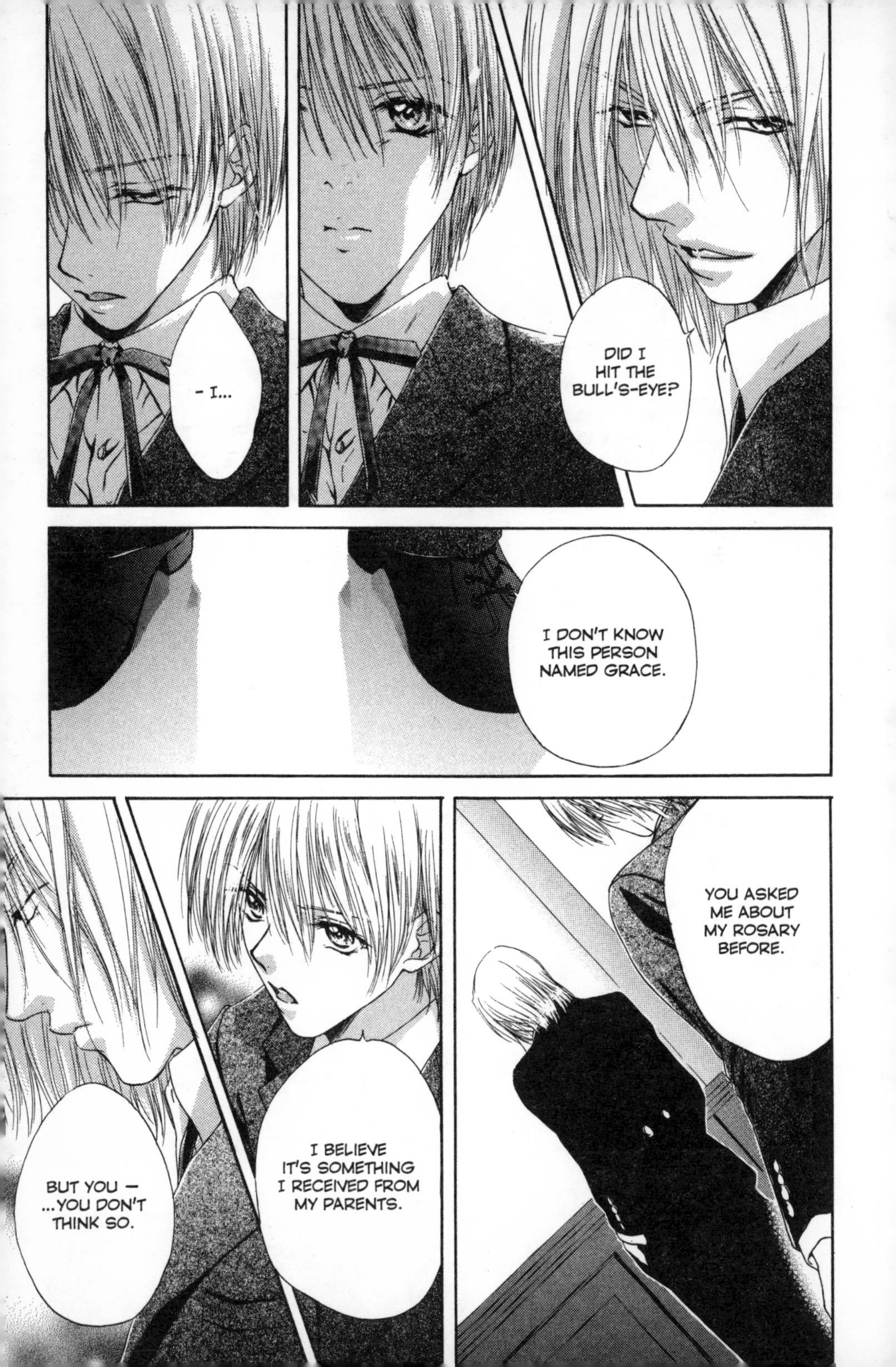
DID I HIT THE BULL'S-EYE?
- I...
I DON'T KNOW THIS PERSON NAMED GRACE.
YOU ASKED ME ABOUT MY ROSARY BEFORE.
I BELIEVE IT'S SOMETHING I RECEIVED FROM MY PARENTS.
BUT YOU — ...YOU DON'T THINK SO.

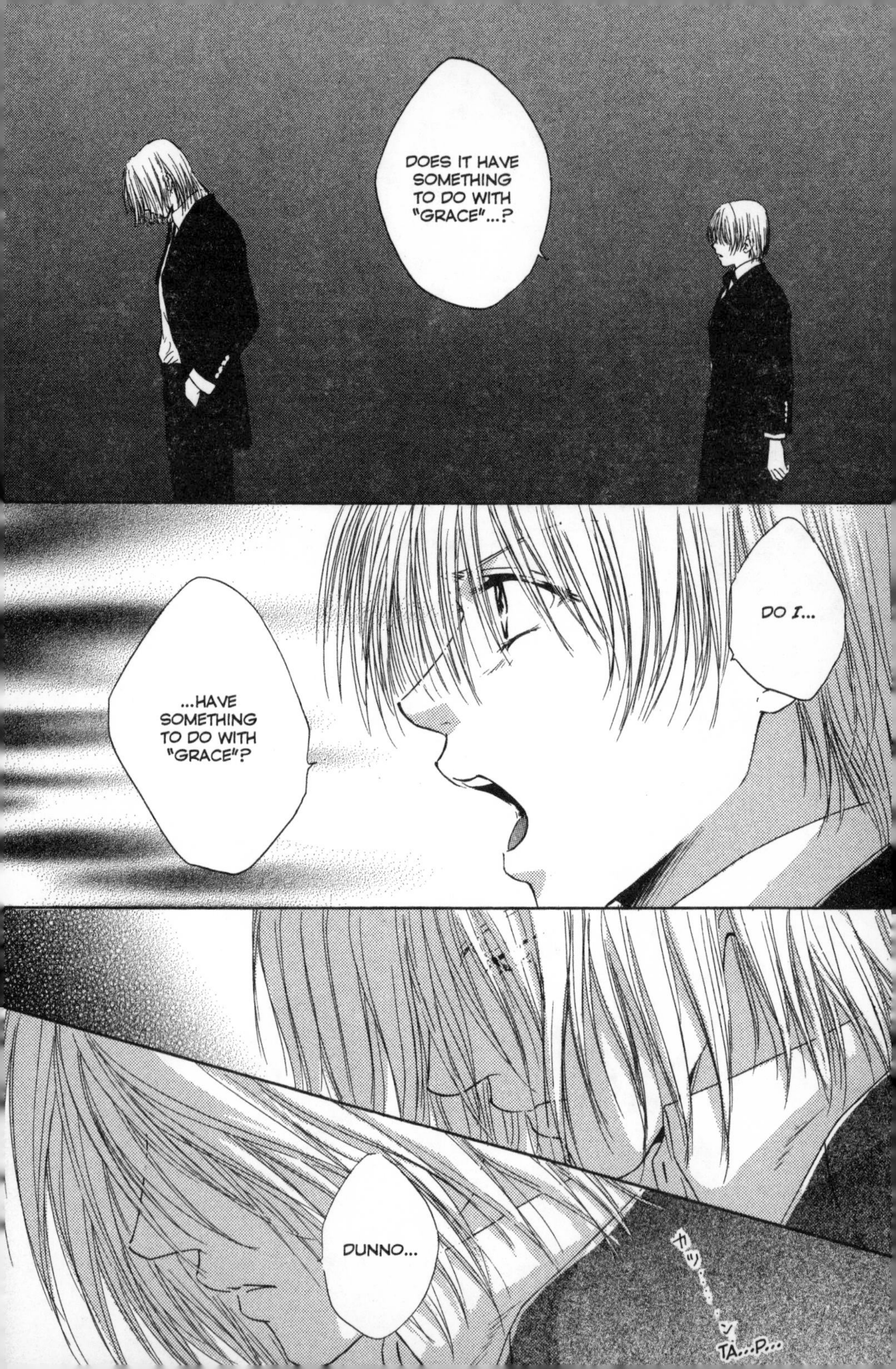
DOES IT HAVE SOMETHING TO DO WITH "GRACE"...?
DO I...
...HAVE SOMETHING TO DO WITH "GRACE"?
DUNNO...
TA...P...

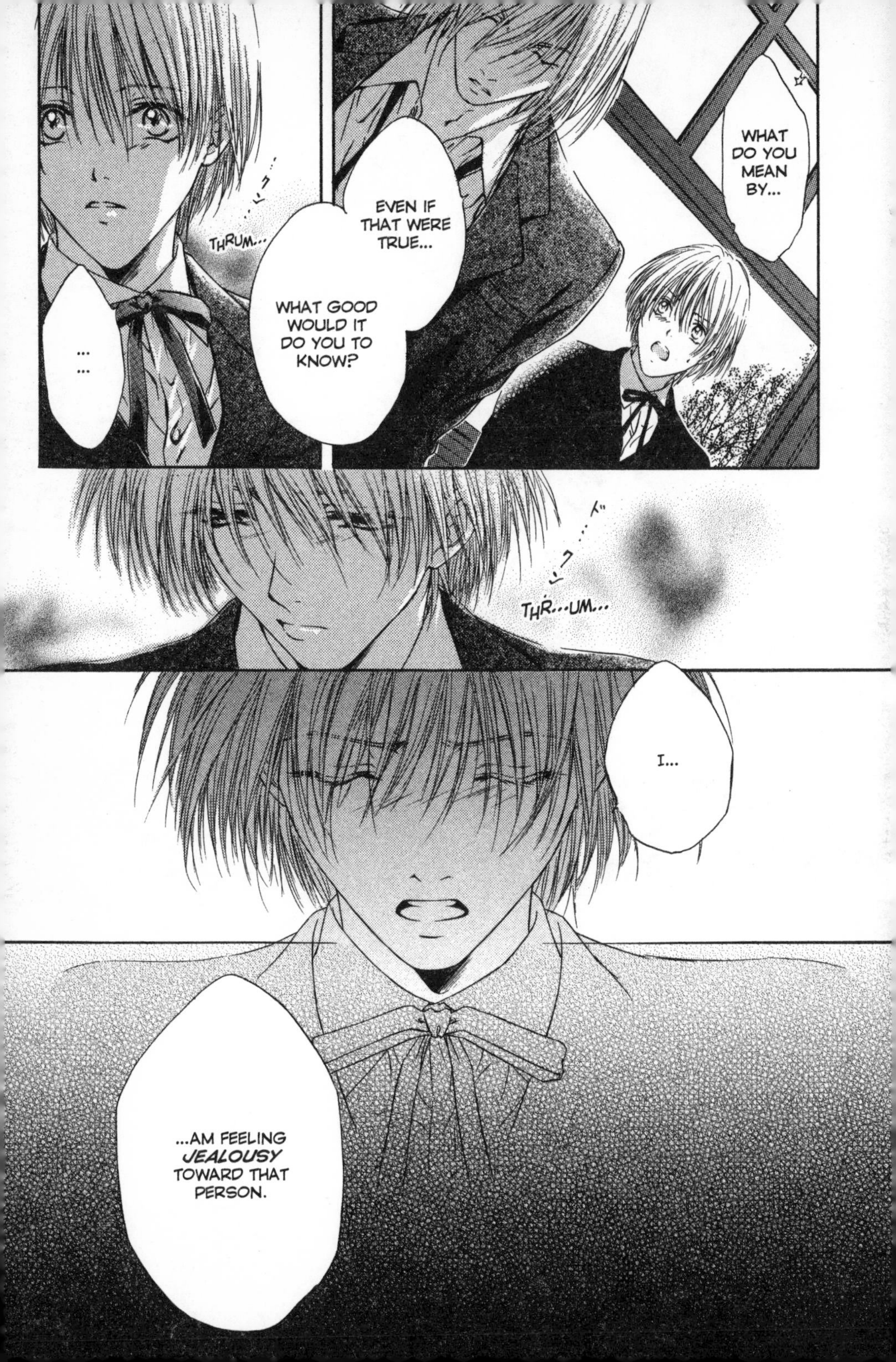

WHAT DO YOU MEAN BY...
EVEN IF THAT WERE TRUE...
WHAT GOOD WOULD IT DO YOU TO KNOW?
THRUM...
... ...
THR...UM...
I...
...AM FEELING *JEALOUSY* TOWARD THAT PERSON.

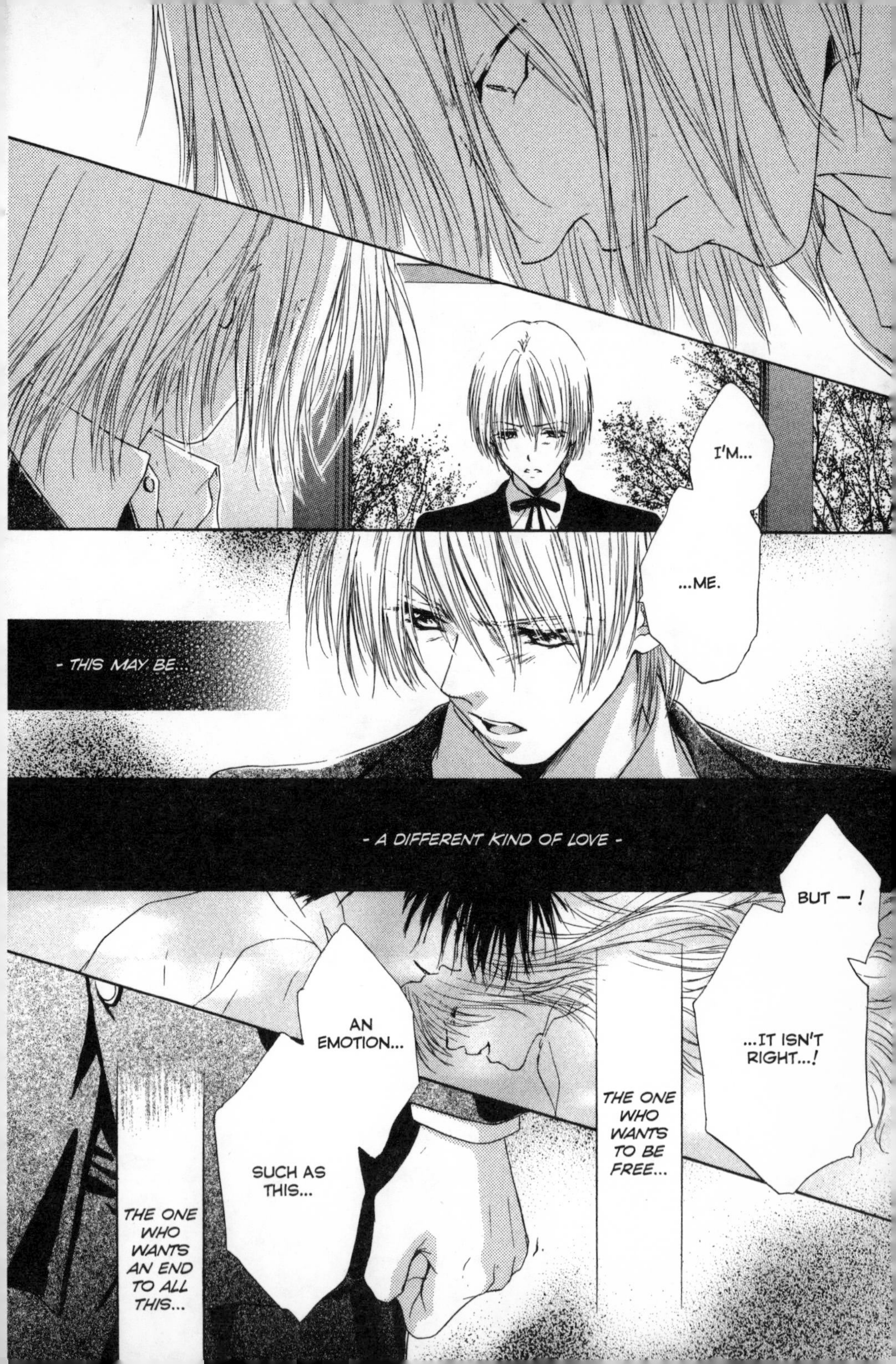
I'M...
...ME.
- THIS MAY BE...
- A DIFFERENT KIND OF LOVE -
BUT — !
...IT ISN'T RIGHT...!
THE ONE WHO WANTS TO BE FREE...
AN EMOTION...
SUCH AS THIS...
THE ONE WHO WANTS AN END TO ALL THIS...

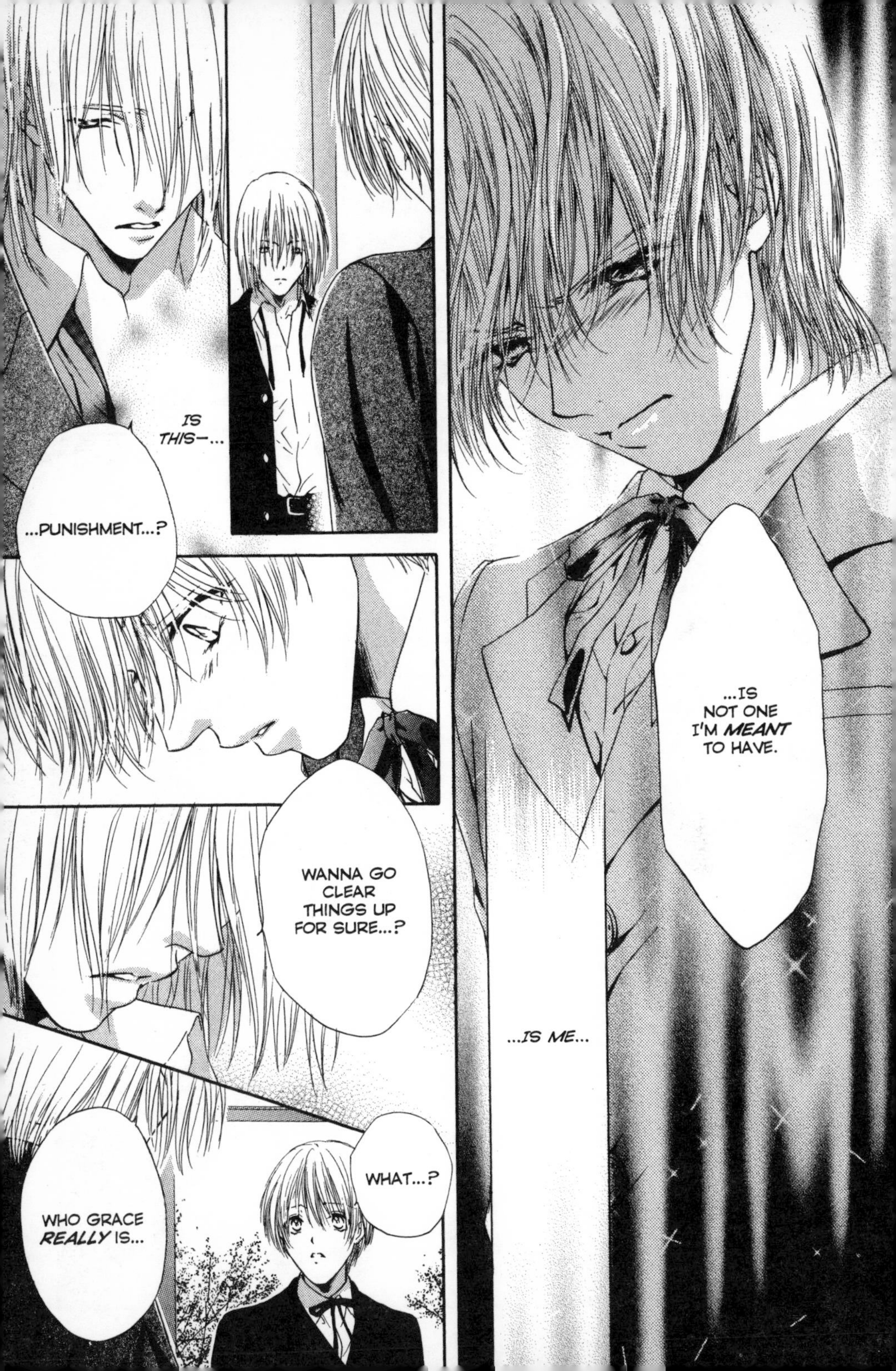
...IS NOT ONE I'M *MEANT* TO HAVE.
...IS ME...
IS THIS—...
...PUNISHMENT...?
WANNA GO CLEAR THINGS UP FOR SURE...?
WHAT...?
WHO GRACE *REALLY* IS...

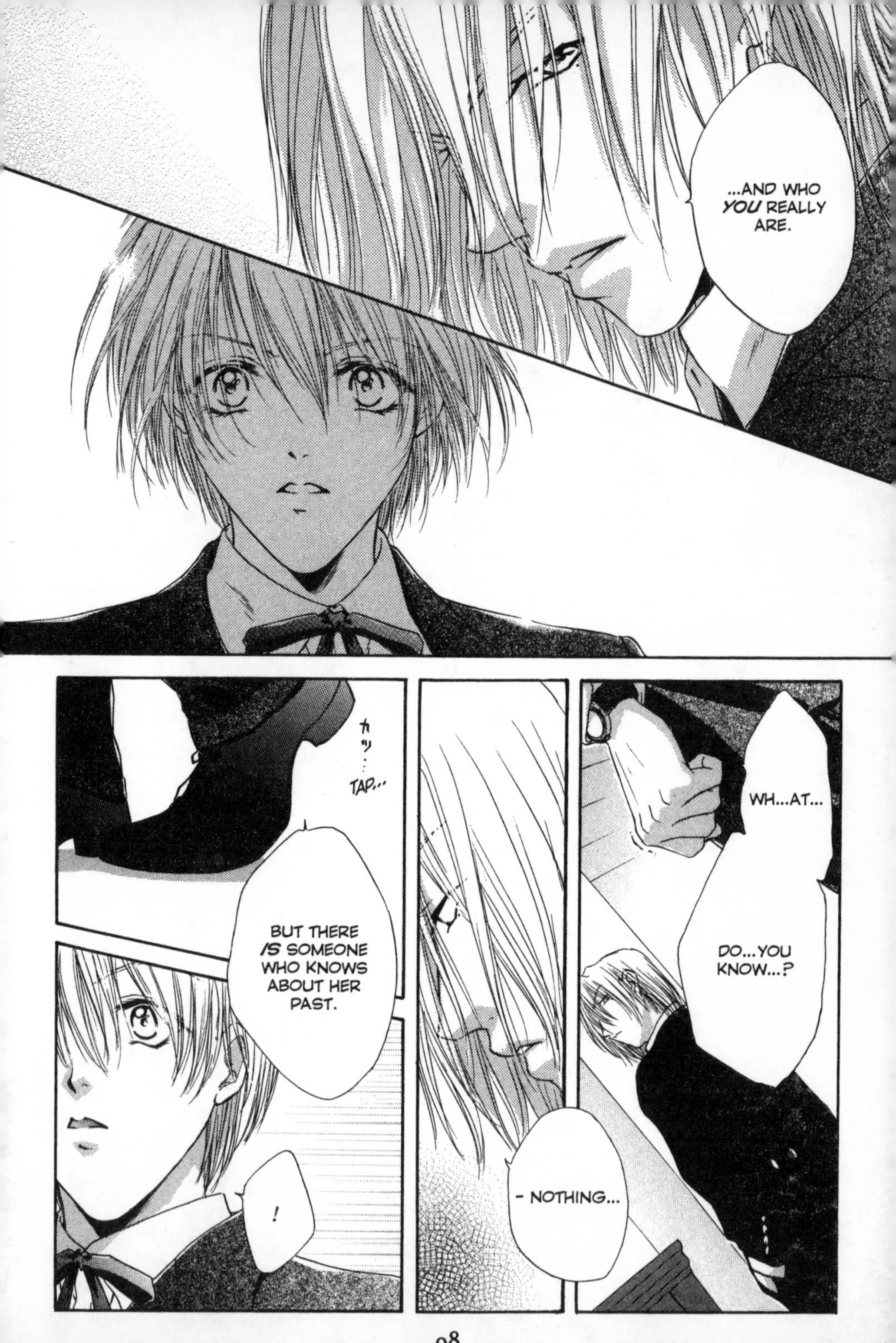
...AND WHO *YOU* REALLY ARE.
WH...AT...
DO...YOU KNOW...?
- NOTHING...
カッ…
TAP...
BUT THERE *IS* SOMEONE WHO KNOWS ABOUT HER PAST.
!

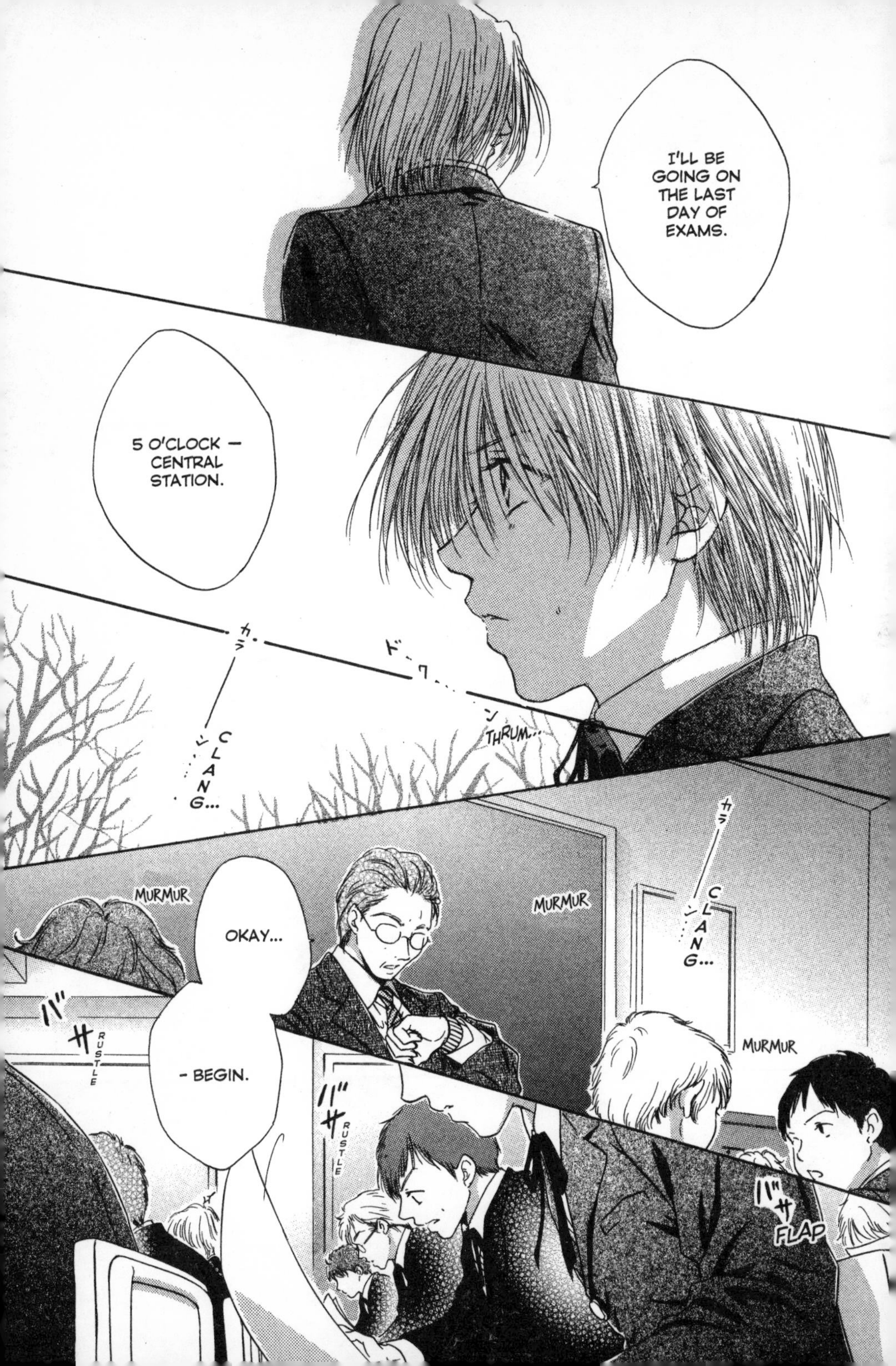
I'LL BE GOING ON THE LAST DAY OF EXAMS.
5 O'CLOCK — CENTRAL STATION.
THRUM...
CLANG...
CLANG...
MURMUR
MURMUR
OKAY...
- BEGIN.
MURMUR
FLAP
RUSTLE
RUSTLE

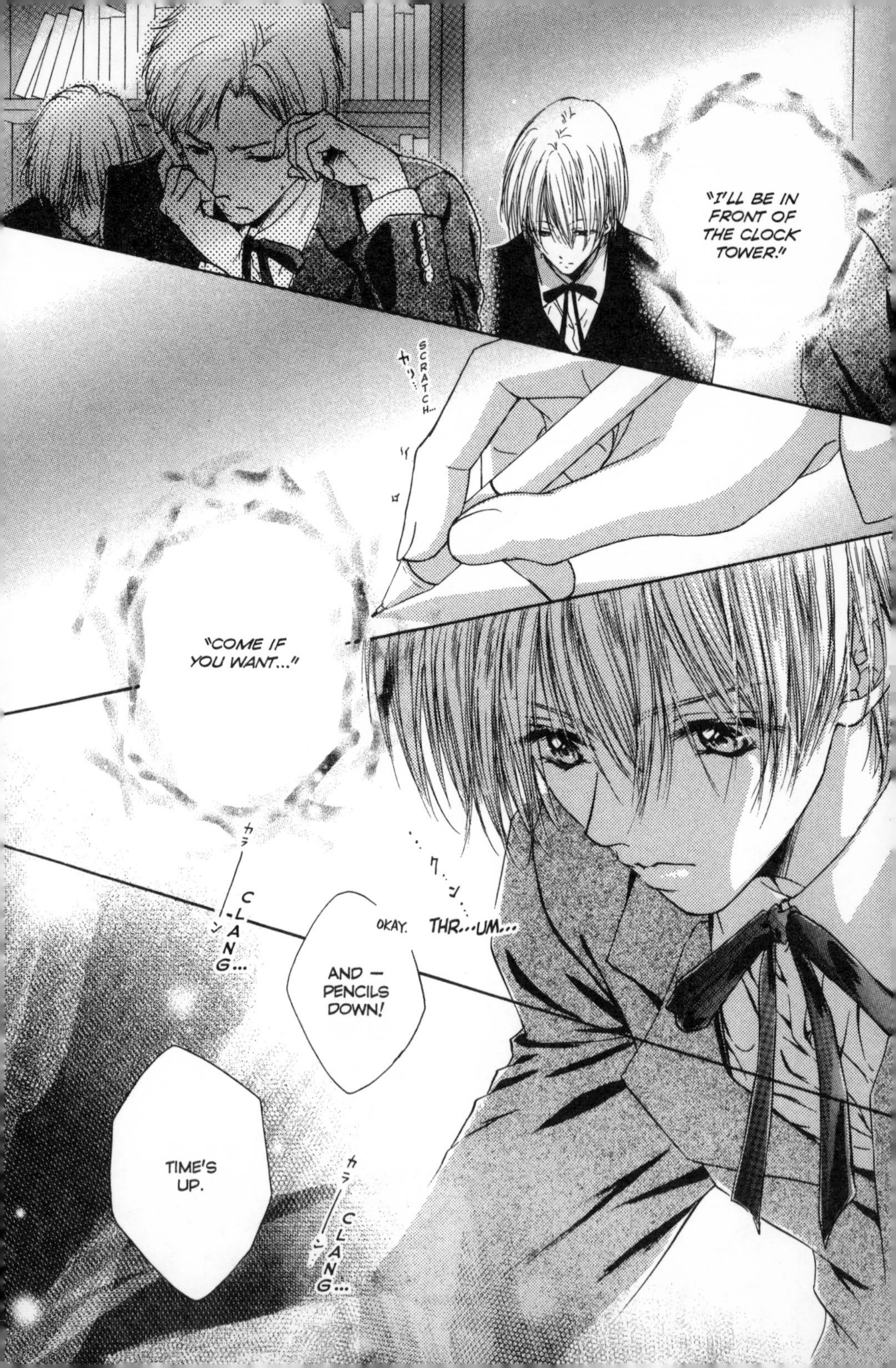
"I'LL BE IN FRONT OF THE CLOCK TOWER."
SCRATCH...
"COME IF YOU WANT..."
THR...UM...
OKAY.
AND — PENCILS DOWN!
CLANG...
TIME'S UP.
CLANG...

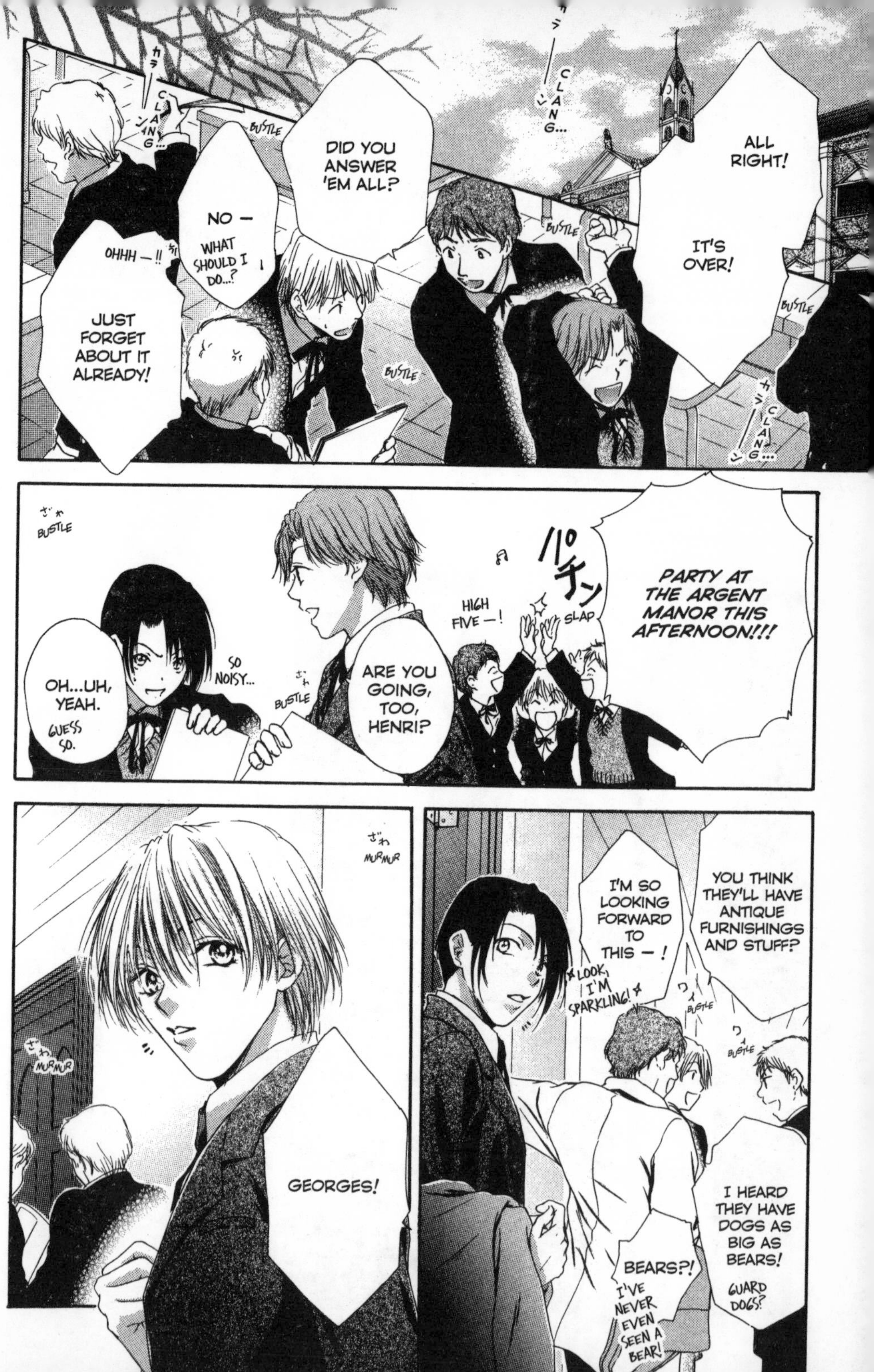
CLANG...
ALL RIGHT!
IT'S OVER!
BUSTLE
BUSTLE
CLANG...
DID YOU ANSWER 'EM ALL?
NO —
WHAT SHOULD I DO...?
OHHH —!!
BUSTLE
CLANG...
JUST FORGET ABOUT IT ALREADY!
BUSTLE
PARTY AT THE ARGENT MANOR THIS AFTERNOON!!!
パチン
SLAP
HIGH FIVE —!
ARE YOU GOING, TOO, HENRI?
BUSTLE
SO NOISY...
OH...UH, YEAH.
GUESS SO.
BUSTLE
YOU THINK THEY'LL HAVE ANTIQUE FURNISHINGS AND STUFF?
I'M SO LOOKING FORWARD TO THIS —!
LOOK, I'M SPARKLING!
BUSTLE
BUSTLE
I HEARD THEY HAVE DOGS AS BIG AS BEARS!
GUARD DOGS?
BEARS?!
I'VE NEVER EVEN SEEN A BEAR!
MURMUR
GEORGES!
MURMUR

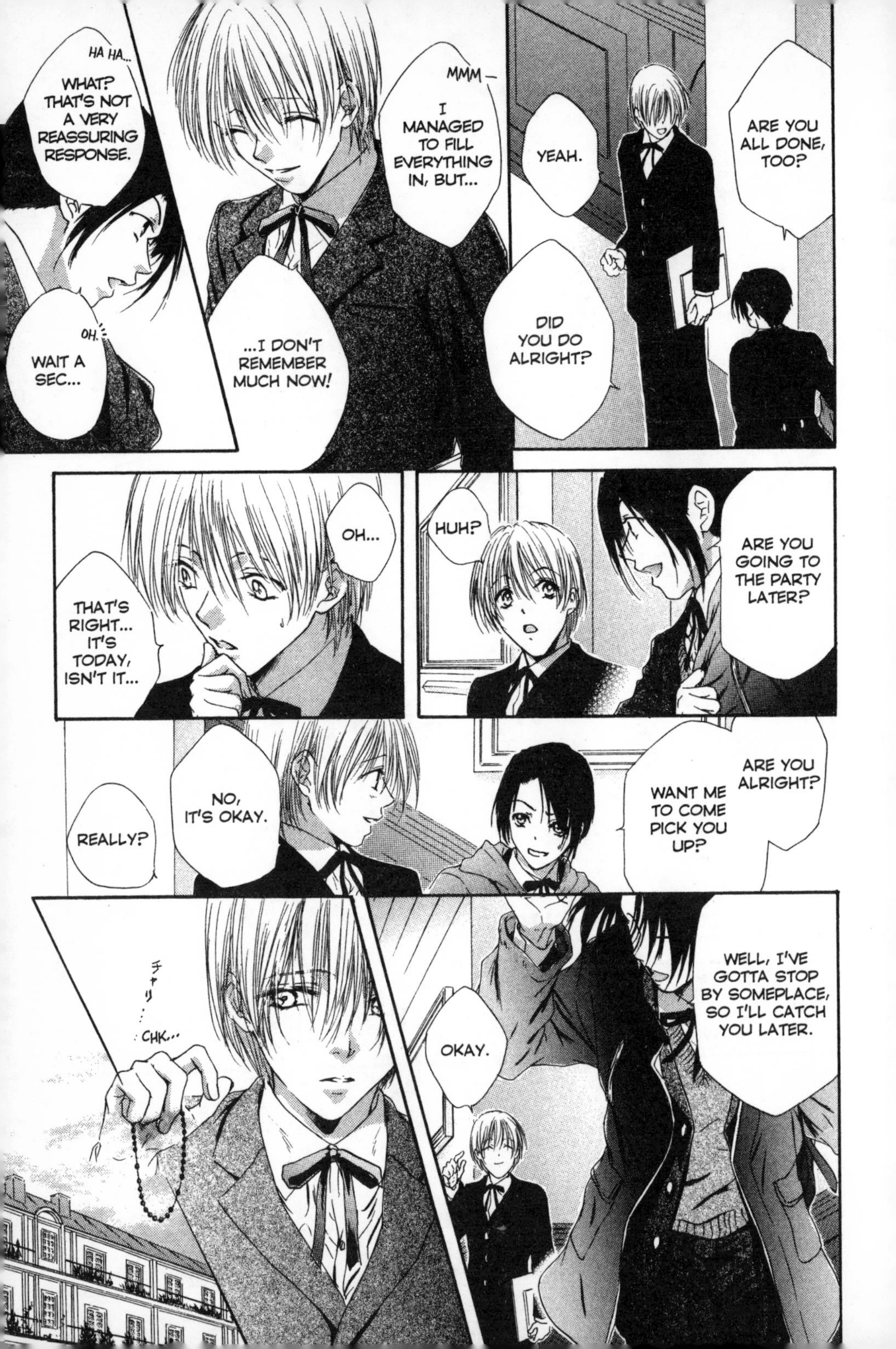
ARE YOU ALL DONE, TOO?
YEAH.
DID YOU DO ALRIGHT?
MMM—
I MANAGED TO FILL EVERYTHING IN, BUT...
...I DON'T REMEMBER MUCH NOW!
HA HA...
WHAT? THAT'S NOT A VERY REASSURING RESPONSE.
OH.
WAIT A SEC...
ARE YOU GOING TO THE PARTY LATER?
HUH?
OH...
THAT'S RIGHT... IT'S TODAY, ISN'T IT...
ARE YOU ALRIGHT?
WANT ME TO COME PICK YOU UP?
NO, IT'S OKAY.
REALLY?
WELL, I'VE GOTTA STOP BY SOMEPLACE, SO I'LL CATCH YOU LATER.
OKAY.
チャリ...
CHK...

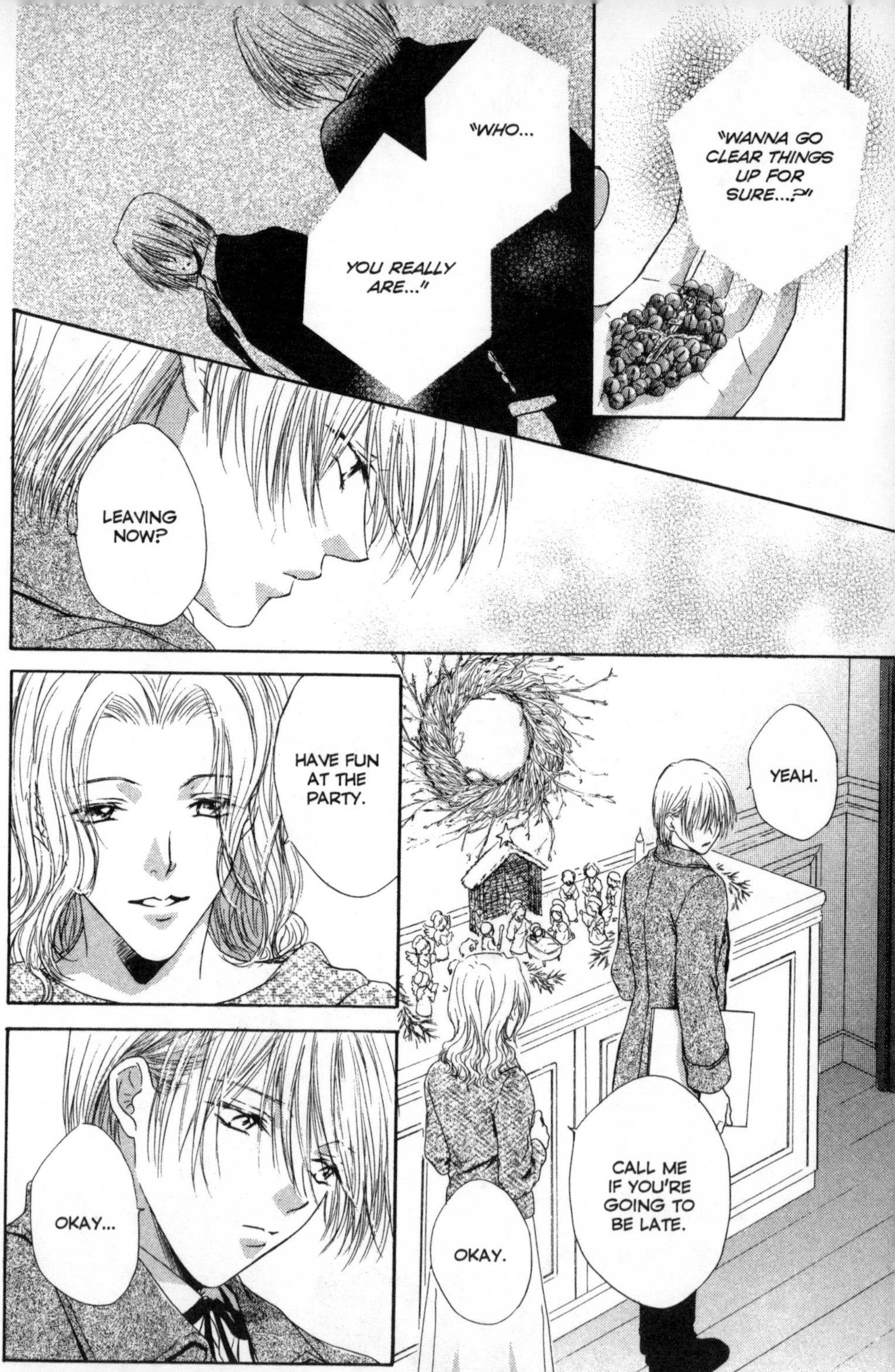
"WANNA GO CLEAR THINGS UP FOR SURE...?"
"WHO...
YOU REALLY ARE..."
LEAVING NOW?
YEAH.
CALL ME IF YOU'RE GOING TO BE LATE.
OKAY.
HAVE FUN AT THE PARTY.
OKAY...

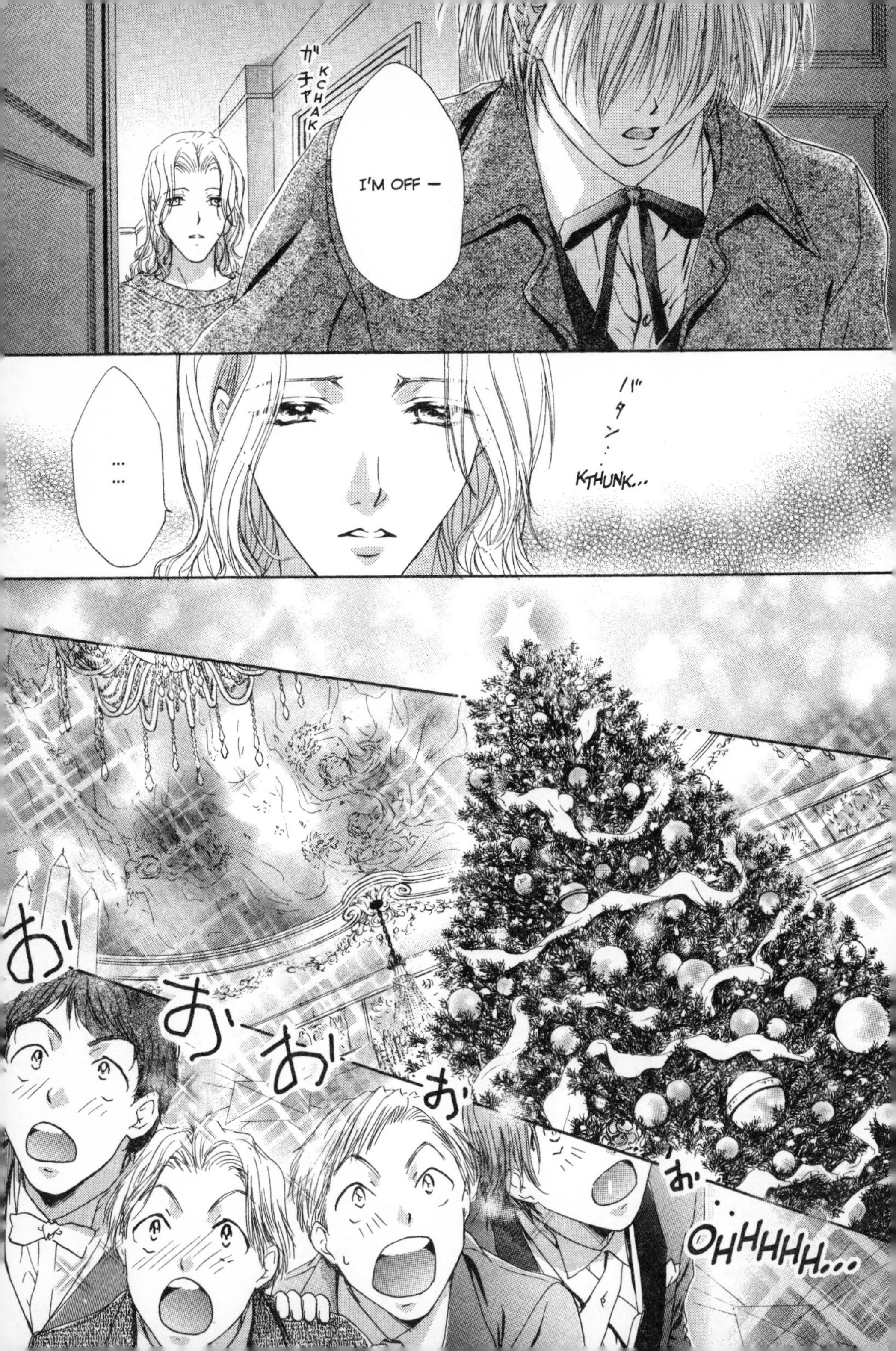
ガチャ
KCHAK
I'M OFF —
バタン‥
KTHUNK...
...
...
お!
おー
お!
お
おー‥
OHHHHH...

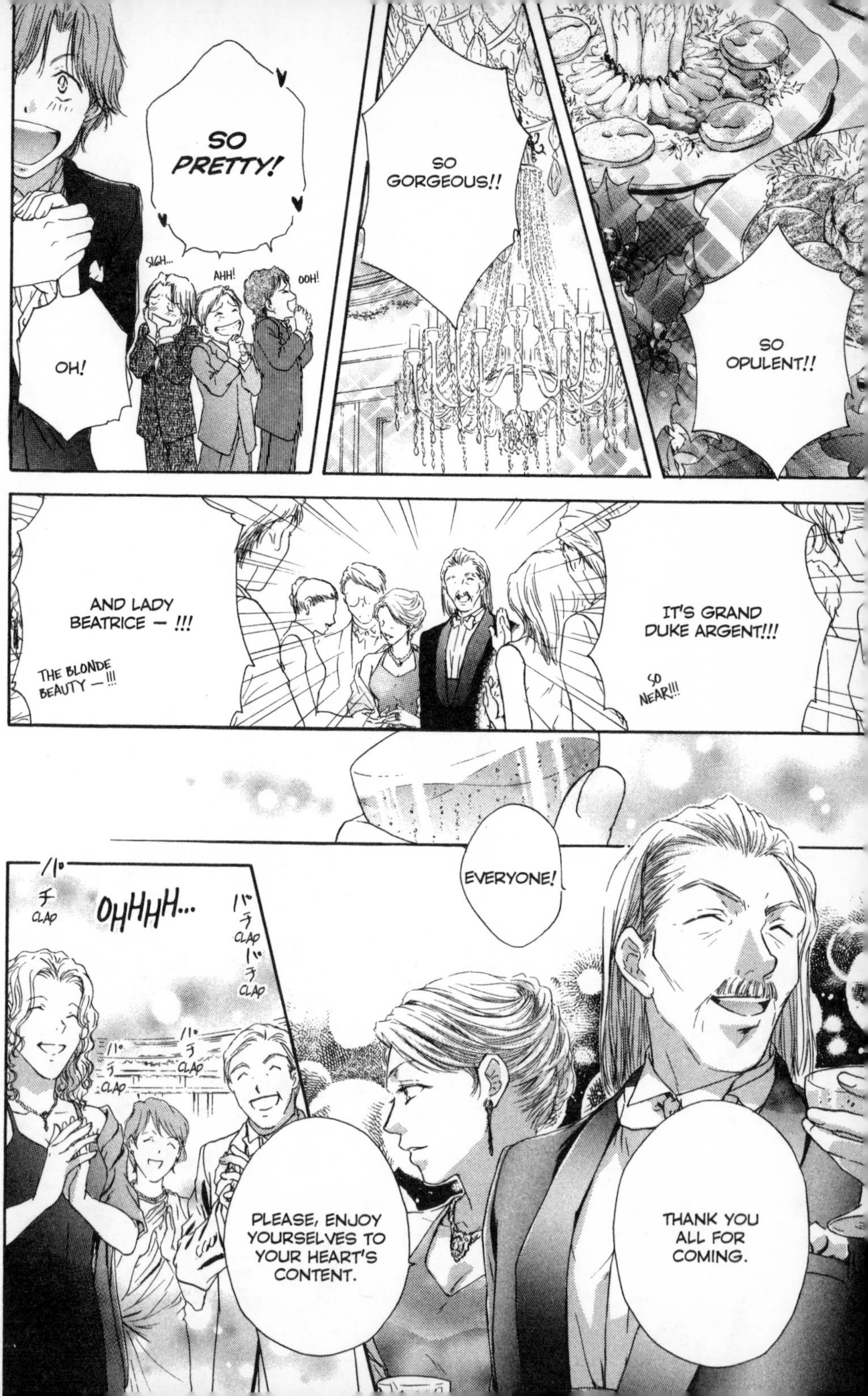
SO OPULENT!!
SO GORGEOUS!!
SO PRETTY!
OOH!
AHH!
SIGH...
OH!
IT'S GRAND DUKE ARGENT!!!
SO NEAR!!!
AND LADY BEATRICE — !!!
THE BLONDE BEAUTY — !!!
EVERYONE!
THANK YOU ALL FOR COMING.
PLEASE, ENJOY YOURSELVES TO YOUR HEART'S CONTENT.
パチ CLAP
パチ CLAP
パチ CLAP
OHHHH...
パチ CLAP
パチ CLAP

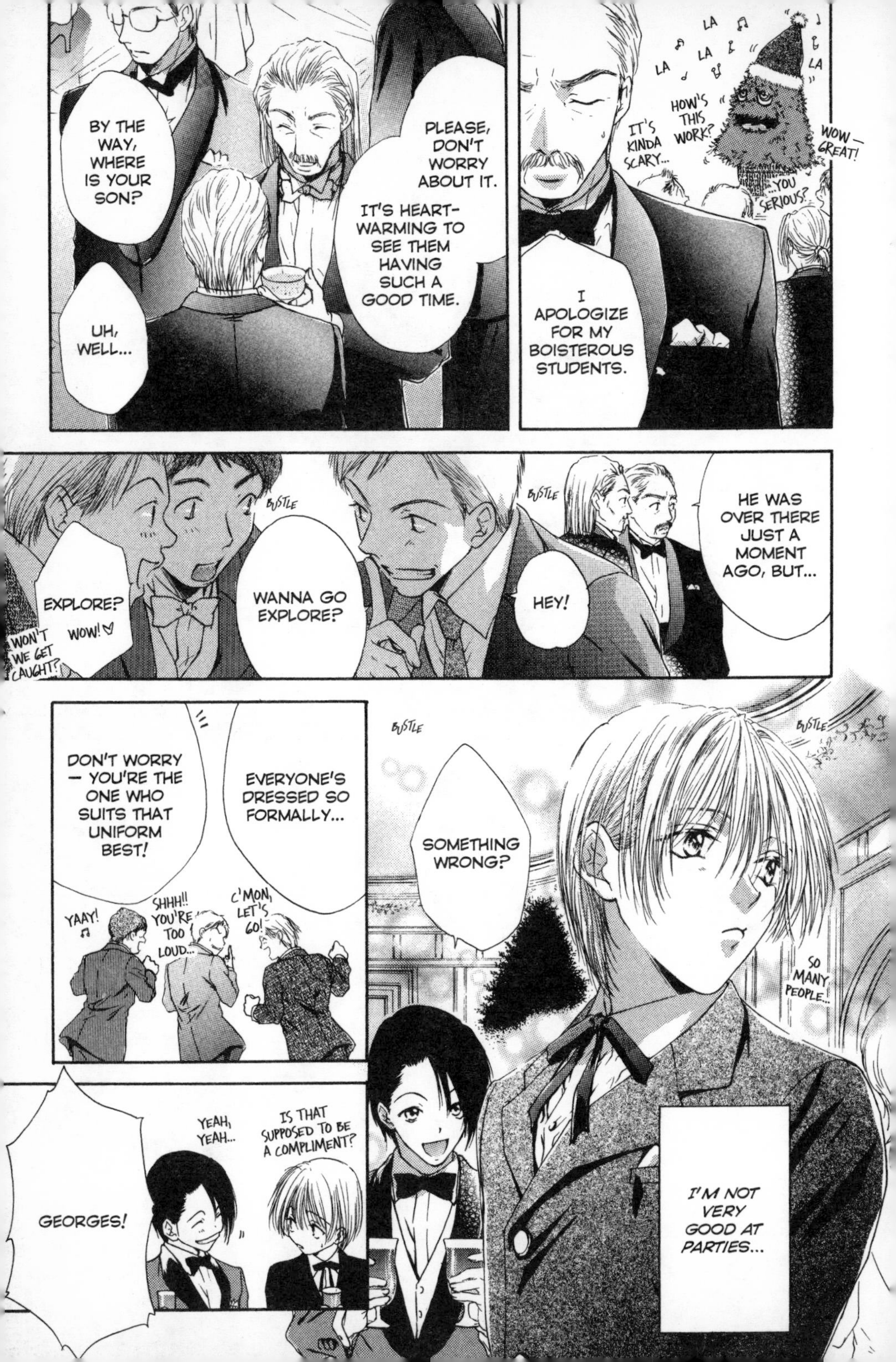

I APOLOGIZE FOR MY BOISTEROUS STUDENTS.
LA LA LA LA
HOW'S THIS WORK?
IT'S KINDA SCARY...
WOW—GREAT!
...YOU SERIOUS?
PLEASE, DON'T WORRY ABOUT IT.
IT'S HEART-WARMING TO SEE THEM HAVING SUCH A GOOD TIME.
BY THE WAY, WHERE IS YOUR SON?
UH, WELL...
HE WAS OVER THERE JUST A MOMENT AGO, BUT...
BUSTLE
HEY!
WANNA GO EXPLORE?
BUSTLE
EXPLORE?
WOW!♡
WON'T WE GET CAUGHT?
BUSTLE
BUSTLE
SO MANY PEOPLE...
SOMETHING WRONG?
I'M NOT VERY GOOD AT PARTIES...
EVERYONE'S DRESSED SO FORMALLY...
DON'T WORRY — YOU'RE THE ONE WHO SUITS THAT UNIFORM BEST!
C'MON, LET'S GO!
SHHH!! YOU'RE TOO LOUD...
YAAY!♫
IS THAT SUPPOSED TO BE A COMPLIMENT?
YEAH, YEAH...
GEORGES!

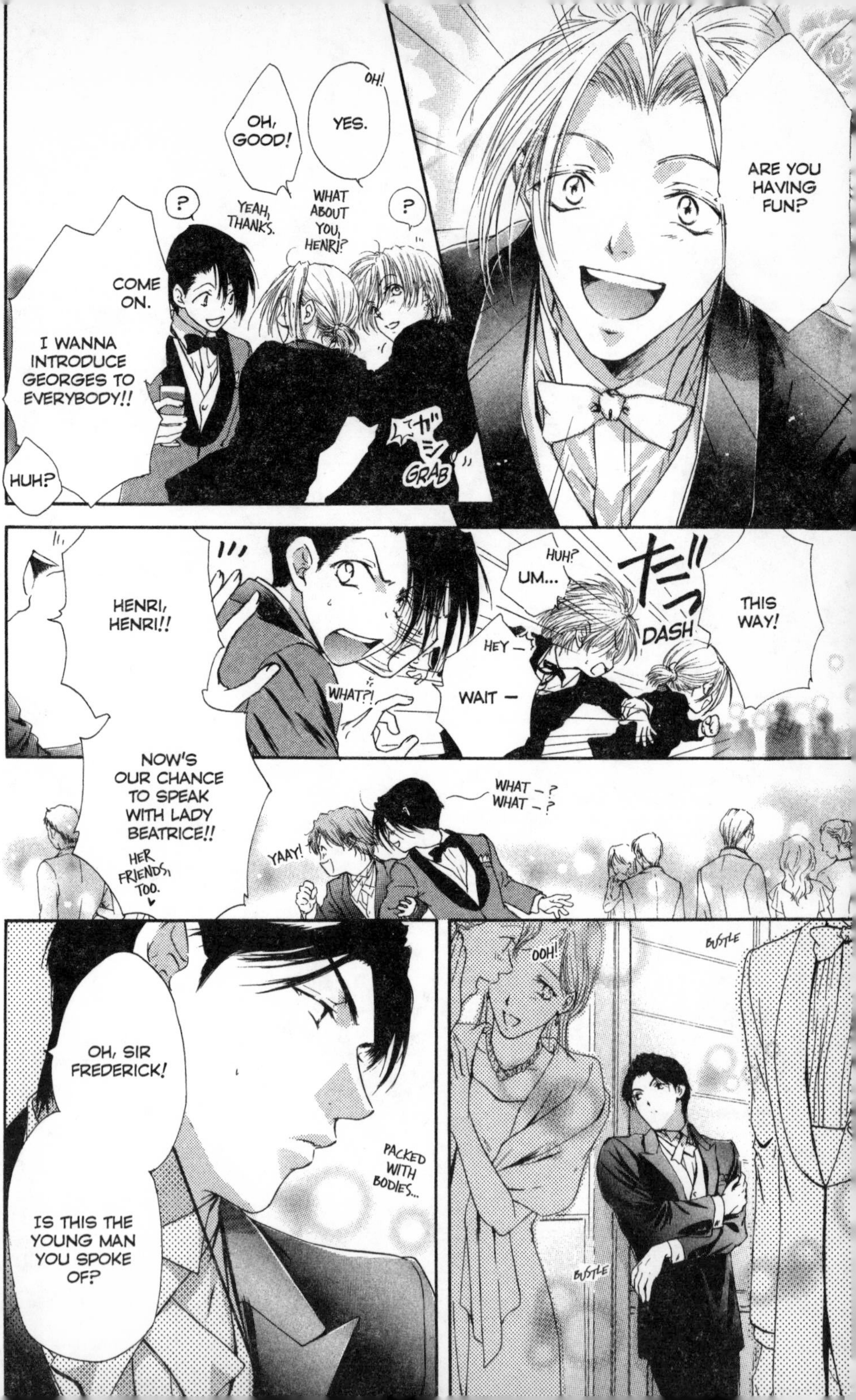

ARE YOU HAVING FUN?
OH!
YES.
OH, GOOD!
WHAT ABOUT YOU, HENRI?
?
YEAH, THANKS.
?
COME ON.
I WANNA INTRODUCE GEORGES TO EVERYBODY!!
GRAB
HUH?
THIS WAY!
HUH?
UM...
DASH
HEY —
WAIT —
HENRI, HENRI!!
WHAT?!
WHAT —?
WHAT —?
YAAY!
NOW'S OUR CHANCE TO SPEAK WITH LADY BEATRICE!!
HER FRIENDS, TOO.
BUSTLE
OOH!
BUSTLE
OH, SIR FREDERICK!
PACKED WITH BODIES...
IS THIS THE YOUNG MAN YOU SPOKE OF?

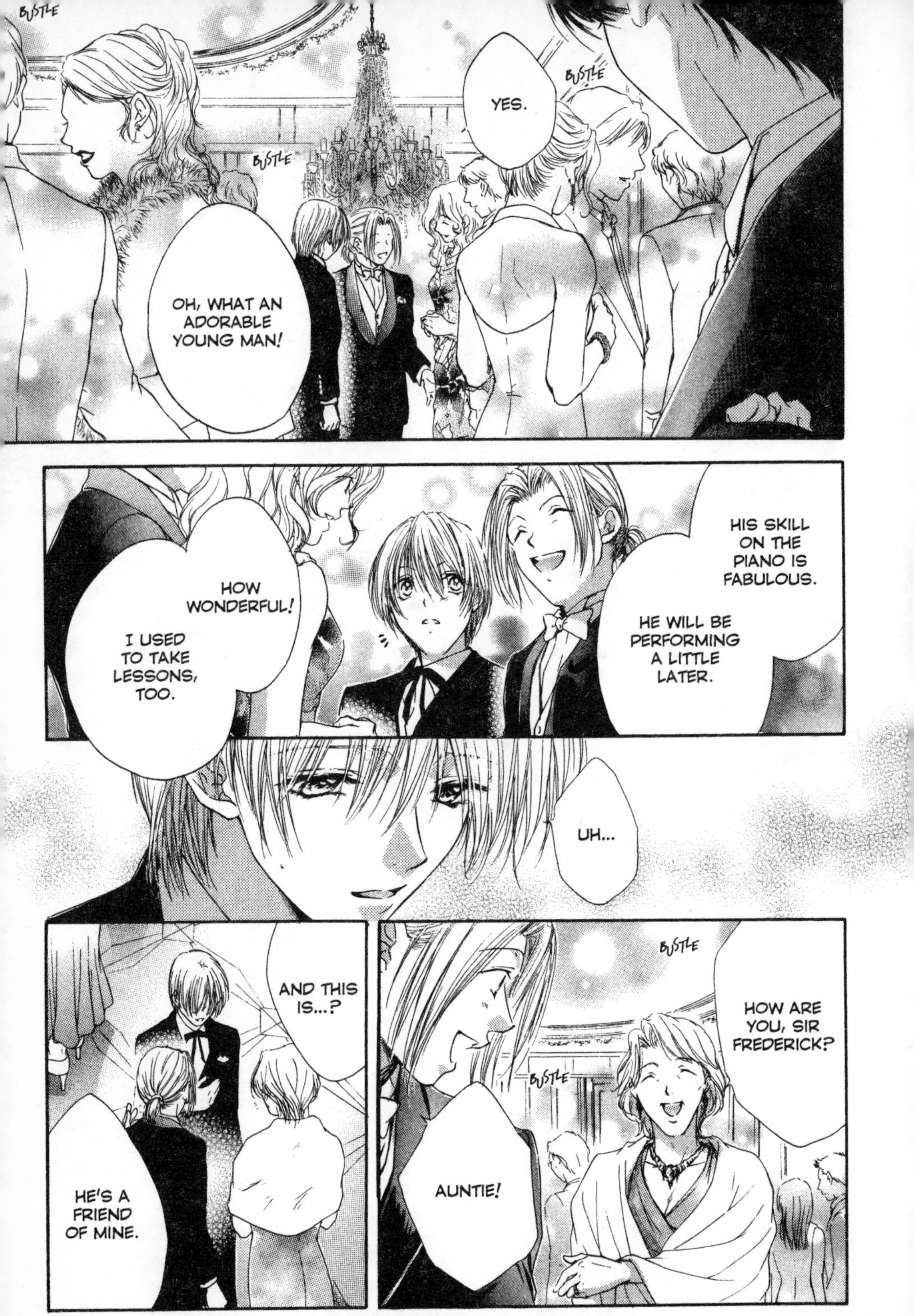
BUSTLE
YES.
BUSTLE
BUSTLE
OH, WHAT AN ADORABLE YOUNG MAN!
HIS SKILL ON THE PIANO IS FABULOUS.
HE WILL BE PERFORMING A LITTLE LATER.
HOW WONDERFUL!
I USED TO TAKE LESSONS, TOO.
UH...
BUSTLE
HOW ARE YOU, SIR FREDERICK?
BUSTLE
AUNTIE!
AND THIS IS...?
HE'S A FRIEND OF MINE.

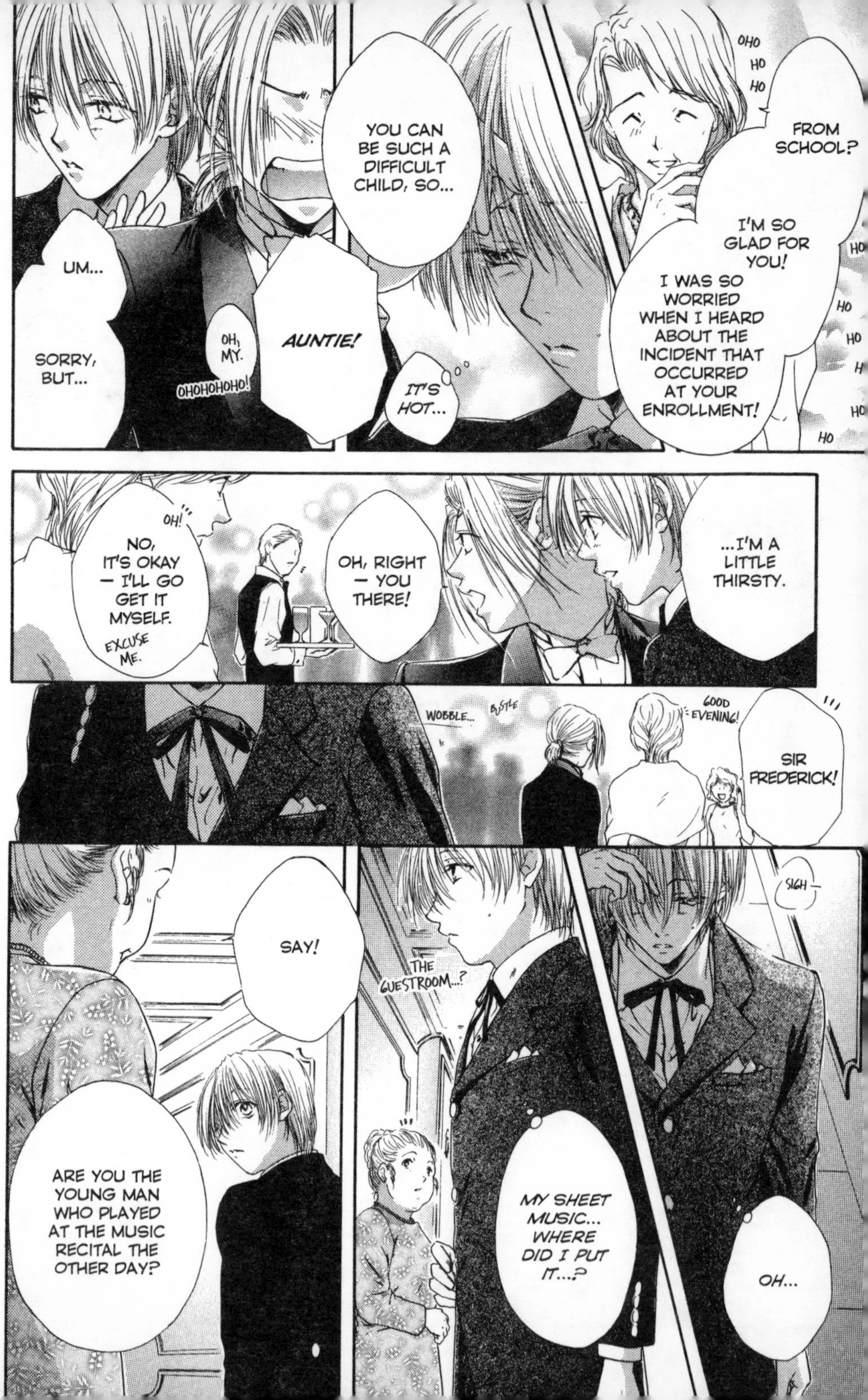
OHO HO HO
FROM SCHOOL?
I'M SO GLAD FOR YOU!
I WAS SO WORRIED WHEN I HEARD ABOUT THE INCIDENT THAT OCCURRED AT YOUR ENROLLMENT!
HO HO HO H HO HO
YOU CAN BE SUCH A DIFFICULT CHILD, SO...
IT'S HOT...
AUNTIE!
OH, MY.
OHOHOHOHO!
UM...
SORRY, BUT...
...I'M A LITTLE THIRSTY.
OH, RIGHT — YOU THERE!
OH!
NO, IT'S OKAY — I'LL GO GET IT MYSELF.
EXCUSE ME.
SIR FREDERICK!
GOOD EVENING!
BUSTLE
WOBBLE...
SIGH
OH...
MY SHEET MUSIC... WHERE DID I PUT IT...?
THE GUESTROOM...?
SAY!
ARE YOU THE YOUNG MAN WHO PLAYED AT THE MUSIC RECITAL THE OTHER DAY?

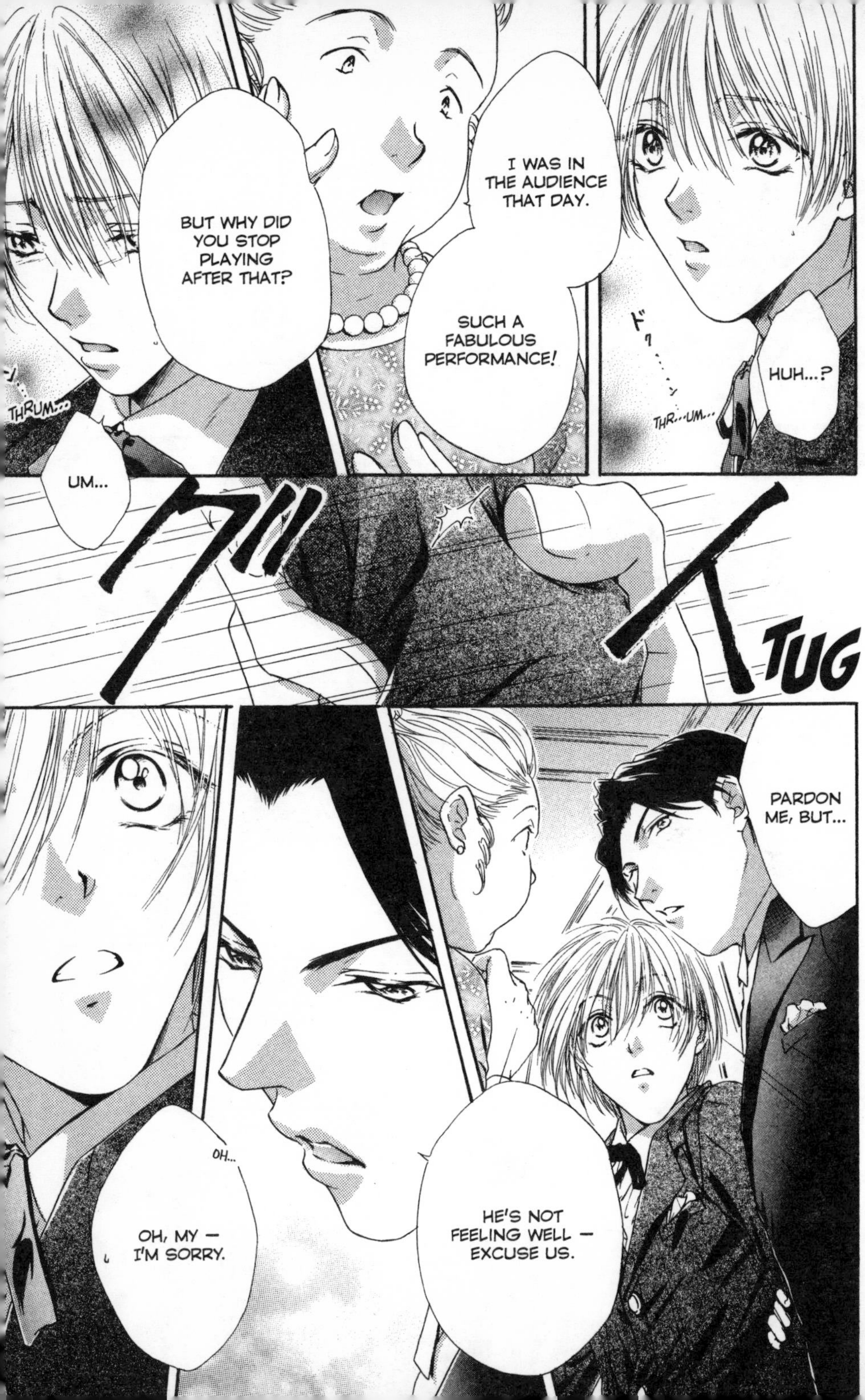
HUH...?
THR...UM...
I WAS IN THE AUDIENCE THAT DAY.
SUCH A FABULOUS PERFORMANCE!
BUT WHY DID YOU STOP PLAYING AFTER THAT?
THRUM...
UM...
グイ
TUG
PARDON ME, BUT...
HE'S NOT FEELING WELL — EXCUSE US.
OH...
OH, MY — I'M SORRY.

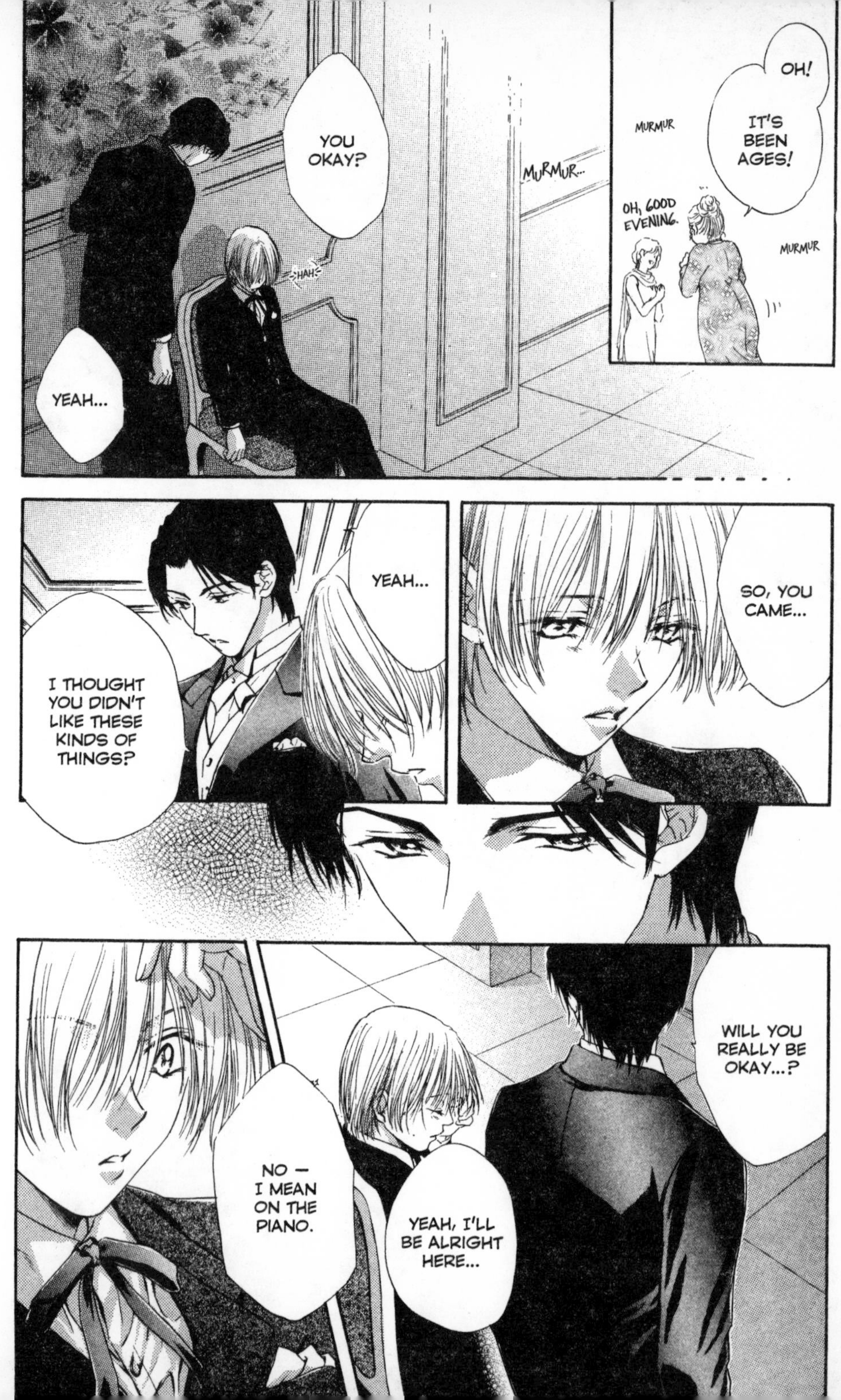
OH! IT'S BEEN AGES!
MURMUR
OH, GOOD EVENING.
MURMUR
MURMUR...
YOU OKAY?
HAH
YEAH...
SO, YOU CAME...
YEAH...
I THOUGHT YOU DIDN'T LIKE THESE KINDS OF THINGS?
WILL YOU REALLY BE OKAY...?
YEAH, I'LL BE ALRIGHT HERE...
NO — I MEAN ON THE PIANO.

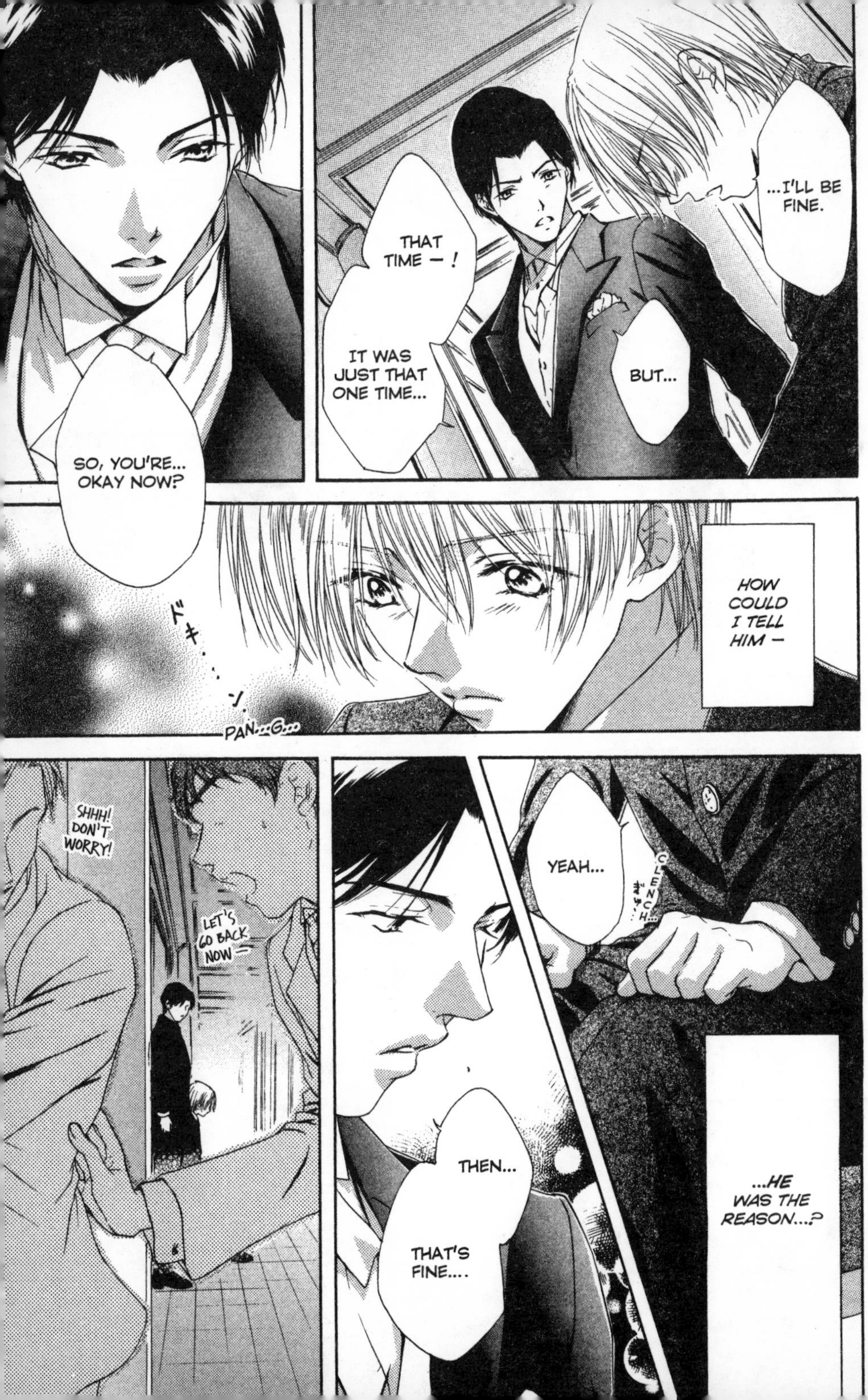
...I'LL BE FINE.
BUT...
THAT TIME —!
IT WAS JUST THAT ONE TIME...
SO, YOU'RE... OKAY NOW?
HOW COULD I TELL HIM —
ドキ...ン
PAN...G...
YEAH...
CLENCH...
...HE WAS THE REASON...?
THEN...
THAT'S FINE....
SHHH! DON'T WORRY!
LET'S GO BACK NOW —

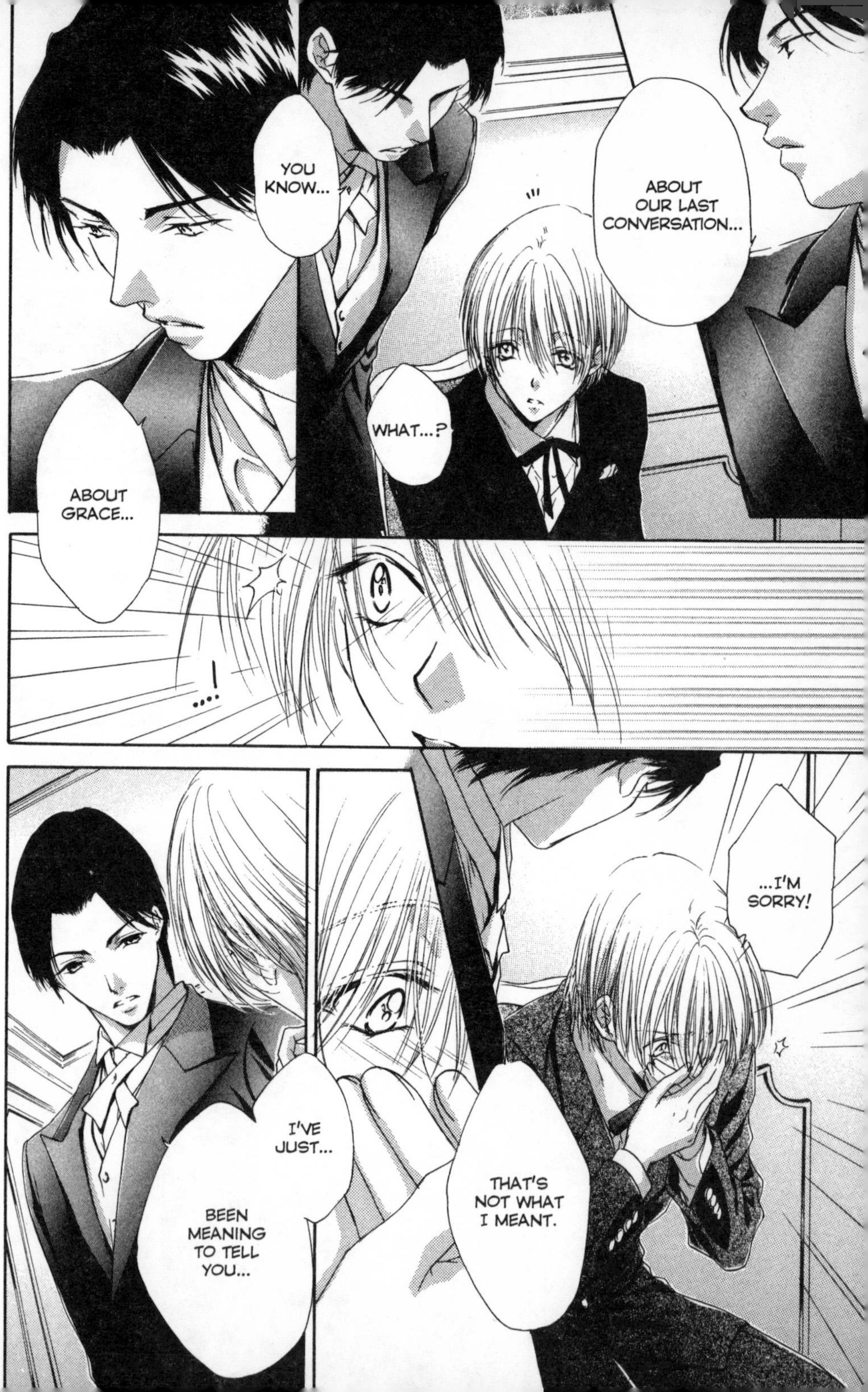
ABOUT OUR LAST CONVERSATION...
YOU KNOW...
WHAT...?
ABOUT GRACE...
...!
...I'M SORRY!
THAT'S NOT WHAT I MEANT.
I'VE JUST...
BEEN MEANING TO TELL YOU...

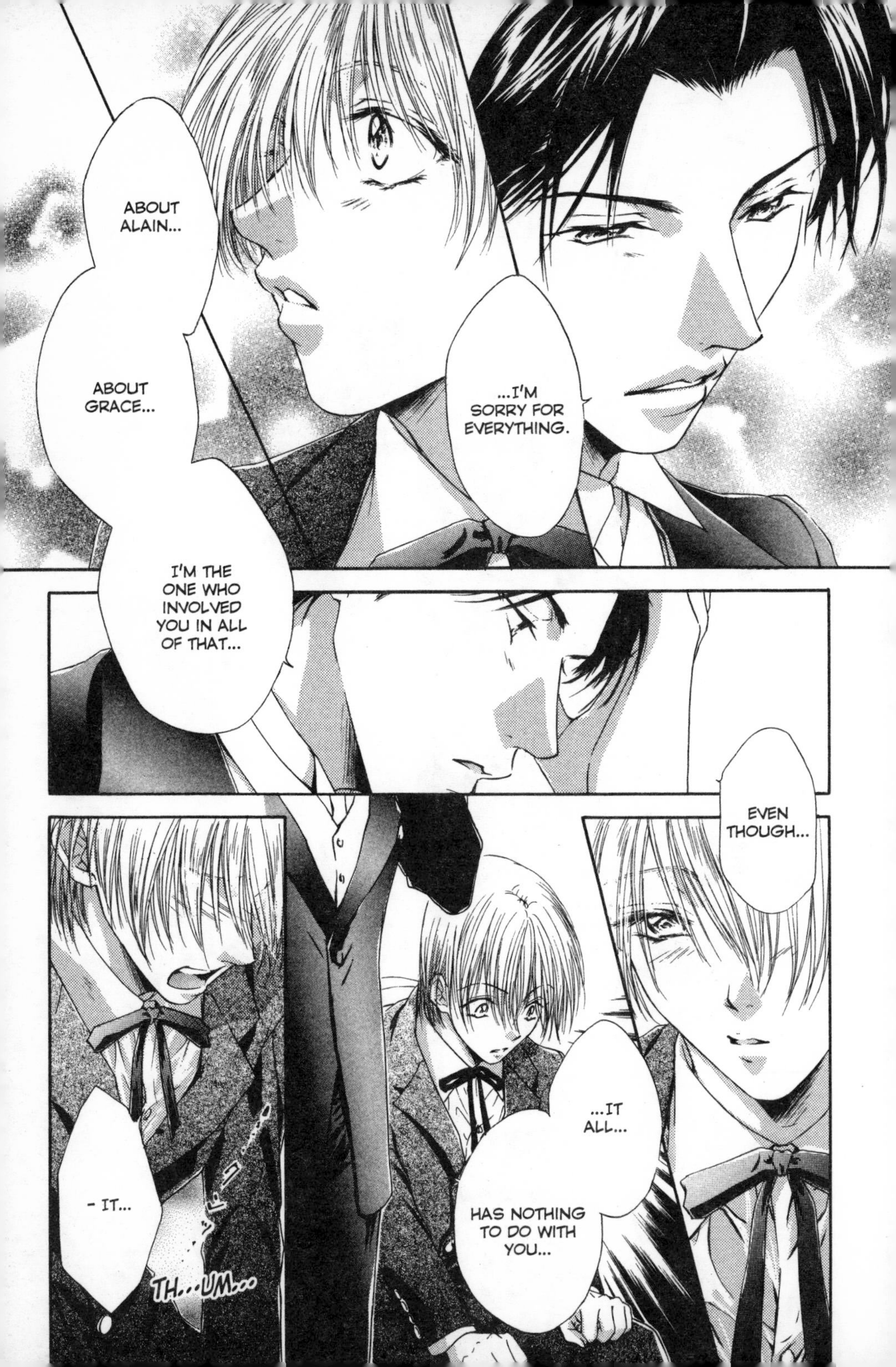
ABOUT ALAIN...
ABOUT GRACE...
I'M THE ONE WHO INVOLVED YOU IN ALL OF THAT...
...I'M SORRY FOR EVERYTHING.
EVEN THOUGH...
...IT ALL...
HAS NOTHING TO DO WITH YOU...
- IT...
TH...UM...

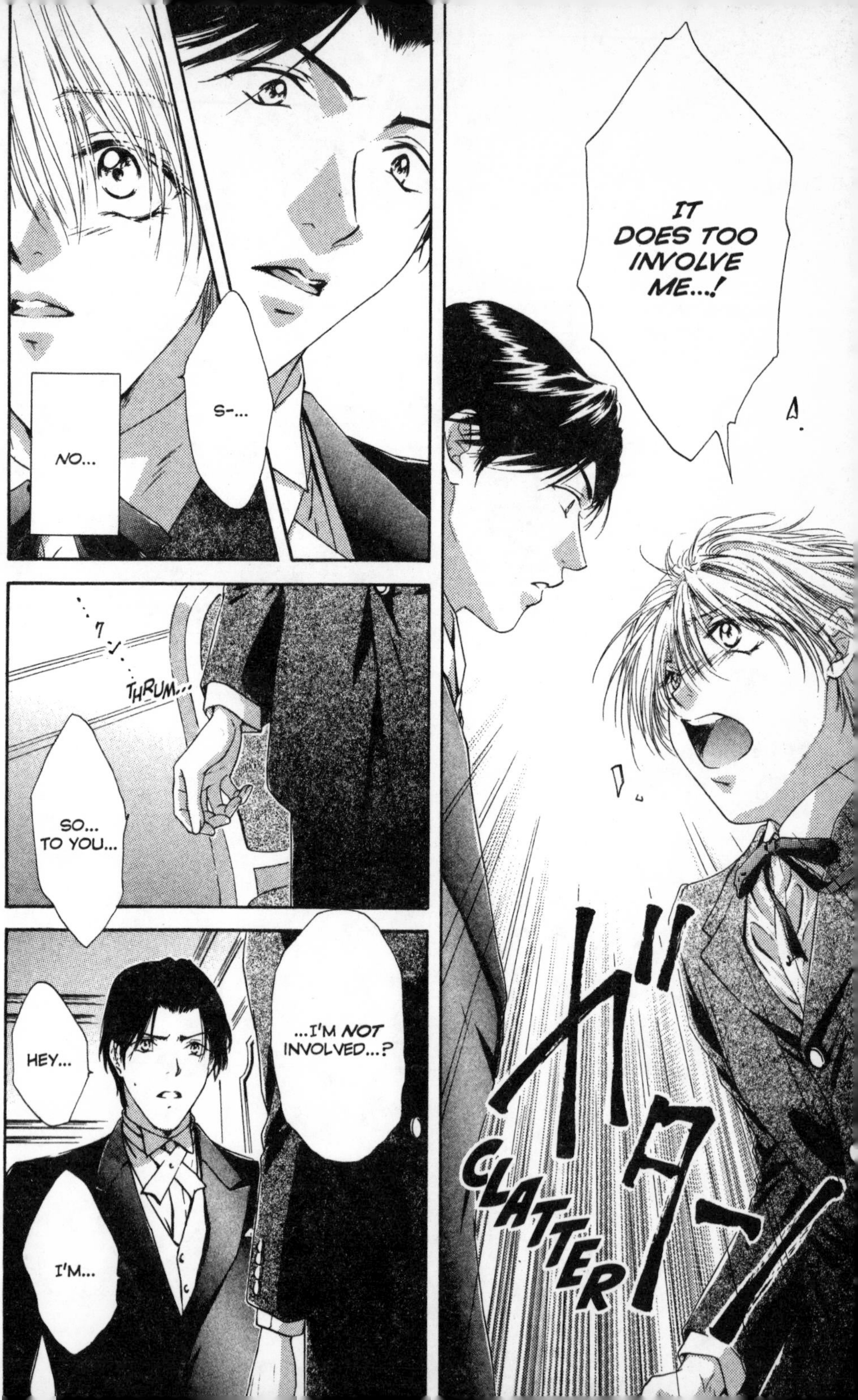
IT DOES TOO INVOLVE ME...!
CLATTER
S-...
NO...
THRUM...
SO... TO YOU...
...I'M NOT INVOLVED...?
HEY...
I'M...

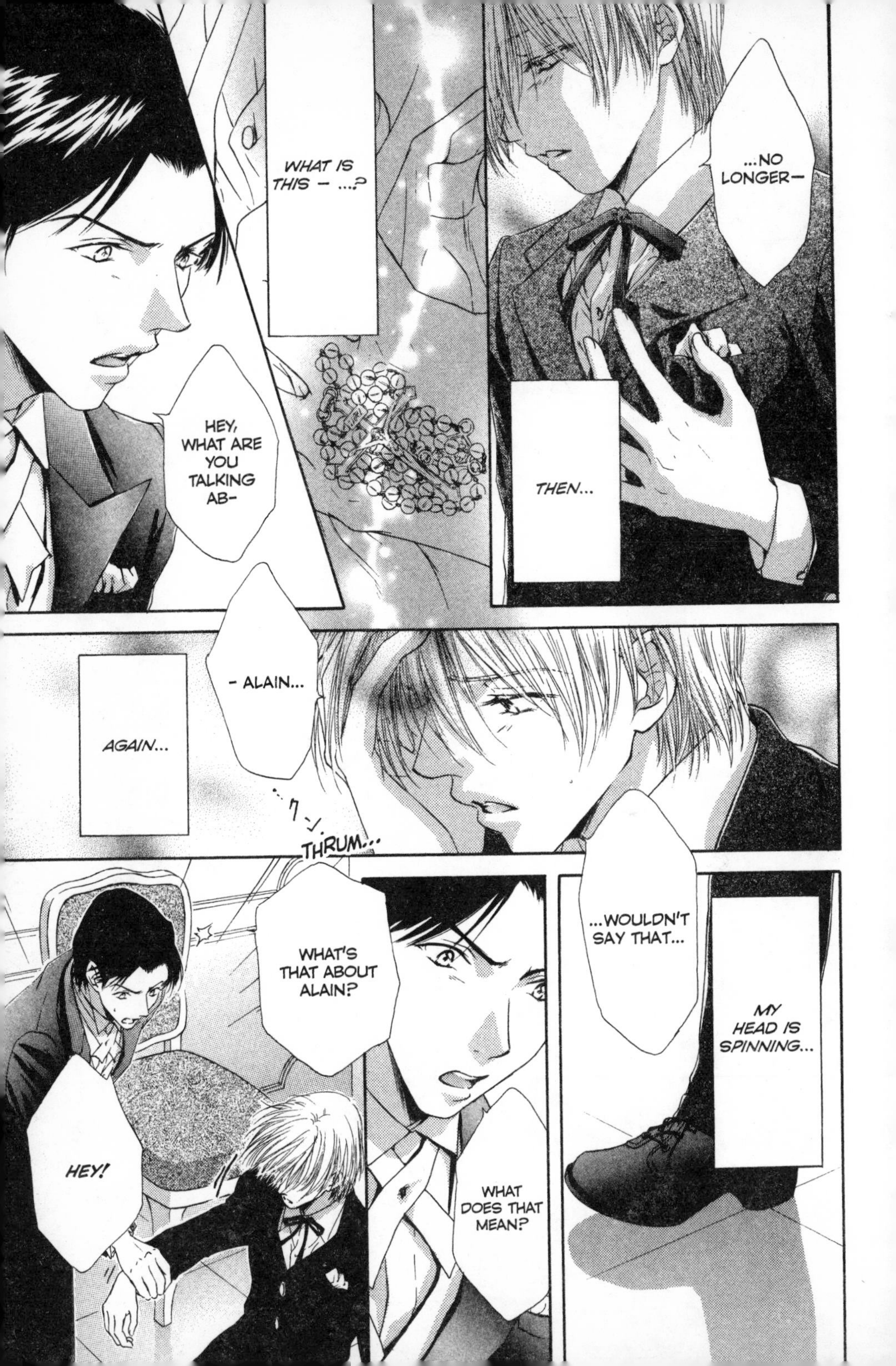
...NO LONGER—
THEN...
WHAT IS THIS – ...?
HEY, WHAT ARE YOU TALKING AB-
- ALAIN...
AGAIN...
THRUM...
...WOULDN'T SAY THAT...
MY HEAD IS SPINNING...
WHAT'S THAT ABOUT ALAIN?
WHAT DOES THAT MEAN?
HEY!

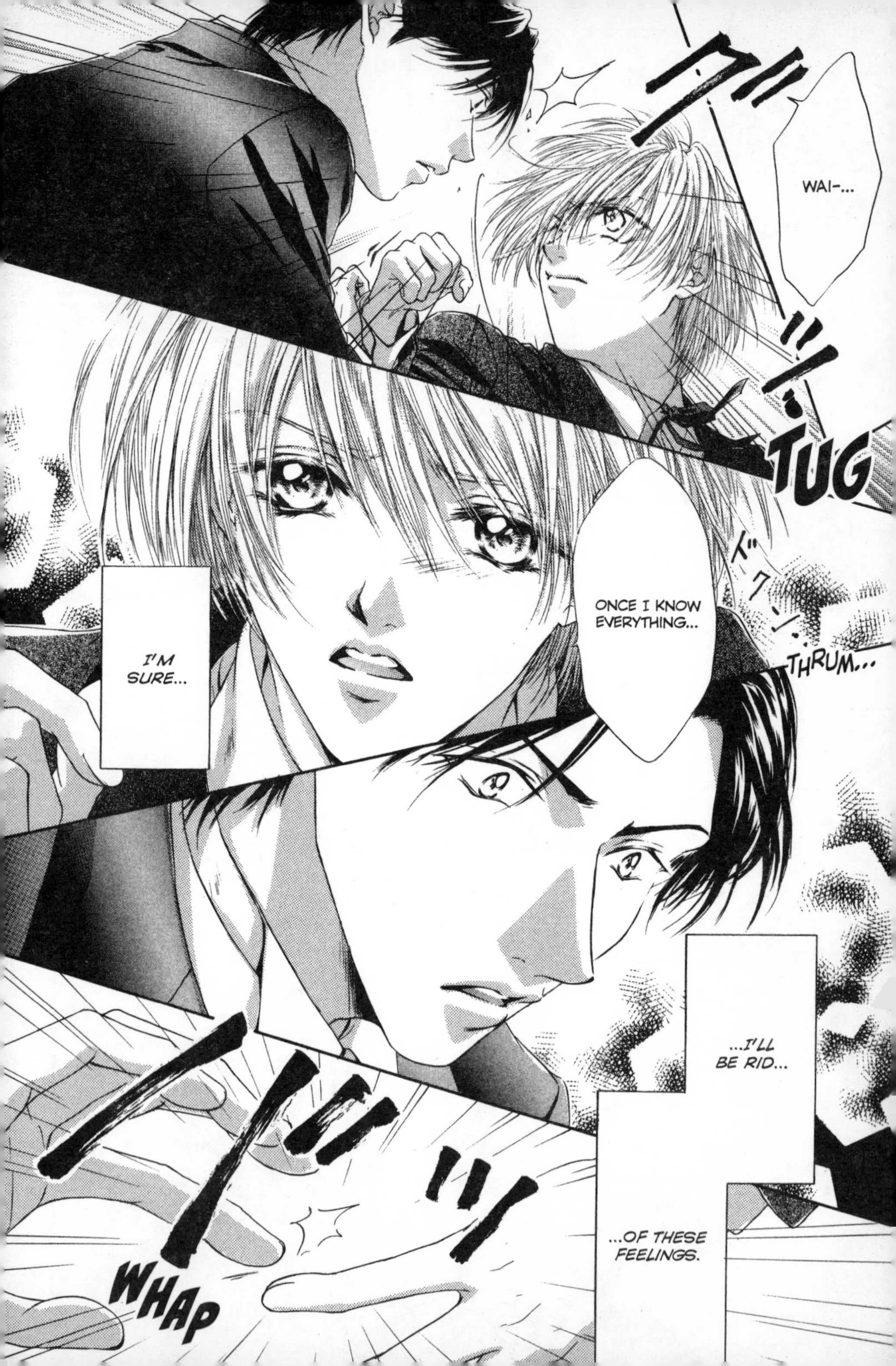
WAI-...
TUG
ONCE I KNOW EVERYTHING...
THRUM...
I'M SURE...
...I'LL BE RID...
...OF THESE FEELINGS.
WHAP

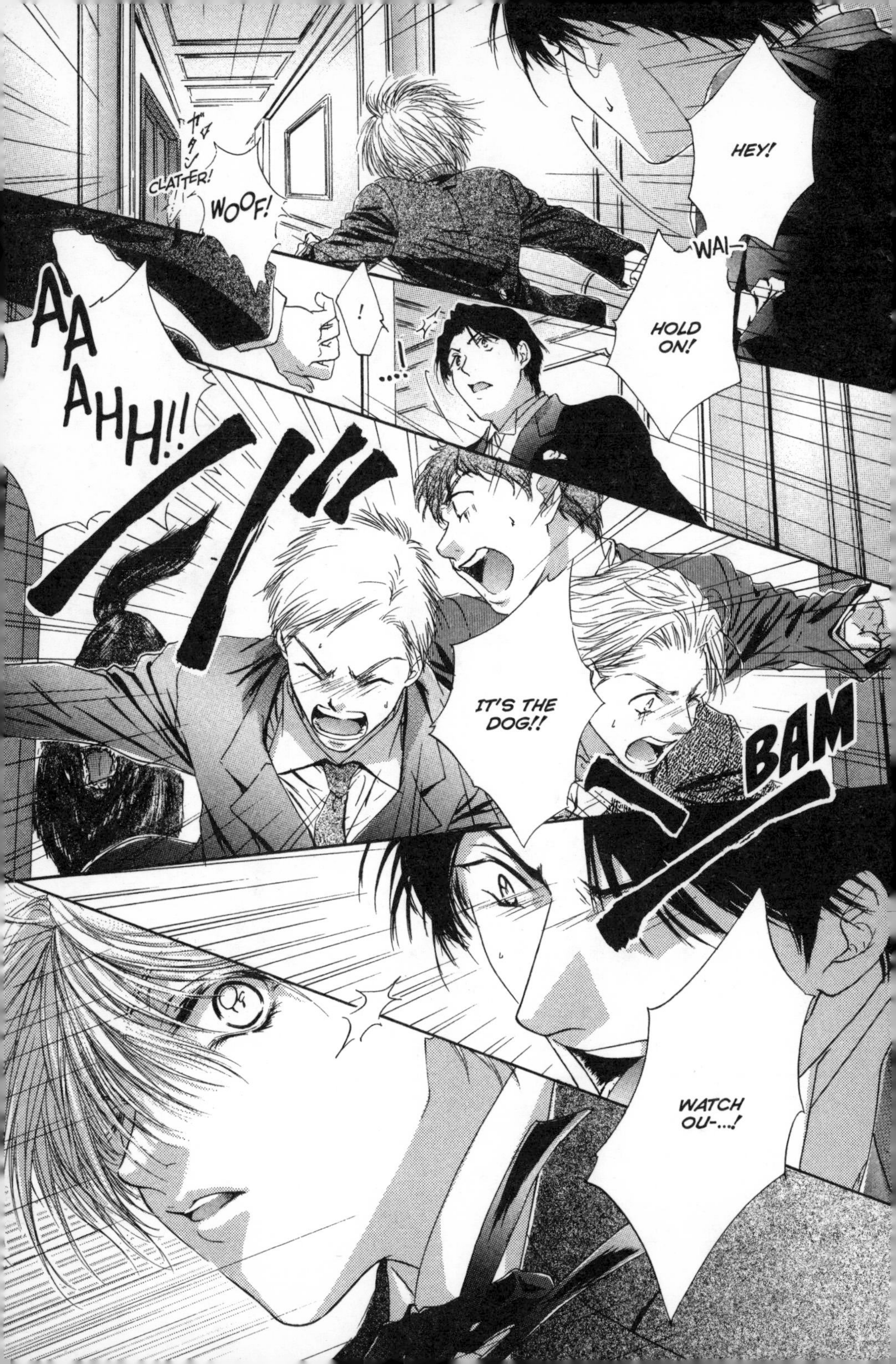
HEY!
WAI—
HOLD ON!
ガタン
CLATTER!
WOOF!
!
...!
AAAHH!!
IT'S THE DOG!!
BAM
WATCH OU-...!

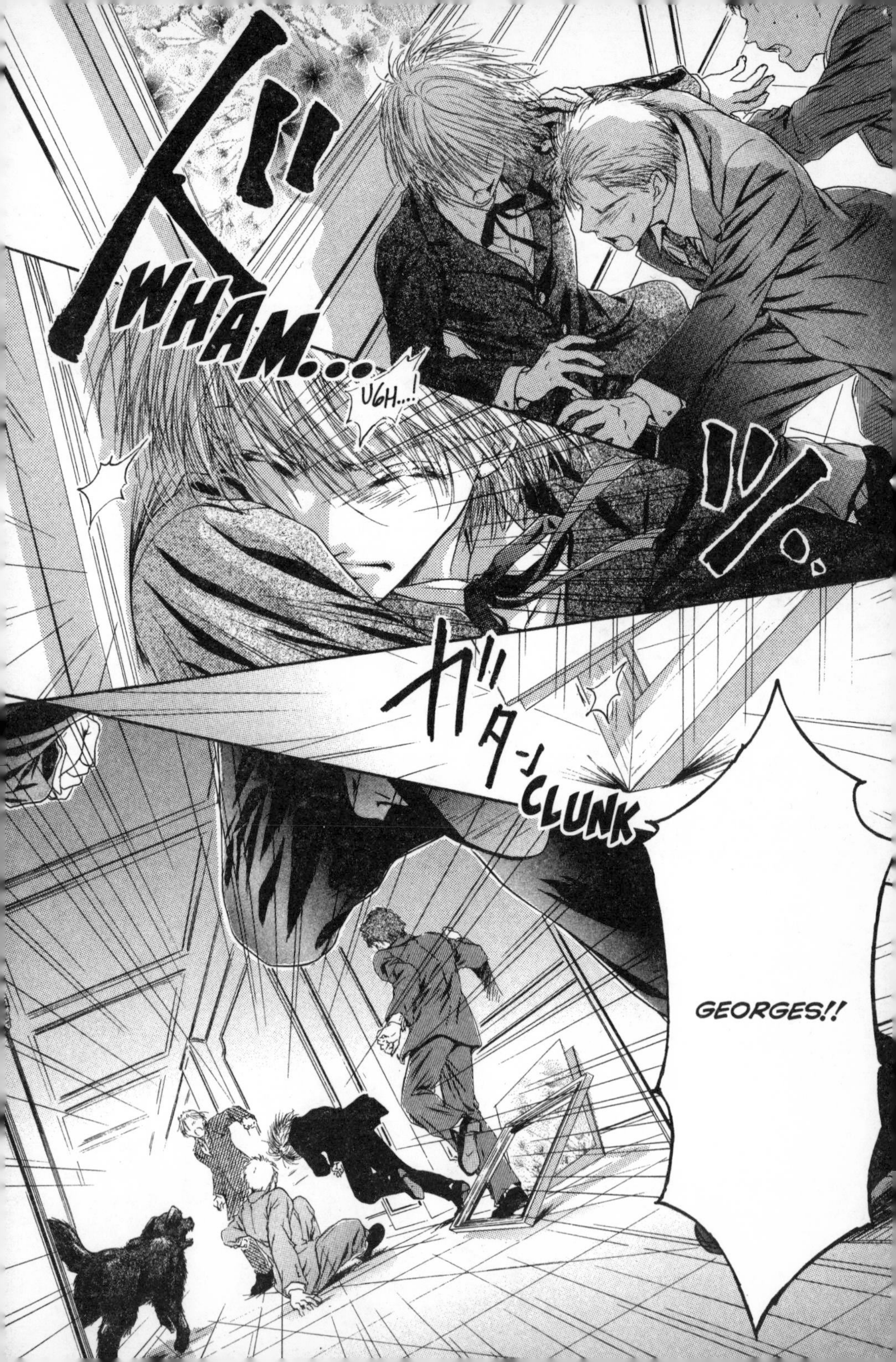
ド
WHAM...
UGH...!
ッ。
ガターン
CLUNK
GEORGES!!

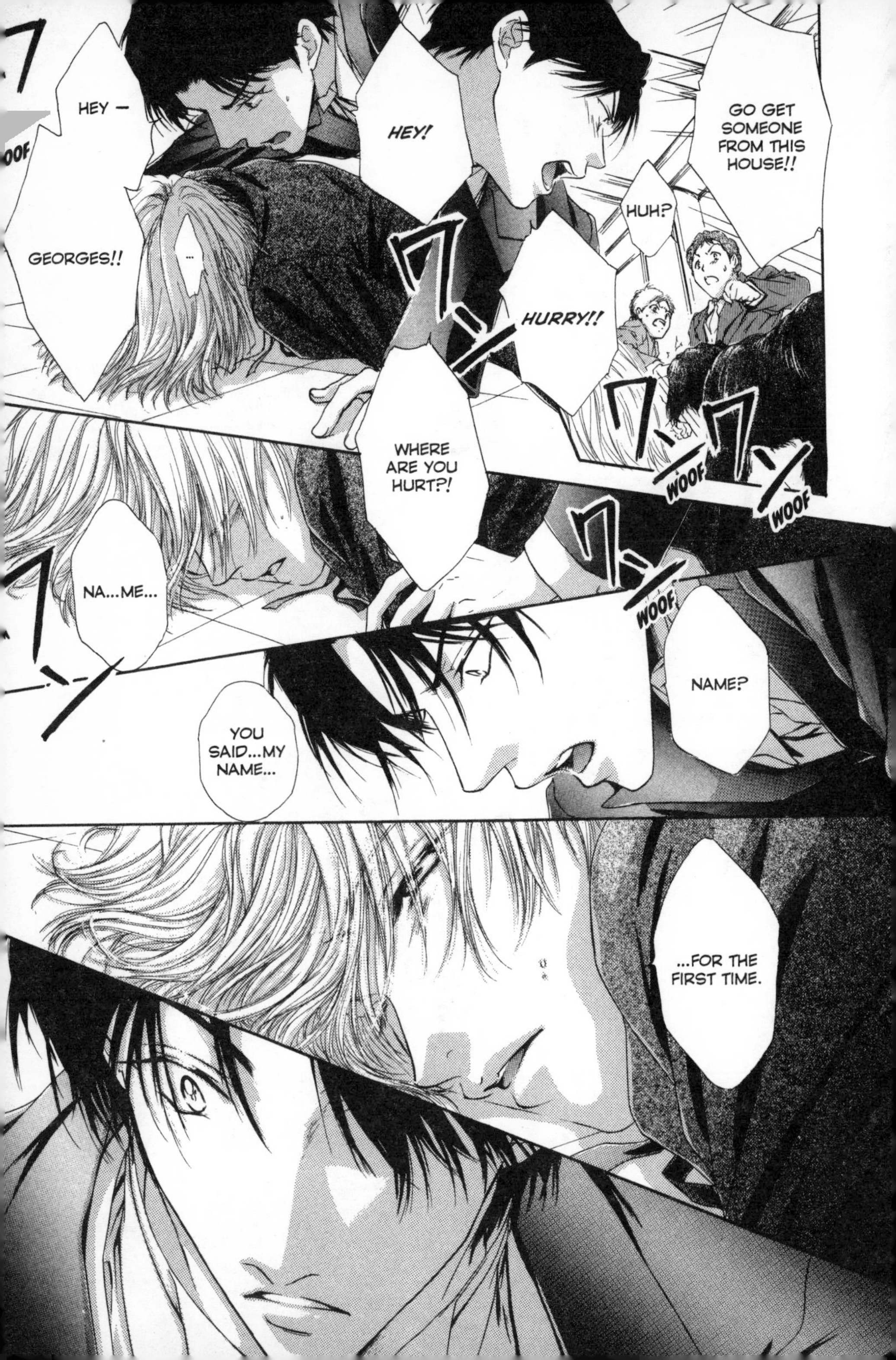
GO GET SOMEONE FROM THIS HOUSE!!
HEY!
HUH?
HEY —
HURRY!!
GEORGES!!
...
OOF
WOOF
WOOF
WHERE ARE YOU HURT?!
WOOF
NA...ME...
NAME?
YOU SAID...MY NAME...
...FOR THE FIRST TIME.

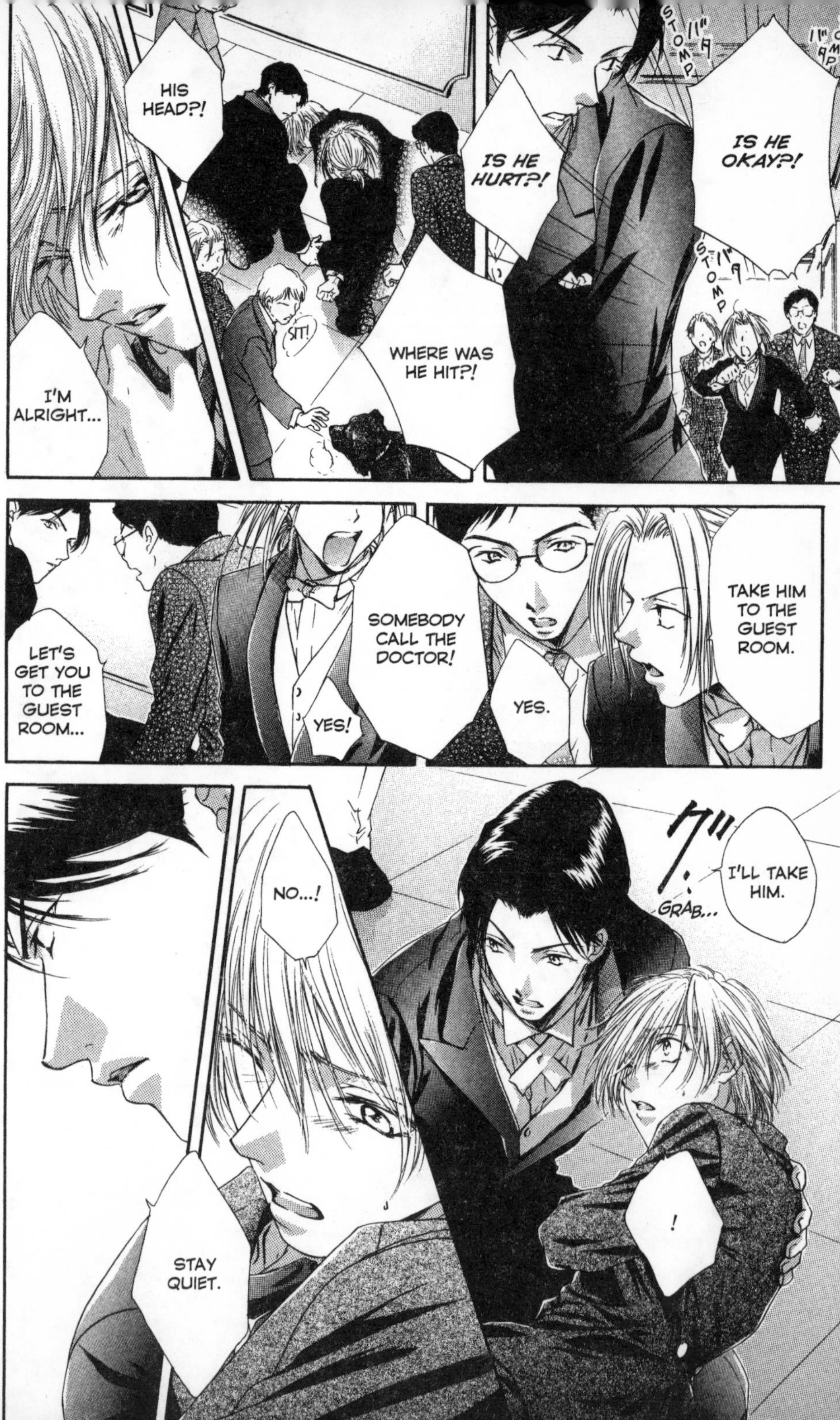
STOMP
STOMP
IS HE OKAY?!
IS HE HURT?!
STOMP
HIS HEAD?!
WHERE WAS HE HIT?!
SIT!
I'M ALRIGHT...
TAKE HIM TO THE GUEST ROOM.
YES.
SOMEBODY CALL THE DOCTOR!
YES!
LET'S GET YOU TO THE GUEST ROOM...
I'LL TAKE HIM.
GRAB...
NO...!
!
STAY QUIET.

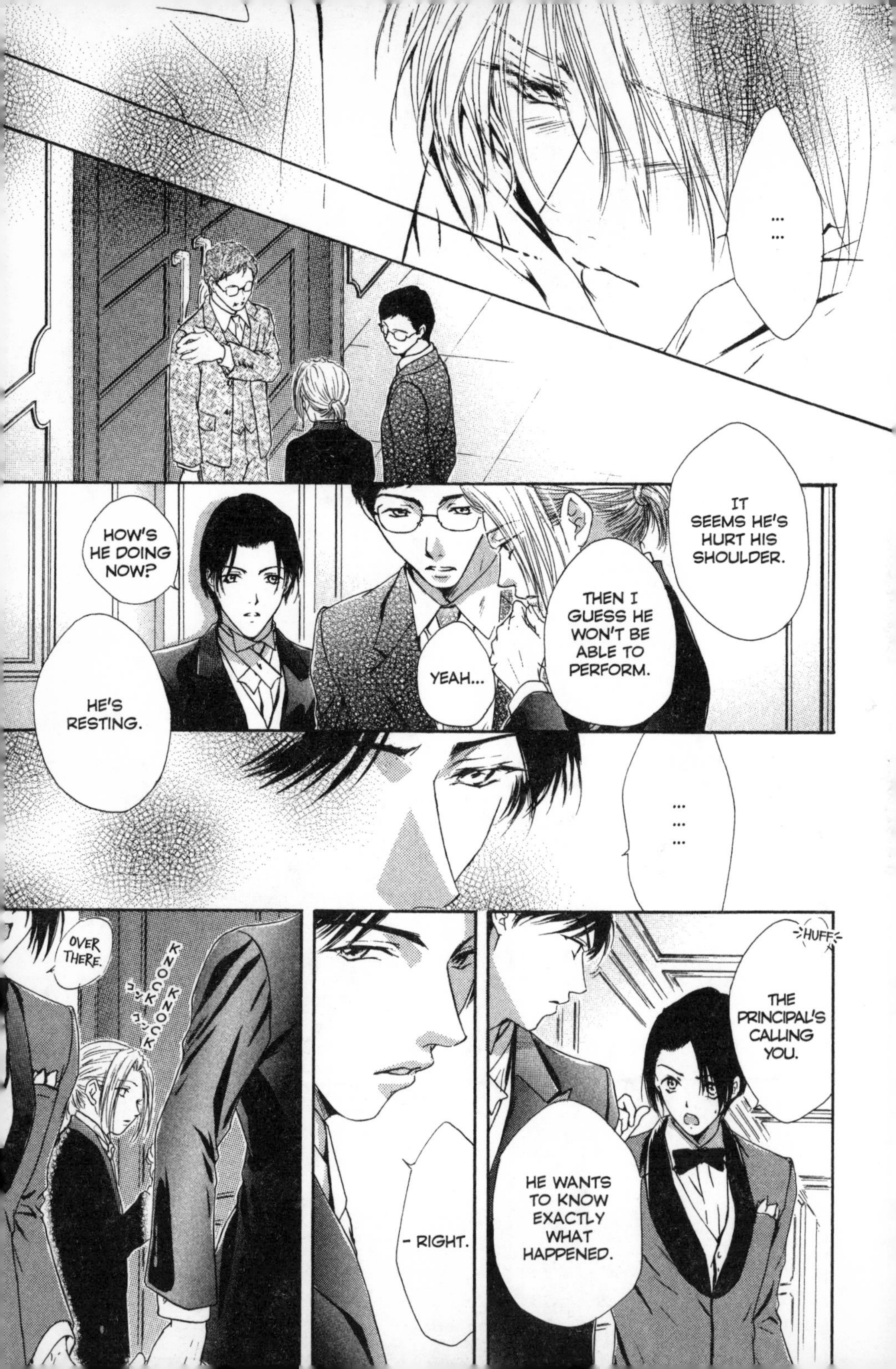

...
...
IT SEEMS HE'S HURT HIS SHOULDER.
THEN I GUESS HE WON'T BE ABLE TO PERFORM.
YEAH...
HOW'S HE DOING NOW?
HE'S RESTING.
...
...
...
HUFF
THE PRINCIPAL'S CALLING YOU.
HE WANTS TO KNOW EXACTLY WHAT HAPPENED.
- RIGHT.
OVER THERE.
KNOCK KNOCK

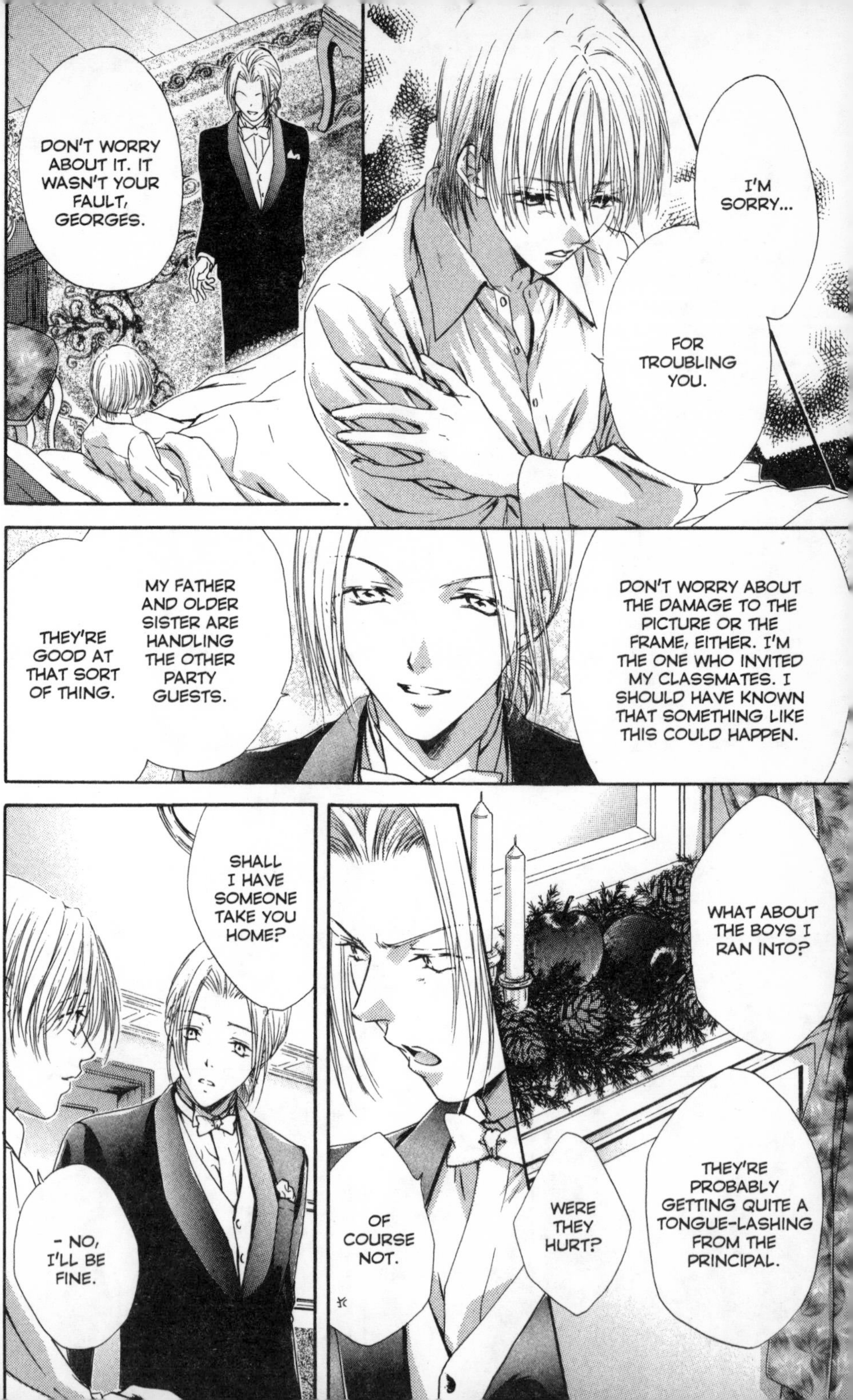
I'M SORRY...
FOR TROUBLING YOU.
DON'T WORRY ABOUT IT. IT WASN'T YOUR FAULT, GEORGES.
DON'T WORRY ABOUT THE DAMAGE TO THE PICTURE OR THE FRAME, EITHER. I'M THE ONE WHO INVITED MY CLASSMATES. I SHOULD HAVE KNOWN THAT SOMETHING LIKE THIS COULD HAPPEN.
MY FATHER AND OLDER SISTER ARE HANDLING THE OTHER PARTY GUESTS.
THEY'RE GOOD AT THAT SORT OF THING.
WHAT ABOUT THE BOYS I RAN INTO?
THEY'RE PROBABLY GETTING QUITE A TONGUE-LASHING FROM THE PRINCIPAL.
WERE THEY HURT?
OF COURSE NOT.
SHALL I HAVE SOMEONE TAKE YOU HOME?
- NO, I'LL BE FINE.

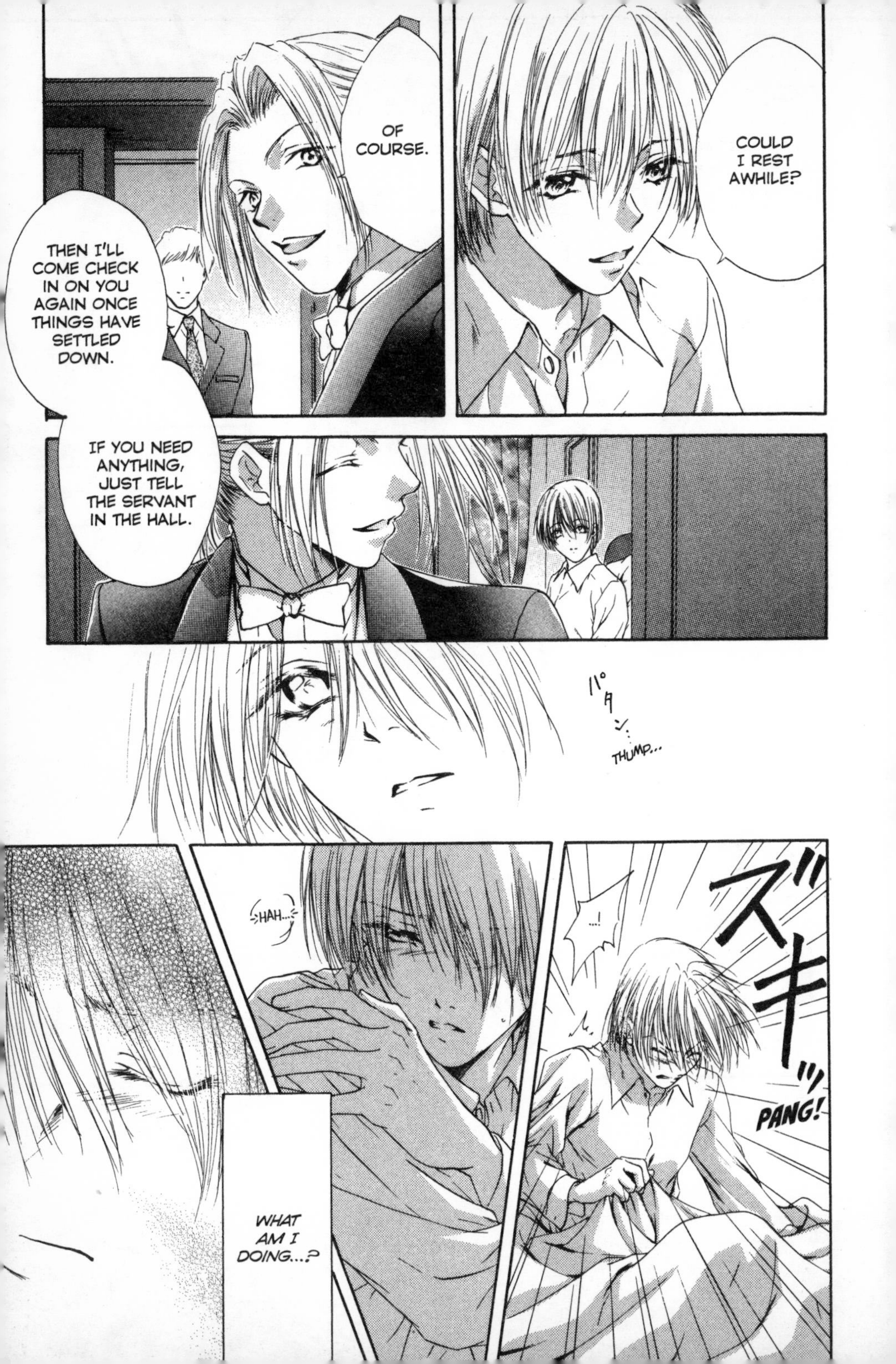
COULD I REST AWHILE?
OF COURSE.
THEN I'LL COME CHECK IN ON YOU AGAIN ONCE THINGS HAVE SETTLED DOWN.
IF YOU NEED ANYTHING, JUST TELL THE SERVANT IN THE HALL.
パタン…
THUMP...
ズキッ
PANG!
...!
HAH...
WHAT AM I DOING...?

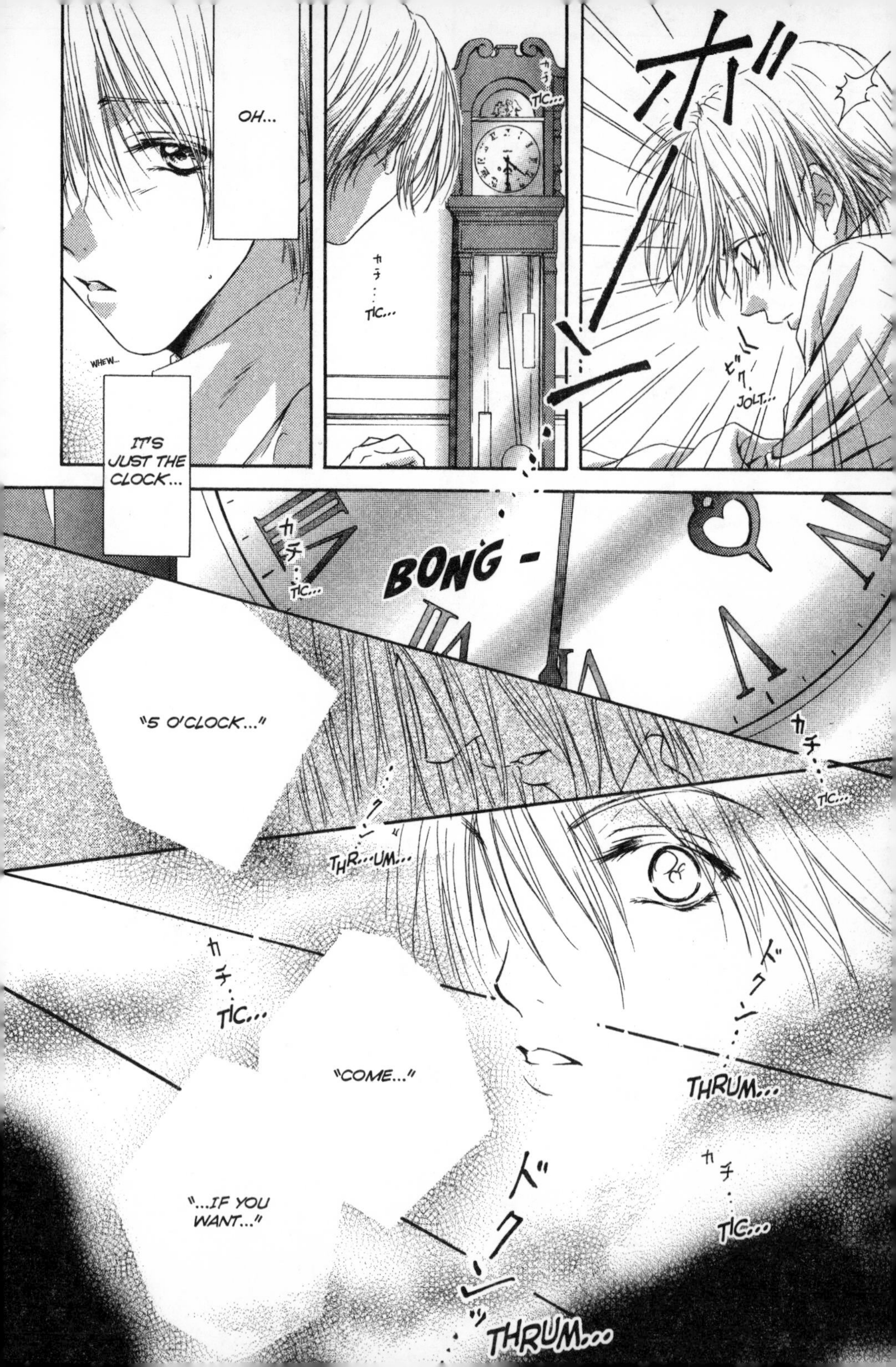

ボーン
ビク
JOLT...
カチ
TIC...
カチ...
TIC...
OH...
WHEW...
IT'S JUST THE CLOCK...
BONG -
カチ...
TIC...
"5 O'CLOCK..."
カチ...
TIC...
THR...UM...
カチ.
TIC...
THRUM...
"COME..."
"...IF YOU WANT..."
カチ...
TIC...
ドクン
THRUM...

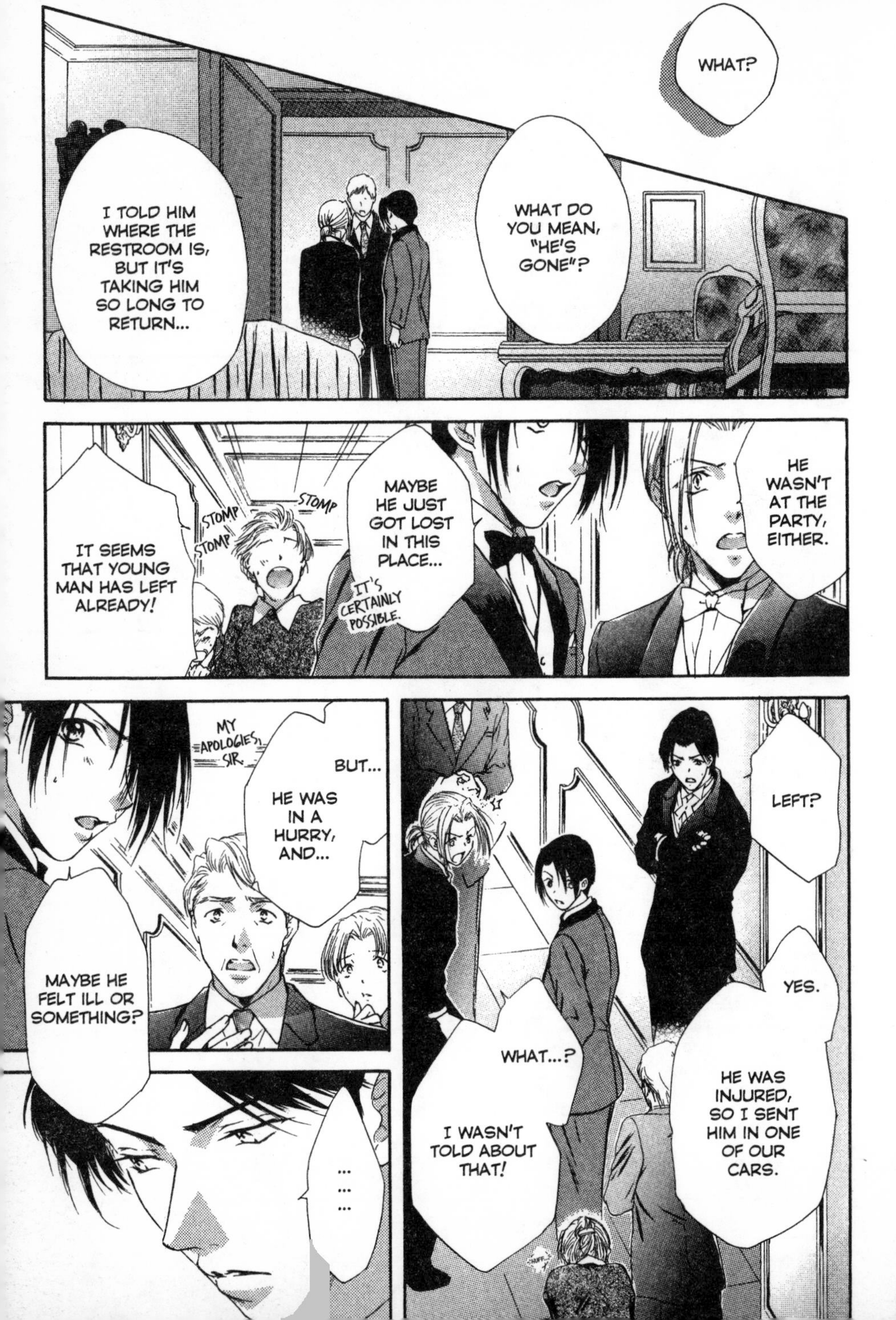
WHAT?
WHAT DO YOU MEAN, "HE'S GONE"?
I TOLD HIM WHERE THE RESTROOM IS, BUT IT'S TAKING HIM SO LONG TO RETURN...
HE WASN'T AT THE PARTY, EITHER.
MAYBE HE JUST GOT LOST IN THIS PLACE...
IT'S CERTAINLY POSSIBLE.
STOMP
STOMP
STOMP
IT SEEMS THAT YOUNG MAN HAS LEFT ALREADY!
LEFT?
YES.
HE WAS INJURED, SO I SENT HIM IN ONE OF OUR CARS.
WHAT...?
I WASN'T TOLD ABOUT THAT!
MY APOLOGIES, SIR.
BUT...
HE WAS IN A HURRY, AND...
MAYBE HE FELT ILL OR SOMETHING?
... ...

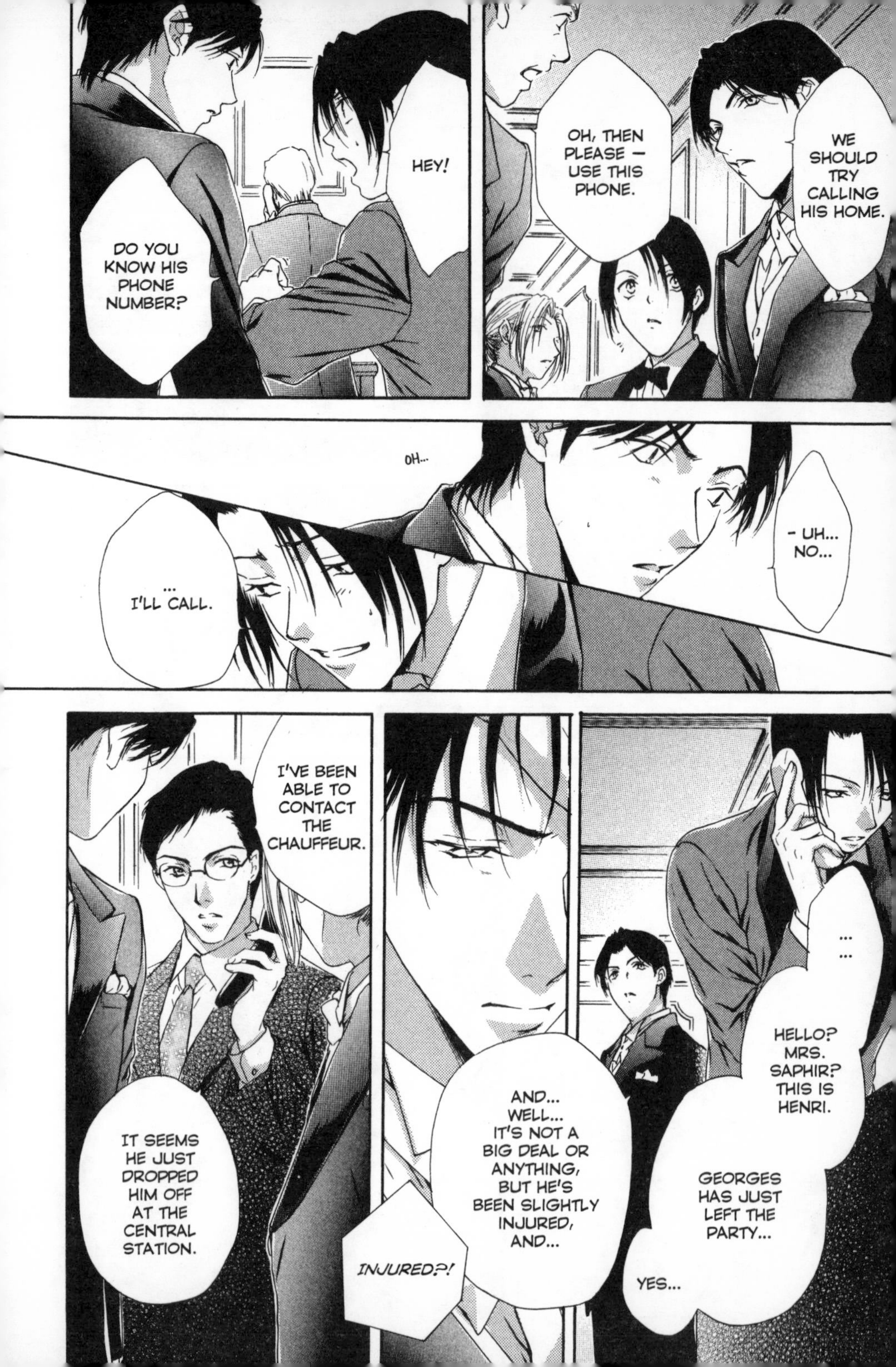
WE SHOULD TRY CALLING HIS HOME.
OH, THEN PLEASE — USE THIS PHONE.
HEY!
DO YOU KNOW HIS PHONE NUMBER?
- UH... NO...
OH...
... I'LL CALL.
... ...
HELLO? MRS. SAPHIR? THIS IS HENRI.
GEORGES HAS JUST LEFT THE PARTY...
YES...
AND... WELL... IT'S NOT A BIG DEAL OR ANYTHING, BUT HE'S BEEN SLIGHTLY INJURED, AND...
INJURED?!
I'VE BEEN ABLE TO CONTACT THE CHAUFFEUR.
IT SEEMS HE JUST DROPPED HIM OFF AT THE CENTRAL STATION.

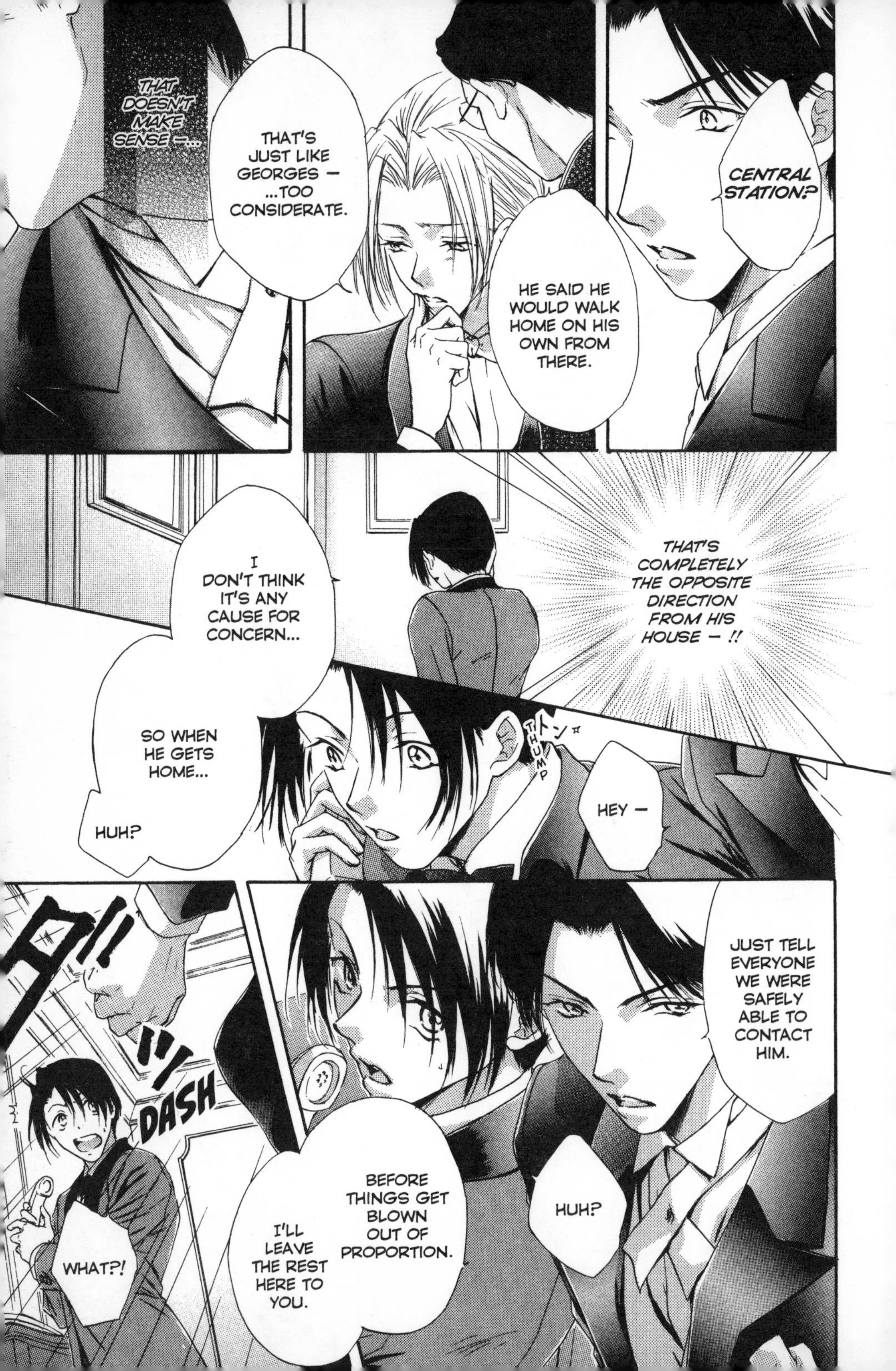
CENTRAL STATION?
HE SAID HE WOULD WALK HOME ON HIS OWN FROM THERE.
THAT'S JUST LIKE GEORGES — ...TOO CONSIDERATE.
THAT DOESN'T MAKE SENSE —...
THAT'S COMPLETELY THE OPPOSITE DIRECTION FROM HIS HOUSE — !!
I DON'T THINK IT'S ANY CAUSE FOR CONCERN...
SO WHEN HE GETS HOME...
HEY —
THUMP
HUH?
JUST TELL EVERYONE WE WERE SAFELY ABLE TO CONTACT HIM.
HUH?
BEFORE THINGS GET BLOWN OUT OF PROPORTION.
I'LL LEAVE THE REST HERE TO YOU.
DASH
WHAT?!

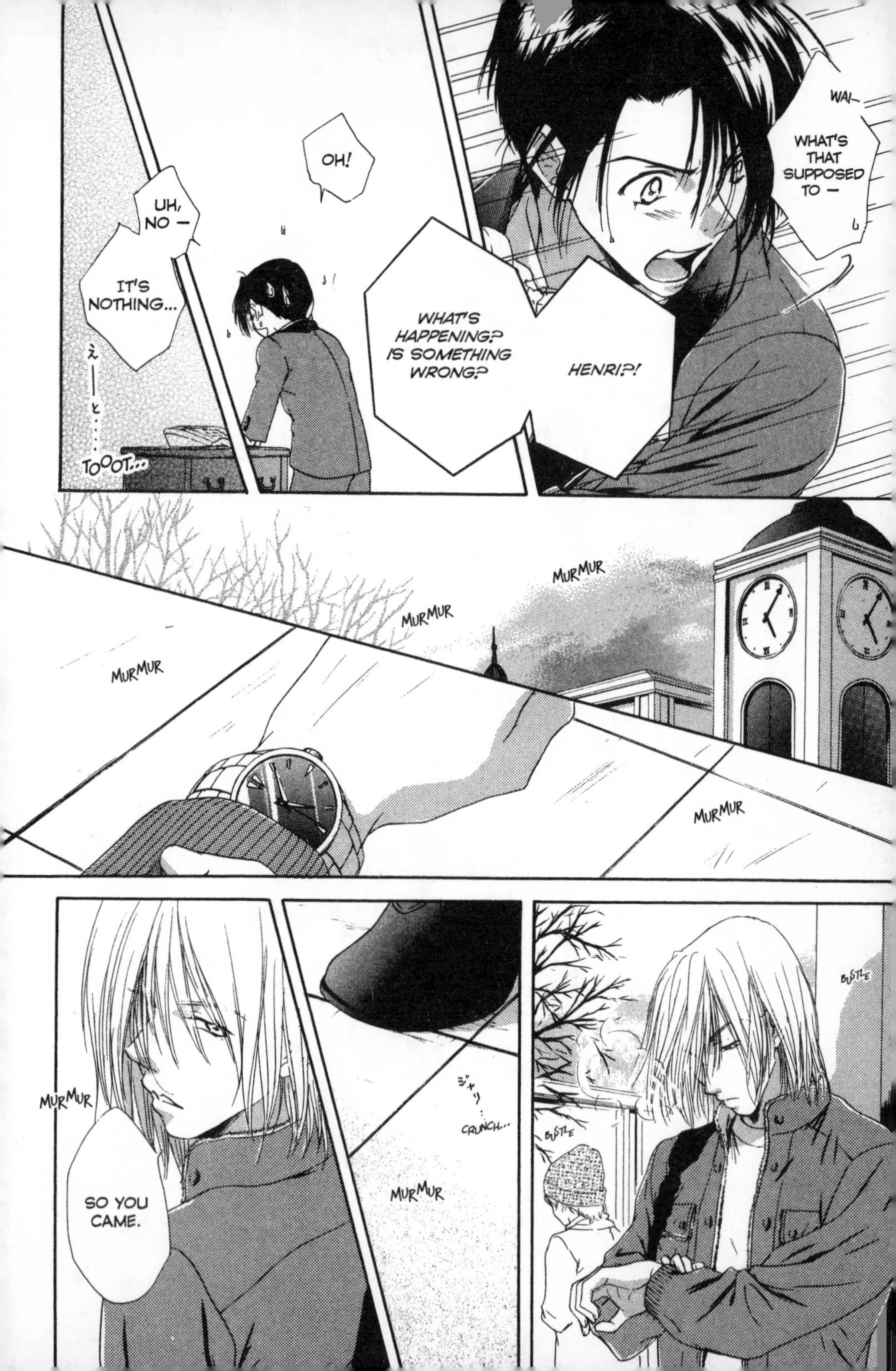
WAI—
WHAT'S THAT SUPPOSED TO —
HENRI?!
WHAT'S HAPPENING? IS SOMETHING WRONG?
OH!
UH, NO —
IT'S NOTHING...
えーーと・・・
TOOOT...
MURMUR
MURMUR
MURMUR
MURMUR
BUSTLE
BUSTLE
ジャリ…
CRUNCH...
MURMUR
MURMUR
SO YOU CAME.

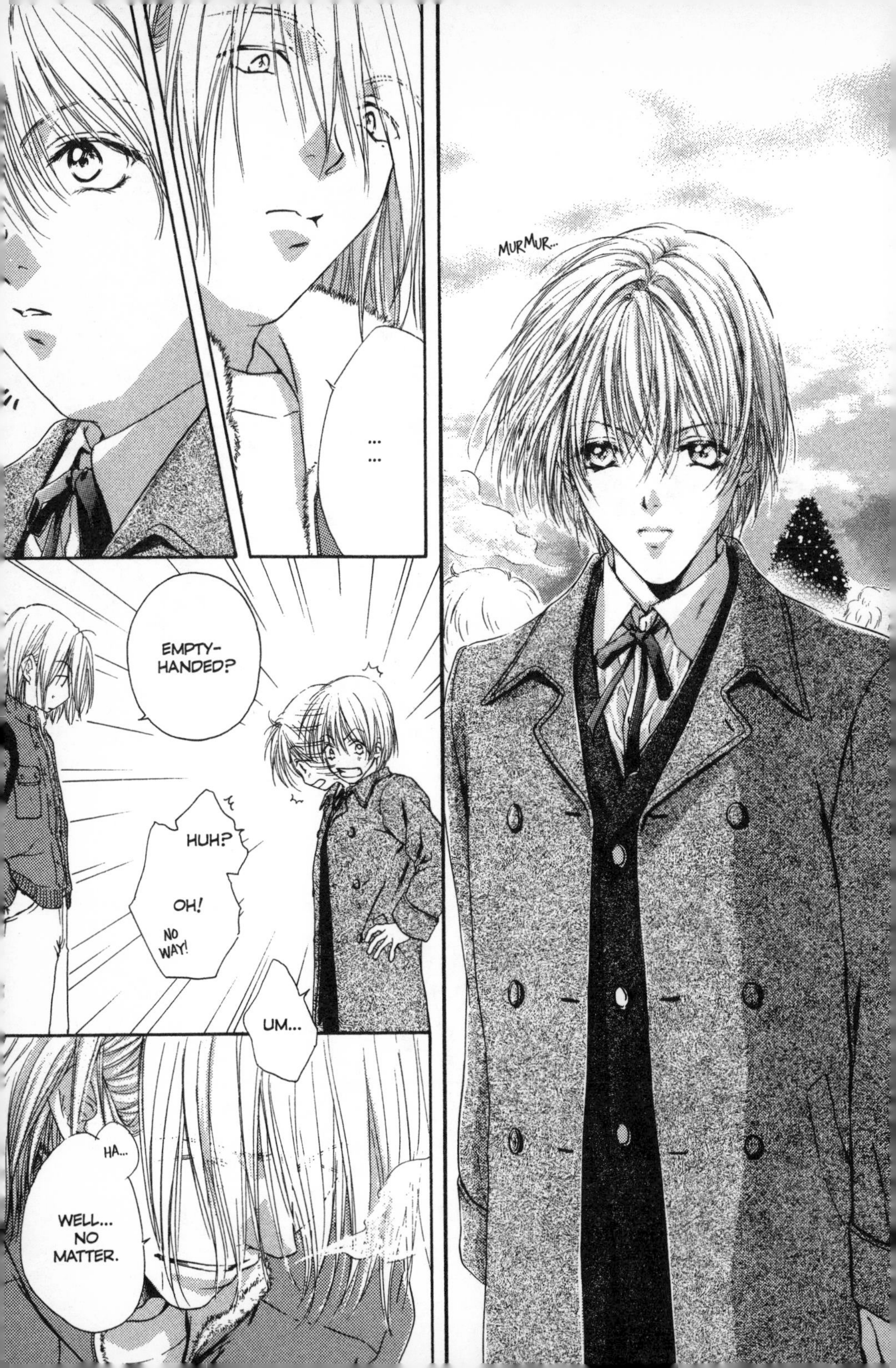
MURMUR...
...
...
EMPTY-HANDED?
HUH?
OH!
NO WAY!
UM...
HA...
WELL... NO MATTER.

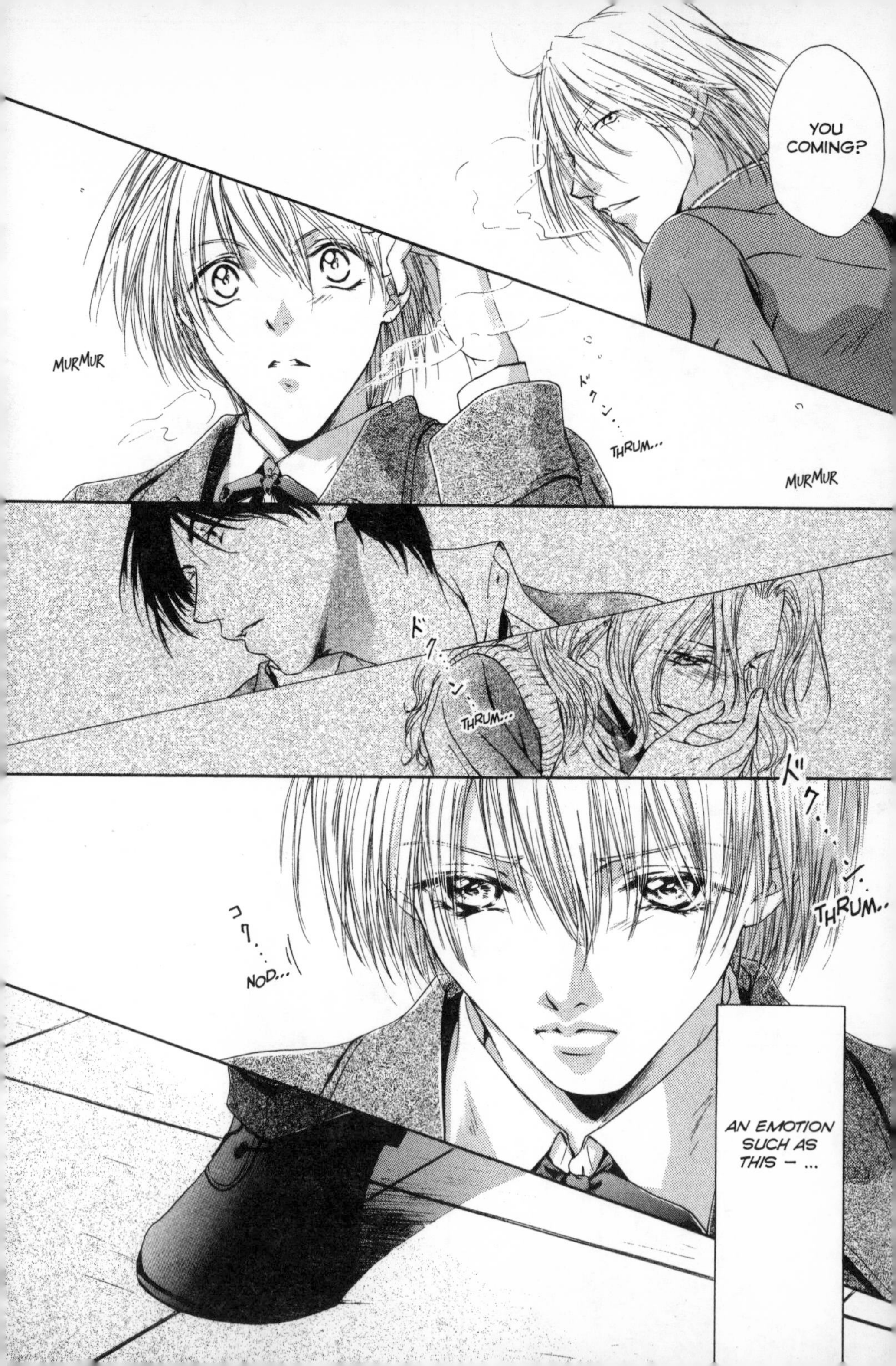
YOU COMING?
ドクン…
THRUM...
MURMUR
MURMUR
ドクン…
THRUM...
ドクン…
THRUM...
コク…
NOD...
AN EMOTION SUCH AS THIS – ...

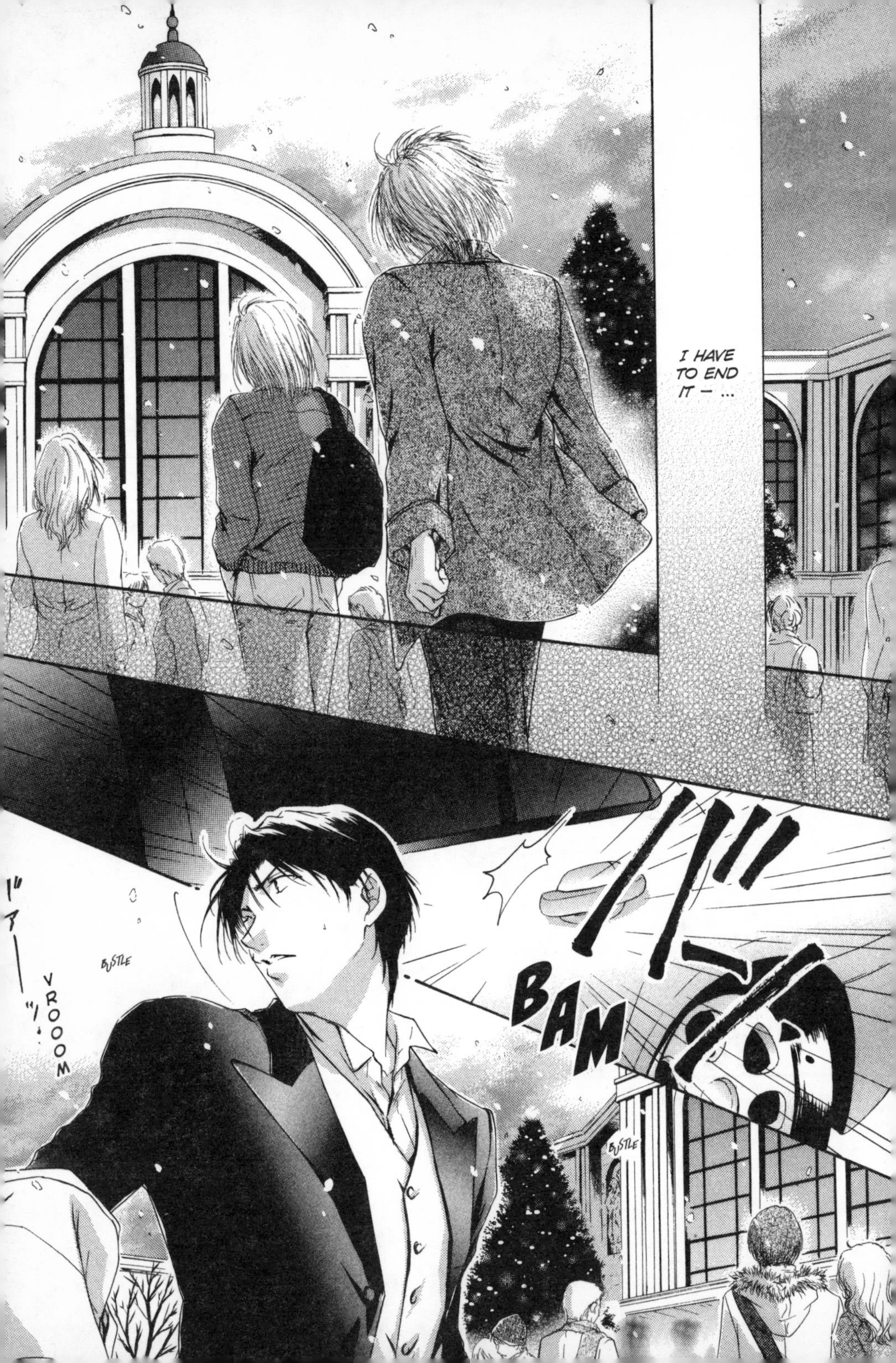
I HAVE TO END IT — ...
BAM
BUSTLE
VROOOM
BUSTLE

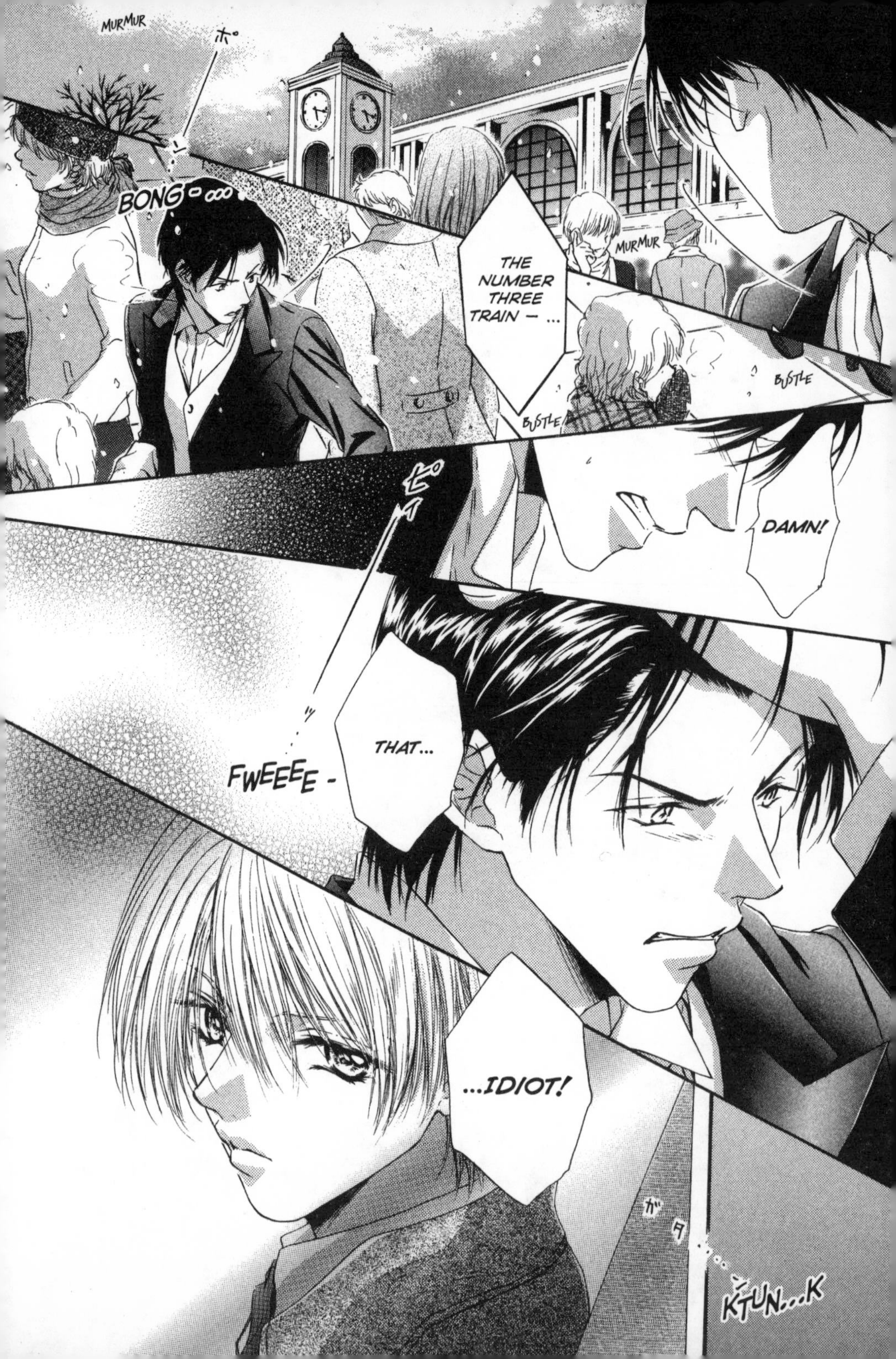

MURMUR
THE NUMBER THREE TRAIN — ...
BUSTLE
BUSTLE
MURMUR
ポ
ン
BONG-...
DAMN!
ピー
ッ
FWEEEE -
THAT...
...IDIOT!
ガタ
KTUN...K

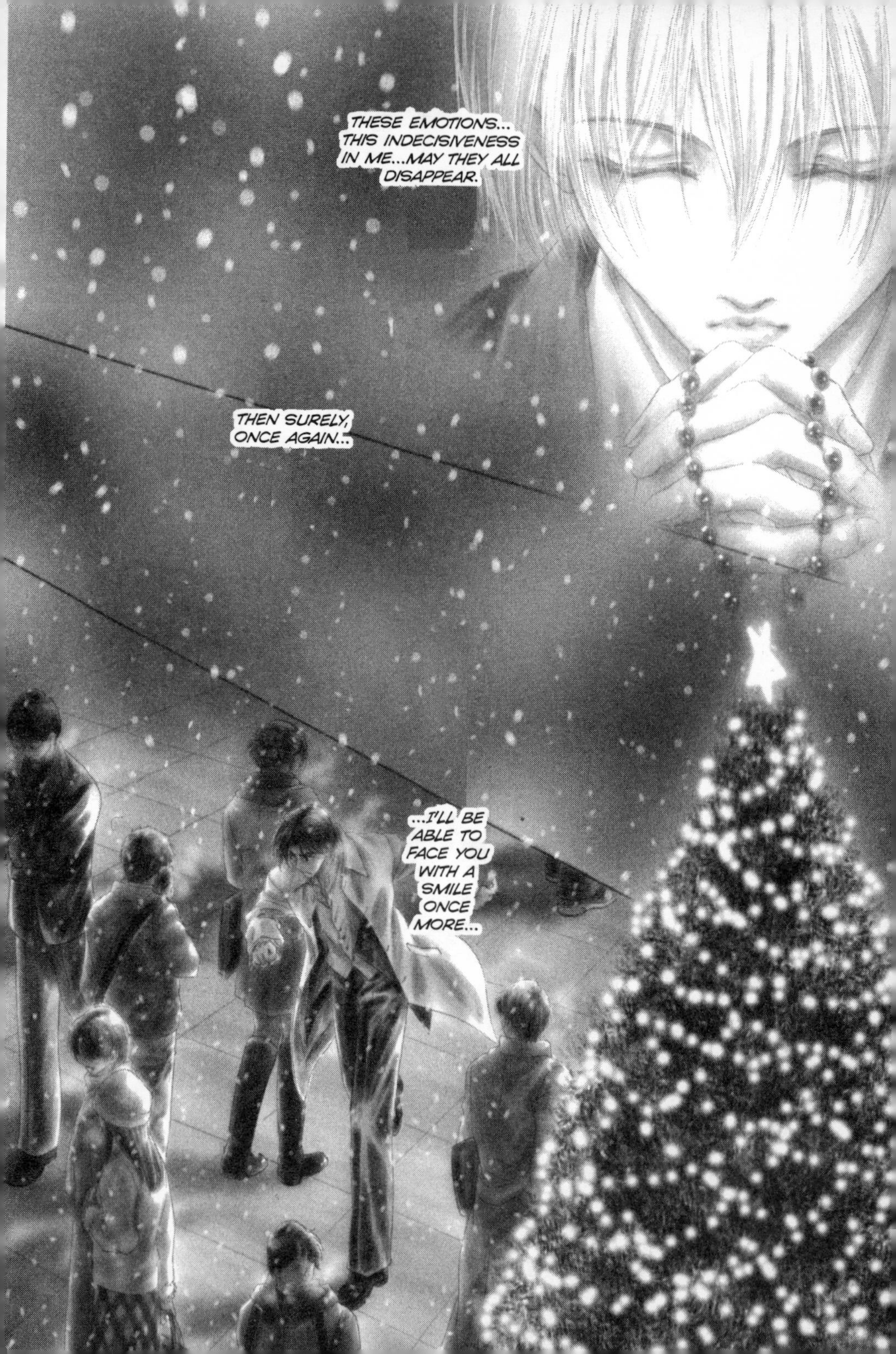
THESE EMOTIONS... THIS INDECISIVENESS IN ME...MAY THEY ALL DISAPPEAR.
THEN SURELY, ONCE AGAIN...
...I'LL BE ABLE TO FACE YOU WITH A SMILE ONCE MORE...

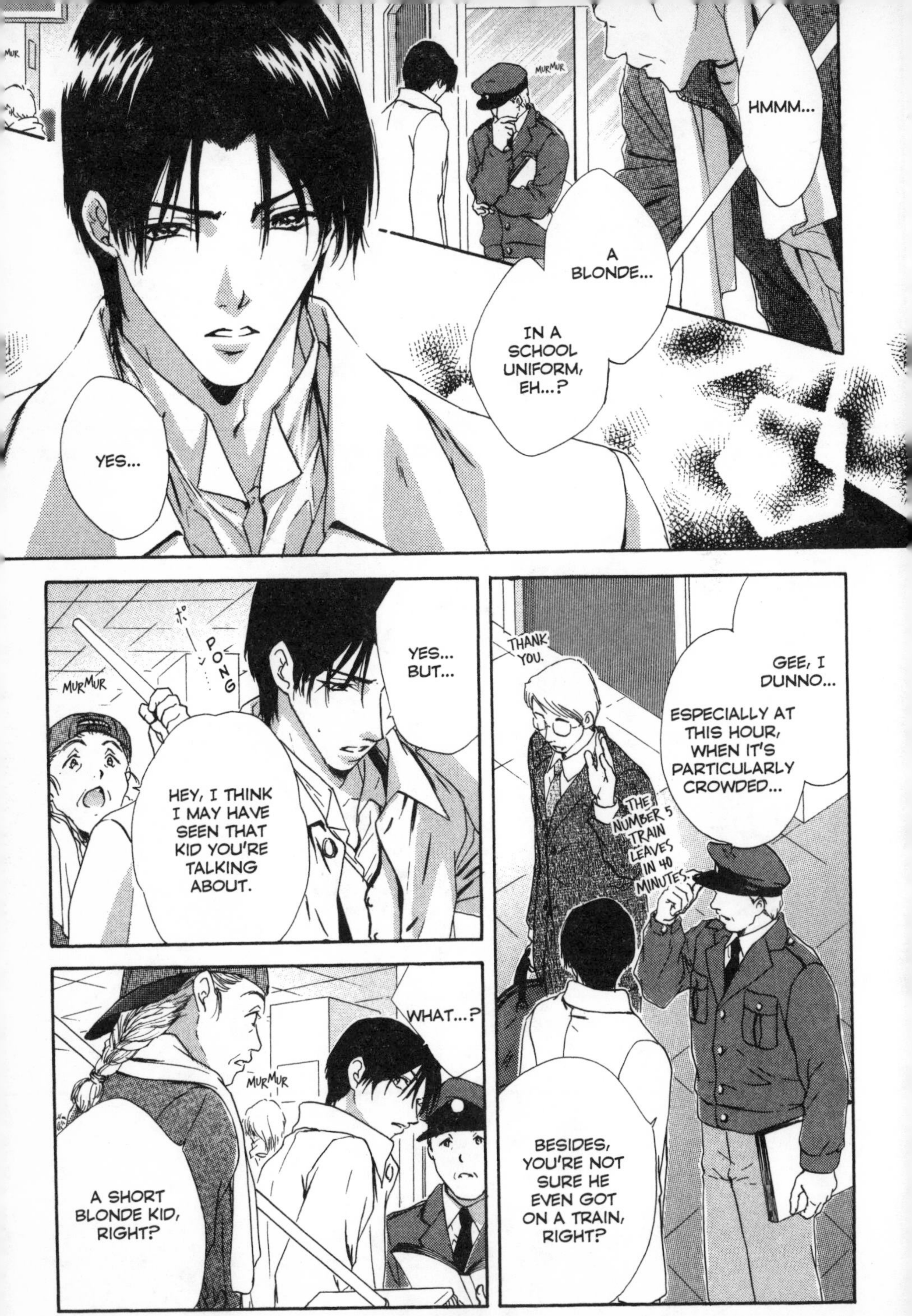
MURMUR
HMMM...
A BLONDE...
IN A SCHOOL UNIFORM, EH...?
YES...
GEE, I DUNNO...
ESPECIALLY AT THIS HOUR, WHEN IT'S PARTICULARLY CROWDED...
THANK YOU.
THE NUMBER 5 TRAIN LEAVES IN 40 MINUTES.
BESIDES, YOU'RE NOT SURE HE EVEN GOT ON A TRAIN, RIGHT?
YES... BUT...
PONG
MURMUR
HEY, I THINK I MAY HAVE SEEN THAT KID YOU'RE TALKING ABOUT.
WHAT...?
MURMUR
A SHORT BLONDE KID, RIGHT?

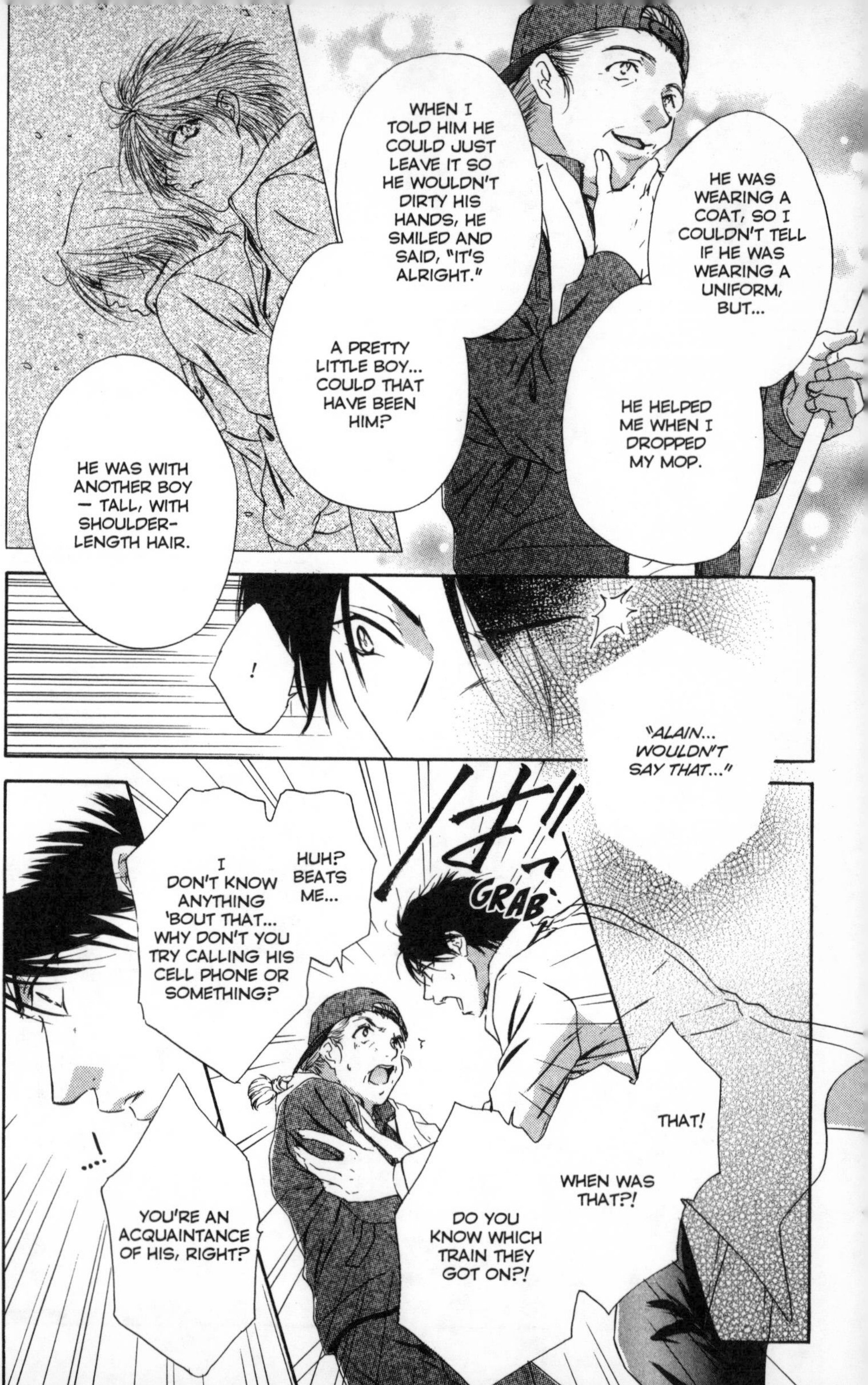
HE WAS WEARING A COAT, SO I COULDN'T TELL IF HE WAS WEARING A UNIFORM, BUT...
HE HELPED ME WHEN I DROPPED MY MOP.
WHEN I TOLD HIM HE COULD JUST LEAVE IT SO HE WOULDN'T DIRTY HIS HANDS, HE SMILED AND SAID, "IT'S ALRIGHT."
A PRETTY LITTLE BOY... COULD THAT HAVE BEEN HIM?
HE WAS WITH ANOTHER BOY — TALL, WITH SHOULDER-LENGTH HAIR.
"ALAIN... WOULDN'T SAY THAT..."
!
GRAB
THAT!
WHEN WAS THAT?!
DO YOU KNOW WHICH TRAIN THEY GOT ON?!
HUH? BEATS ME...
I DON'T KNOW ANYTHING 'BOUT THAT... WHY DON'T YOU TRY CALLING HIS CELL PHONE OR SOMETHING?
...!
YOU'RE AN ACQUAINTANCE OF HIS, RIGHT?

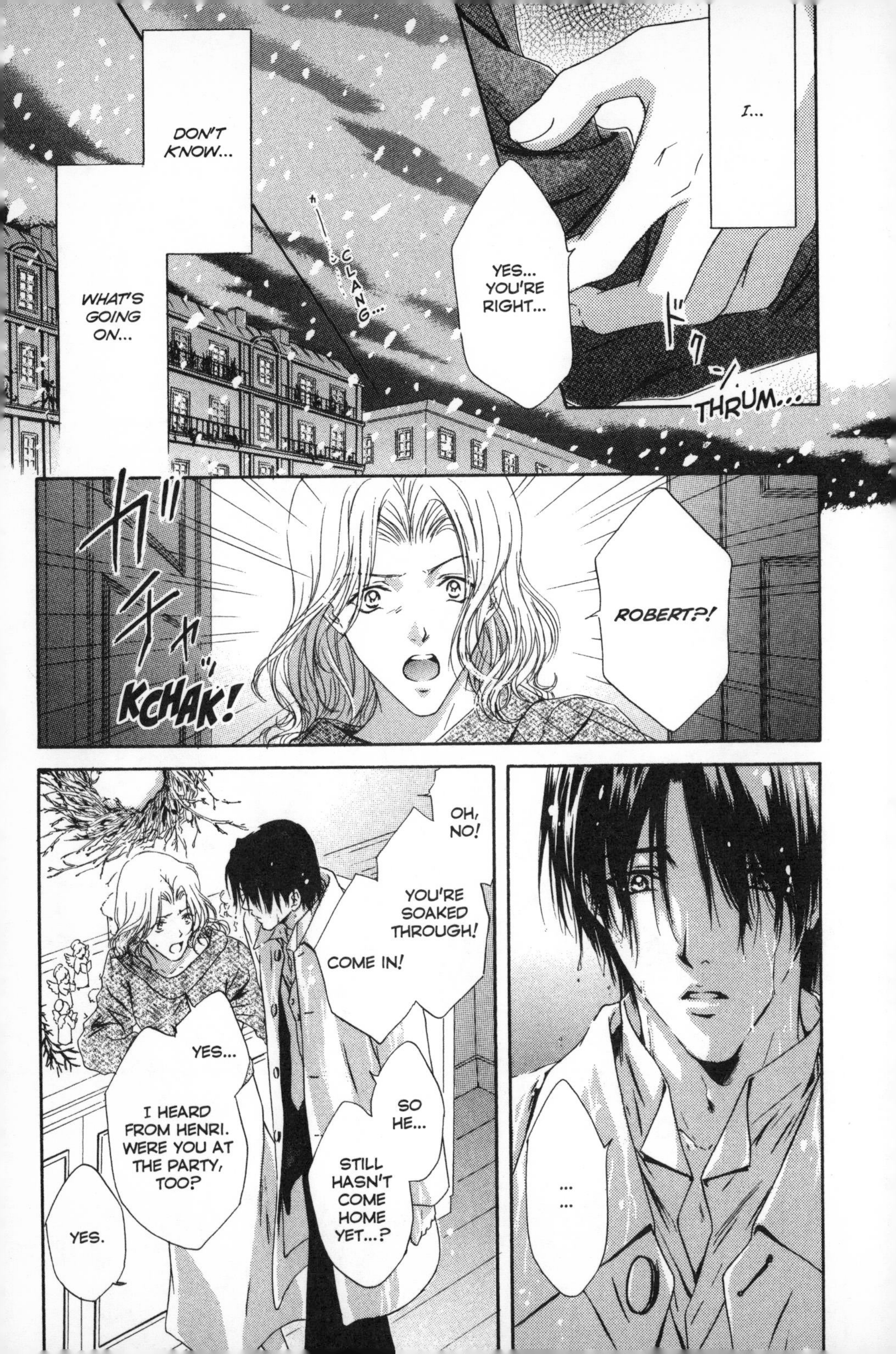
I...
YES... YOU'RE RIGHT...
THRUM...
CLANG...
DON'T KNOW...
WHAT'S GOING ON...
ROBERT?!
KCHAK!
... ...
OH, NO!
YOU'RE SOAKED THROUGH!
COME IN!
SO HE...
STILL HASN'T COME HOME YET...?
YES...
I HEARD FROM HENRI. WERE YOU AT THE PARTY, TOO?
YES.

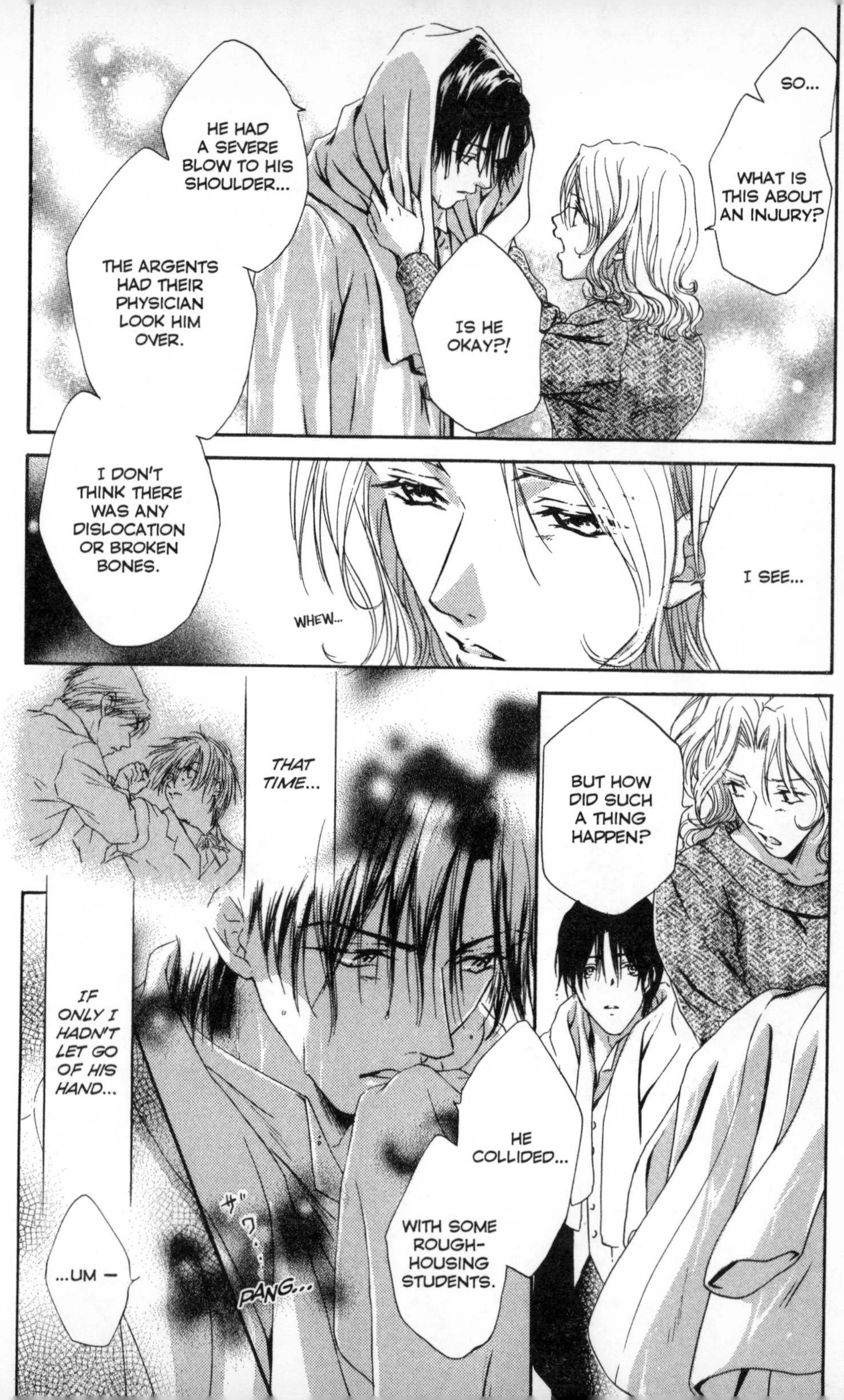
SO...
WHAT IS THIS ABOUT AN INJURY?
IS HE OKAY?!
HE HAD A SEVERE BLOW TO HIS SHOULDER...
THE ARGENTS HAD THEIR PHYSICIAN LOOK HIM OVER.
I DON'T THINK THERE WAS ANY DISLOCATION OR BROKEN BONES.
WHEW...
I SEE...
BUT HOW DID SUCH A THING HAPPEN?
THAT TIME...
HE COLLIDED...
WITH SOME ROUGH-HOUSING STUDENTS.
ザワ...
PANG...
IF ONLY I HADN'T LET GO OF HIS HAND...
...UM —

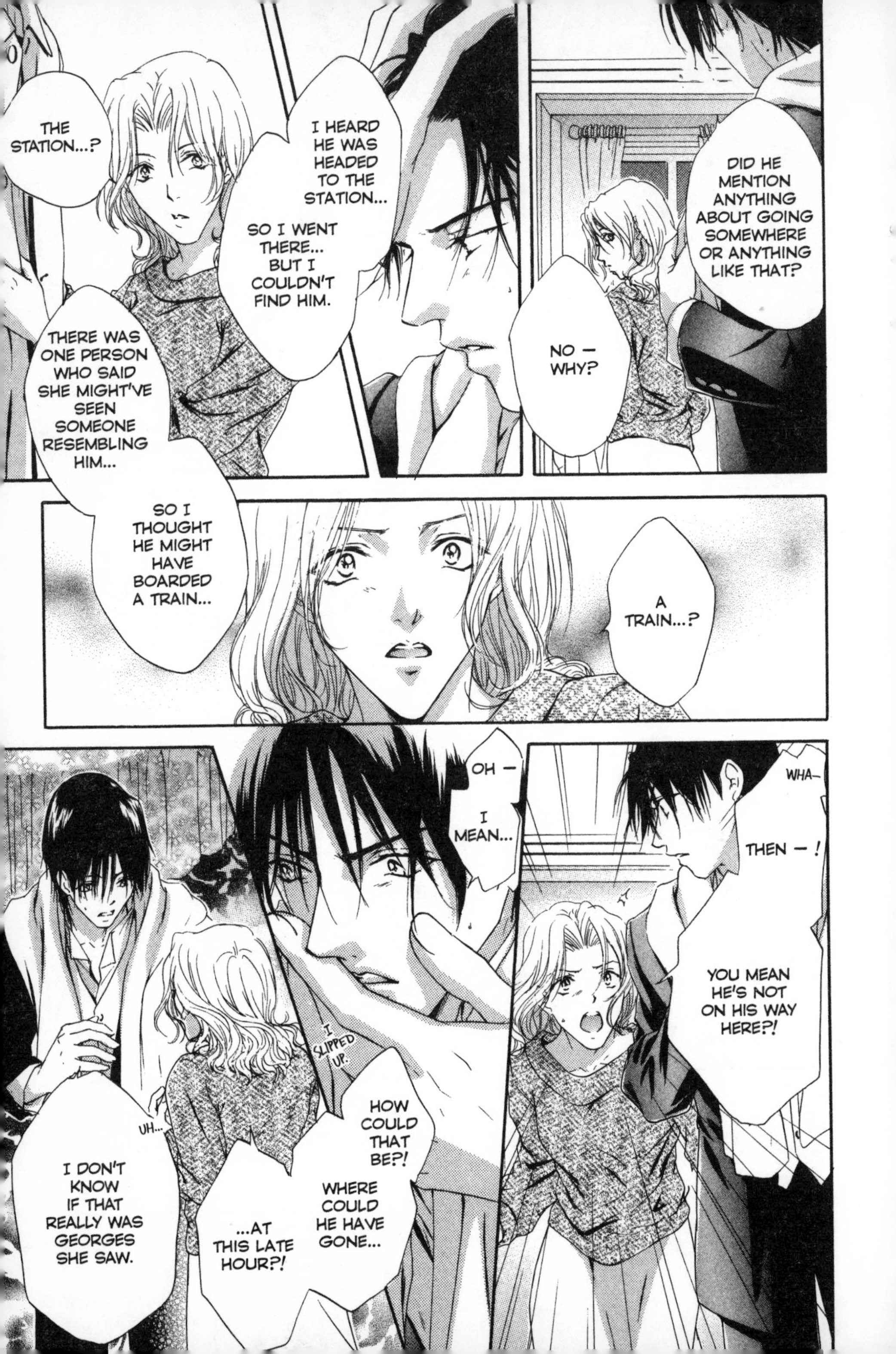
DID HE MENTION ANYTHING ABOUT GOING SOMEWHERE OR ANYTHING LIKE THAT?
NO — WHY?
I HEARD HE WAS HEADED TO THE STATION...
SO I WENT THERE... BUT I COULDN'T FIND HIM.
THE STATION...?
THERE WAS ONE PERSON WHO SAID SHE MIGHT'VE SEEN SOMEONE RESEMBLING HIM...
SO I THOUGHT HE MIGHT HAVE BOARDED A TRAIN...
A TRAIN...?
WHA-
THEN —!
YOU MEAN HE'S NOT ON HIS WAY HERE?!
OH —
I MEAN...
I SLIPPED UP.
HOW COULD THAT BE?!
WHERE COULD HE HAVE GONE...
...AT THIS LATE HOUR?!
UH...
I DON'T KNOW IF THAT REALLY WAS GEORGES SHE SAW.

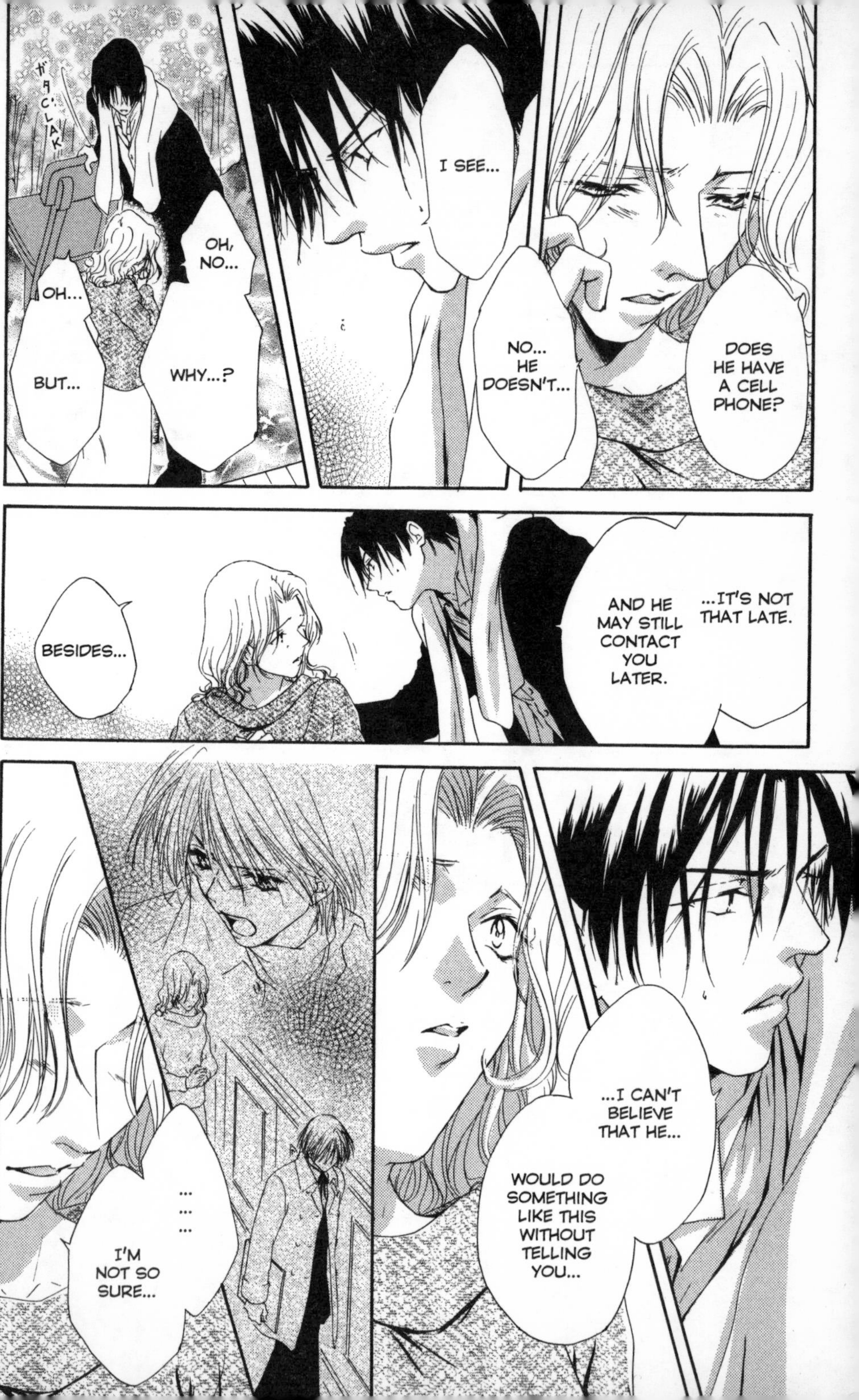
DOES HE HAVE A CELL PHONE?
NO... HE DOESN'T...
I SEE...
ガタッ CLAK
OH, NO...
WHY...?
OH...
BUT...
...IT'S NOT THAT LATE.
AND HE MAY STILL CONTACT YOU LATER.
BESIDES...
...I CAN'T BELIEVE THAT HE...
WOULD DO SOMETHING LIKE THIS WITHOUT TELLING YOU...
......
I'M NOT SO SURE...

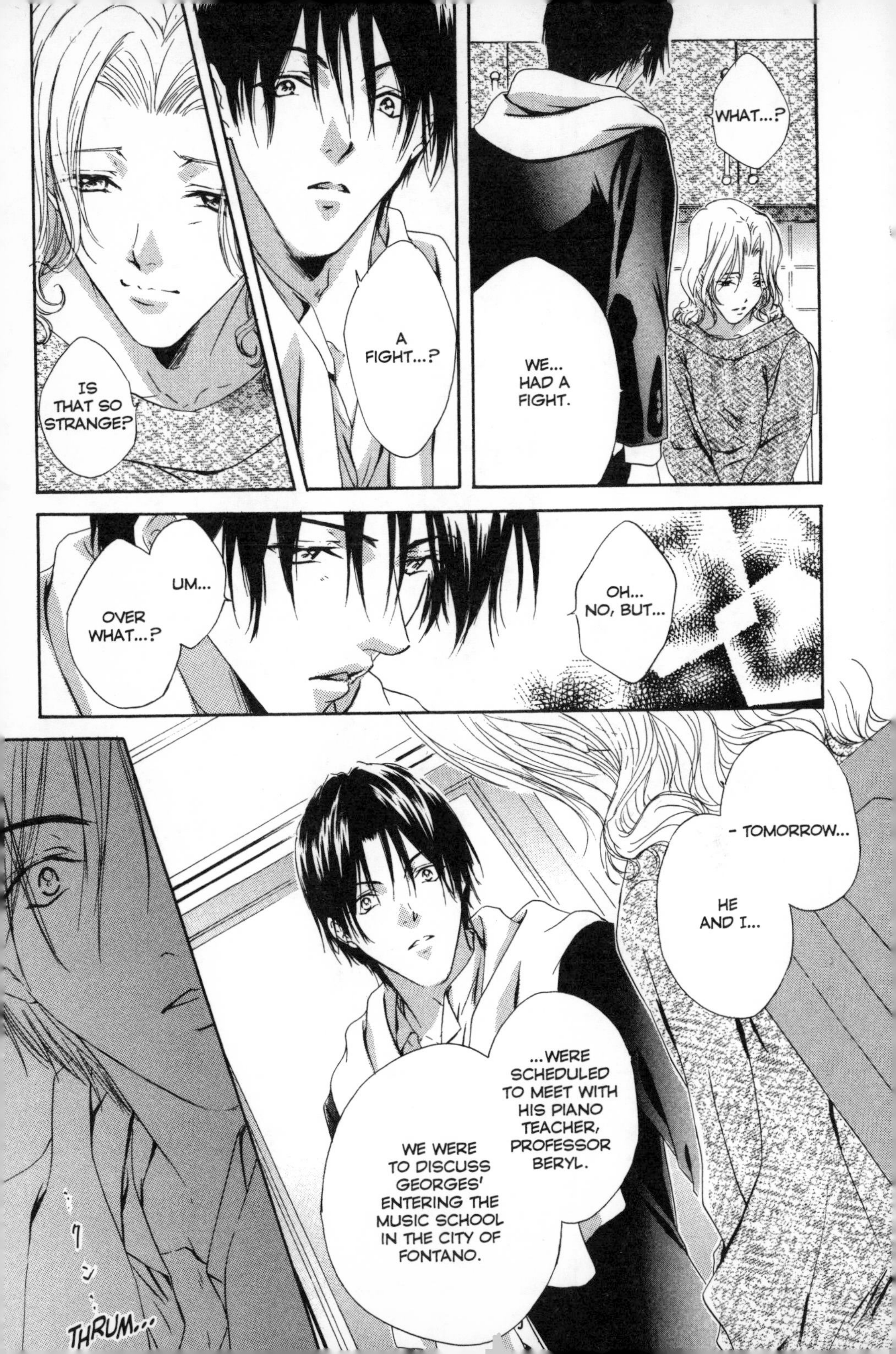
WHAT...?
WE... HAD A FIGHT.
A FIGHT...?
IS THAT SO STRANGE?
OH... NO, BUT...
UM... OVER WHAT...?
- TOMORROW... HE AND I...
...WERE SCHEDULED TO MEET WITH HIS PIANO TEACHER, PROFESSOR BERYL.
WE WERE TO DISCUSS GEORGES' ENTERING THE MUSIC SCHOOL IN THE CITY OF FONTANO.
THRUM...

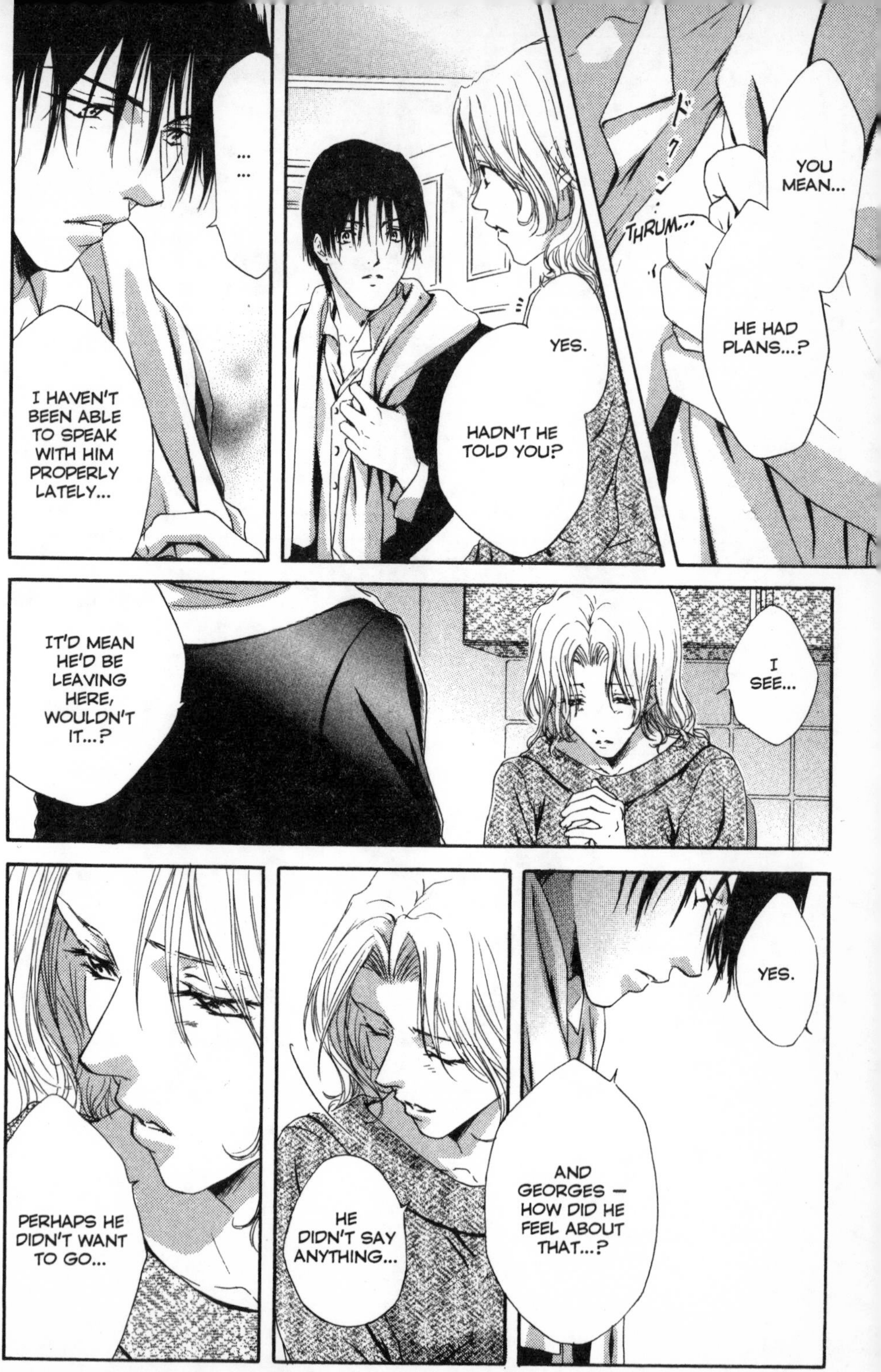
YOU MEAN...
ドクン…
THRUM...
HE HAD PLANS...?
YES.
HADN'T HE TOLD YOU?
...
...
I HAVEN'T BEEN ABLE TO SPEAK WITH HIM PROPERLY LATELY...
I SEE...
IT'D MEAN HE'D BE LEAVING HERE, WOULDN'T IT...?
YES.
AND GEORGES — HOW DID HE FEEL ABOUT THAT...?
HE DIDN'T SAY ANYTHING...
PERHAPS HE DIDN'T WANT TO GO...

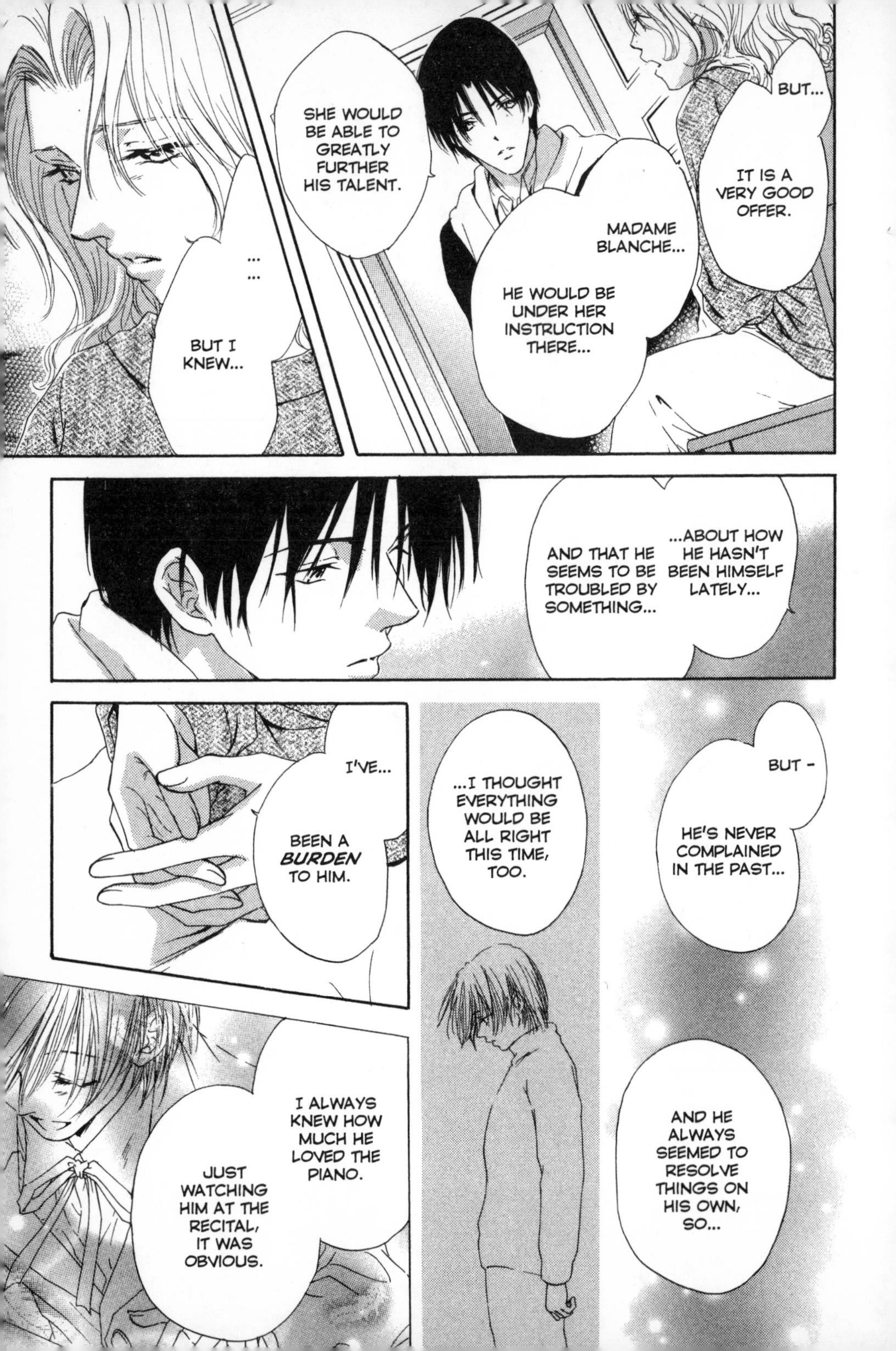
BUT...
IT IS A VERY GOOD OFFER.
MADAME BLANCHE...
HE WOULD BE UNDER HER INSTRUCTION THERE...
SHE WOULD BE ABLE TO GREATLY FURTHER HIS TALENT.
......
BUT I KNEW...
...ABOUT HOW HE HASN'T BEEN HIMSELF LATELY...
AND THAT HE SEEMS TO BE TROUBLED BY SOMETHING...
BUT -
HE'S NEVER COMPLAINED IN THE PAST...
AND HE ALWAYS SEEMED TO RESOLVE THINGS ON HIS OWN, SO...
...I THOUGHT EVERYTHING WOULD BE ALL RIGHT THIS TIME, TOO.
I'VE...
BEEN A *BURDEN* TO HIM.
I ALWAYS KNEW HOW MUCH HE LOVED THE PIANO.
JUST WATCHING HIM AT THE RECITAL, IT WAS OBVIOUS.

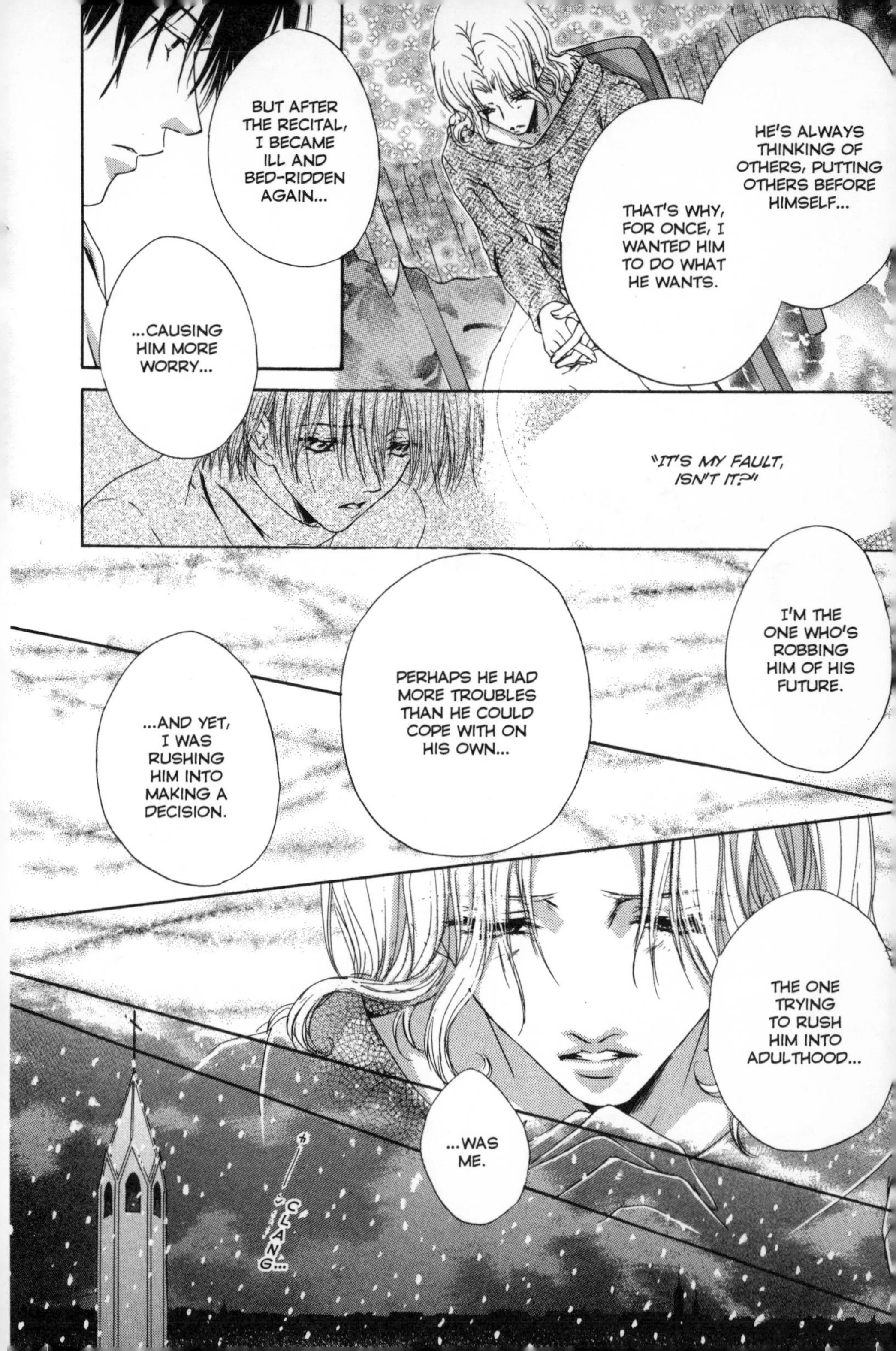
HE'S ALWAYS THINKING OF OTHERS, PUTTING OTHERS BEFORE HIMSELF...
THAT'S WHY, FOR ONCE, I WANTED HIM TO DO WHAT HE WANTS.
BUT AFTER THE RECITAL, I BECAME ILL AND BED-RIDDEN AGAIN...
...CAUSING HIM MORE WORRY...
"IT'S MY FAULT, ISN'T IT?"
I'M THE ONE WHO'S ROBBING HIM OF HIS FUTURE.
PERHAPS HE HAD MORE TROUBLES THAN HE COULD COPE WITH ON HIS OWN...
...AND YET, I WAS RUSHING HIM INTO MAKING A DECISION.
THE ONE TRYING TO RUSH HIM INTO ADULTHOOD...
...WAS ME.
CLANG...

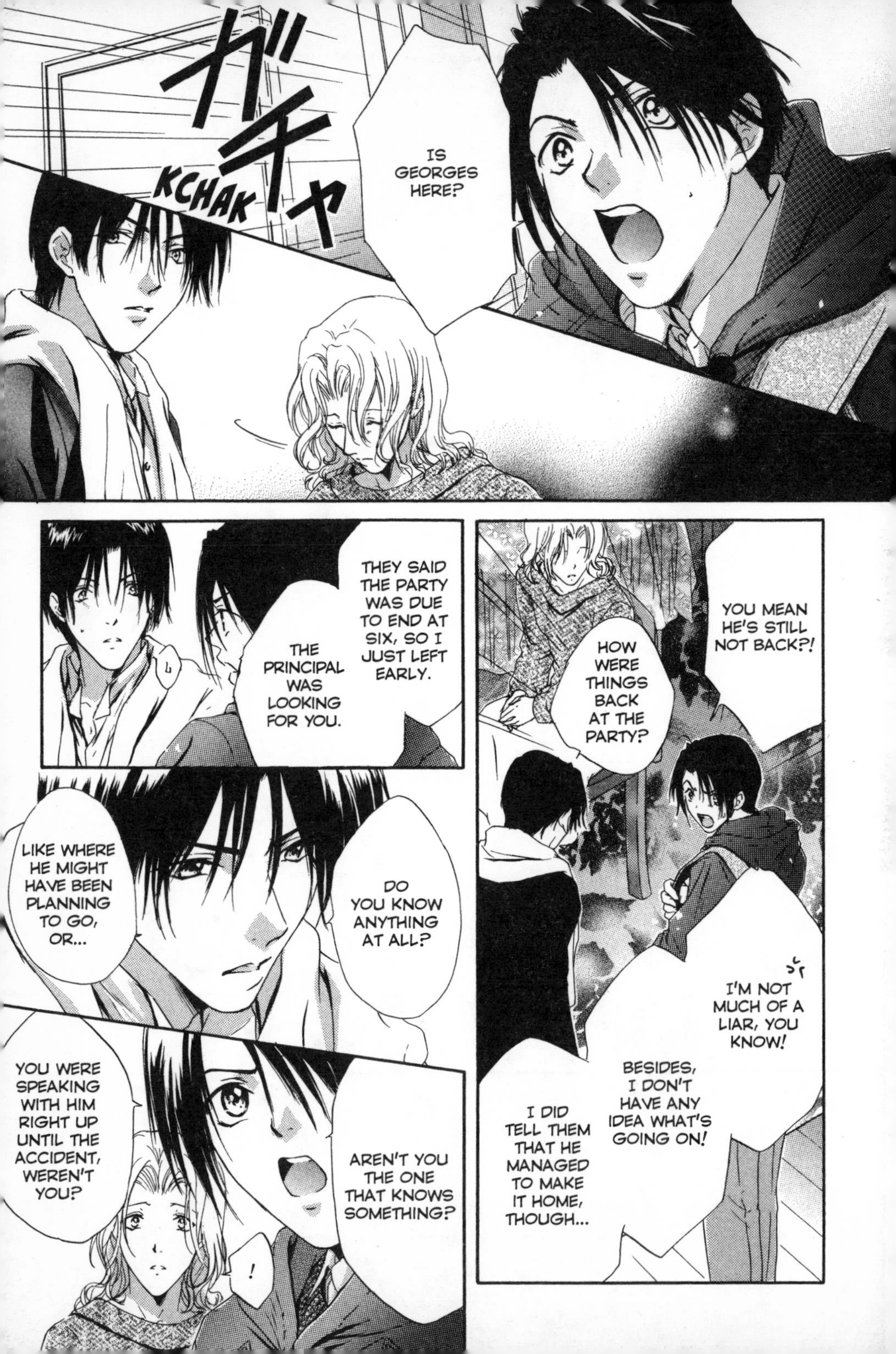

IS GEORGES HERE?
ガチャ
KCHAK
YOU MEAN HE'S STILL NOT BACK?!
HOW WERE THINGS BACK AT THE PARTY?
I'M NOT MUCH OF A LIAR, YOU KNOW!
BESIDES, I DON'T HAVE ANY IDEA WHAT'S GOING ON!
I DID TELL THEM THAT HE MANAGED TO MAKE IT HOME, THOUGH...
THEY SAID THE PARTY WAS DUE TO END AT SIX, SO I JUST LEFT EARLY.
THE PRINCIPAL WAS LOOKING FOR YOU.
DO YOU KNOW ANYTHING AT ALL?
LIKE WHERE HE MIGHT HAVE BEEN PLANNING TO GO, OR...
AREN'T YOU THE ONE THAT KNOWS SOMETHING?
YOU WERE SPEAKING WITH HIM RIGHT UP UNTIL THE ACCIDENT, WEREN'T YOU?
!

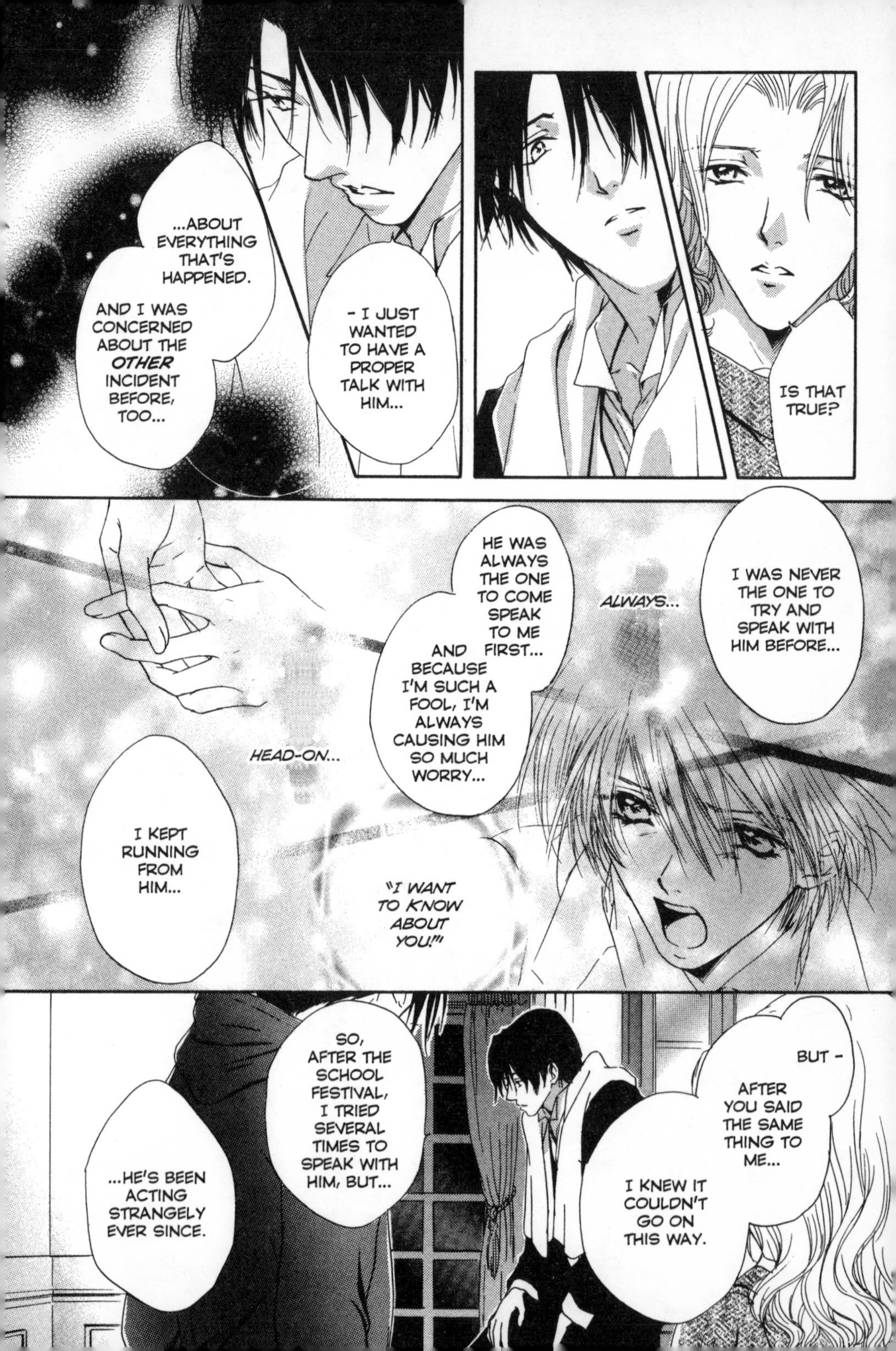
IS THAT TRUE?
- I JUST WANTED TO HAVE A PROPER TALK WITH HIM...
...ABOUT EVERYTHING THAT'S HAPPENED.
AND I WAS CONCERNED ABOUT THE *OTHER* INCIDENT BEFORE, TOO...
I WAS NEVER THE ONE TO TRY AND SPEAK WITH HIM BEFORE...
ALWAYS...
HE WAS ALWAYS THE ONE TO COME SPEAK TO ME FIRST...
AND BECAUSE I'M SUCH A FOOL, I'M ALWAYS CAUSING HIM SO MUCH WORRY...
HEAD-ON...
I KEPT RUNNING FROM HIM...
"I WANT TO KNOW ABOUT YOU!"
BUT -
AFTER YOU SAID THE SAME THING TO ME...
I KNEW IT COULDN'T GO ON THIS WAY.
SO, AFTER THE SCHOOL FESTIVAL, I TRIED SEVERAL TIMES TO SPEAK WITH HIM, BUT...
...HE'S BEEN ACTING STRANGELY EVER SINCE.

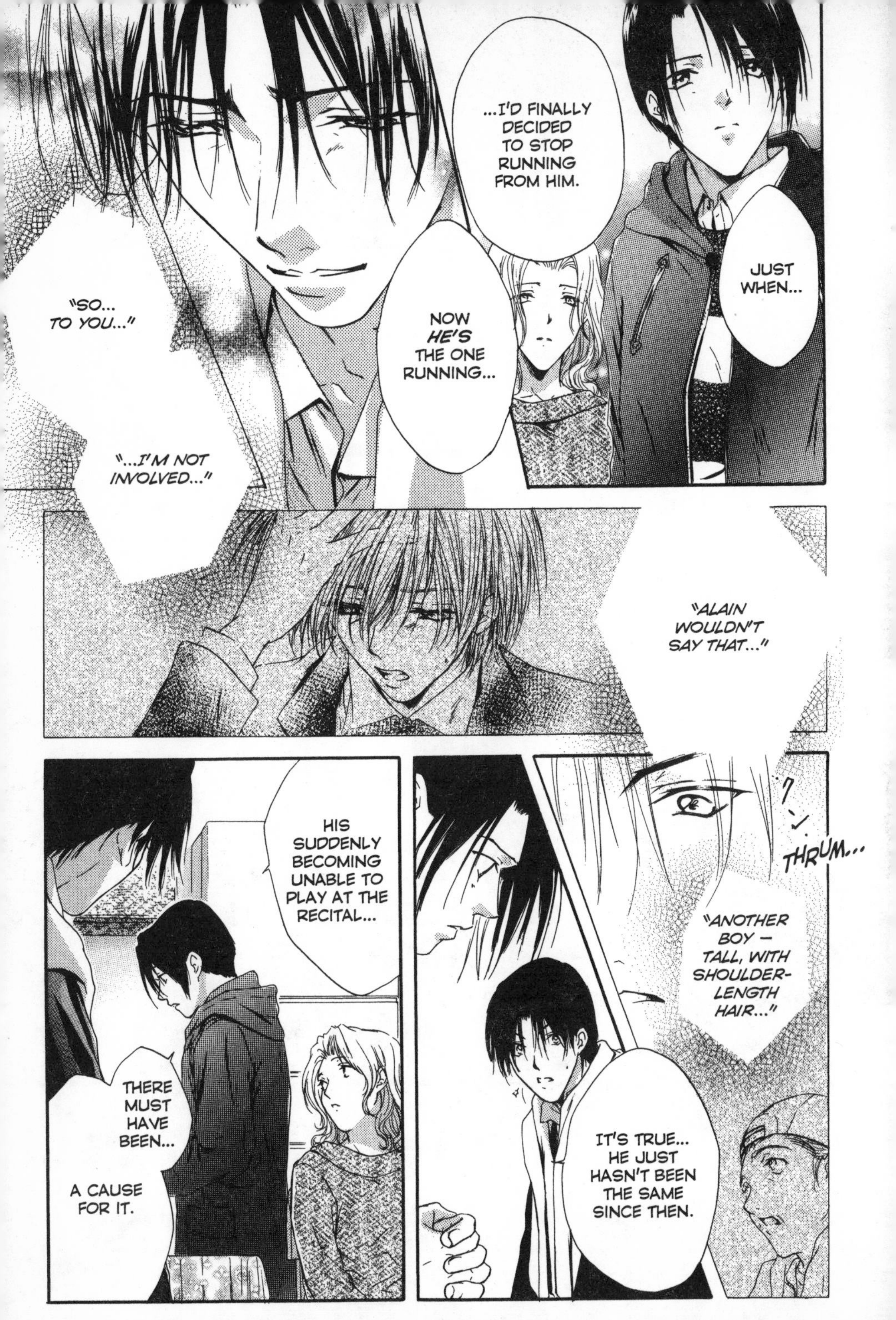
JUST WHEN...
...I'D FINALLY DECIDED TO STOP RUNNING FROM HIM.
NOW *HE'S* THE ONE RUNNING...
"SO... TO YOU..."
"...I'M NOT INVOLVED..."
"ALAIN WOULDN'T SAY THAT..."
THRUM...
"ANOTHER BOY — TALL, WITH SHOULDER-LENGTH HAIR..."
IT'S TRUE... HE JUST HASN'T BEEN THE SAME SINCE THEN.
HIS SUDDENLY BECOMING UNABLE TO PLAY AT THE RECITAL...
THERE MUST HAVE BEEN...
A CAUSE FOR IT.

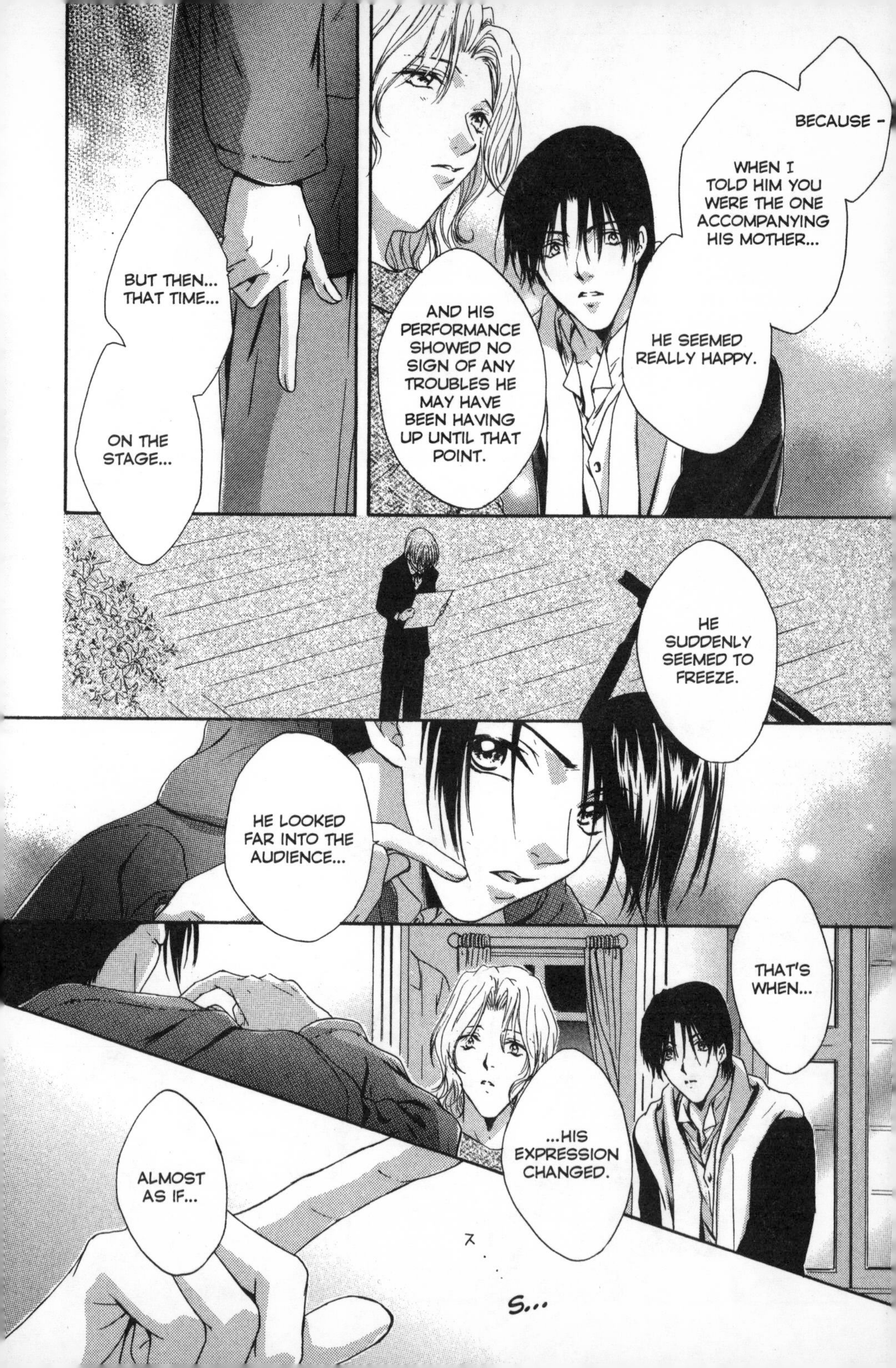
BECAUSE -
WHEN I TOLD HIM YOU WERE THE ONE ACCOMPANYING HIS MOTHER...
HE SEEMED REALLY HAPPY.
AND HIS PERFORMANCE SHOWED NO SIGN OF ANY TROUBLES HE MAY HAVE BEEN HAVING UP UNTIL THAT POINT.
BUT THEN... THAT TIME...
ON THE STAGE...
HE SUDDENLY SEEMED TO FREEZE.
HE LOOKED FAR INTO THE AUDIENCE...
THAT'S WHEN...
...HIS EXPRESSION CHANGED.
ALMOST AS IF...
ス
S...

...BECOMING
AWARE...

...OF
SOMETHING
HE SAW
THERE.

JOLT

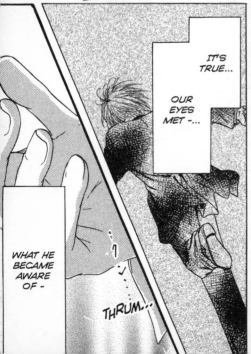

IT'S
TRUE...

OUR
EYES
MET -...

WHAT HE
BECAME
AWARE
OF -

THRUM...

THAT
TIME...

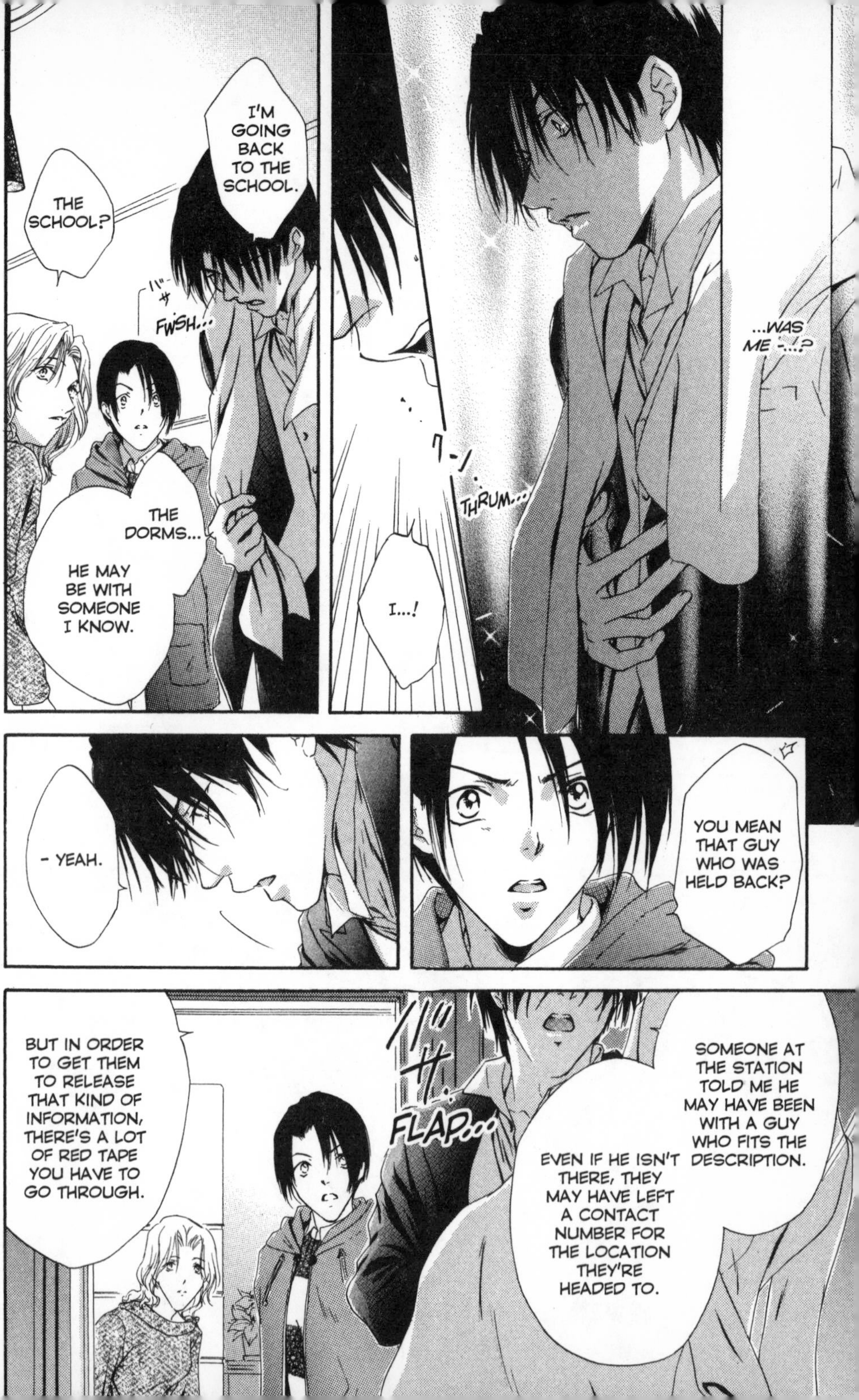
...WAS ME -...!?
I...!
THRUM...
I'M GOING BACK TO THE SCHOOL.
THE SCHOOL?
FWSH...
THE DORMS...
HE MAY BE WITH SOMEONE I KNOW.
YOU MEAN THAT GUY WHO WAS HELD BACK?
- YEAH.
SOMEONE AT THE STATION TOLD ME HE MAY HAVE BEEN WITH A GUY WHO FITS THE DESCRIPTION.
EVEN IF HE ISN'T THERE, THEY MAY HAVE LEFT A CONTACT NUMBER FOR THE LOCATION THEY'RE HEADED TO.
FLAP...
BUT IN ORDER TO GET THEM TO RELEASE THAT KIND OF INFORMATION, THERE'S A LOT OF RED TAPE YOU HAVE TO GO THROUGH.

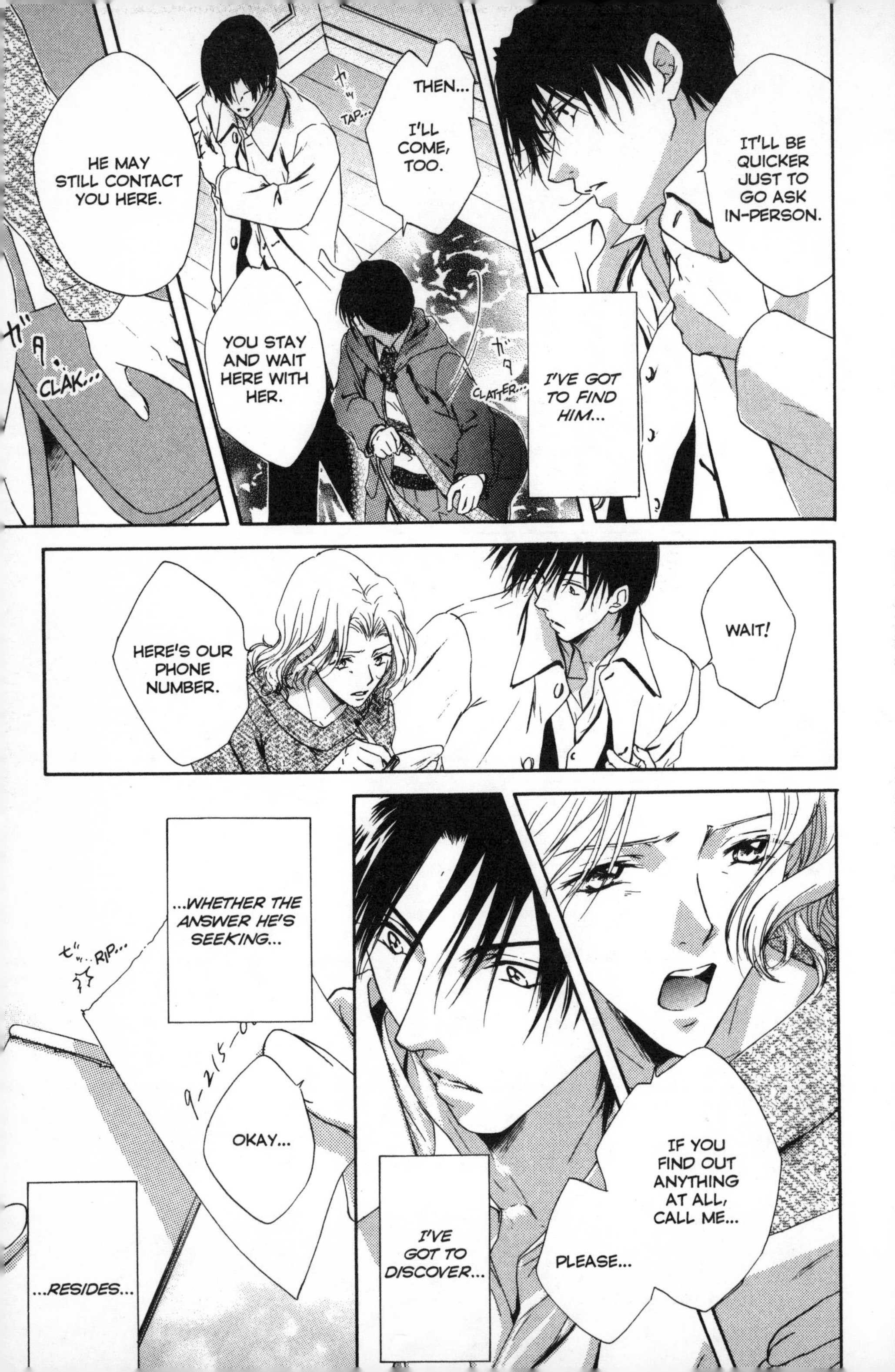
IT'LL BE QUICKER JUST TO GO ASK IN-PERSON.
I'VE GOT TO FIND HIM...
THEN...
I'LL COME, TOO.
TAP...
YOU STAY AND WAIT HERE WITH HER.
CLATTER...
HE MAY STILL CONTACT YOU HERE.
CLAK...
WAIT!
HERE'S OUR PHONE NUMBER.
IF YOU FIND OUT ANYTHING AT ALL, CALL ME...
PLEASE...
I'VE GOT TO DISCOVER...
...WHETHER THE ANSWER HE'S SEEKING...
RIP...
OKAY...
...RESIDES...

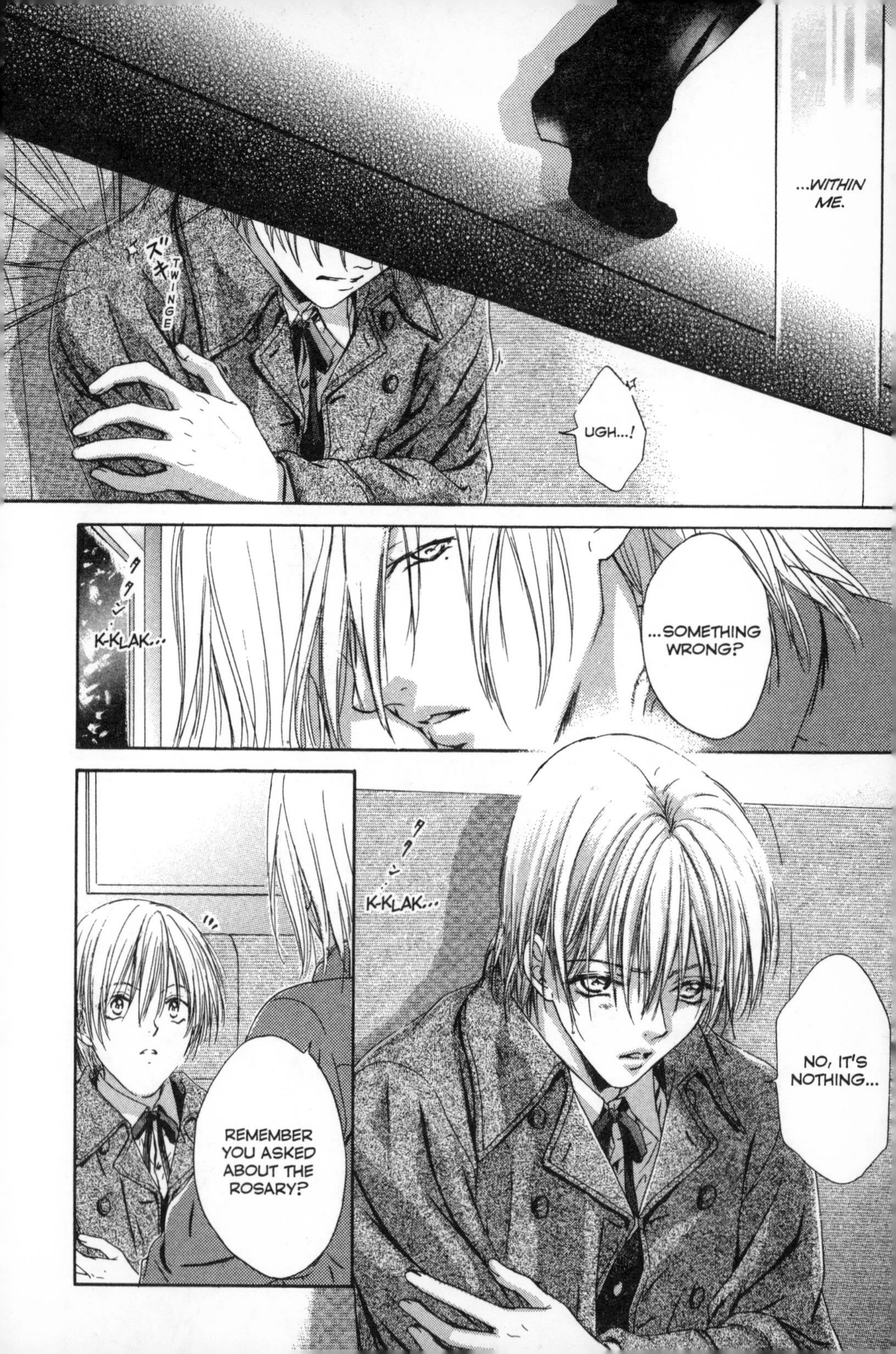
...WITHIN ME.
ズキ TWINGE
UGH...!
...SOMETHING WRONG?
タタン K-KLAK...
NO, IT'S NOTHING...
タタン K-KLAK...
REMEMBER YOU ASKED ABOUT THE ROSARY?

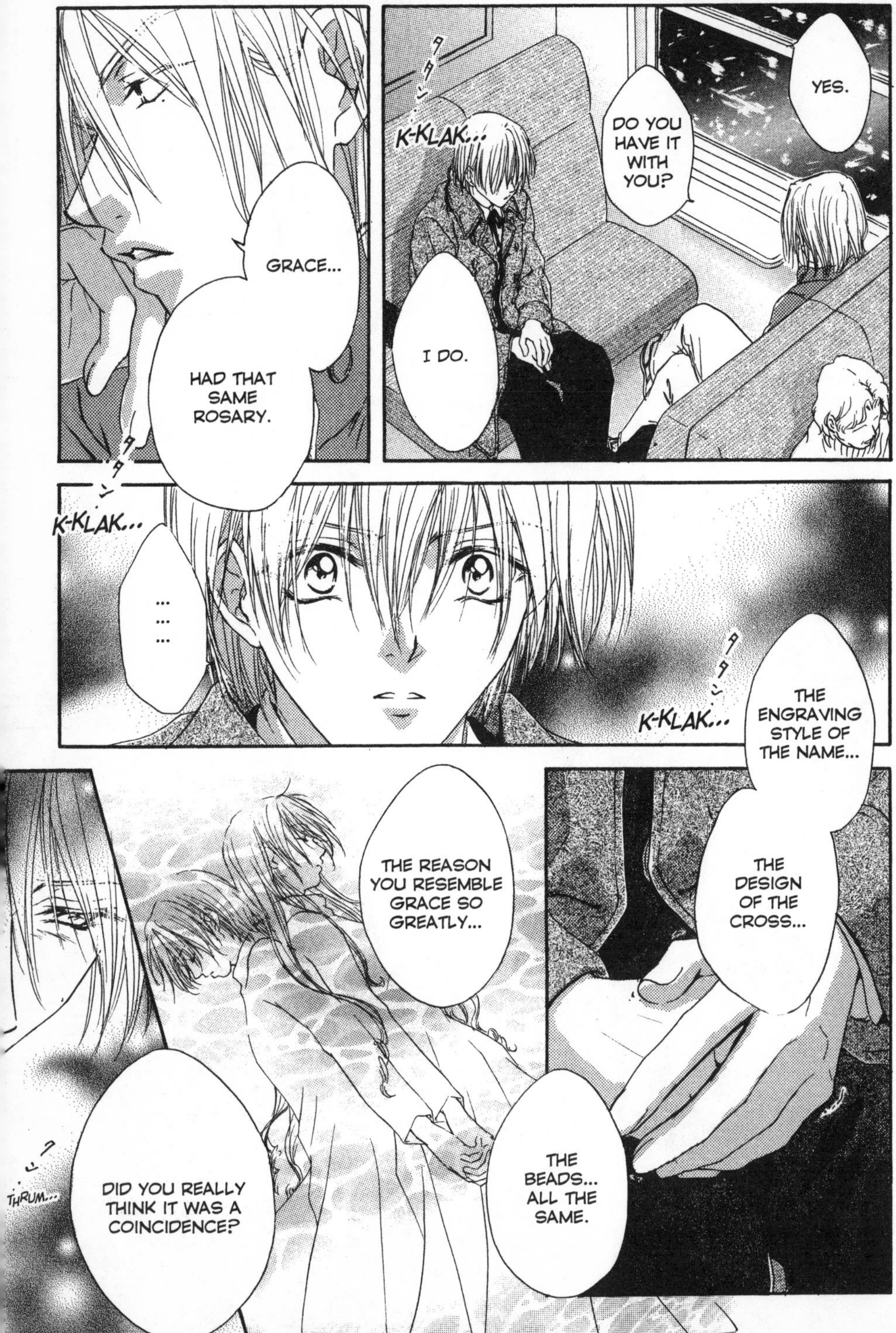
YES.
DO YOU HAVE IT WITH YOU?
K-KLAK...
I DO.
GRACE...
HAD THAT SAME ROSARY.
K-KLAK...
K-KLAK...
...
...
...
THE ENGRAVING STYLE OF THE NAME...
THE DESIGN OF THE CROSS...
THE BEADS... ALL THE SAME.
THE REASON YOU RESEMBLE GRACE SO GREATLY...
DID YOU REALLY THINK IT WAS A COINCIDENCE?
THRUM...

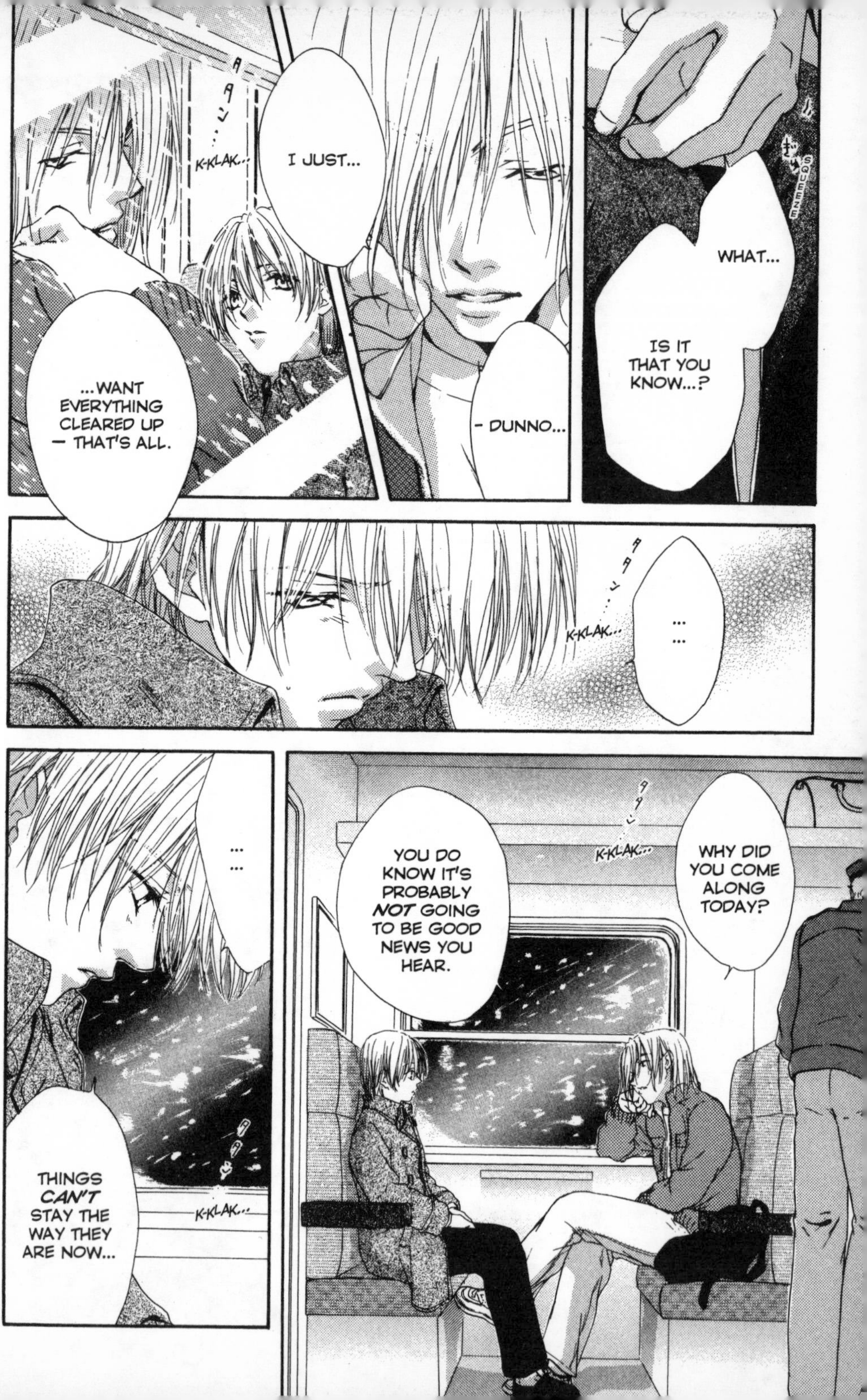
SQUEEZE
WHAT...
IS IT THAT YOU KNOW...?
- DUNNO...
I JUST...
K-KLAK...
...WANT EVERYTHING CLEARED UP — THAT'S ALL.
K-KLAK...
... ...
WHY DID YOU COME ALONG TODAY?
K-KLAK...
YOU DO KNOW IT'S PROBABLY *NOT* GOING TO BE GOOD NEWS YOU HEAR.
... ...
K-KLAK...
THINGS *CAN'T* STAY THE WAY THEY ARE NOW...

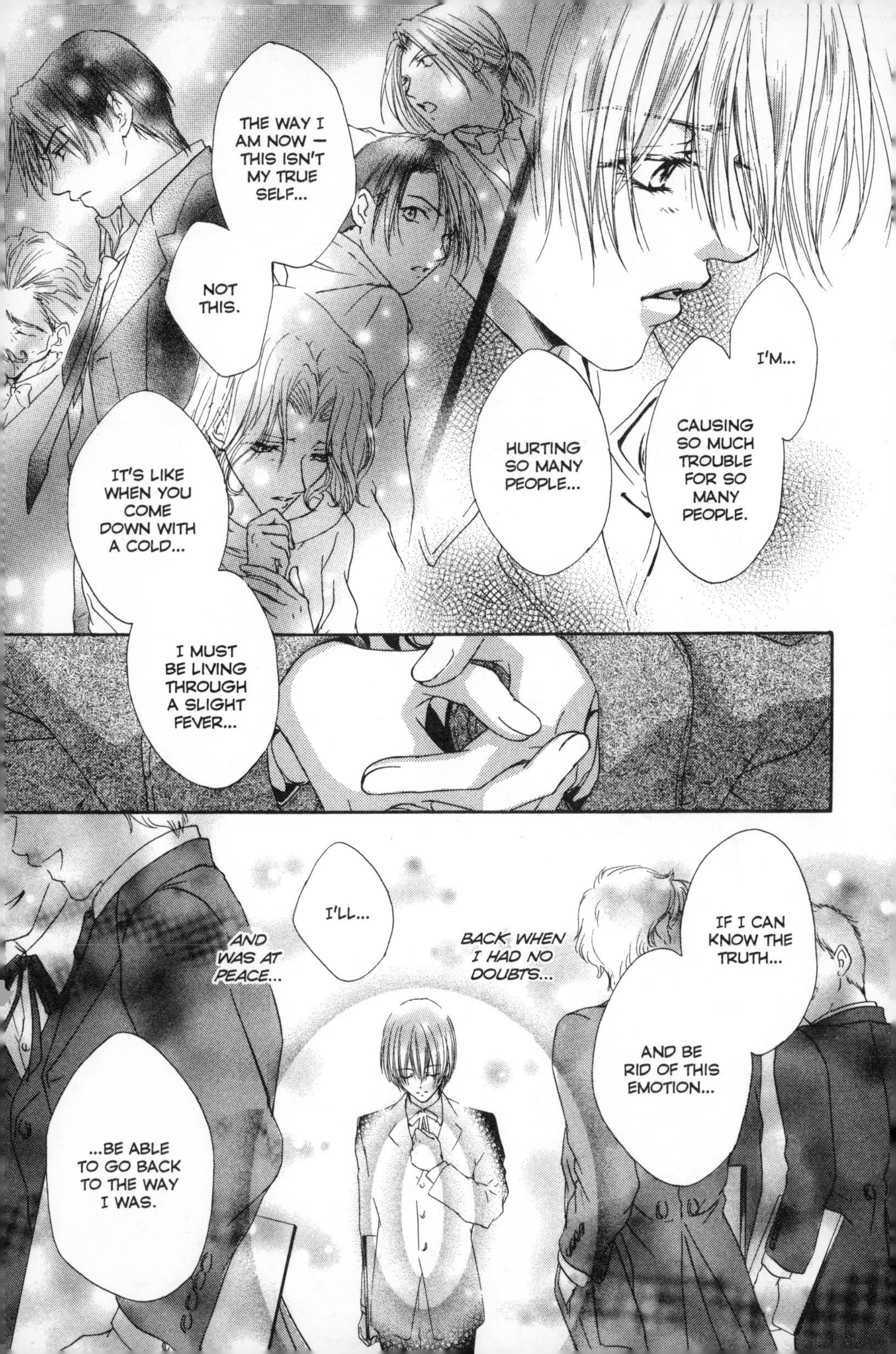
I'M...
CAUSING SO MUCH TROUBLE FOR SO MANY PEOPLE.
HURTING SO MANY PEOPLE...
THE WAY I AM NOW — THIS ISN'T MY TRUE SELF...
NOT THIS.
IT'S LIKE WHEN YOU COME DOWN WITH A COLD...
I MUST BE LIVING THROUGH A SLIGHT FEVER...
IF I CAN KNOW THE TRUTH...
AND BE RID OF THIS EMOTION...
I'LL...
...BE ABLE TO GO BACK TO THE WAY I WAS.
BACK WHEN I HAD NO DOUBTS...
AND WAS AT PEACE...

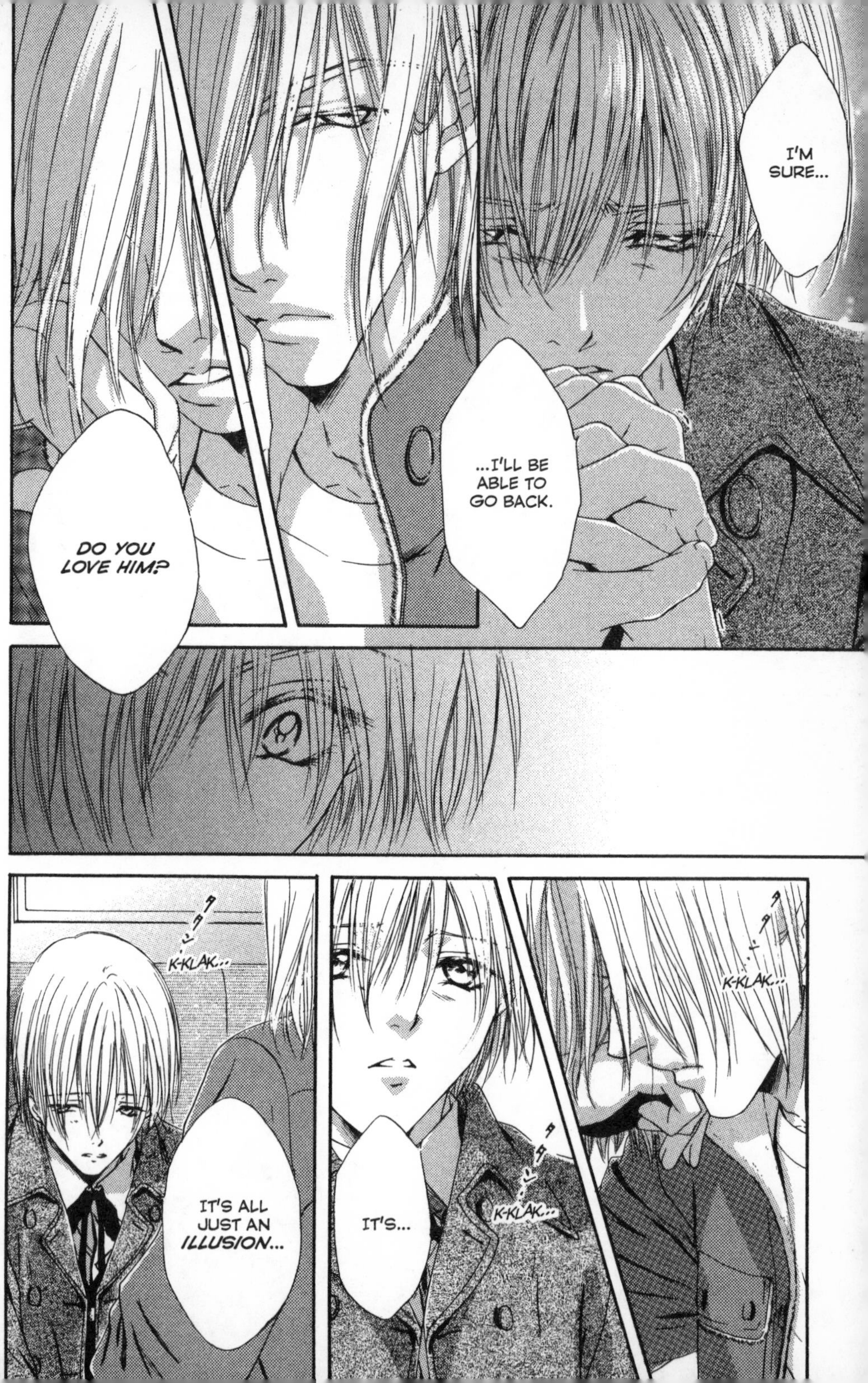
I'M SURE...
...I'LL BE ABLE TO GO BACK.
DO YOU LOVE HIM?
K-KLAK...
IT'S...
K-KLAK...
K-KLAK...
IT'S ALL JUST AN *ILLUSION*...

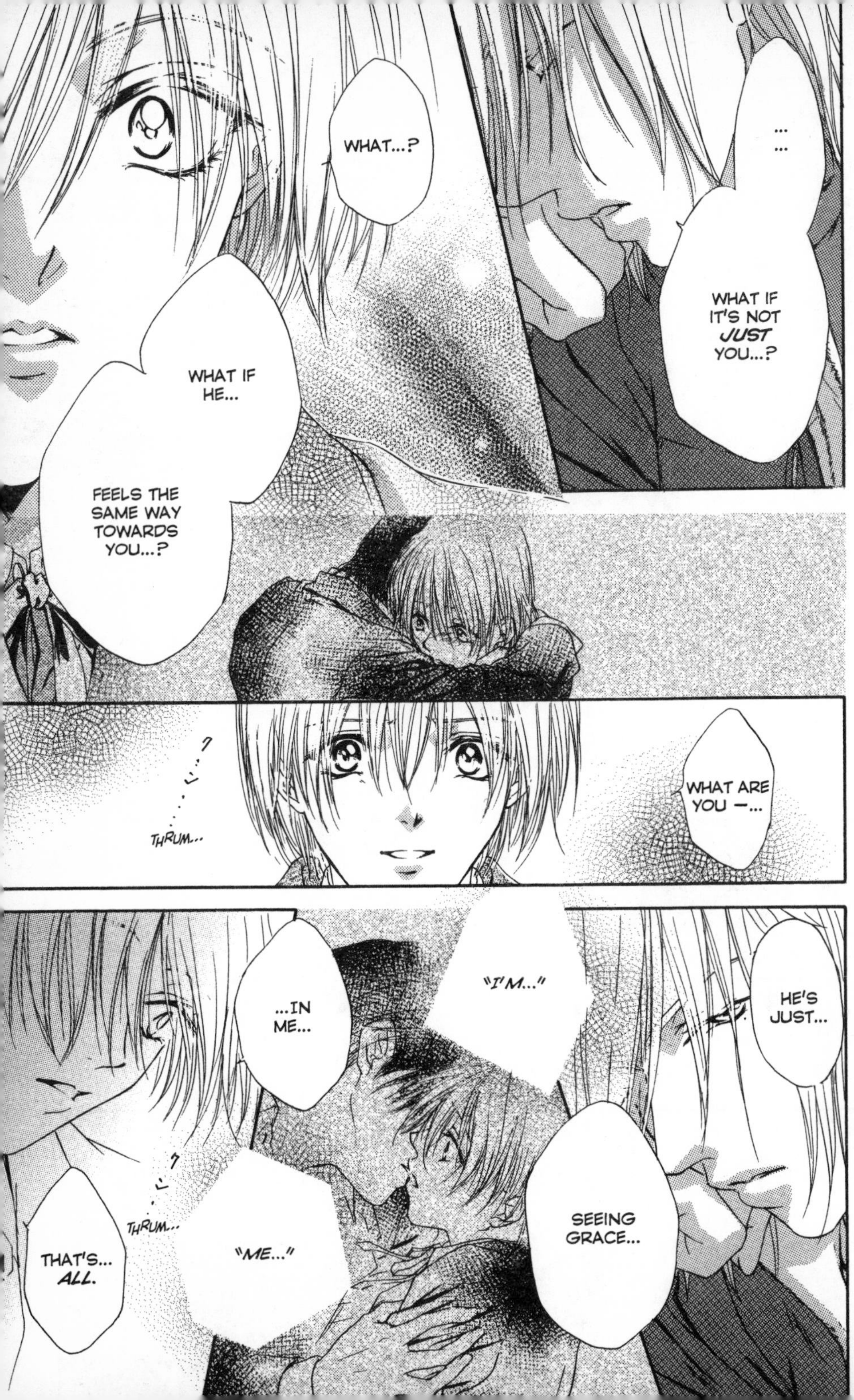
……
WHAT IF IT'S NOT *JUST* YOU...?
WHAT...?
WHAT IF HE...
FEELS THE SAME WAY TOWARDS YOU...?
WHAT ARE YOU —...
THRUM...
HE'S JUST...
SEEING GRACE...
"I'M..."
...IN ME...
"ME..."
THRUM...
THAT'S... *ALL.*

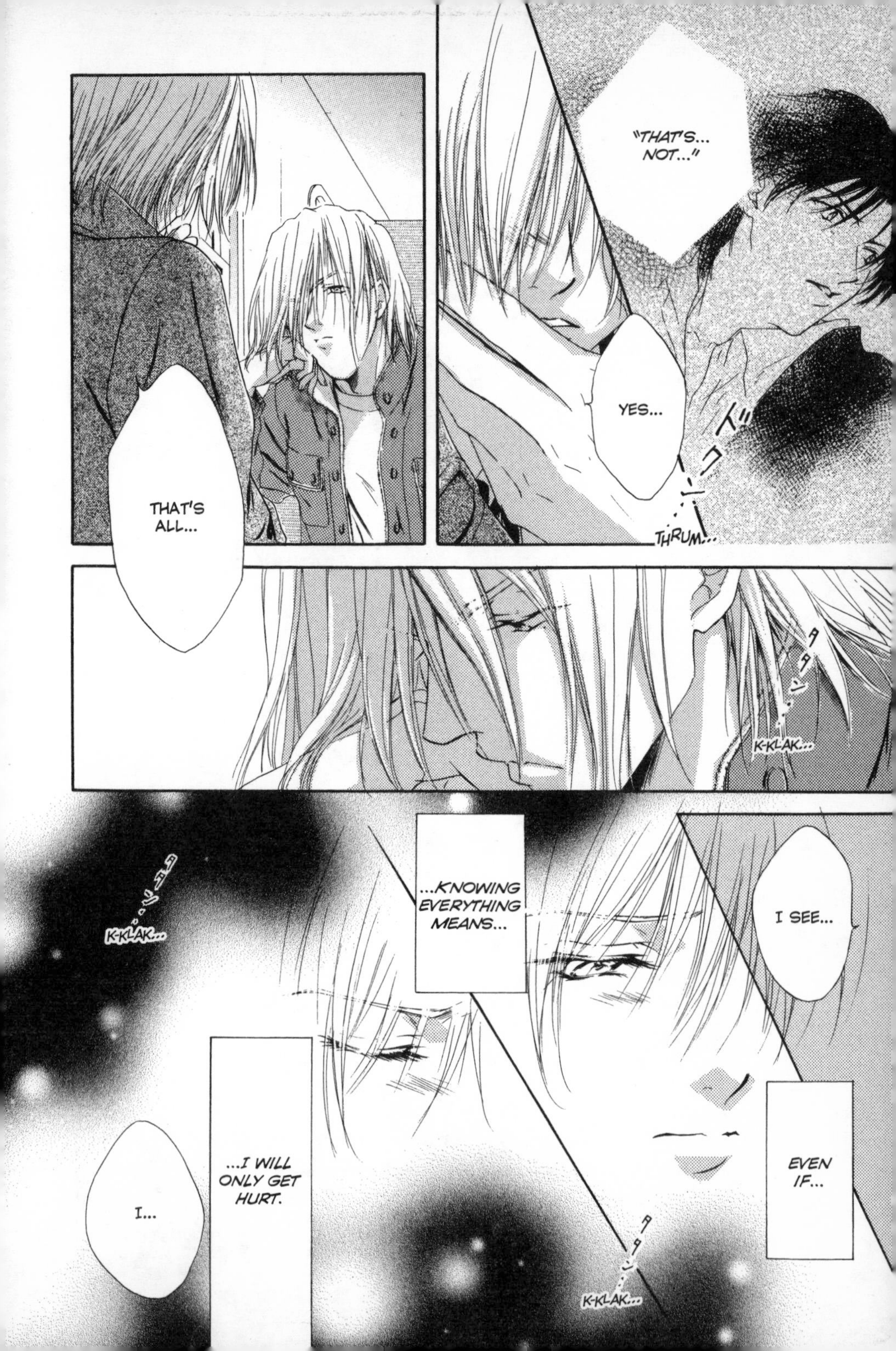
"THAT'S... NOT..."
YES...
THRUM...
THAT'S ALL...
K-KLAK...
I SEE...
...KNOWING EVERYTHING MEANS...
EVEN IF...
K-KLAK...
...I WILL ONLY GET HURT.
I...
K-KLAK...

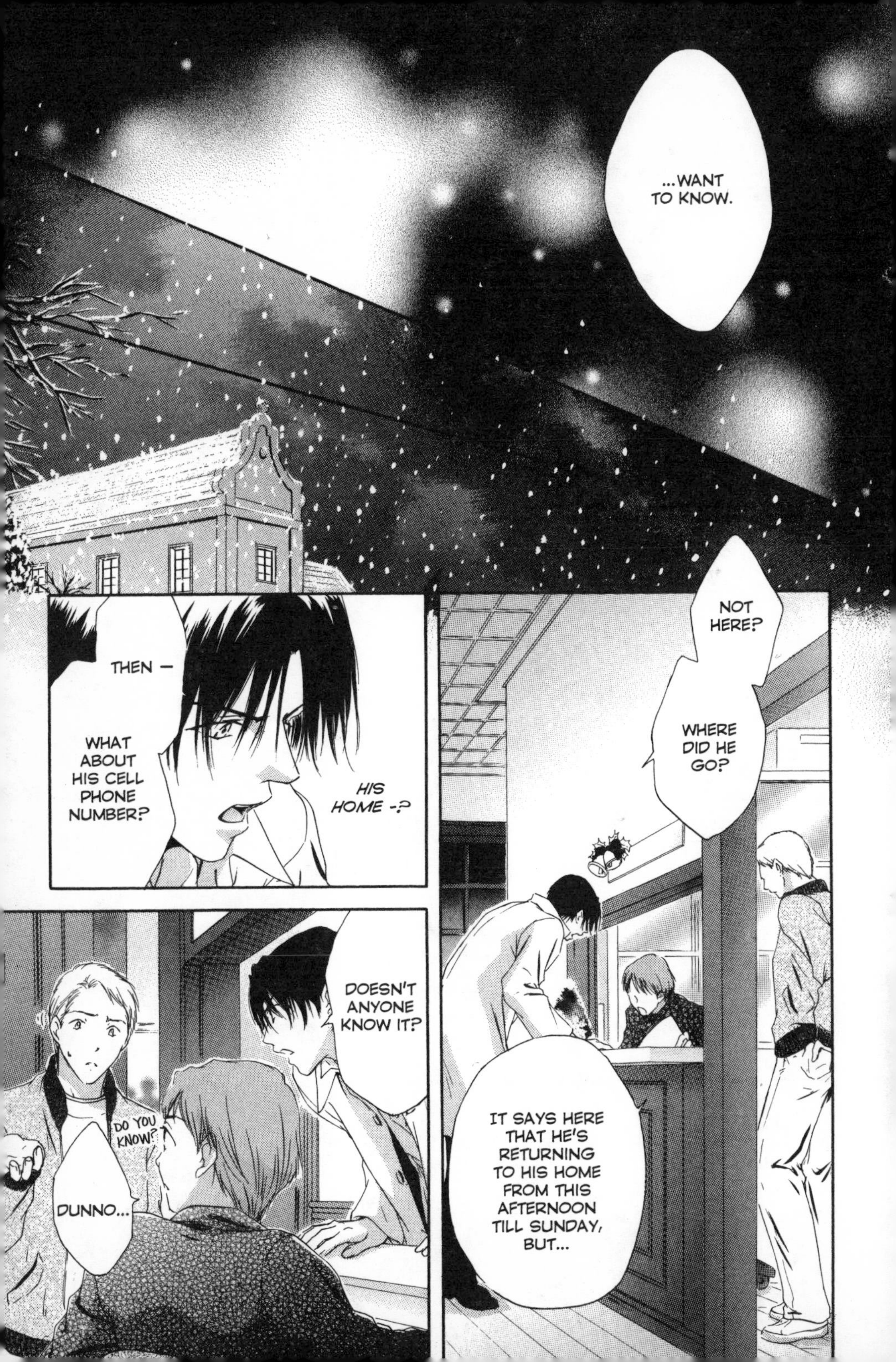
...WANT TO KNOW.
NOT HERE?
WHERE DID HE GO?
IT SAYS HERE THAT HE'S RETURNING TO HIS HOME FROM THIS AFTERNOON TILL SUNDAY, BUT...
THEN —
HIS HOME -?
WHAT ABOUT HIS CELL PHONE NUMBER?
DOESN'T ANYONE KNOW IT?
DO YOU KNOW?
DUNNO...

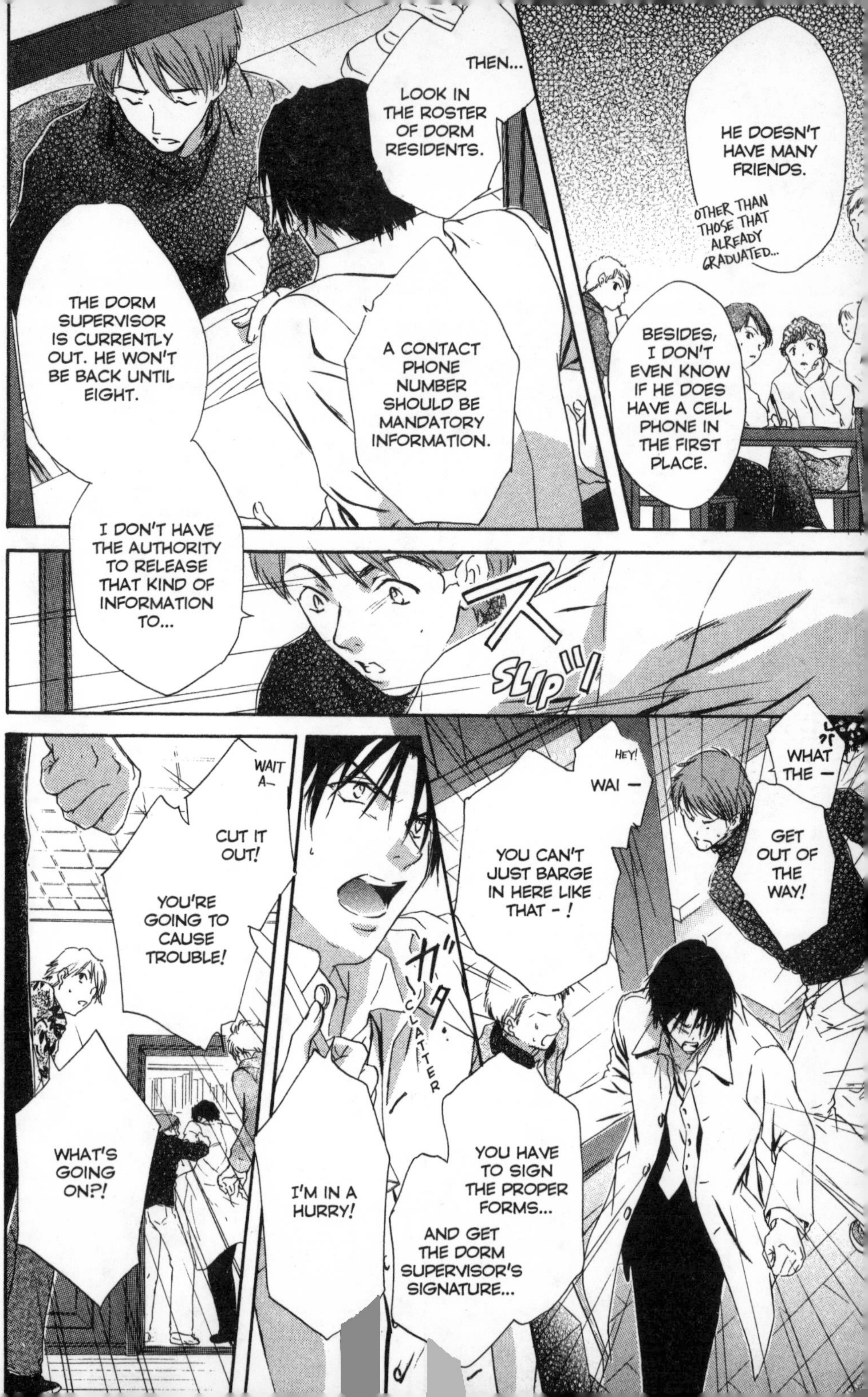
HE DOESN'T HAVE MANY FRIENDS.
OTHER THAN THOSE THAT ALREADY GRADUATED...
BESIDES, I DON'T EVEN KNOW IF HE DOES HAVE A CELL PHONE IN THE FIRST PLACE.
THEN...
LOOK IN THE ROSTER OF DORM RESIDENTS.
A CONTACT PHONE NUMBER SHOULD BE MANDATORY INFORMATION.
THE DORM SUPERVISOR IS CURRENTLY OUT. HE WON'T BE BACK UNTIL EIGHT.
I DON'T HAVE THE AUTHORITY TO RELEASE THAT KIND OF INFORMATION TO...
SLIP
WHAT THE —
GET OUT OF THE WAY!
HEY!
WAI —
YOU CAN'T JUST BARGE IN HERE LIKE THAT — !
YOU HAVE TO SIGN THE PROPER FORMS...
AND GET THE DORM SUPERVISOR'S SIGNATURE...
CLATTER
I'M IN A HURRY!
WAIT A—
CUT IT OUT!
YOU'RE GOING TO CAUSE TROUBLE!
WHAT'S GOING ON?!

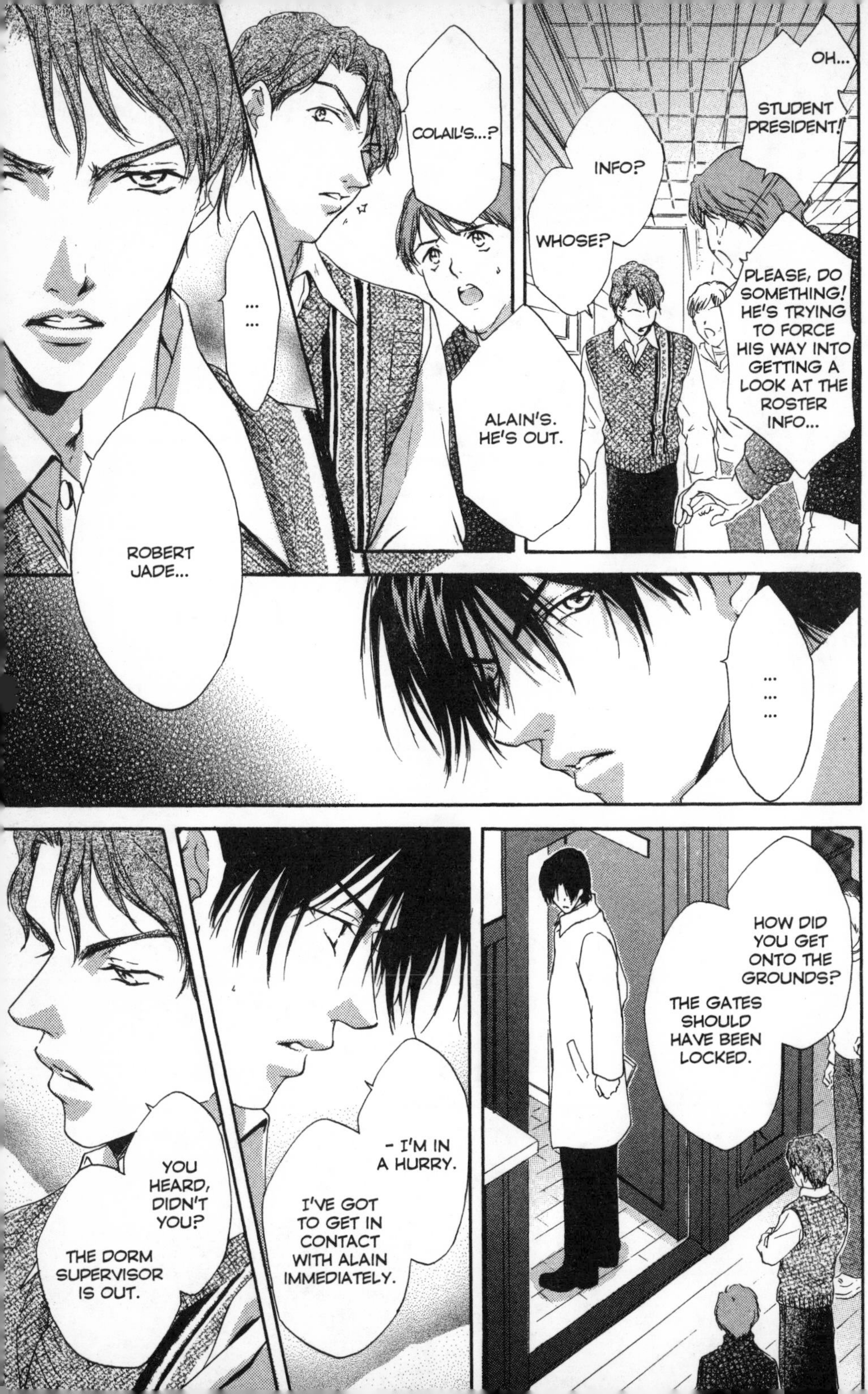
OH...
STUDENT PRESIDENT!
PLEASE, DO SOMETHING! HE'S TRYING TO FORCE HIS WAY INTO GETTING A LOOK AT THE ROSTER INFO...
INFO?
WHOSE?
ALAIN'S. HE'S OUT.
COLAIL'S...?
... ...
ROBERT JADE...
... ...
HOW DID YOU GET ONTO THE GROUNDS?
THE GATES SHOULD HAVE BEEN LOCKED.
- I'M IN A HURRY.
I'VE GOT TO GET IN CONTACT WITH ALAIN IMMEDIATELY.
YOU HEARD, DIDN'T YOU?
THE DORM SUPERVISOR IS OUT.

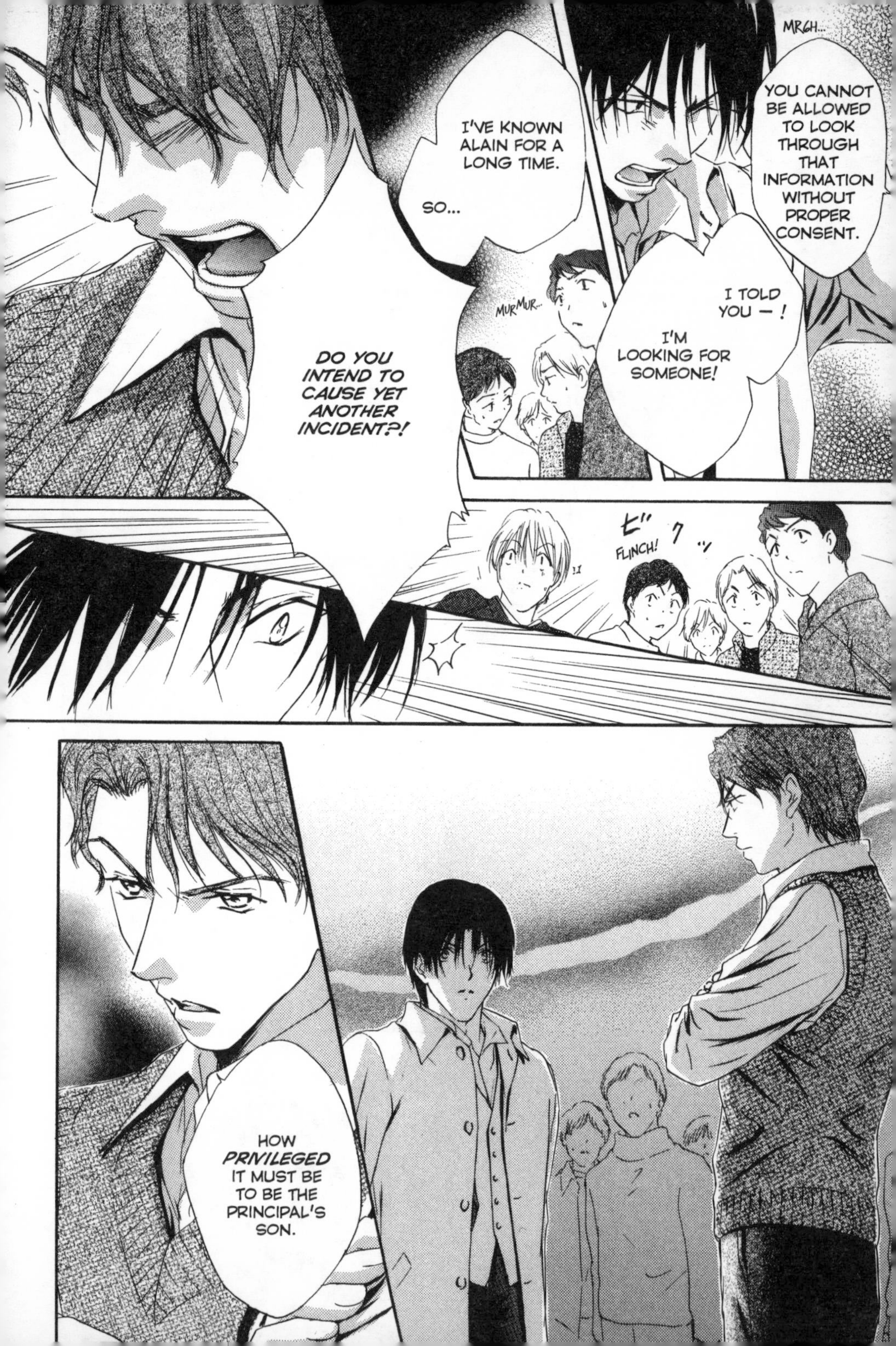
MRGH...
YOU CANNOT BE ALLOWED TO LOOK THROUGH THAT INFORMATION WITHOUT PROPER CONSENT.
I TOLD YOU —!
I'M LOOKING FOR SOMEONE!
MURMUR...
I'VE KNOWN ALAIN FOR A LONG TIME.
SO...
DO YOU INTEND TO CAUSE YET ANOTHER INCIDENT?!
ビクッ
FLINCH!
HOW *PRIVILEGED* IT MUST BE TO BE THE PRINCIPAL'S SON.

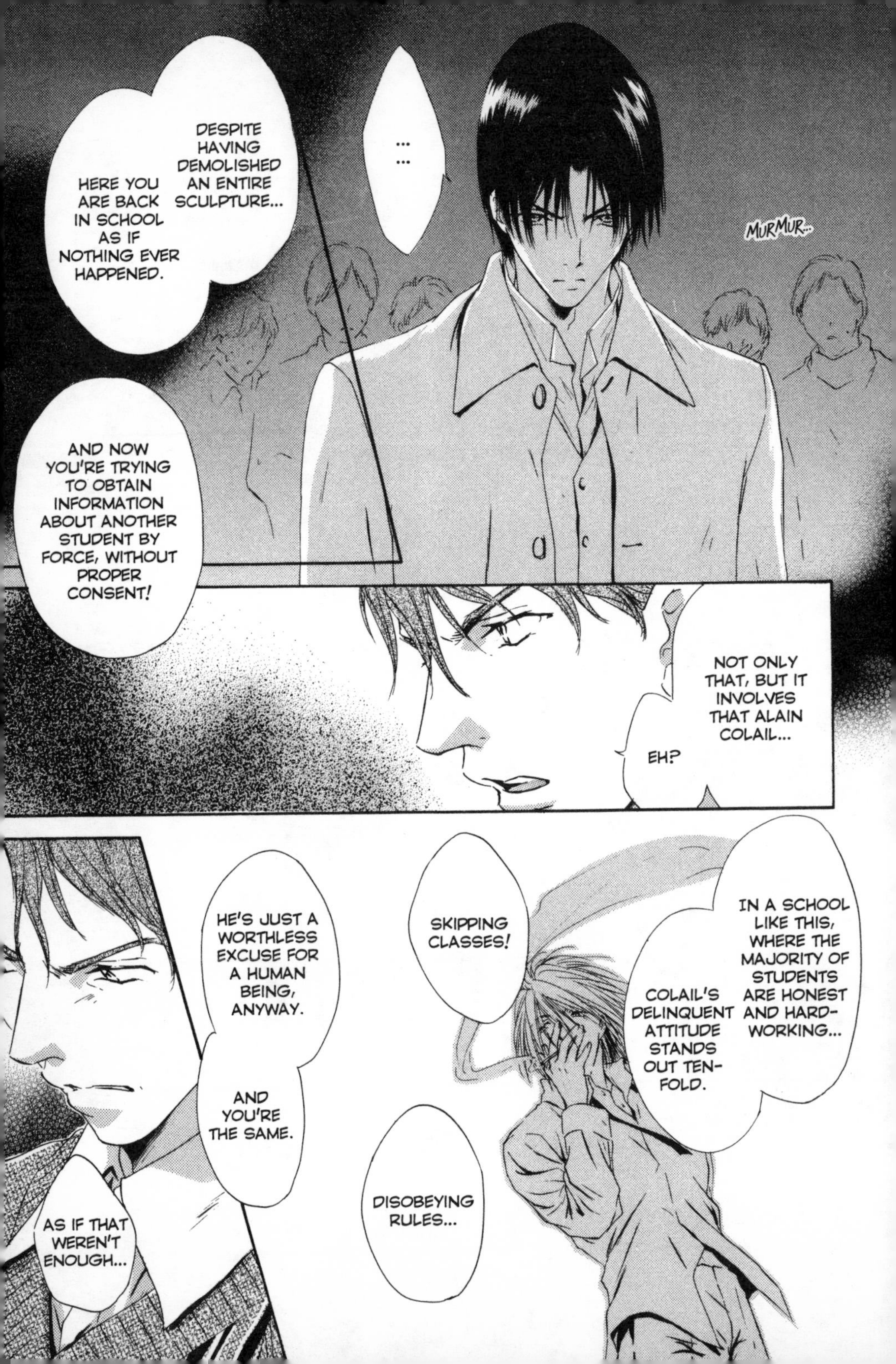
MURMUR...
...
...
DESPITE HAVING DEMOLISHED AN ENTIRE SCULPTURE...
HERE YOU ARE BACK IN SCHOOL AS IF NOTHING EVER HAPPENED.
AND NOW YOU'RE TRYING TO OBTAIN INFORMATION ABOUT ANOTHER STUDENT BY FORCE, WITHOUT PROPER CONSENT!
NOT ONLY THAT, BUT IT INVOLVES THAT ALAIN COLAIL...
EH?
IN A SCHOOL LIKE THIS, WHERE THE MAJORITY OF STUDENTS ARE HONEST AND HARD-WORKING...
COLAIL'S DELINQUENT ATTITUDE STANDS OUT TEN-FOLD.
SKIPPING CLASSES!
DISOBEYING RULES...
HE'S JUST A WORTHLESS EXCUSE FOR A HUMAN BEING, ANYWAY.
AND YOU'RE THE SAME.
AS IF THAT WEREN'T ENOUGH...

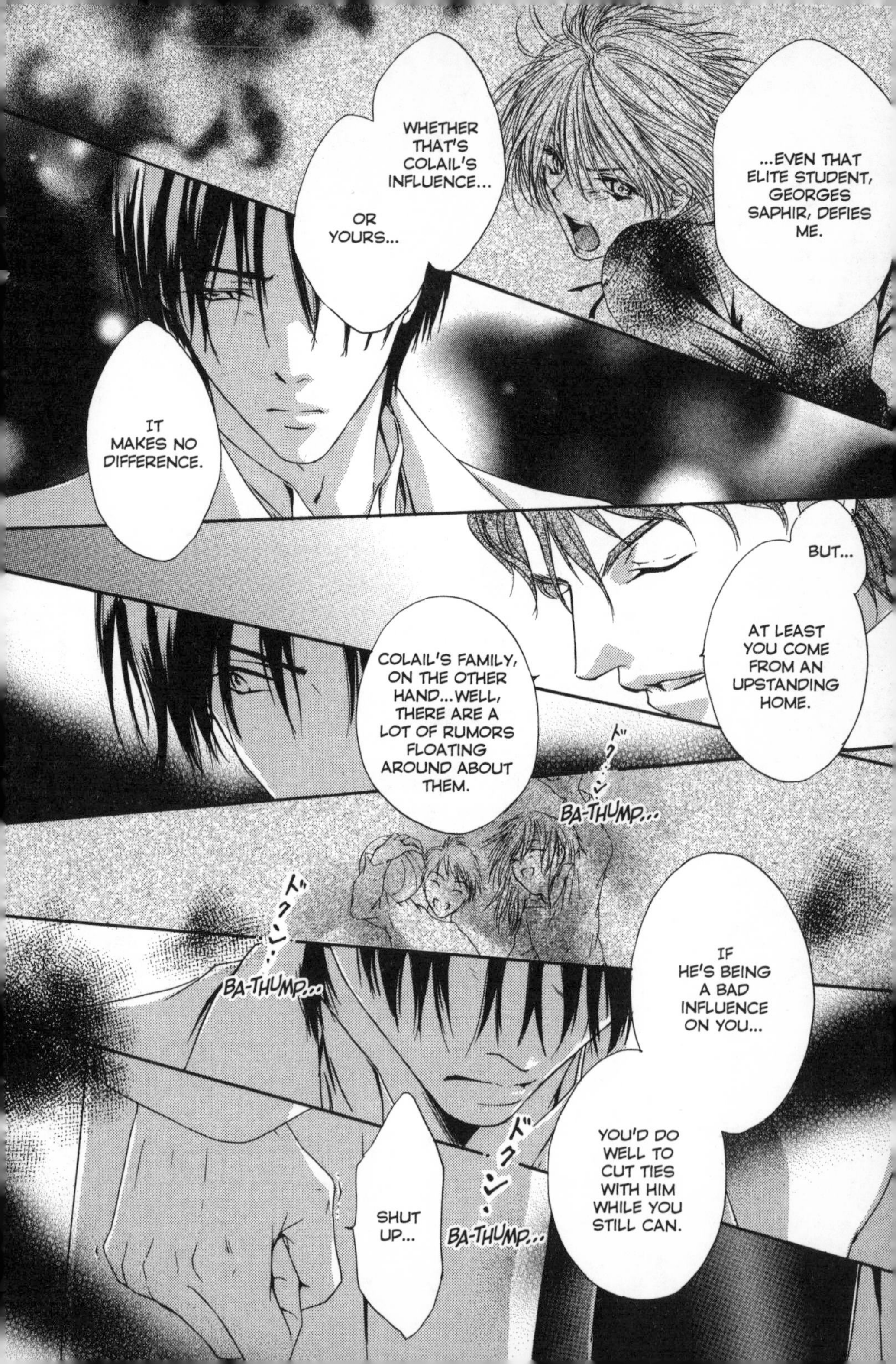
...EVEN THAT ELITE STUDENT, GEORGES SAPHIR, DEFIES ME.
WHETHER THAT'S COLAIL'S INFLUENCE...
OR YOURS...
IT MAKES NO DIFFERENCE.
BUT...
AT LEAST YOU COME FROM AN UPSTANDING HOME.
COLAIL'S FAMILY, ON THE OTHER HAND...WELL, THERE ARE A LOT OF RUMORS FLOATING AROUND ABOUT THEM.
ドクン
BA-THUMP...
IF HE'S BEING A BAD INFLUENCE ON YOU...
ドクン
BA-THUMP...
YOU'D DO WELL TO CUT TIES WITH HIM WHILE YOU STILL CAN.
ドクン
BA-THUMP...
SHUT UP...

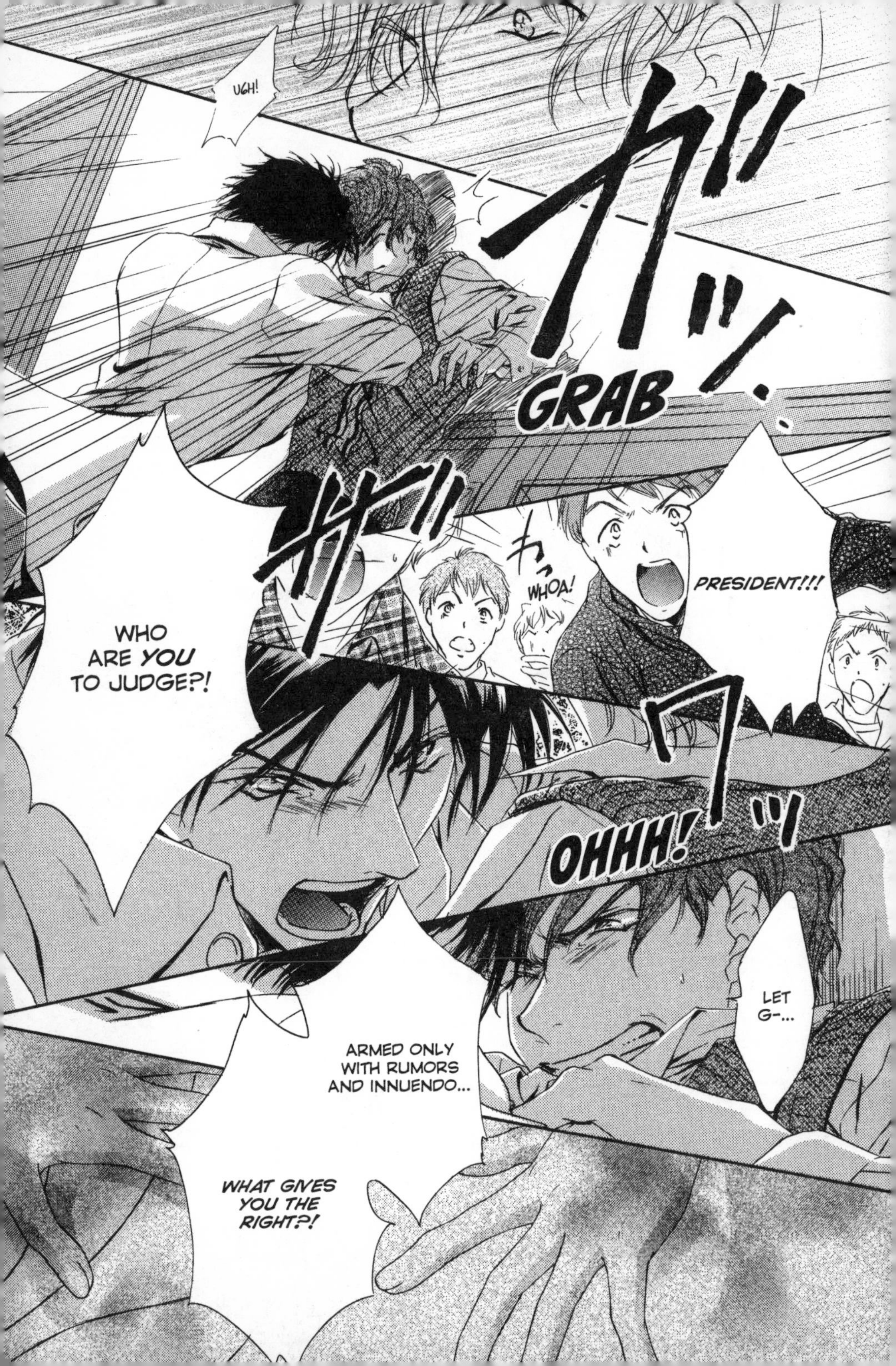
UGH!
GRAB
PRESIDENT!!!
WHOA!
WHO ARE *YOU* TO JUDGE?!
OHHH!
LET G-...
ARMED ONLY WITH RUMORS AND INNUENDO...
WHAT GIVES YOU THE RIGHT?!

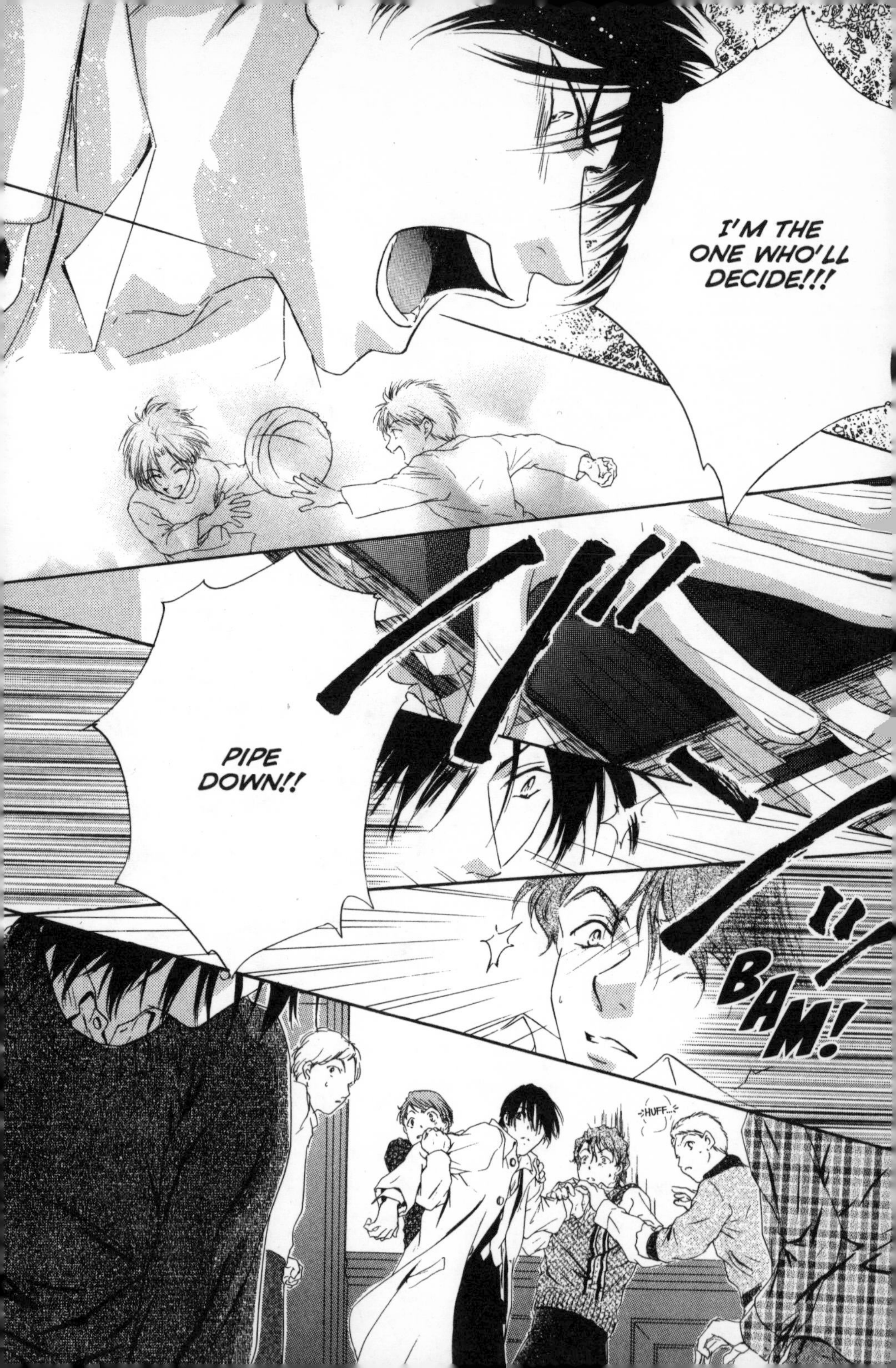
I'M THE ONE WHO'LL DECIDE!!!
PIPE DOWN!!
BAM!
HUFF...

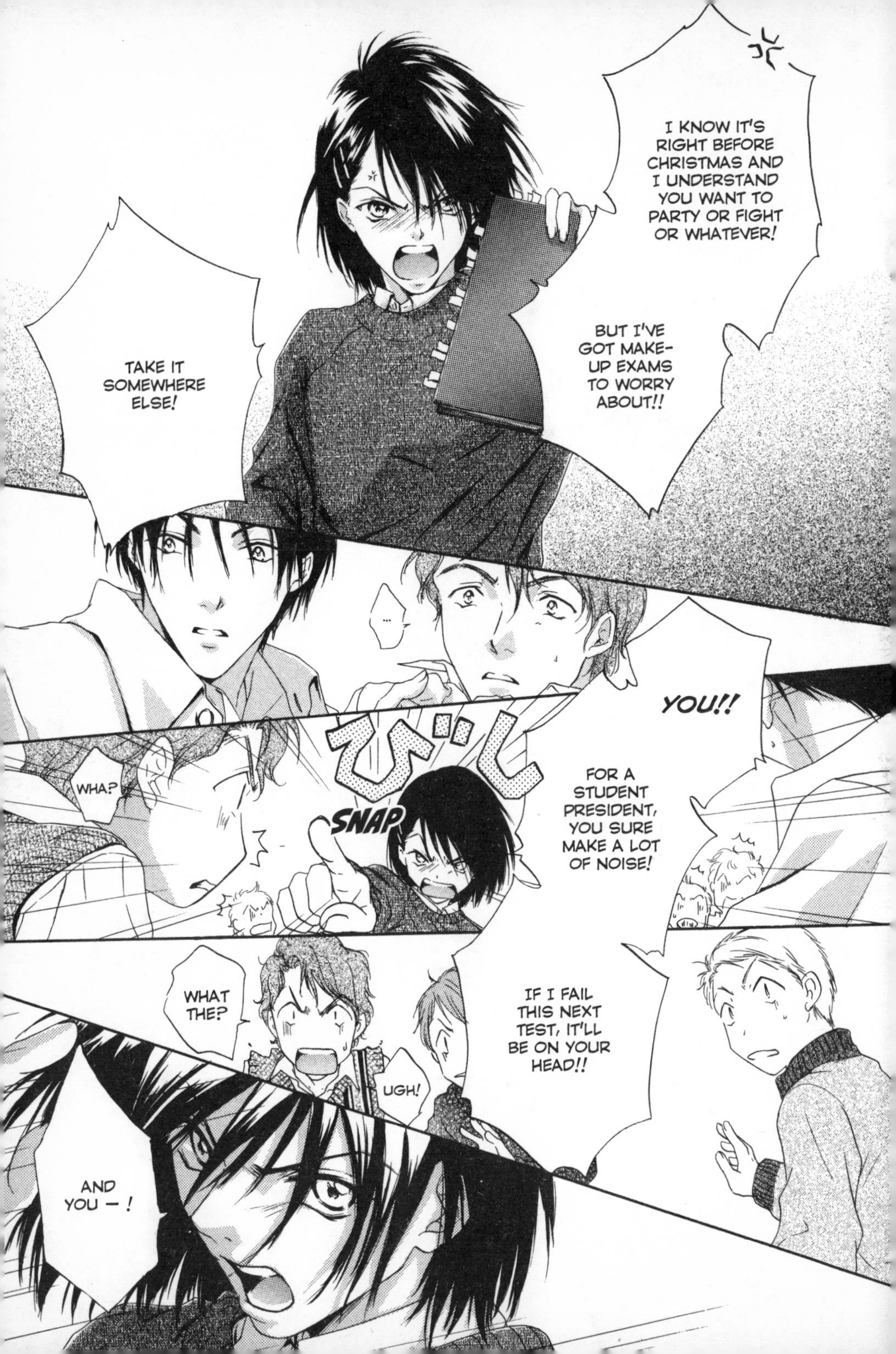
I KNOW IT'S RIGHT BEFORE CHRISTMAS AND I UNDERSTAND YOU WANT TO PARTY OR FIGHT OR WHATEVER!
BUT I'VE GOT MAKE-UP EXAMS TO WORRY ABOUT!!
TAKE IT SOMEWHERE ELSE!
...
YOU!!
FOR A STUDENT PRESIDENT, YOU SURE MAKE A LOT OF NOISE!
びし
SNAP
WHA?
IF I FAIL THIS NEXT TEST, IT'LL BE ON YOUR HEAD!!
UGH!
WHAT THE?
AND YOU — !

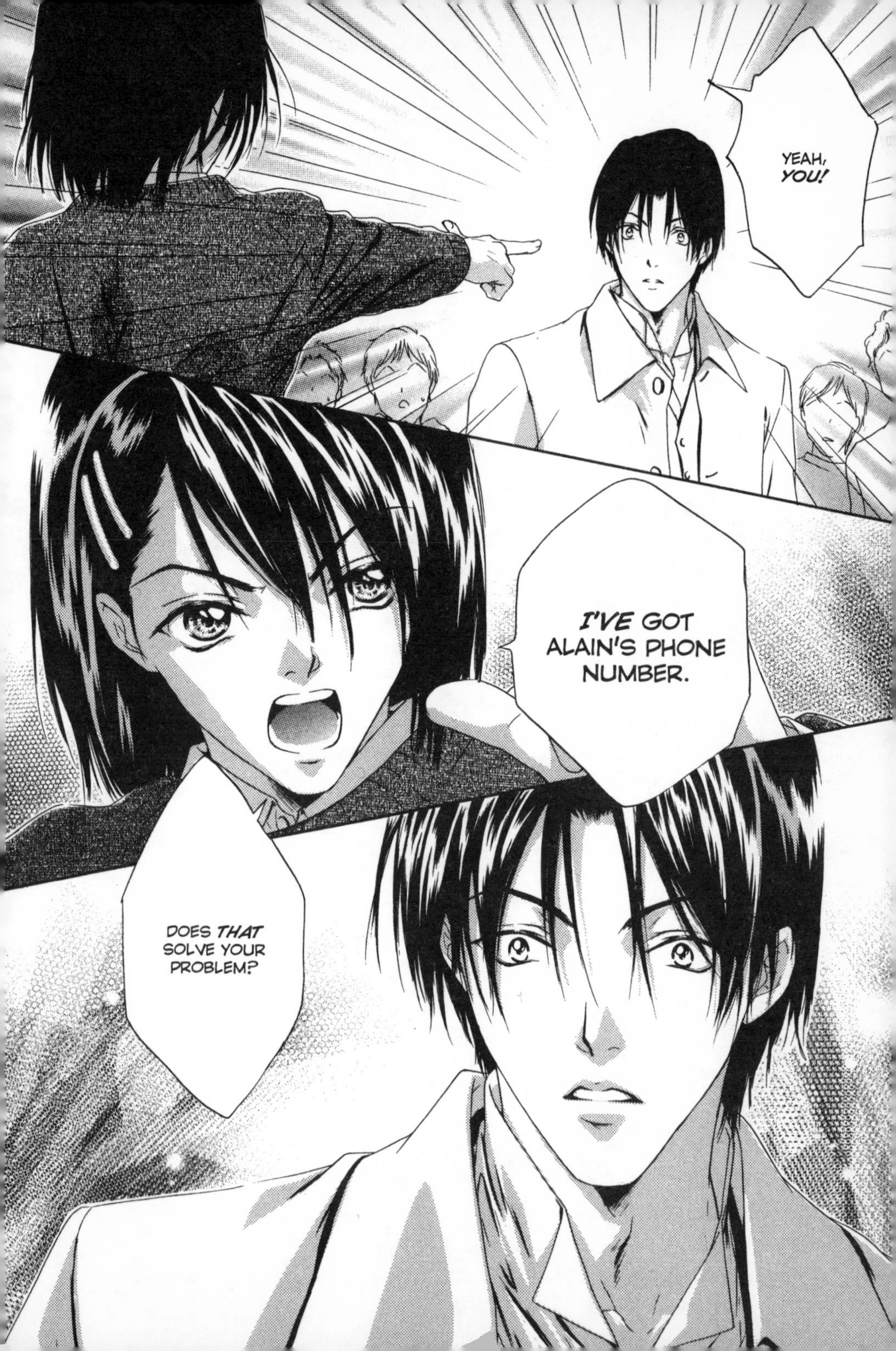
YEAH, *YOU!*
I'VE GOT ALAIN'S PHONE NUMBER.
DOES *THAT* SOLVE YOUR PROBLEM?

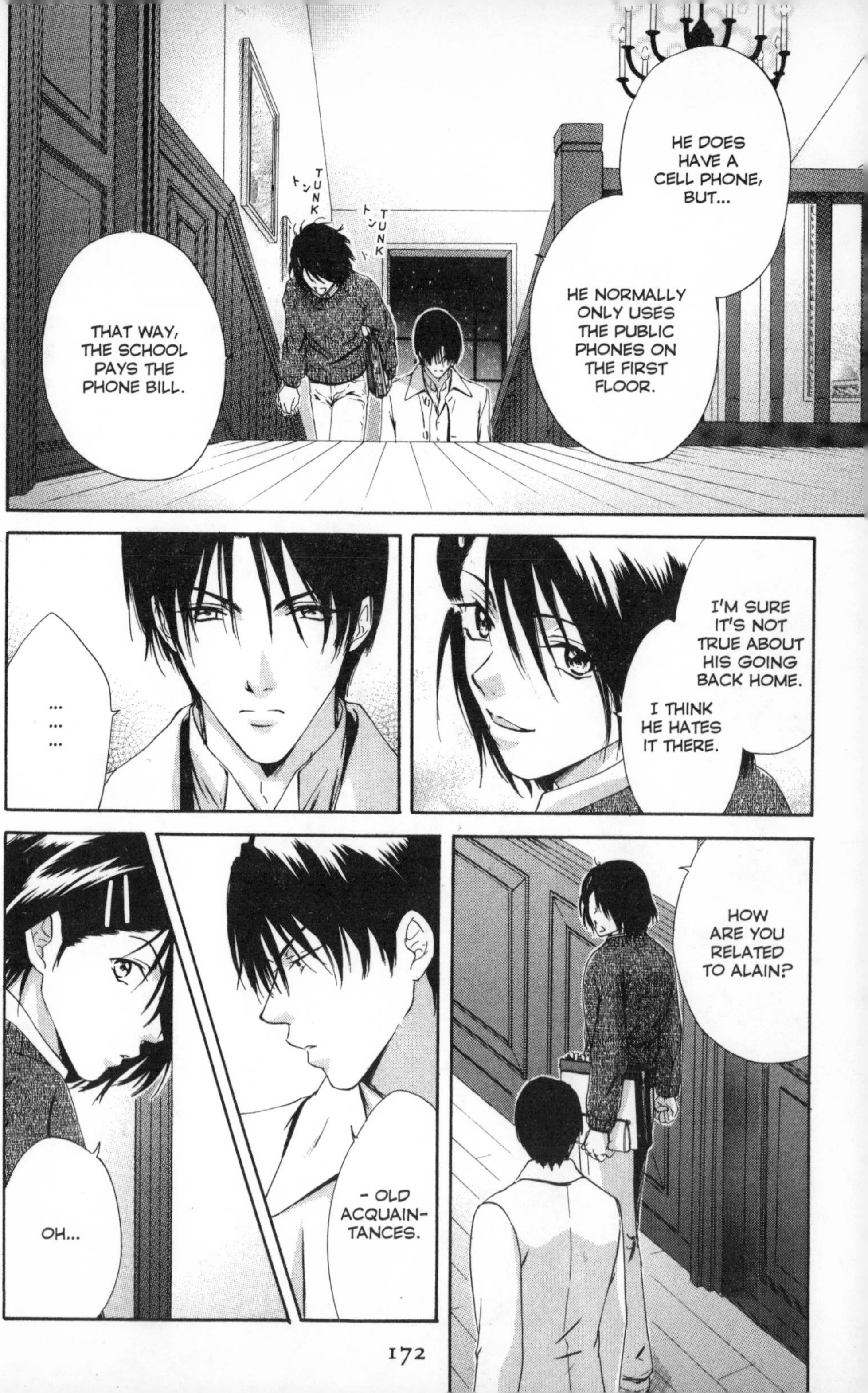
HE DOES HAVE A CELL PHONE, BUT...
HE NORMALLY ONLY USES THE PUBLIC PHONES ON THE FIRST FLOOR.
TUNK トン
TUNK トン
THAT WAY, THE SCHOOL PAYS THE PHONE BILL.
I'M SURE IT'S NOT TRUE ABOUT HIS GOING BACK HOME.
I THINK HE HATES IT THERE.
... ...
HOW ARE YOU RELATED TO ALAIN?
- OLD ACQUAINTANCES.
OH...

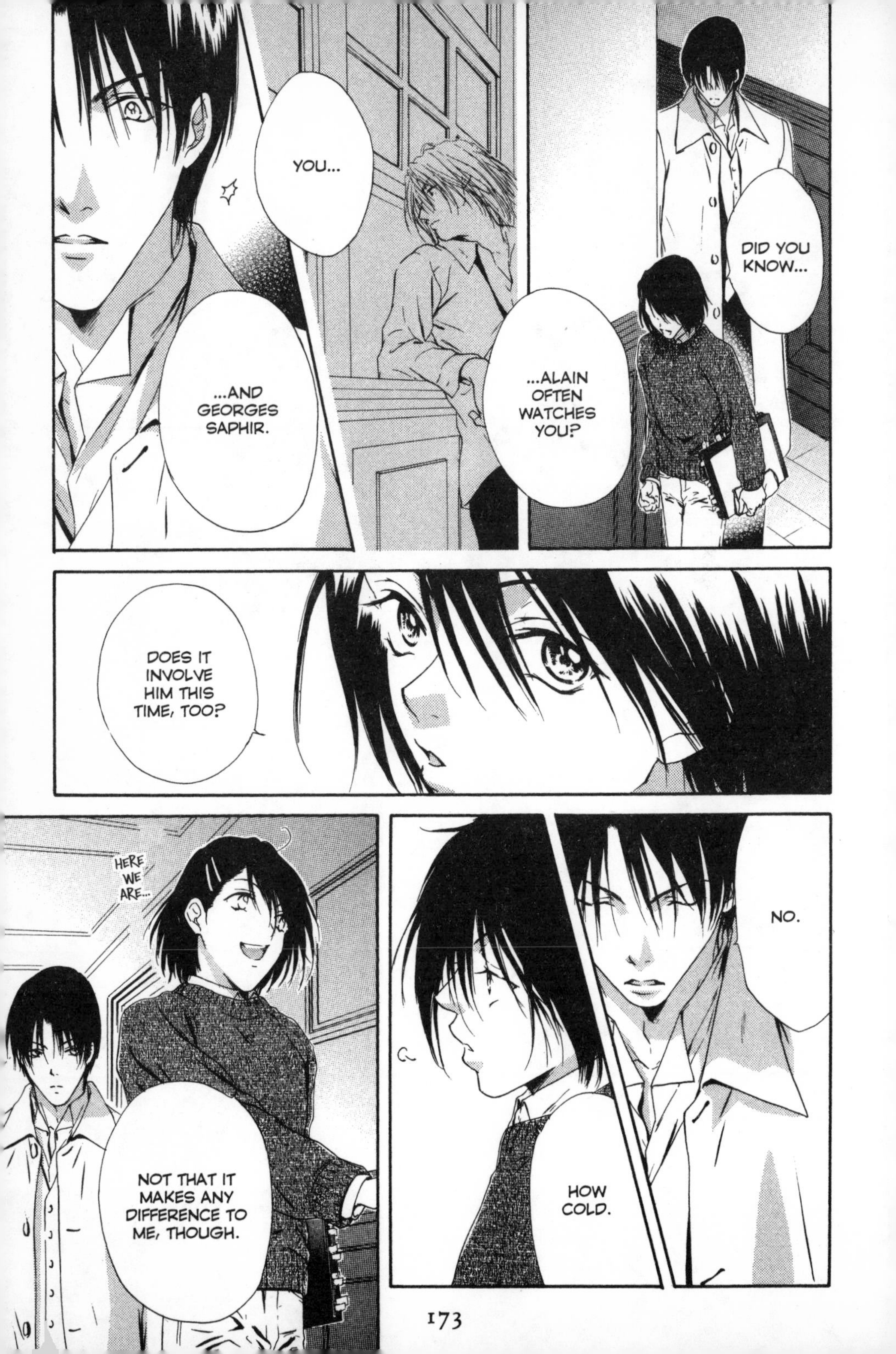
DID YOU KNOW...
...ALAIN OFTEN WATCHES YOU?
YOU...
...AND GEORGES SAPHIR.
DOES IT INVOLVE HIM THIS TIME, TOO?
NO.
HOW COLD.
HERE WE ARE...
NOT THAT IT MAKES ANY DIFFERENCE TO ME, THOUGH.

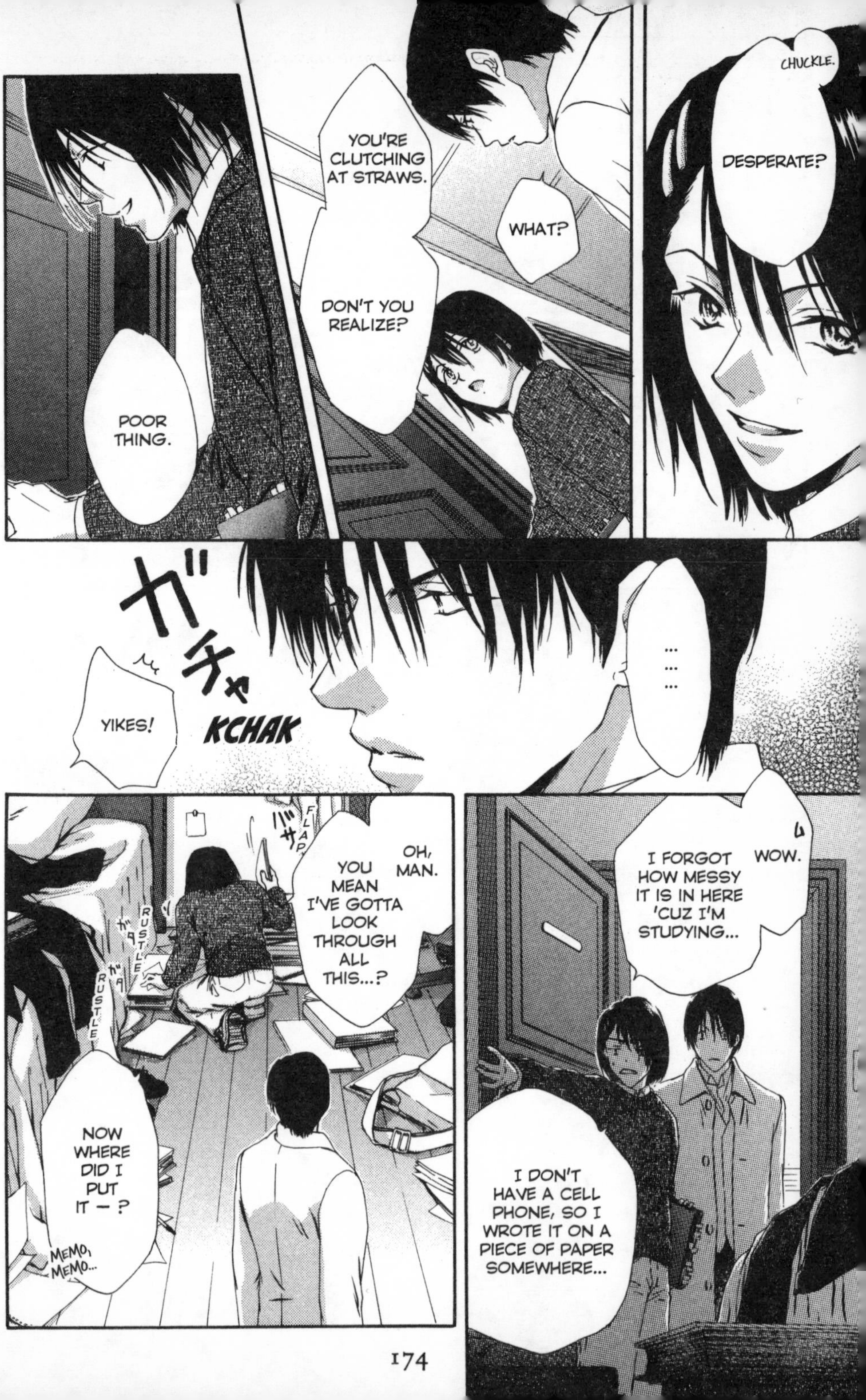
CHUCKLE.
DESPERATE?
YOU'RE CLUTCHING AT STRAWS.
WHAT?
DON'T YOU REALIZE?
POOR THING.
...
...
...
KCHAK
YIKES!
WOW.
I FORGOT HOW MESSY IT IS IN HERE 'CUZ I'M STUDYING...
I DON'T HAVE A CELL PHONE, SO I WROTE IT ON A PIECE OF PAPER SOMEWHERE...
FLAP
OH, MAN.
YOU MEAN I'VE GOTTA LOOK THROUGH ALL THIS...?
RUSTLE
RUSTLE
NOW WHERE DID I PUT IT — ?
MEMO, MEMO...

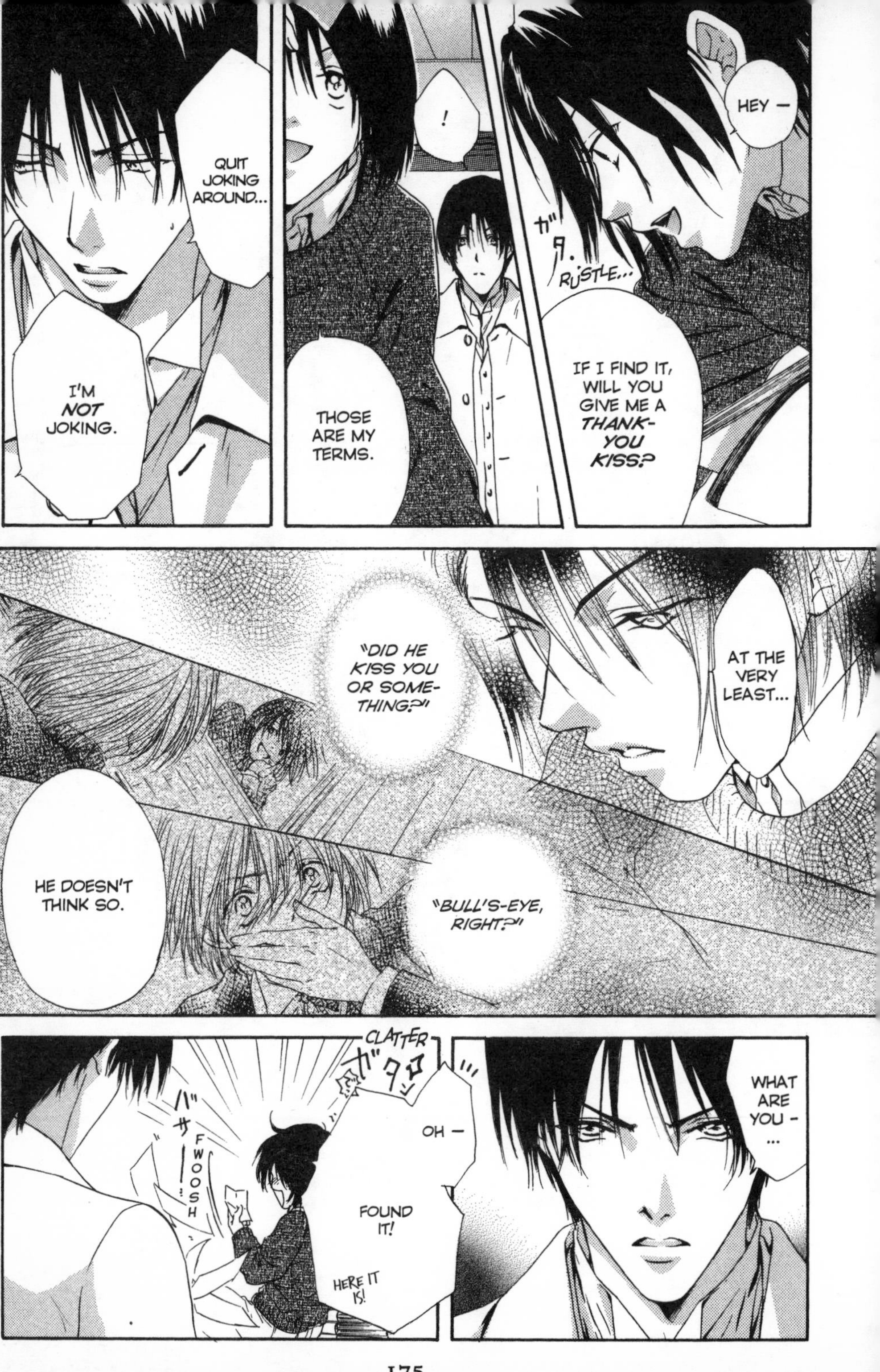
HEY —
ガタ.
RUSTLE...
IF I FIND IT, WILL YOU GIVE ME A THANK-YOU KISS?
!
THOSE ARE MY TERMS.
QUIT JOKING AROUND...
I'M NOT JOKING.
AT THE VERY LEAST...
"DID HE KISS YOU OR SOMETHING?"
"BULL'S-EYE, RIGHT?"
HE DOESN'T THINK SO.
WHAT ARE YOU - ...
CLATTER
ガタン
OH —
FOUND IT!
HERE IT IS!
バサ
FWOOSH

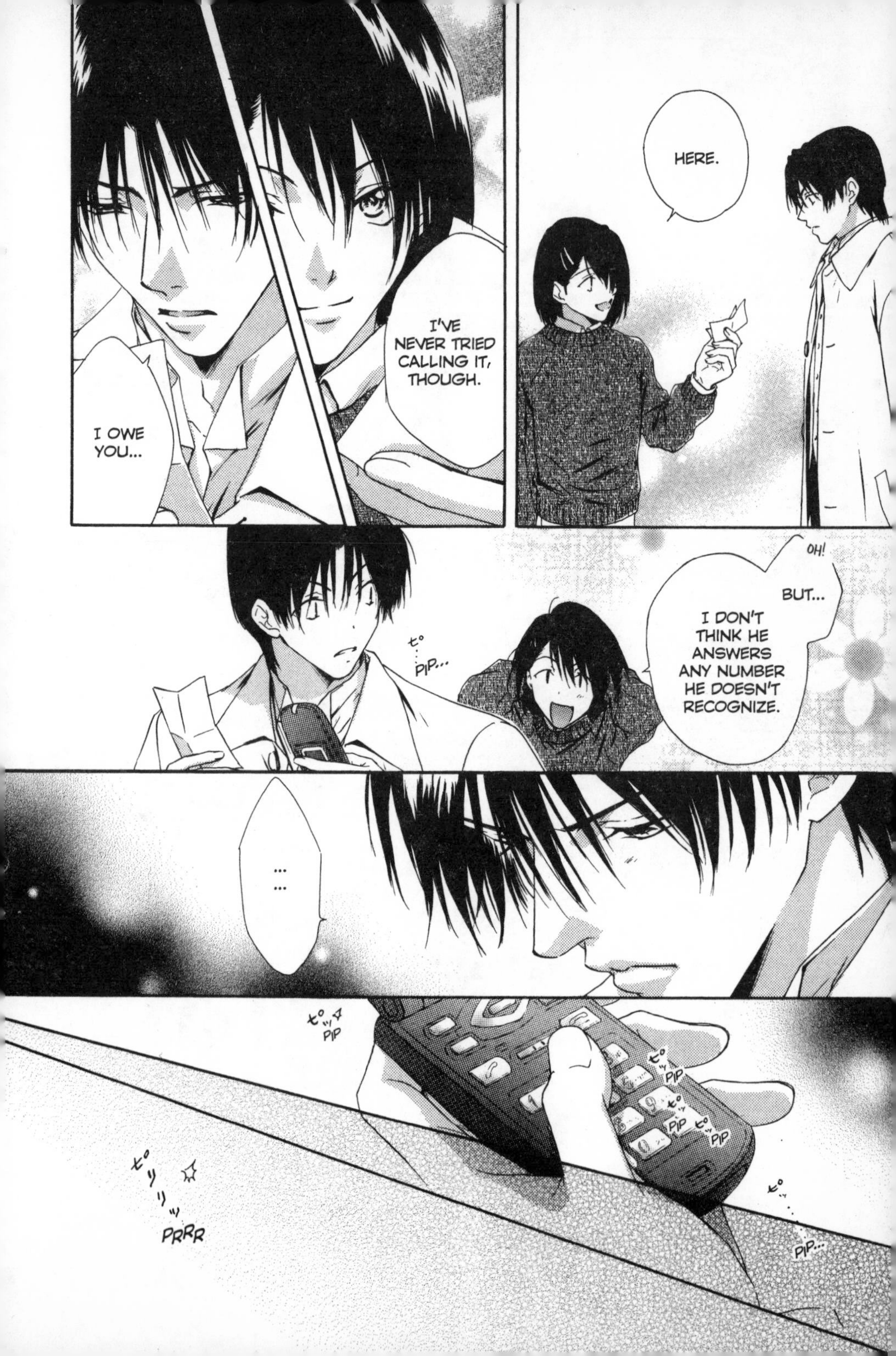
HERE.
I'VE NEVER TRIED CALLING IT, THOUGH.
I OWE YOU...
OH!
BUT...
I DON'T THINK HE ANSWERS ANY NUMBER HE DOESN'T RECOGNIZE.
ピ... PIP...
... ...
ピッ PIP
ピッ PIP
ピッ PIP
ピッ PIP
ピ... PIP...
ピリリッ PRRR

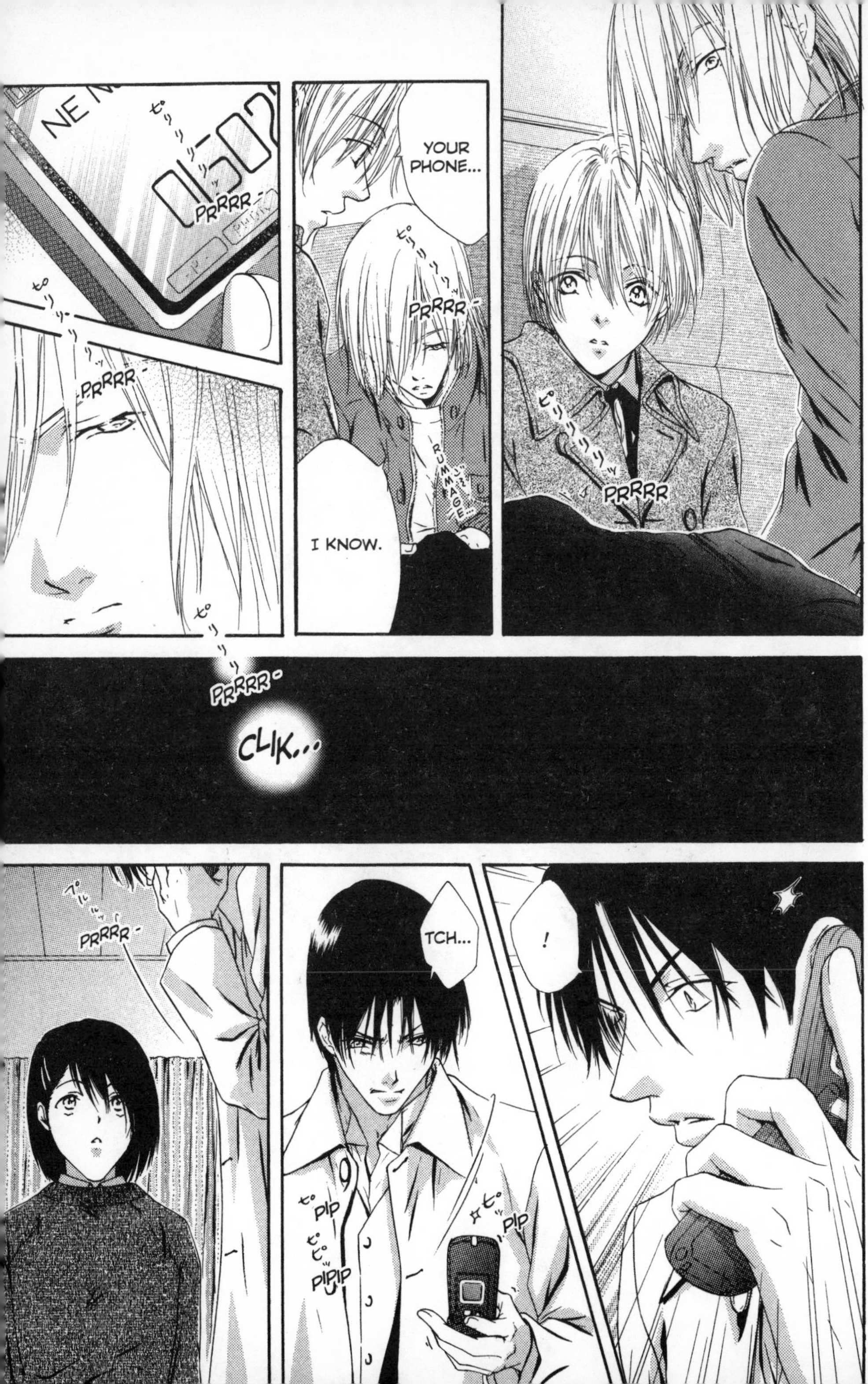
PRRRR
YOUR PHONE...
PRRRR-
I KNOW.
RUMMAGE...
NE N
0150?
PRRRR-
PRRRR-
PRRRR-
CLIK...
!
TCH...
PIP
PIP
PIPIP
PRRRR-

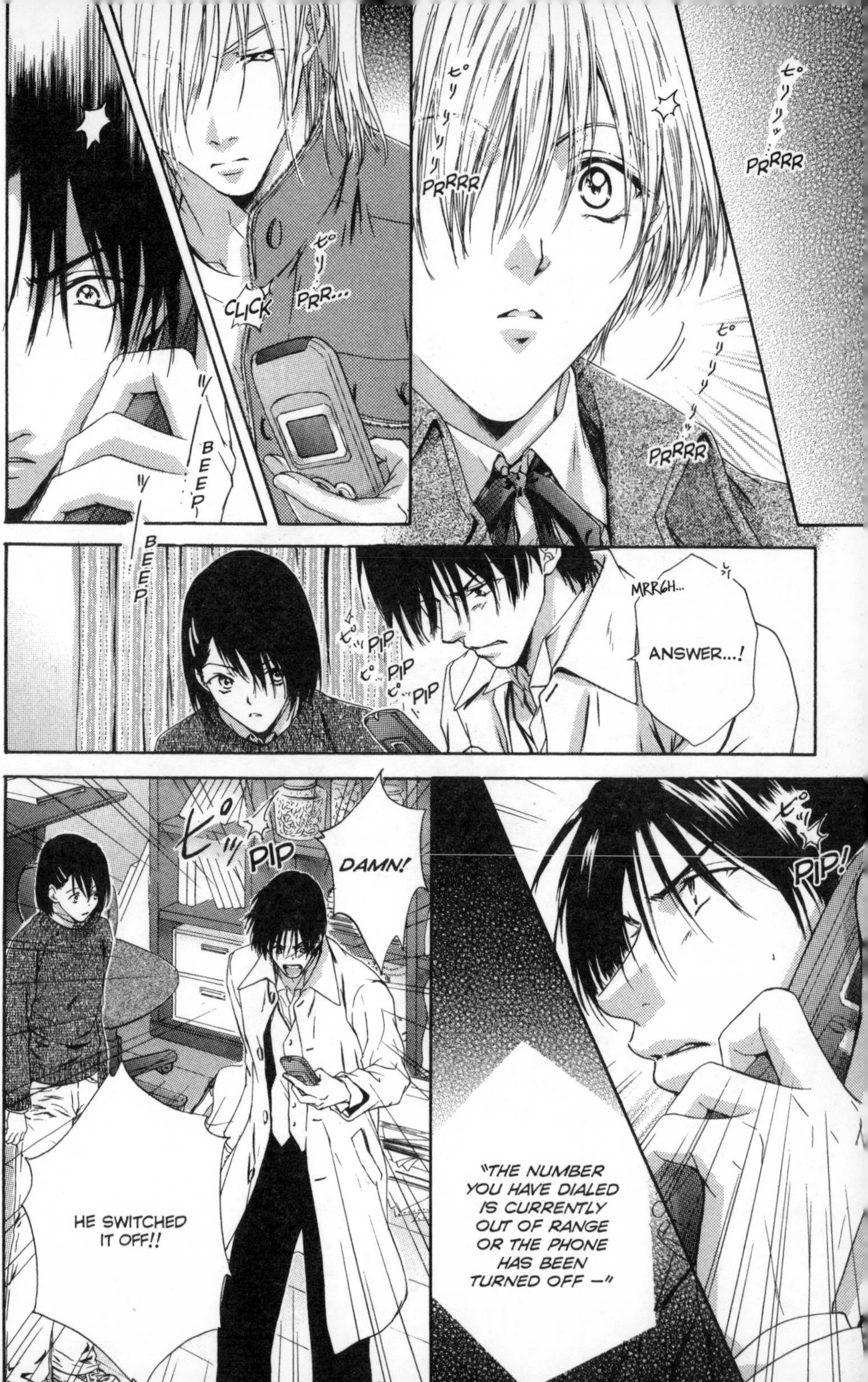
ピリリッ… PRRRR
ピリリリ PRRRR
ピリリリリ… PRRRR
ピリ… PRR…
CLICK
ツ BEEP
ツ BEEP
MRRGH…
ANSWER…!
ピッ PIP
ピッ PIP
ピッ PIP
ピッ PIP!
"THE NUMBER YOU HAVE DIALED IS CURRENTLY OUT OF RANGE OR THE PHONE HAS BEEN TURNED OFF —"
DAMN!
ピッ PIP
HE SWITCHED IT OFF!!

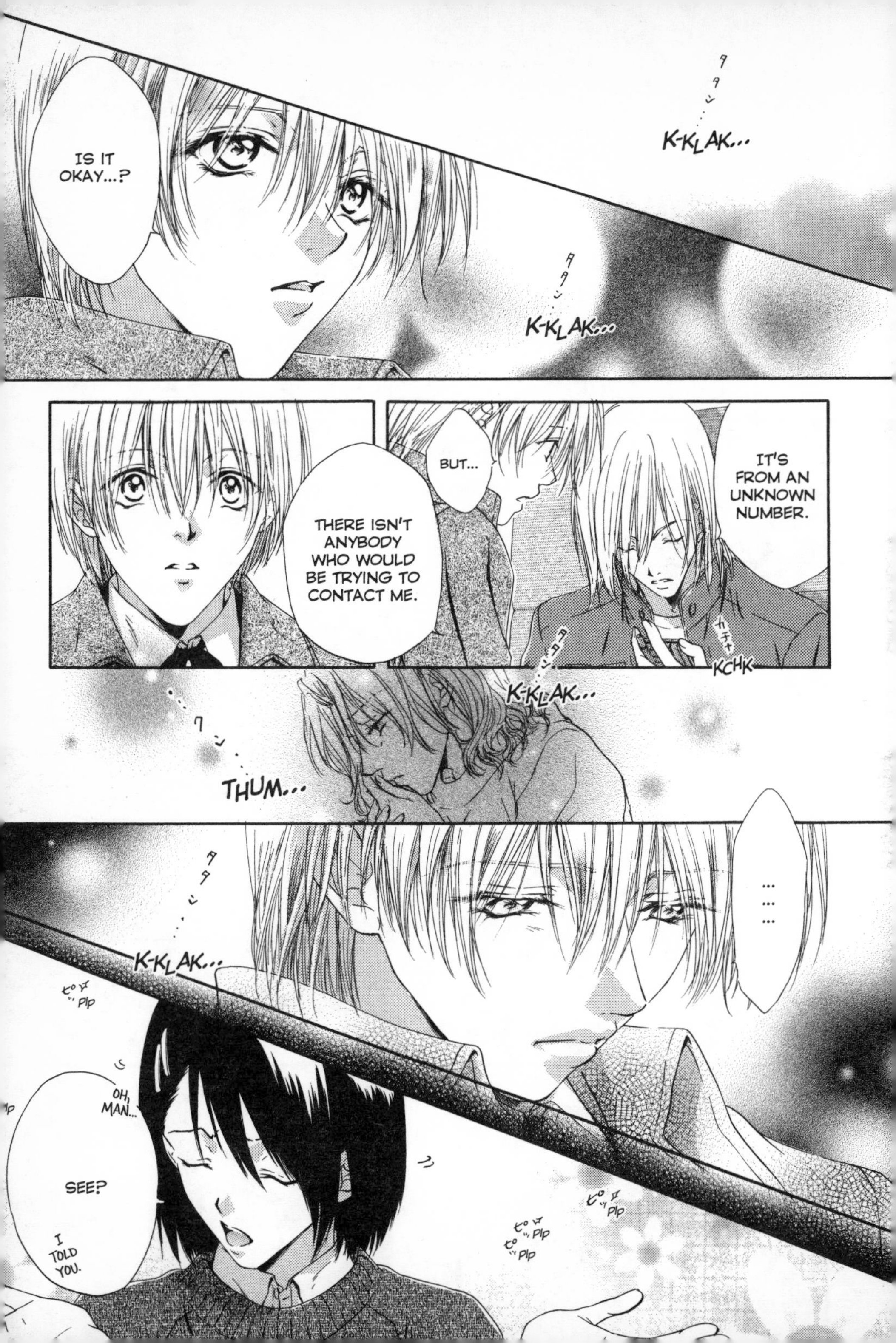
K-KLAK...
IS IT OKAY...?
K-KLAK...
IT'S FROM AN UNKNOWN NUMBER.
BUT...
KCHK
THERE ISN'T ANYBODY WHO WOULD BE TRYING TO CONTACT ME.
K-KLAK...
THUM...
....
K-KLAK...
PIP
OH, MAN...
SEE?
I TOLD YOU.
PIP
PIP
PIP

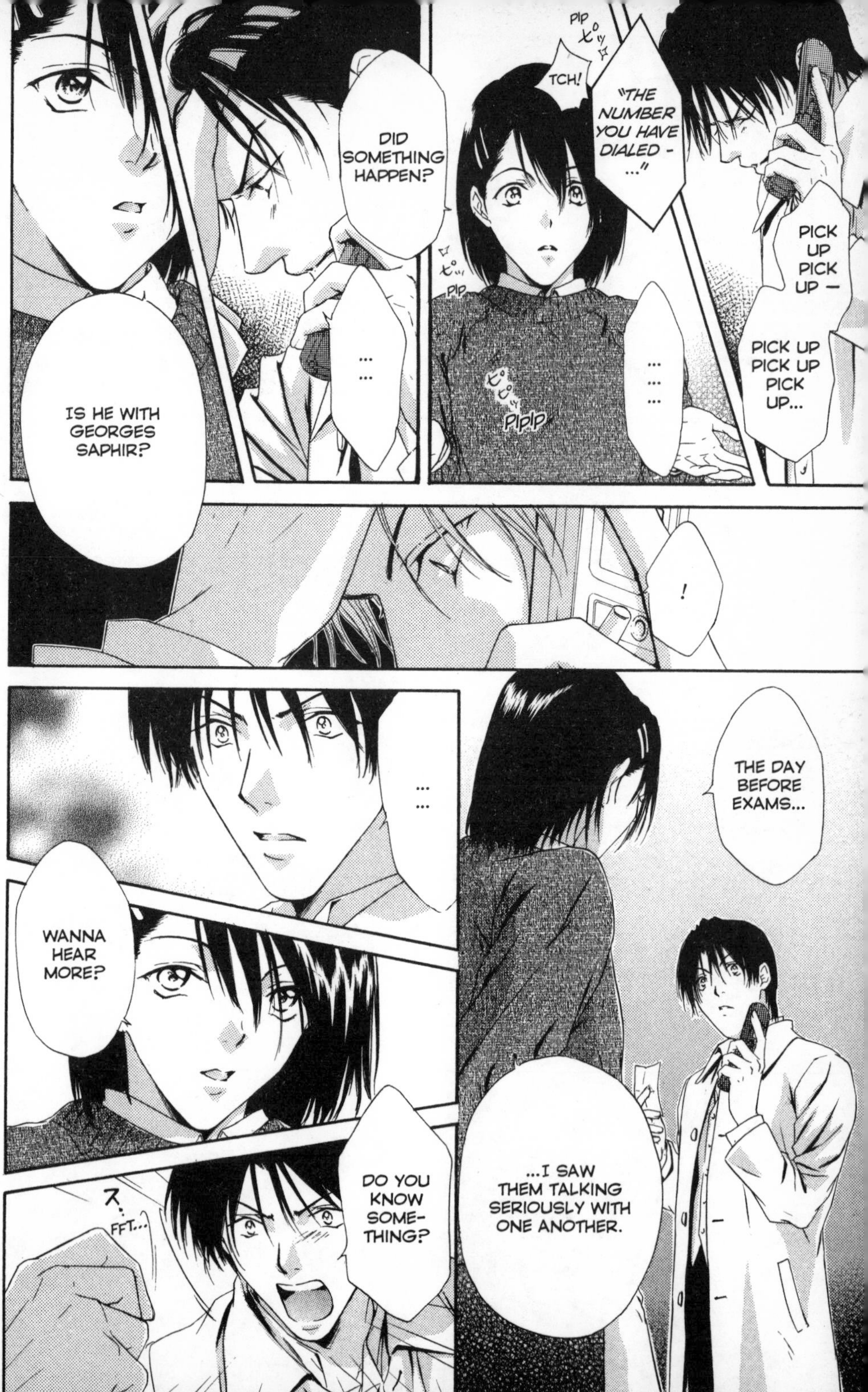
PICK UP PICK UP PICK UP —
PICK UP PICK UP PICK UP...
PIP
"THE NUMBER YOU HAVE DIALED - ..."
TCH!
PIP
PIPIP
......
DID SOMETHING HAPPEN?
... ...
IS HE WITH GEORGES SAPHIR?
!
THE DAY BEFORE EXAMS...
...I SAW THEM TALKING SERIOUSLY WITH ONE ANOTHER.
... ...
WANNA HEAR MORE?
DO YOU KNOW SOME-THING?
FFT...

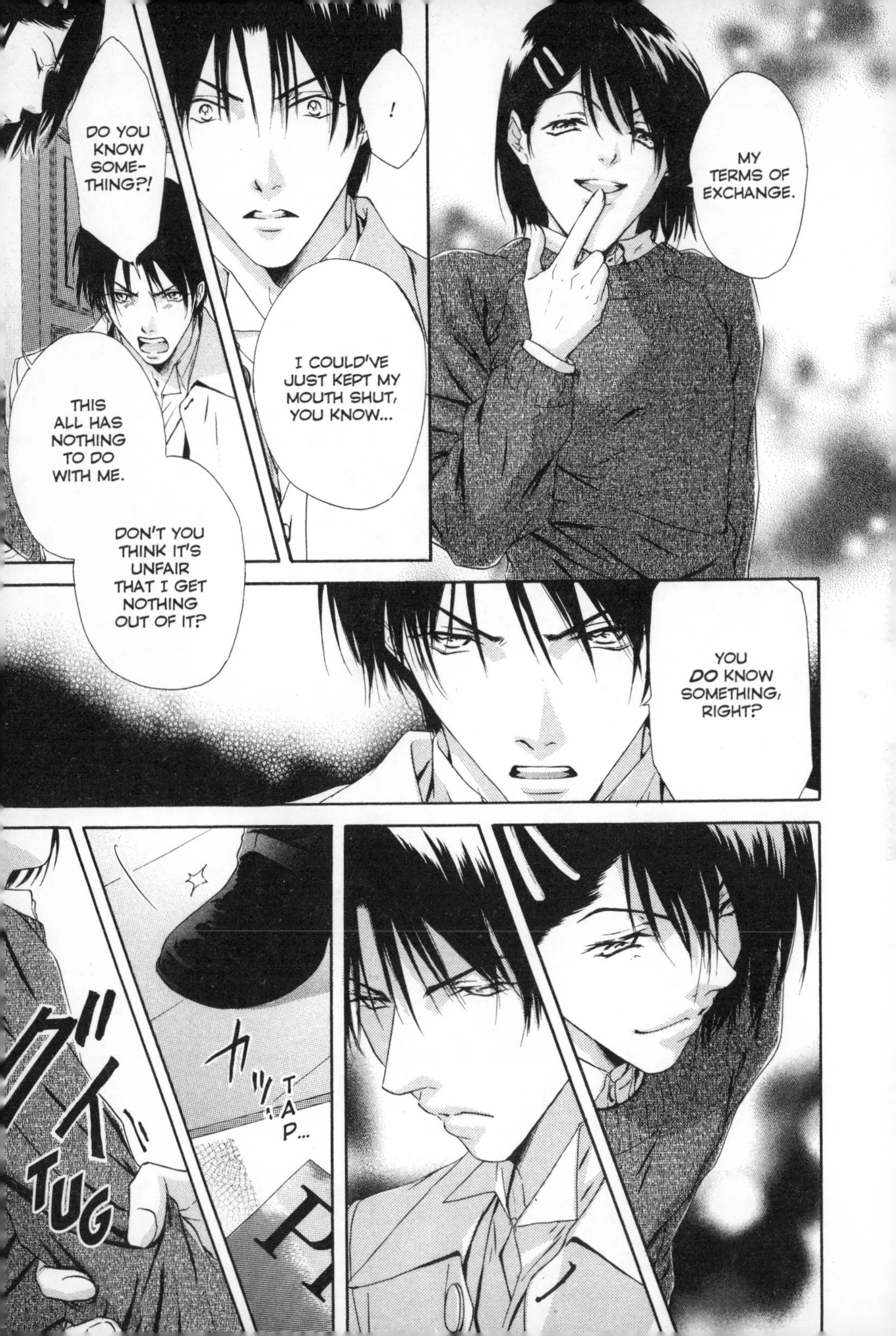
MY TERMS OF EXCHANGE.
!
I COULD'VE JUST KEPT MY MOUTH SHUT, YOU KNOW...
DO YOU KNOW SOME-THING?!
THIS ALL HAS NOTHING TO DO WITH ME.
DON'T YOU THINK IT'S UNFAIR THAT I GET NOTHING OUT OF IT?
YOU *DO* KNOW SOMETHING, RIGHT?
カッ
TAP...
グイ
TUG

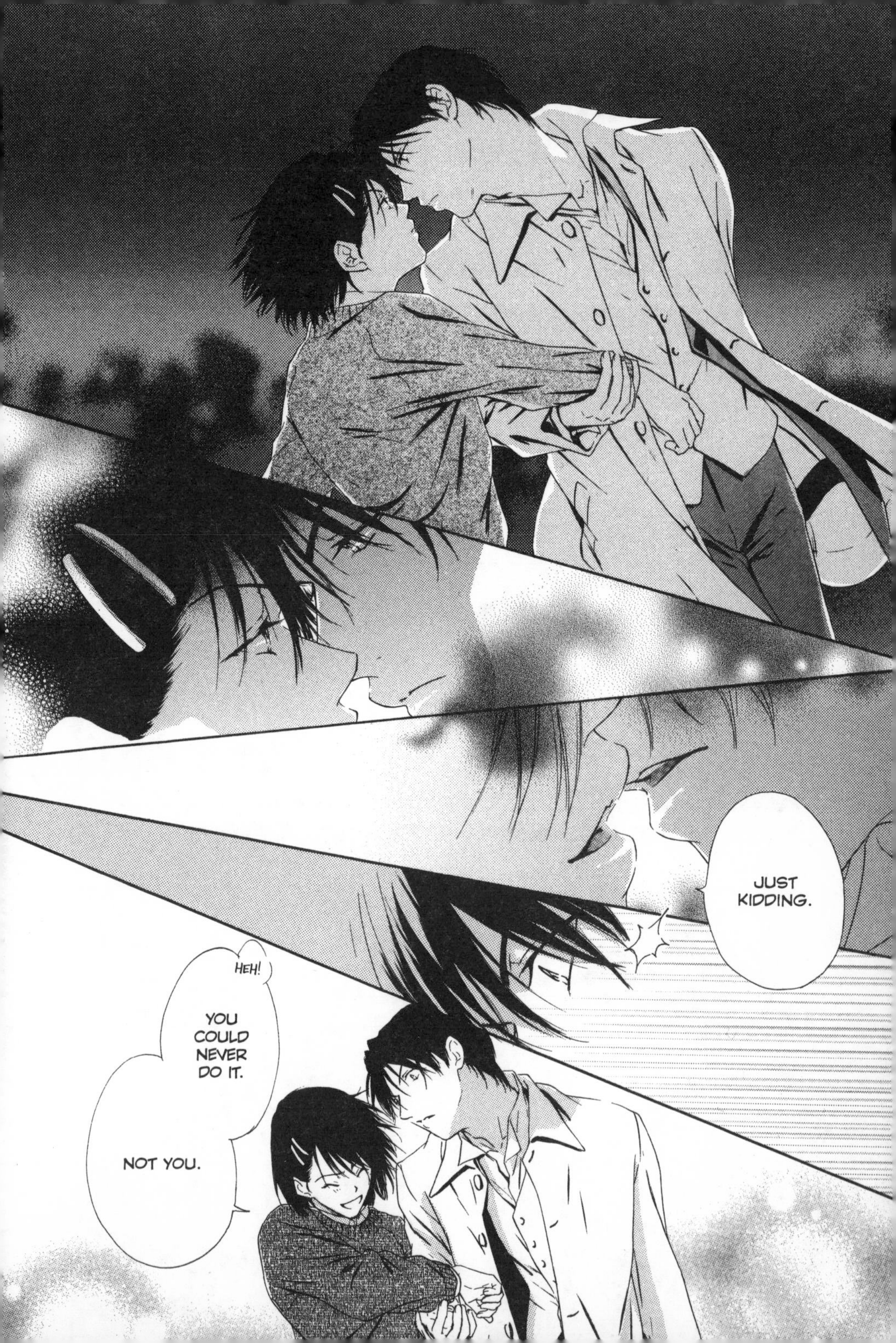
JUST KIDDING.
HEH!
YOU COULD NEVER DO IT.
NOT YOU.

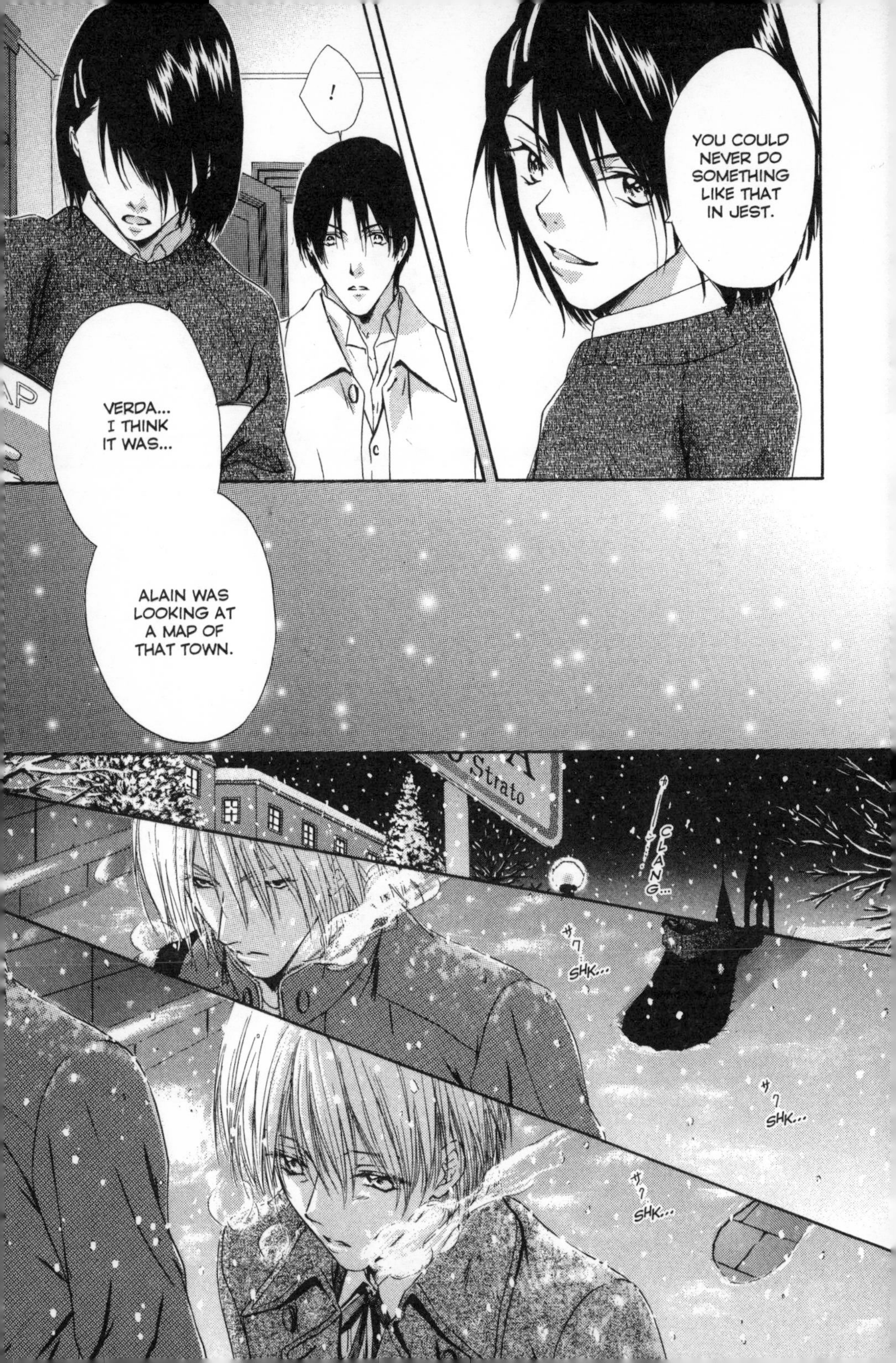

YOU COULD NEVER DO SOMETHING LIKE THAT IN JEST.
!
VERDA... I THINK IT WAS...
ALAIN WAS LOOKING AT A MAP OF THAT TOWN.
Strato
CLANG...
SHK...
SHK...
SHK...

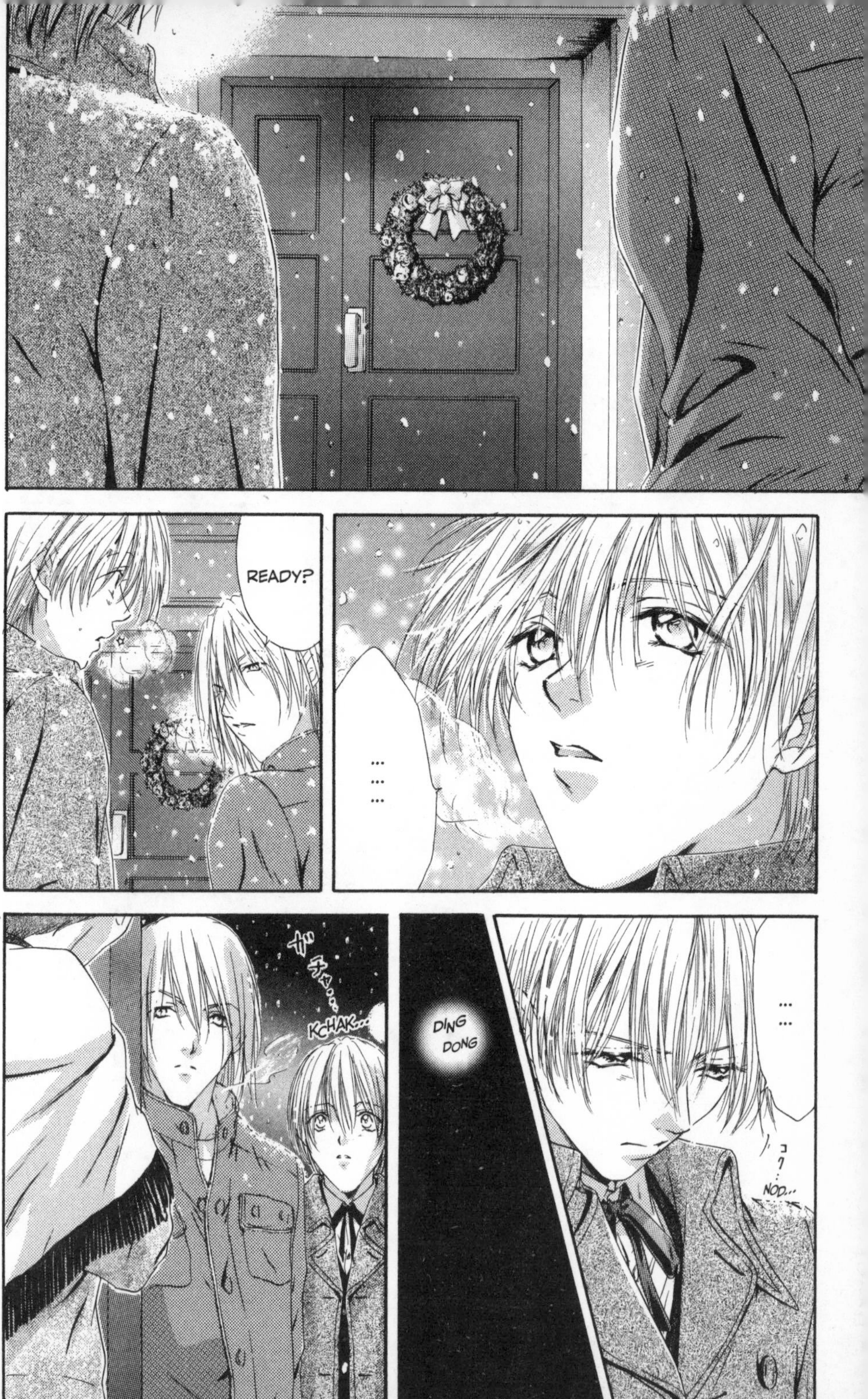

...
...
...
READY?
...
...
コク...
NOD...
DING DONG
ガチャ...
KCHAK...

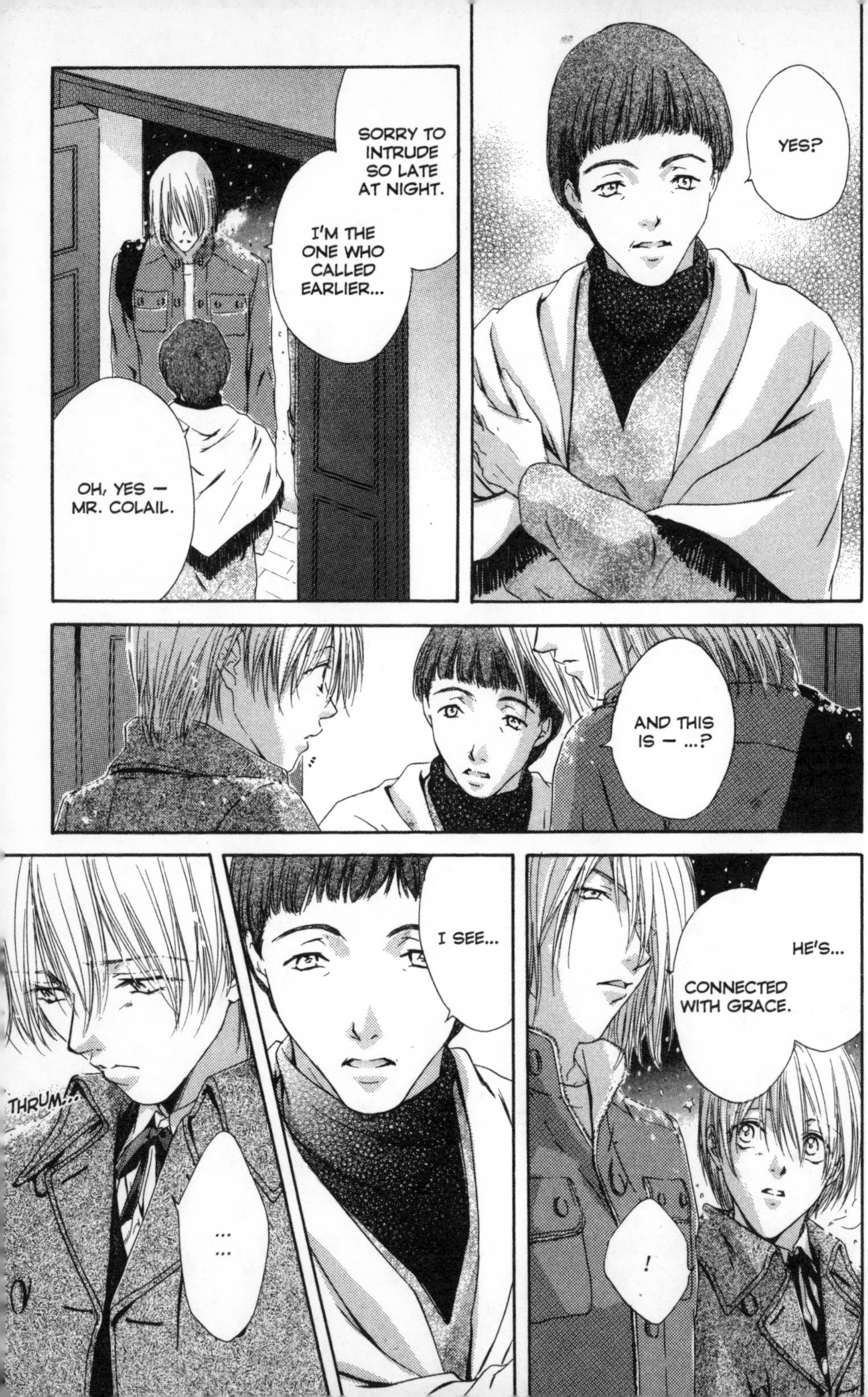
YES?
SORRY TO INTRUDE SO LATE AT NIGHT.
I'M THE ONE WHO CALLED EARLIER...
OH, YES — MR. COLAIL.
AND THIS IS — ...?
HE'S...
CONNECTED WITH GRACE.
!
I SEE...
THRUM...
...
...

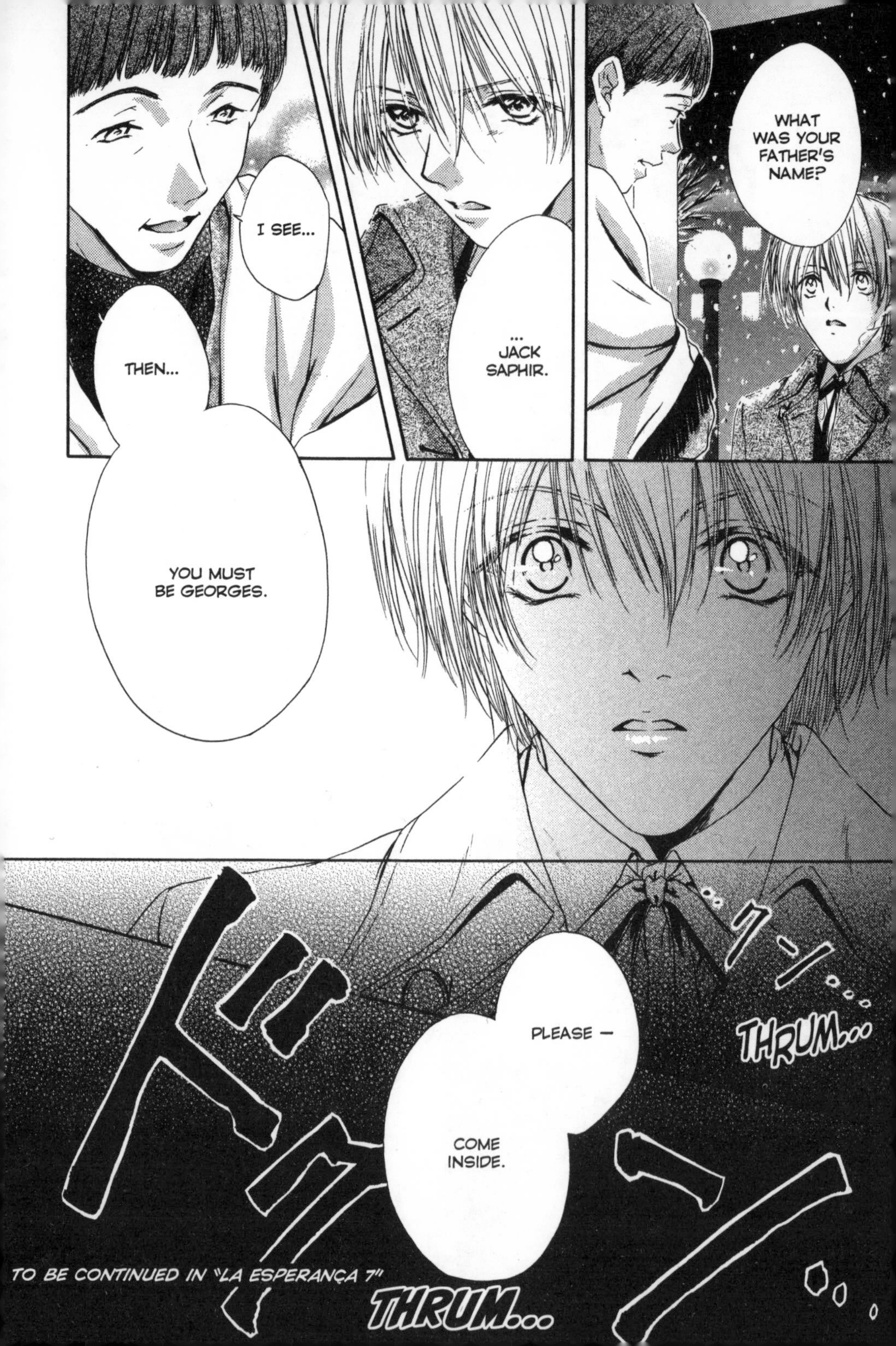
WHAT WAS YOUR FATHER'S NAME?
... JACK SAPHIR.
I SEE...
THEN...
YOU MUST BE GEORGES.
THRUM...
PLEASE —
COME INSIDE.
THRUM...
TO BE CONTINUED IN "LA ESPERANÇA 7"

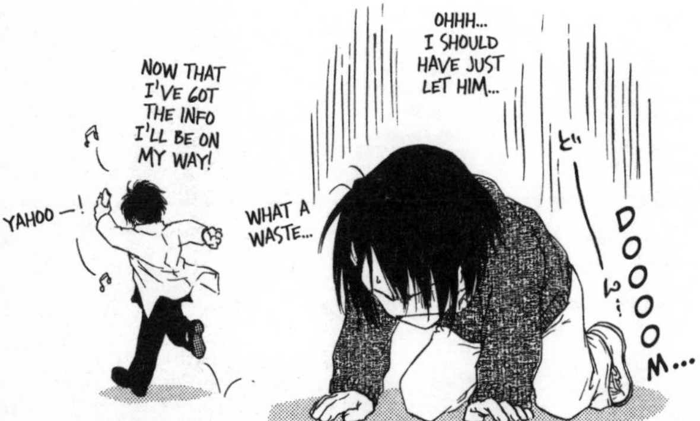
OHHH... I SHOULD HAVE JUST LET HIM...
どーん!!
DOOOOM...
WHAT A WASTE...
NOW THAT I'VE GOT THE INFO I'LL BE ON MY WAY!
YAHOO—!

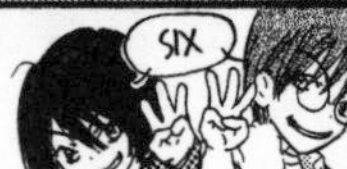
SIX

PROMENADE

HELLO. CHIGUSA KAWAI HERE. HERE IS VOLUME 6 OF "LA ESPERANZA". THE MAIN COLOR FOR THE COVER OF THIS VOLUME 6 IS PURPLE. THE FOCUS IS ON GEORGES. EARLIER, I RECEIVED THE COMMENT, "ROBERT HAS HIS OWN SOLO COVER...BUT GEORGES DOESN'T, EVEN THOUGH HE'S THE MAIN CHARACTER. I FEEL SORRY FOR HIM," SO I DECIDED TO GIVE GEORGIE HIS OWN...BUT IN THE END, HE TURNED OUT NOT TO BE ALONE ON THE COVER AFTER ALL. I DECIDED ON THE COLOR PURPLE BECAUSE I THOUGHT IT WOULD MAKE THE BLONDE HAIR STAND OUT. I STILL HAVEN'T SEEN THE FINAL PRINT SO I'M NOT SURE HOW IT TURNED OUT, BUT IF IT LOOKS NICE I WILL BE PLEASED. SINCE THERE AREN'T MANY NEW CHARACTERS TO INTRODUCE THIS TIME AROUND, THE ILLUSTRATIONS WILL FOCUS ON THE DIFFERENT SCHOOL UNIFORM DESIGNS.

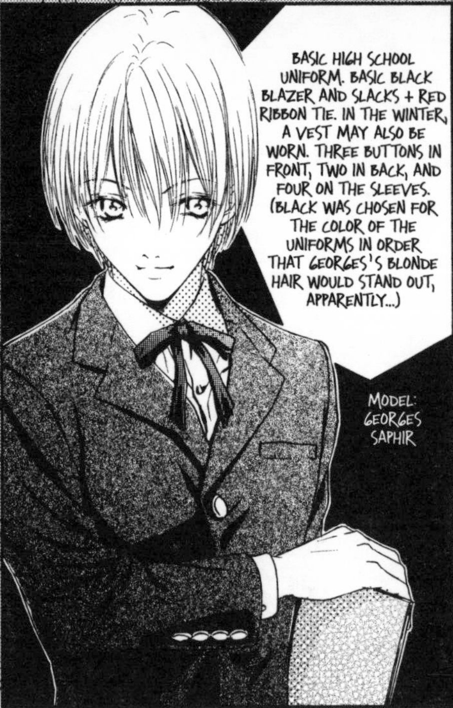
BASIC HIGH SCHOOL UNIFORM. BASIC BLACK BLAZER AND SLACKS + RED RIBBON TIE. IN THE WINTER, A VEST MAY ALSO BE WORN. THREE BUTTONS IN FRONT, TWO IN BACK, AND FOUR ON THE SLEEVES. (BLACK WAS CHOSEN FOR THE COLOR OF THE UNIFORMS IN ORDER THAT GEORGES'S BLONDE HAIR WOULD STAND OUT, APPARENTLY...)
MODEL: GEORGES SAPHIR

◎ CHAPTER 13 ROSARIO VOL.1 – VOL.6

→ THE "ROSARIO ARC" ENDED UP TAKING AN ENTIRE VOLUME. THE STORY OCCURS SOMETIME BETWEEN THE SEASONS OF AUTUMN AND WINTER. IT'S A VERY OPPRESSIVE FEELING TO HAVE TO DRAW SNOWY LANDSCAPES IN THE MIDDLE OF SUMMER... "WHY ARE YOU GUYS WEARING SUCH HEAVY, STIFLING CLOTHING?!" IS WHAT I KEPT ASKING AS I DREW. THE LAST CHAPTER IN THE PREVIOUS VOLUME ENDED ON A, "HUUUH?!" NOTE, SO THIS VOLUME IS THE CONTINUATION. (IF YOU'RE SAYING, "I DON'T GET WHAT'S GOING ON!" YOU MUST RUN OUT AND GET VOLUME 5!)
CHRISTMAS PARTY AT THE ARGENT'S. PARTY = FORMAL WEAR. THEREFORE, ELEGANCE AND REFINEMENT SHOULD ABOUND...BUT NO! THE MAIN CHARACTERS WHO ATTEND ARE ALL MALE...SIGH. AFTER ALL, IT'S THE WOMEN WHO LEND ELEGANCE TO THE BALL. A MAN'S ROLE IS TO HELP SET OFF THE WOMAN'S BEAUTY. TUXEDOS EVERYWHERE... DRESSES HAVE MANY VARIATIONS IN STYLE, BUT NOT SO WITH TUXEDOS...

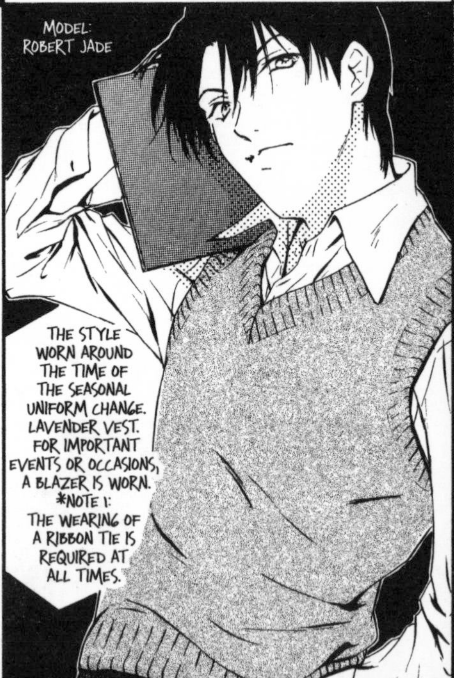
MODEL: ROBERT JADE
THE STYLE WORN AROUND THE TIME OF THE SEASONAL UNIFORM CHANGE. LAVENDER VEST. FOR IMPORTANT EVENTS OR OCCASIONS, A BLAZER IS WORN.
*NOTE 1: THE WEARING OF A RIBBON TIE IS REQUIRED AT ALL TIMES.

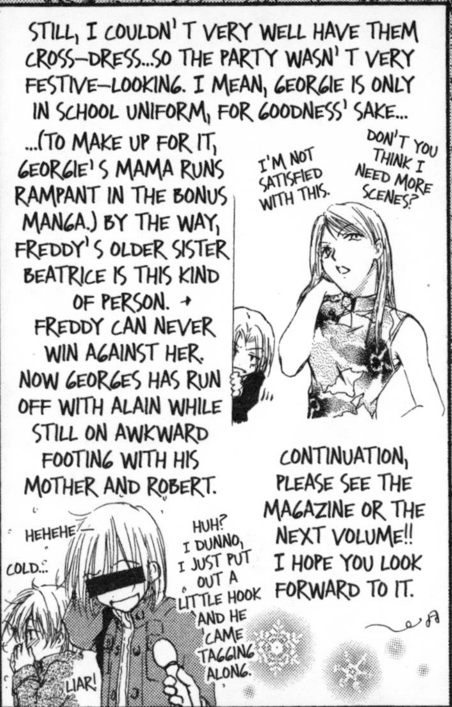
STILL, I COULDN'T VERY WELL HAVE THEM CROSS-DRESS...SO THE PARTY WASN'T VERY FESTIVE-LOOKING. I MEAN, GEORGIE IS ONLY IN SCHOOL UNIFORM, FOR GOODNESS' SAKE...
...(TO MAKE UP FOR IT, GEORGIE'S MAMA RUNS RAMPANT IN THE BONUS MANGA.) BY THE WAY, FREDDY'S OLDER SISTER BEATRICE IS THIS KIND OF PERSON. → FREDDY CAN NEVER WIN AGAINST HER. NOW GEORGES HAS RUN OFF WITH ALAIN WHILE STILL ON AWKWARD FOOTING WITH HIS MOTHER AND ROBERT.
DON'T YOU THINK I NEED MORE SCENES?
I'M NOT SATISFIED WITH THIS.
CONTINUATION, PLEASE SEE THE MAGAZINE OR THE NEXT VOLUME!! I HOPE YOU LOOK FORWARD TO IT.
HUH? I DUNNO, I JUST PUT OUT A LITTLE HOOK AND HE CAME TAGGING ALONG.
HEHEHE—
COLD...
LIAR!

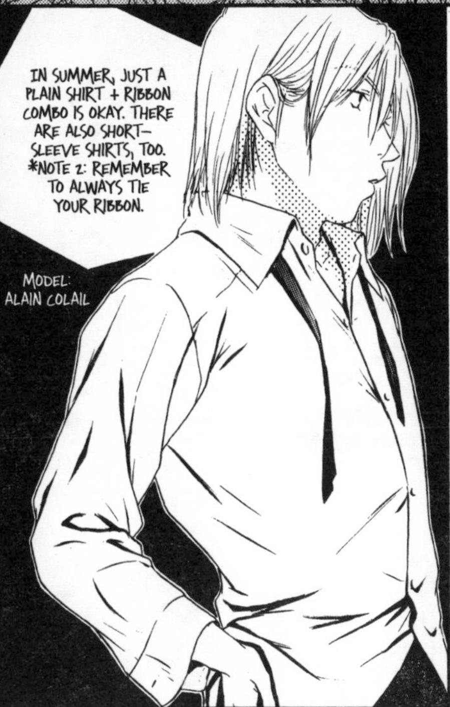
IN SUMMER, JUST A PLAIN SHIRT + RIBBON COMBO IS OKAY. THERE ARE ALSO SHORT-SLEEVE SHIRTS, TOO. *NOTE 2: REMEMBER TO ALWAYS TIE YOUR RIBBON.
MODEL: ALAIN COLAIL

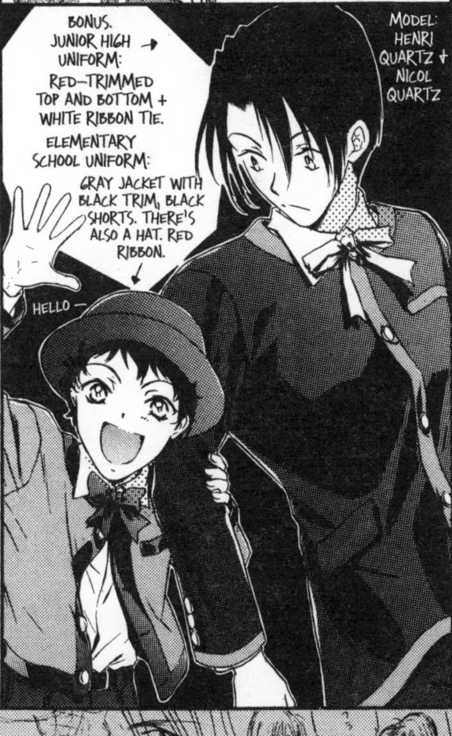
MODEL: HENRI QUARTZ + NICOL QUARTZ
BONUS. JUNIOR HIGH → UNIFORM: RED-TRIMMED TOP AND BOTTOM + WHITE RIBBON TIE.
ELEMENTARY SCHOOL UNIFORM: GRAY JACKET WITH BLACK TRIM, BLACK SHORTS. THERE'S ALSO A HAT. RED RIBBON. ↓
HELLO—

TO EVERYONE WHO WRITES ME — THANK YOU VERY MUCH. YOUR LETTERS PROVIDE MUCH ENCOURAGEMENT. AND TO THOSE OF YOU WHO ARE SECRET SUPPORTERS, THANK YOU ALL AS WELL. I HOPE YOU'LL ALL CONTINUE TO SUPPORT ME IN FUTURE, TOO.

THIS IS A BIT OF SAD NEWS, BUT THE NEXT VOLUME OF LA ESPERANCA IS SLATED TO BE THE LAST. (YOU NEVER CAN TELL, THOUGH...HAHAHA...) I STILL HAVEN'T ROUGHED OUT THE SCRIPT FOR THE FINALE SO I DON'T QUITE KNOW HOW IT'S ALL GOING TO WRAP UP YET — BUT I PLAN ON TYING UP ALL THE LOOSE ENDS, SO IF YOU COULD FOLLOW ME ALONG UNTIL THE END, IT'D BE MUCH APPRECIATED!

THE NEXT VOLUME SHOULD BE OUT A LITTLE QUICKER. THANK YOU FOR READING THIS FAR.

WELL THEN, SEE YOU AGAIN NEXT TIME.

2005. 7. Chigusa Kawai

BGM: YASUKATSU OSHIMA

SPECIAL THANKS TO: R. OCHI

La Esperança

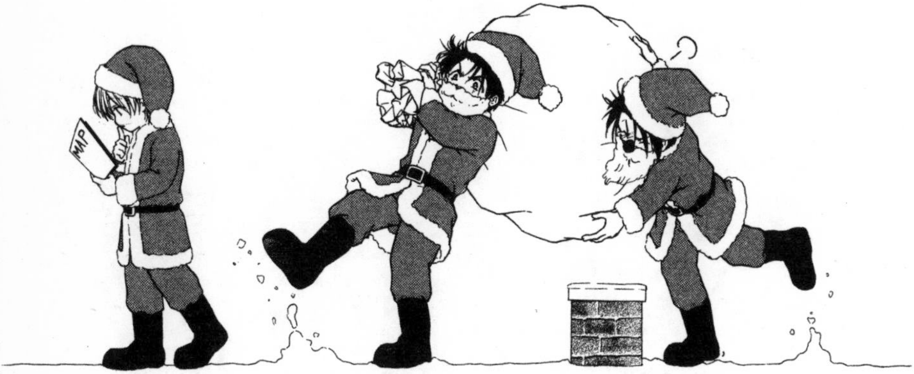
MAP

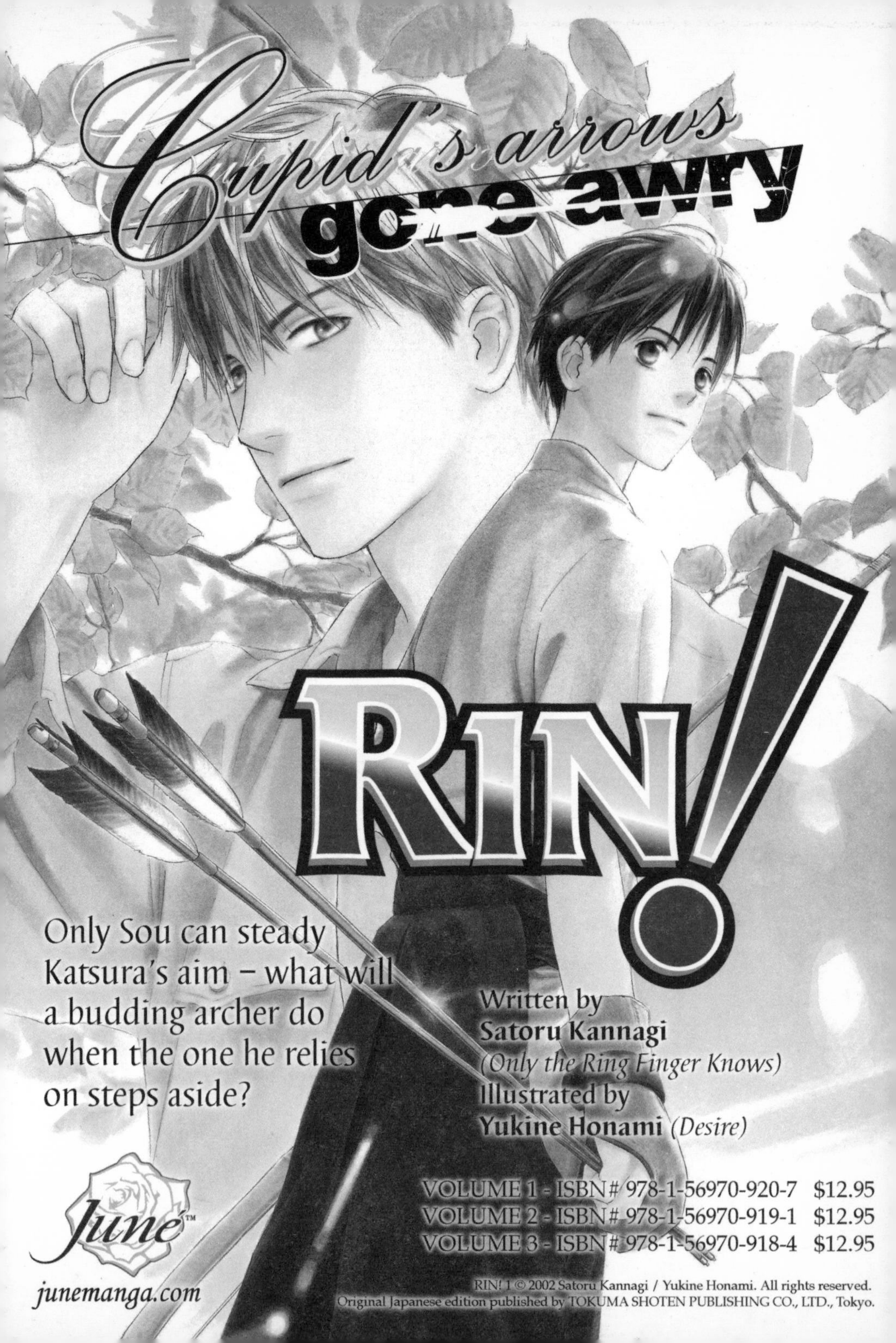
Cupid's arrows
gone awry
RIN!
Only Sou can steady Katsura's aim – what will a budding archer do when the one he relies on steps aside?
Written by
Satoru Kannagi
(Only the Ring Finger Knows)
Illustrated by
Yukine Honami (Desire)
VOLUME 1 - ISBN# 978-1-56970-920-7 $12.95
VOLUME 2 - ISBN# 978-1-56970-919-1 $12.95
VOLUME 3 - ISBN# 978-1-56970-918-4 $12.95
June™
junemanga.com
RIN! 1 © 2002 Satoru Kannagi / Yukine Honami. All rights reserved.
Original Japanese edition published by TOKUMA SHOTEN PUBLISHING CO., LTD., Tokyo.

He has no luck.
He has no name.
Sometimes letting go of the past...
requires finding love in the present.
SEVEN
BY MOMOKO TENZEN
June™
junemanga.com
ISBN# 978-1-56970-849-1 $12.95
SEVEN © Momoko Tenzen 2004.
Originally published in Japan in 2004 by TAIYOH TOSHO Co., Ltd.

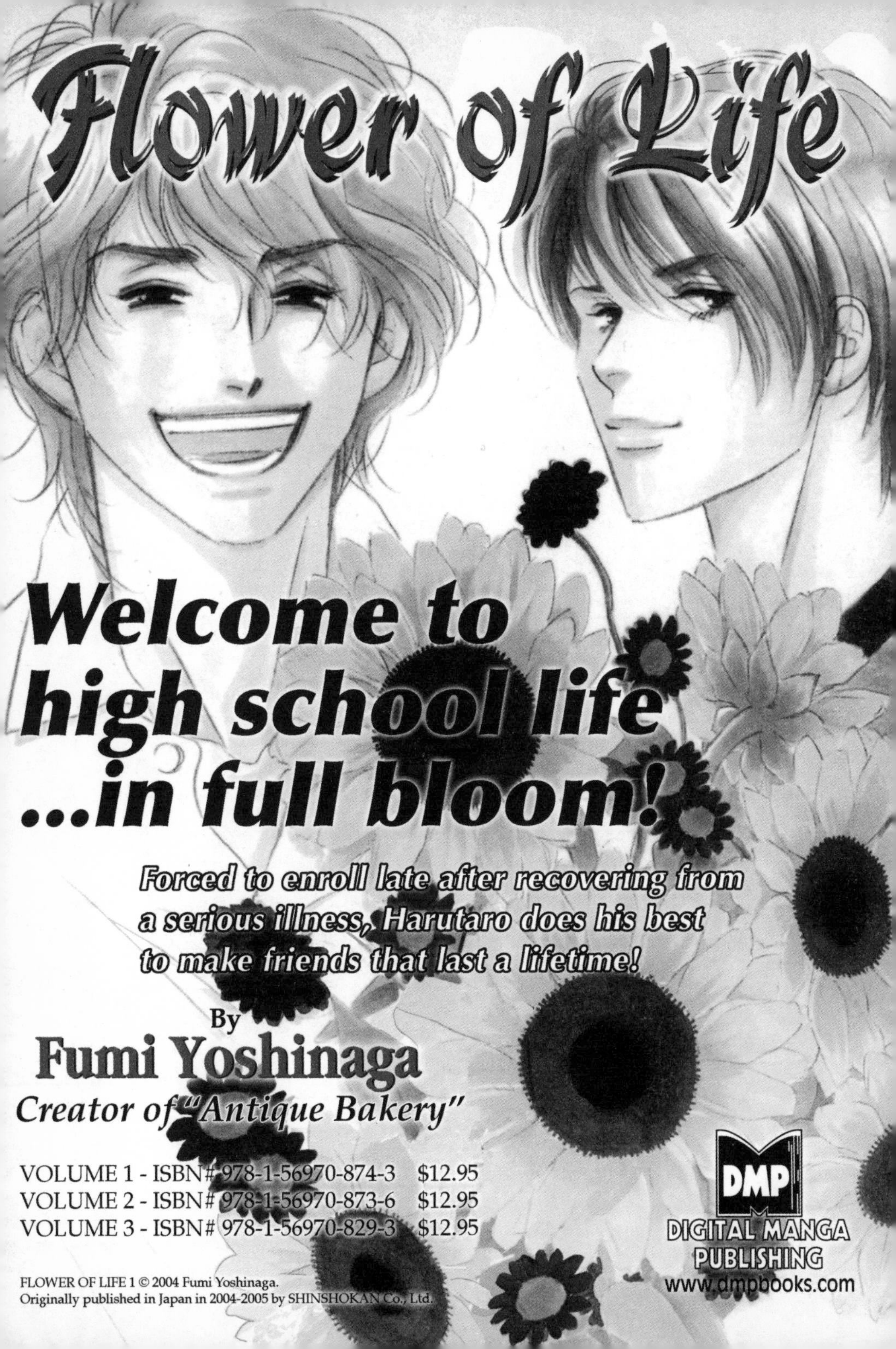
Flower of Life
Welcome to high school life ...in full bloom!
Forced to enroll late after recovering from a serious illness, Harutaro does his best to make friends that last a lifetime!
By
Fumi Yoshinaga
Creator of "Antique Bakery"
VOLUME 1 - ISBN# 978-1-56970-874-3 $12.95
VOLUME 2 - ISBN# 978-1-56970-873-6 $12.95
VOLUME 3 - ISBN# 978-1-56970-829-3 $12.95
DMP
DIGITAL MANGA PUBLISHING
www.dmpbooks.com
FLOWER OF LIFE 1 © 2004 Fumi Yoshinaga.
Originally published in Japan in 2004-2005 by SHINSHOKAN Co., Ltd.

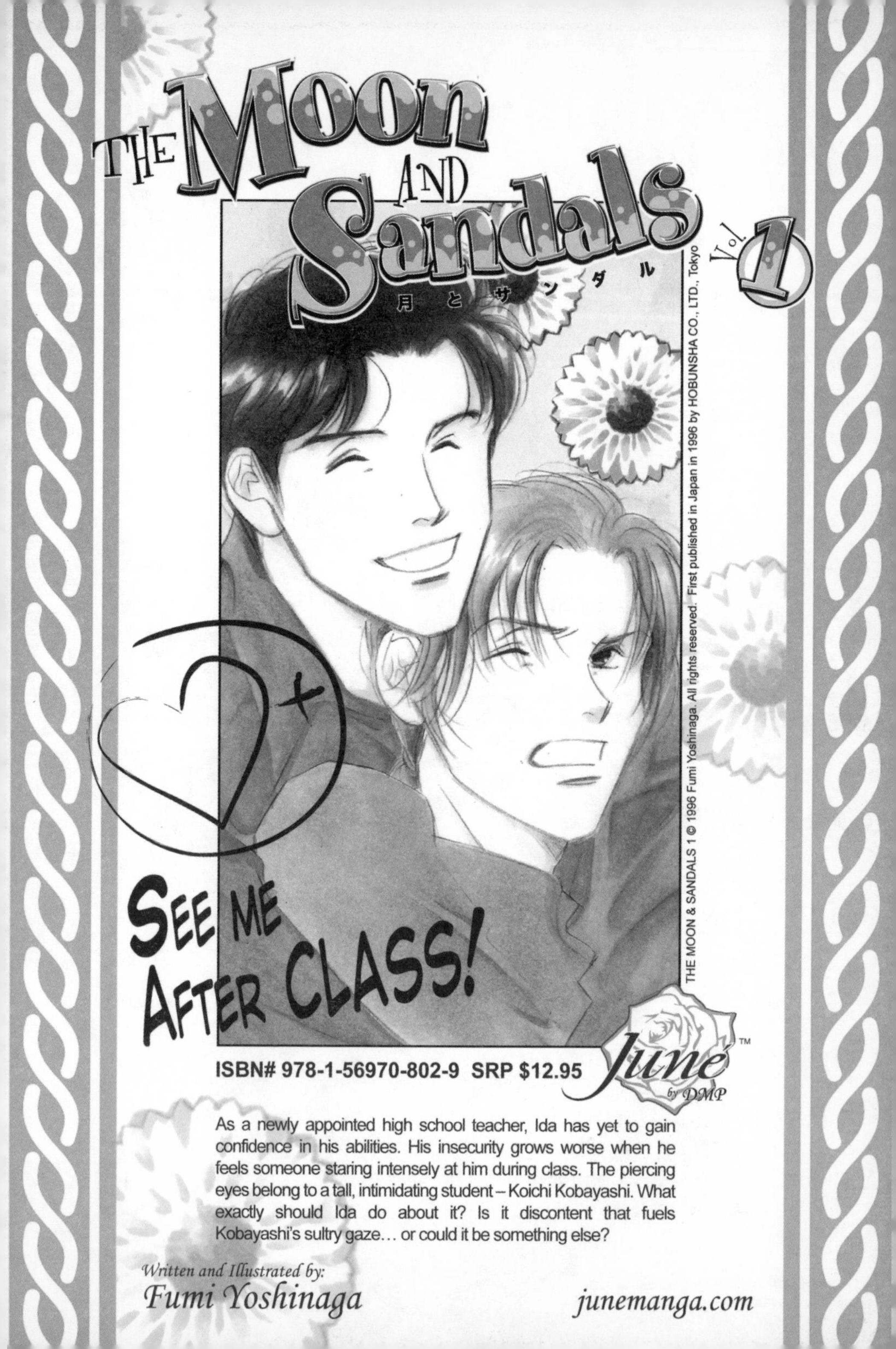
THE Moon AND Sandals
月とサンダル
Vol. 1
SEE ME AFTER CLASS!

ISBN# 978-1-56970-802-9 SRP $12.95

June™ by DMP

As a newly appointed high school teacher, Ida has yet to gain confidence in his abilities. His insecurity grows worse when he feels someone staring intensely at him during class. The piercing eyes belong to a tall, intimidating student – Koichi Kobayashi. What exactly should Ida do about it? Is it discontent that fuels Kobayashi's sultry gaze… or could it be something else?

Written and Illustrated by:
Fumi Yoshinaga

junemanga.com

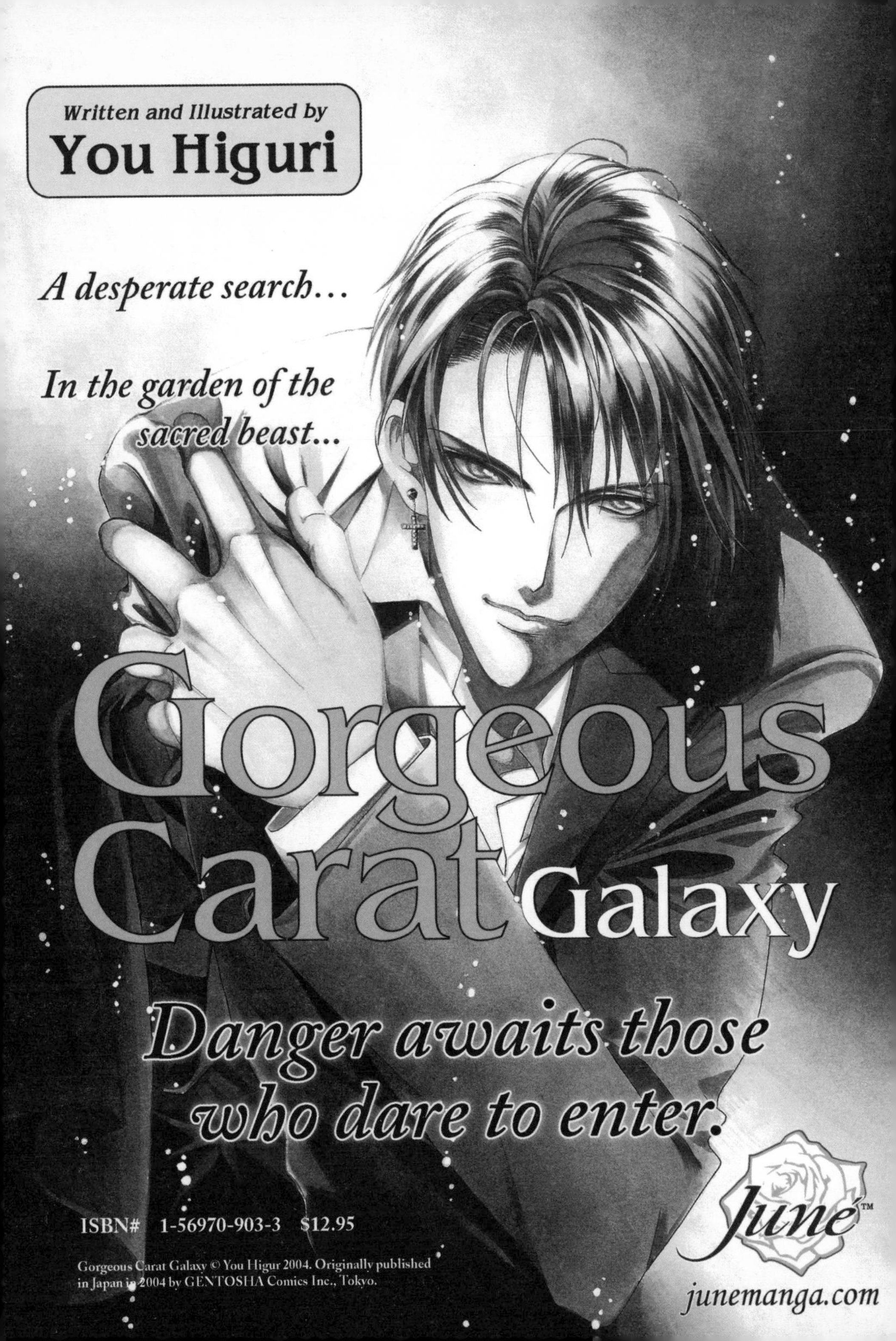
Written and Illustrated by
You Higuri
A desperate search…
In the garden of the sacred beast…
Gorgeous Carat Galaxy
Danger awaits those who dare to enter.
June™
ISBN# 1-56970-903-3 $12.95
Gorgeous Carat Galaxy © You Higur 2004. Originally published in Japan in 2004 by GENTOSHA Comics Inc., Tokyo.
junemanga.com

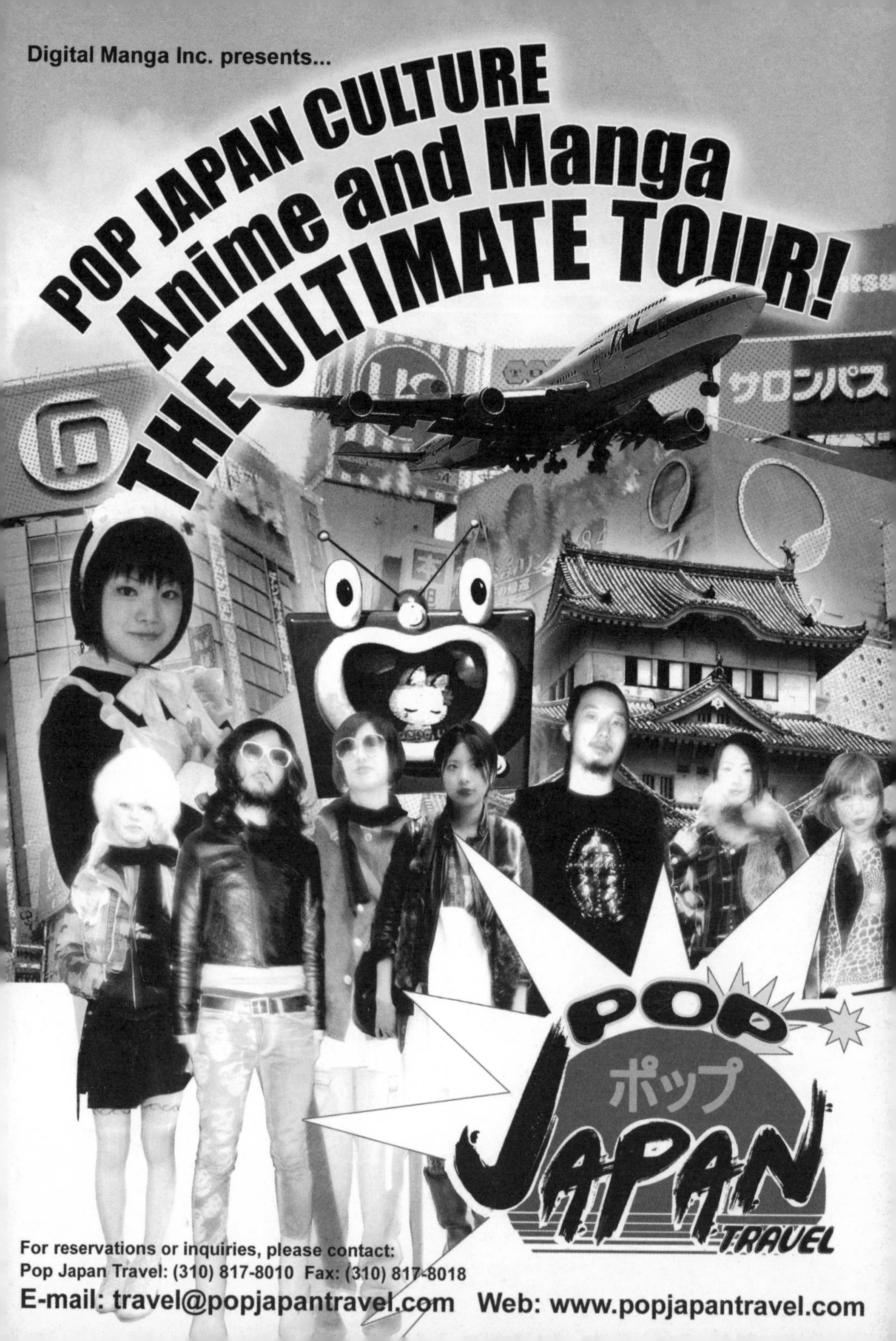
Digital Manga Inc. presents...
POP JAPAN CULTURE
Anime and Manga
THE ULTIMATE TOUR!
サロンパス
POP
ポップ
JAPAN
TRAVEL
For reservations or inquiries, please contact:
Pop Japan Travel: (310) 817-8010 Fax: (310) 817-8018
E-mail: travel@popjapantravel.com Web: www.popjapantravel.com

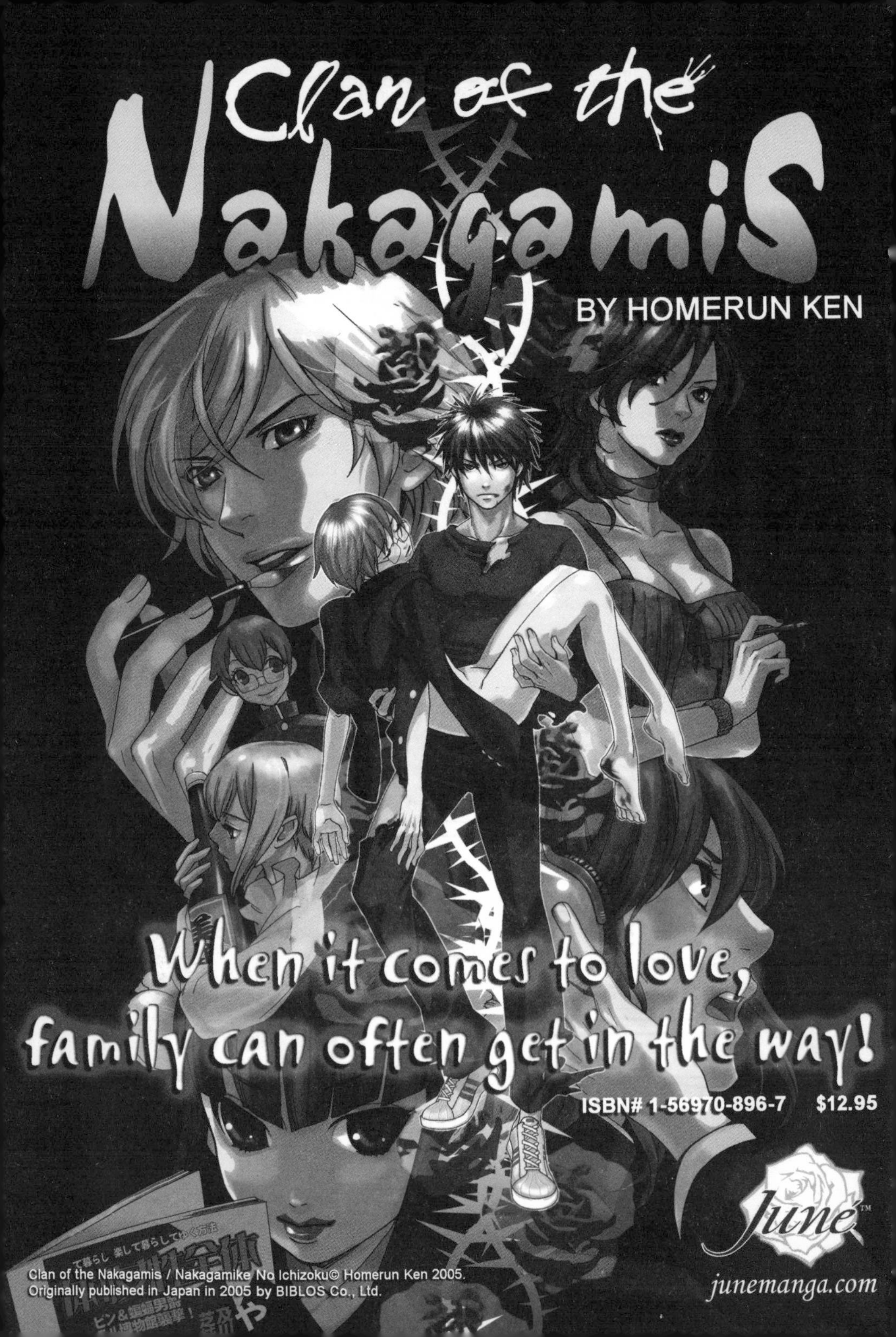
Clan of the Nakagamis
BY HOMERUN KEN
When it comes to love, family can often get in the way!
ISBN# 1-56970-896-7 $12.95
Juné™
Clan of the Nakagamis / Nakagamike No Ichizoku© Homerun Ken 2005.
Originally published in Japan in 2005 by BIBLOS Co., Ltd.
junemanga.com

STOP

This is the back of the book! Start from the other side.

NATIVE MANGA readers read manga from **right to left**.

If you run into our **Native Manga** logo on any of our books... you'll know that this manga is published in it's true original native Japanese right to ~~reading~~ format, ~~as~~ intended. ~~read from~~ the other ~~side of~~ the book ~~and begin~~ reading ~~right~~ to left, ~~top to bottom~~.

~~Check out the~~ diagram ~~to see how~~ its done. ~~Follow It Up!~~

MANGA

~~READS~~ RIGHT TO LEFT